HUSBAND MATERIAL

XAVIER MAYNE

Dreamspinner Press

Published by
Dreamspinner Press
5032 Capital Circle SW
Suite 2, PMB# 279
Tallahassee, FL 32305-7886
USA
http://www.dreamspinnerpress.com/

Husband Material
© 2014 Xavier Mayne.

Cover Art
© 2014 Aaron Anderson.
aaronbydesign55@gmail.com
Cover content is for illustrative purposes only and any person depicted on the cover is a model.

ISBN: 978-1-62798-370-9
Digital ISBN: 978-1-62798-369-3

Printed in the United States of America
First Edition
January 2014

Always, for J.

ACKNOWLEDGMENTS

I first must thank Andi, the amazing editor, whose patient and perceptive work on *Frat House Troopers* showed me how to do more things right this time through.

Of all of the people who read my work and give me their generous and thoughtful feedback, the dearest to me is my sister, Gretchen, whose support I appreciate more than I can ever convey.

AUTHOR'S NOTE

One final note to readers who obtained this copy of my work through file sharing. If you "pirated" my work because you cannot afford to buy it yourself, or because you live in a place where purchasing such content is illegal, then you have my fervent wish for improved circumstances in the future. If you downloaded it because you weren't sure you would like it enough to pay for it, I hope you will. For anyone else—who perhaps thinks that books should be free to those who can find them—I would simply ask that you consider the many hours I spent writing this work instead of cooking for my family or taking my dog for the walk she so desperately wants; reflect on the efforts of all of the people at Dreamspinner who worked to bring this book to you, edited and designed and packaged for your e-reader of choice; and, finally, think of all of those people who don't write books—books you might have enjoyed—because they aren't confident they can make a living when so many people think books are "free." I hope you will consider the retail price of this book reasonable recompense for our labors.

CHAPTER ONE

THE GAME IS AFOOT

THE LONG, black car snaked its way through midmorning traffic. Its occupants, six men who, until stepping into the limousine moments ago at the airport hotel, had never laid eyes on one another, sat silent as the southern California landscape slowly rolled past the tinted windows. They were gladiators, already girded for battle, and unless there was advantage to be had in conversation, they would not indulge in any.

Riley wondered how the hell he had gotten here. This was like someone else's life. Someone who made bad choices—big ones. That wasn't him, not at all.

Except that now it was.

These men—and more besides as there were probably two other cars like this one out there on the freeway—would be his competition. He recollected with a twinge of shame that the spoils accruing to the winner would be a person—a woman—who, in full view of a television audience in the millions, would choose a future husband. Maybe she would choose him.

Is that what he wanted? He wasn't sure. His baseball coach in high school used to bellow that if he didn't want to win badly enough, if he couldn't see himself holding the trophy, he never would. But then again he didn't need to visualize being a loser to feel like one, and he'd done that long enough. This was the first page of the new chapter of his life, he reminded himself. And whatever was written on it, and the one after it and the one after that, would have to be better than the chapter he had just closed. He was here to reinvent himself.

In order to do that, he had to win. And to win, he had to beat every man in this car, and the others as well. He had never been what anyone would call an aggressive competitor, or even a very assertive person. But now he had to be. He had to be the kind of person who, unlucky in love, goes on a reality show competition that he can only win by being lucky in love. The kind of guy who takes chances and makes the heroine swoon.

Yes, this was going to be hard. But he was ready for a change, ready for a challenge, and, maybe, ready for love.

He felt the car slowing and then turning. They were climbing a steep driveway, spiraling up the hillside. The ground suddenly leveled out, and they came to a stop next to an identical limousine, already parked, and a third pulled alongside. The doors of all three were opened at once, and the men emerged, blinking, into the bright sunshine.

All eighteen men, ranging in age from their early to late twenties, ranging in physical attractiveness from handsome to godlike, followed the chauffeurs up the steps to a patio that overlooked the valley they had just come from. He glanced from side to side, pretending to be admiring the artful arrangement of flagstones, the careful workmanship of the brick pizza oven. He was aware of at least three cameras on him, watching his movements as he looked around.

If these men were even half as polished on the inside as they were on the outside, he had his work cut out for him.

KAITLYN REGARDED the young man sitting opposite her at the conference table in the production office. He was dressed far above the station of a production intern, but his manner was open and his eyebrows were arched in what she might describe as optimistic anticipation.

She extended her hand.

"So, you're Mr. Palinsha—Palikinsha—" She studied the beautifully designed resume she had grabbed off her desk on the way into the room and tried to force her lips into the bizarre shape this name required. "Mr. Palilikshawi—"

"Please, call me Omar," he said, rising to take her hand.

"That's quite a last name you've got there, Omar," she said, smiling, motioning for him to resume his seat. "Did the person typing your birth certificate drop the keyboard down a staircase?" She sucked in a sudden breath as her internal political correctness sensor started blaring. "I'm sorry," she blurted. "It's been a long day." She slumped into her chair.

Omar grinned good-naturedly. "At least you tried," he said. "Often people don't even attempt it—they blink, twitch a bit, and go right for a joke about the no-fly list."

"You are a remarkably good sport about it," she replied, genuinely impressed with his bearing at such a young age. He acknowledged her compliment with a graceful nod.

She smoothed out the somewhat crumpled resume on the table and blinked hard. She scanned quickly down the page, picking out the essentials.

"How long have you been working with Dr. Preston?" she asked.

"I've been his lab assistant for two years now," he replied.

Kaitlyn knew Drew Preston from her own time at the university—he had long been a fixture of the media department. She hadn't worked with him as closely as Omar seemed to have, but anyone who had lasted for two years as Preston's lackey was clearly made of strong stuff. His e-mail message had recommended Omar in glowing terms.

Her eyes flicked through the rest of his resume. "I see here that you have a good deal of video production experience. But have you worked under anything like the time pressure on a show like this?"

"Dr. Preston has always remarked on my speed in postproduction work, if that's what you mean."

"Well," she continued, "it's one thing when you're working on the long-form stuff that Preston does. But what we do is a whole different deal. We've got to take a week of twenty-four-hour feeds from six dozen cameras and turn them into forty-four minutes of reality, once a week, for three months. And it has to happen in near-real time, because the next week's footage is already piling up as we work."

"If I may ask a naive question," Omar said, with a bow of his head, "why does it have to happen so quickly? Why not just film everything and then spend a month or two pulling together the episodes all at once? You would gain narrative coherence and reduce what Dr. Preston calls the 'crazy time.'"

She smiled. His question wasn't naive at all. "We used to do it that way. And my hair used to not have these lovely silver accents," she added, wryly. "But the powers that be are convinced that 'audience engagement' will save network television, and that means that this season, for the first time, the viewers get to vote on each week's competition—they pick who goes, and they get to pick a bachelor as their favorite of the week. You can't do that with a production delay of more than a day, so now we have to get it done quick."

"But doesn't that lower the quality of the end product?"

Okay, now he was being naive. She couldn't help chuckling.

"This ain't about quality, my good man. You will learn that soon enough." She stood. "Shall we take a quick tour of the facility?" He nodded, and she led him out and down the hall to the nerve center of the show. She opened the door of a control room that could easily have been mistaken for a NASA facility, except that instead of star charts, the monitors showed video feeds of an empty house.

Omar stood scanning the hundred or so displays, blinking as his gaze darted from side to side. Kaitlyn watched for his reaction as he took in the empty kitchen, the deserted bedrooms, the vacant bathrooms. After nearly a minute, he nodded as if he understood something that had eluded him at first.

"So, what do you think?" she asked.

His brow knitted thoughtfully, and he paused before answering. "Many of these cameras will not produce footage that will be usable."

She tried to stifle a smile, and mostly failed. "Why do you say that?"

"Take cameras 2-4 and 2-6," he said, pointing. "They seem to be located in a large shower."

"Yes, they are," she replied. This guy was catching on quickly. "And what about that troubles you?"

"Assuming the contestants are male, and assuming that they will use this shower room...." He glanced at her with his eyebrows up, as if to ask for confirmation.

"Yes, you're right so far," she said, nodding.

"Then the current configuration of the cameras, framing as they do the entire shower from floor to ceiling, will result in footage unsuitable for network television. If the shower is to be used by men, then the cameras must be adjusted to view only the waist up. If women were to use it, then from the clavicles up. I can make the requisite adjustments, if you wish."

"I'm sure you can," she said, smiling. "But we set them this way on purpose. Our only interest is in making sure we record everything. If two of our bachelors start trash-talking in the shower, we want to have it. We'll blur what we need to in order to get it past Standards and Practices. But we don't want to miss anything."

"Will, uh...." Omar stumbled, his poise thrown off for the first time in the interview. "Would I... if I were to be hired, that is, would I—"

"No worries," Kaitlyn cut him off, laughing. "We have a specialist for that. He used to blur blood and guts for the *National Geographic* channel—if he can blur an antelope's entrails at forty-five miles an hour, some dangly bits in the shower is a cakewalk."

Omar was visibly relieved. Despite his apparent squeamishness, Kaitlyn liked Omar. He was quick and seemed capable, and Preston's recommendation didn't hurt either.

"So," she said as they exited the control room, "are you interested?"

He stopped and took a deep breath before answering. "In spite of my reservations about whether I would be making a contribution to the culture of my country by helping produce this... show," he began, then paused for Kaitlyn's giggle to pass, "I think I would learn valuable new skills. Dr. Preston was correct in his assessment of you."

Kaitlyn frowned. "What did Preston say about me?"

"That you were the most talented sellout of your generation."

She turned this over in her mind a moment, then burst out laughing again. "God, what an asshole! But I've been called worse by people I respect less, so I'll take it!"

Omar seemed unsure whether he was supposed to join in this merriment. He waited decorously for her mirth to conclude.

"You in, Omar?" she finally managed.

"Yes, I am," he said solemnly.

"Excellent. The bachelors are arriving as we speak, and the intern who was supposed to be helping me out this season got a better offer this morning from a strip club in Ventura, so we have a shitload of work to do. I hope you didn't think you'd be getting any sleep tonight." She tore off down the hallway, and only after she had reached the corner did she turn back to see him, shell-shocked, motionless where she had left him.

"Come on. Your internship starts now!"

He straightened up and started after her at a jog, an expression of complete bafflement on his face.

CHAPTER TWO
REALITY TV

THE MEN milled around the patio, awaiting instructions. The show had never begun this way, or never seemed to, at any rate; of course, what was broadcast and what actually happened were probably two very different things.

A door opened. From a room that appeared to be made mostly of glass, she stepped.

Now this seemed to him very odd. Normally, the contestants were presented to her one by one in a kind of slow reveal ceremony. But this time she just strode into the midst of them. She was beautiful—they always were—but not in the usual way. Her dirty-blonde hair was up in a ponytail, and she wore sensible clothes—and tennis shoes! What was going on?

She walked up to each man in turn, shook his hand, said a few words, and then moved on to the next. Something was wrong. He stood off to the side to observe the action. The cameras weren't even following her. No, something was definitely wrong.

She came to him last.

"Riley?" she said, not really a question.

"Yes," he said, and held out his hand. She took it, and gave a very businesslike shake.

"I'm Kaitlyn," she said, smiling.

"I'm very pleased to meet you," he said, employing the resonant and confident voice he had decided would play the best when he met Her. He smiled warmly, thankful that his dentist had fit him in for one more whitening last week.

"Me too," she replied. "I'm the supervising producer, and I'd like to have a quick chat with all of the contestants before we get started. How about we start with you?"

Riley's smile betrayed nothing of his surprise. "That would be fine," he assured her. She turned and headed back to the glass room, and he followed.

Once they had settled into a pair of chairs that faced each other, the cameras clicked on and they began.

"So, Riley. Tell me a little about yourself."

He glanced quickly at the red light atop the camera just over her shoulder, then back at her. As he looked earnestly into her eyes, he told the story he had practiced so many times in the mirror.

THE MEN were led downstairs after the completion of the interviews. A broad hallway ran the length of the lower level, with several doors leading off of it. Having been directed to the first of three doors on the left side of the hall, Riley found himself in a large room that contained six beds, three on each side of the room, each no more than two feet from the others. At the far end of the room was a bathroom, equal in size to the room containing the beds. This boasted a long counter with three sinks, a small separate room with a toilet, and a large glass-walled shower. Riley noted with some surprise that there were three showerheads arrayed along the wall, which promised a little less in the privacy department than he had expected.

All around the rooms—both the bedroom and the bathroom—cameras stood watch. Some were mounted in the ceiling, others high on the walls, and the slightly wavy reflection in the mirror above the sinks gave the distinct impression that there were cameras behind, looking across the room at the shower.

As the men had been told they had an hour to settle in, Riley stood in the middle of the bathroom and considered the situation. He could recall no episode from the many seasons he had watched that had even shown the bachelors' bedrooms, much less their bathroom. A queasy suspicion crept into his gut that he now found himself on a very different show than he had anticipated.

"D'ya mind?" came an impatient voice from behind him. "You're blocking my locker," one of the men, in a very expensive suit, grumbled, nodding toward the wall where stood six cubbies.

Riley stepped aside, and the other man opened the first, and most easily accessible, locker and placed his shaving kit inside. It was in no sense "his" locker, but in getting there first, he had established his right to it. The opening moves in this bizarre game were being played.

Back in the bedroom, the rest of the men were unpacking the small suitcase each had been allowed to bring and that had been delivered here from the trunk of the limo. There was a line of armoires along the wall near the door, and just as in the bathroom, each man laid claim to one. One was energetically, and somewhat robotically, arranging his clothes using folding and pressing techniques that would have made the Prince of Wales's valet applaud, while another simply shoved his suitcase under the bed.

All the while red lights flashed and then extinguished on the various cameras, in no order Riley could discern. He could not even be sure the red lights meant anything at all—this entire arrangement was so different from anything he had seen on television that he had to discard all of his assumptions about how it would work. He was starting from scratch, something he had worked hard to avoid.

He was completely absorbed in brainstorming, running scenarios in his head, so it was not until one of the men actually bumped his shoulder as he passed by, naked, that Riley even noticed him.

"Dude, what the hell?" he asked, as the stack of muscle with the allover tan strode toward the bathroom.

"What's your problem?" came the blunt reply. "They said we have an hour, and I'm gonna put mine to good use. I kinda stink after being cooped up in the limo with you losers." He turned and continued his nude promenade to the shower.

"Like we all wanted to see his junk," muttered another of the men, whose sartorial preferences ran along the hemp shorts and puka shell line. He shook his head and turned his attention back to the cliché he was holding, a copy of *On the Road.*

Riley put his clothes away, stowed his shaving kit, and sat back on his bed to strategize. He had now gotten a better sense of at least some of his competitors, and while all had something to recommend them, he didn't think that any of them presented an insurmountable challenge.

He was going to win this thing.

NOW THAT they had settled into the house, the men were slightly more at ease, and Riley was able to get some sense of his competitors from the other limos. He had surveyed their physical characteristics during the first gathering on the terrace and found little to concern him; in fact, several of the contestants would be difficult to tell apart were their eyes not different colors. It didn't hurt that he was in the best physical condition of his twenty-nine years; the gym had been his refuge over the last year as he recovered from being left at the altar by the person whose name he still couldn't say, couldn't even think. Every weight set, every mile on the running track, every sit-up—each was a shovelful of dirt atop the pain that she had left him in.

Aside from the five clones who varied only in eye and hair color and who would be eliminated in early rounds, he knew—unless there was something distinctive about them, they tended to go early—and the five he had already sized up in the limo, there were seven others he needed to know more about. He strolled as casually as he could around the room, ears sharp for intelligent talk, low and soulful voices, anything distinctive. He came up with little until he rounded the final corner of the room and heard two of the men discussing the current political situation in a middle-eastern country in the news for having nearly blown itself to pieces over the weekend in its latest spasm of civil unrest.

"… and if they think that the president is hard to deal with, just wait until he gets whacked and the clerics step into the power vacuum," the shorter one was saying.

"You'd think we'd have learned that by now. This is hardly the first time this has happened," the taller one said in an accent Riley tried to place—Australian? New Zealander?—shaking his head and shrugging his shoulders at the inevitability of it all.

"Gentlemen," Riley said, extending his hand to the taller man first, shaking his strong, tan hand, and then greeting the shorter one similarly. As strong as the first one had been, this one's grip was like a vise. "Nice to hear actual conversation among this somewhat brain-challenged company."

Riley was relieved when the other two men chuckled and nodded. He wanted to be sure he gained their acceptance as they looked to be the most serious competition in the room.

"Name's Riley," he said, in his manliest tone. "And you are—"

"Can I have everyone's attention, please? Attention please!" came a voice from the front of the room—Kaitlyn's voice, he recognized immediately.

"The object of all of your affections will be here shortly, and we would like you to form a line along the terrace to—"

Her voice was immediately drowned out by the scuffle of feet as those closest to the doors rushed to be at the head of the receiving line. They found, however, that the doors were blocked by several gentlemen who were doubtless card-carrying members of the Scary Bouncers Union. There had been an unfortunate incident during the receiving line in season three that resulted in several minor injuries and one contestant rolling down a rocky slope to land in a swimming pool. Now they managed the men more carefully.

Kaitlyn waited for the hubbub to die down. "You will line up in the order in which you were interviewed this afternoon," she managed to say, finally.

Riley, contestant #1, made his way to the door where Kaitlyn waited for him. She nodded to the bruisers who held the door handles, and they released their iron grip and swung the doors open. He walked through, and found his mark on the terrace, where a small piece of blue tape bearing a Sharpied "#1" had been affixed to the flagstone.

A thrill ran through him to realize he would be the first to make a first impression. This was going better than he had let himself hope.

Next to him appeared the tall man with whom he had been attempting to have a conversation moments ago. He nodded his greeting, and the other replied in kind. The rest of the line filled in quickly, and soon they were assembled. Kaitlyn passed by to review the group, and reaching Riley, she waved to the cameramen and quickly ducked out of the shot. A chubby man in a loud Hawaiian shirt made his way with a Steadicam along the group several times, getting a slightly different angle each time he swept sweatily by. After having gotten several takes, the cameraman took up his station at the corner of the terrace.

Two people Riley hadn't seen before walked out of the glass room onto the terrace. The man was dressed in a shiny suit cut in the style of fashionable Europeans half his age. The woman alternately glided and tottered, her breathtakingly high heels no match for the uneven surface of the terrace stones. But a dazzling set of teeth shone between her crimson lips, and as she walked along, she nodded to each of the men as if she had already met them and remembered something charming and significant about them all. One of the conceits of the show was that the two hosts developed a close personal relationship with all involved—the male host empathized with the bachelorette, while the sinuous, gilded female host had the occasional late-night confab with the contestants. It was fake, of course. From watching earlier seasons, Riley strongly suspected that the producers wrote all of the questions and provided them to the hosts to commit to memory before each "spontaneous" conversation.

The hosts stood by the top of the stairs that led up to the terrace from the parking area and waited. Soon a limo appeared, climbing the driveway at a regal pace. It pulled up to the stairs, and the back door was opened by a tuxedoed footman. The bachelorette stepped into the late afternoon sunshine.

Looking like she had stepped out of a Burberry ad at the front of *Vogue*, she was dressed with a surprisingly understated glamour, in contrast to the hosts she would meet at the top of the stairs. The effect was something like a younger daughter of a royal family returning from a not particularly strenuous horse ride.

She climbed the stairs, beaming for the cameras, and greeted the hosts at the top. Then one of the production crew rushed over, explained something with hands waving madly in the air, and the bachelorette returned to the bottom of the stairs and climbed them again, this time more slowly, even stopping to take a break for what looked like internal reflection. Perhaps the producers wanted to portray a young woman with a lot on her mind, who approached her reality show with thoughtfulness and care. On the third try she was, apparently, successful in conveying what the producers wanted to see.

Having successfully mounted the stairs, she made her way to the waiting line of bachelors and began, with the help of the hosts of the show, to introduce herself to the men.

"May I present Daphne, your bachelorette?" the hostess enthused in a breathy voice.

"Pleased to meet you, Daphne. I'm Riley."

"Riley," she replied. "I like that name. Great to meet you." She took his hand, clasped it for a moment, and then was tugged on the elbow by the host of the show to move on.

Riley kept his winning smile fixed on her as she was introduced to the next man, who claimed to be named Shine. But then he recalled the Aussie accent and figured he must actually be named Shane. Shane played the rough-but-sexy outback character to perfection, and Daphne seemed charmed by it.

Riley had met the real competition.

RILEY REVIEWED the day's events as he lay on his bed in the mostly dark dorm (the need for the cameras to have at least some ambient light meant they were never in complete darkness). Meeting Daphne had gone well, especially as he was given the first shot at making a memorable impression. He wished that Shane had been placed in his dorm, not the one across the hall, so Riley could observe him more closely. He hadn't had a chance to even get to know the name of the shorter man he had attempted to introduce himself to—he could be a threat as well.

Riley wondered if he was doing the right thing coming on this show. He had only told one person he was taking an extended break from his job and coming to California for this strange adventure, and that was only two days ago.

"YOU'RE GOING to do *what*?"

Kevin, Riley's friend since childhood, sat looking like a trout—a confused trout. His mouth gaped open, his eyes glassy with incomprehension.

"I'm going to do that show," Riley repeated, more slowly this time, and for good measure, he gestured to the television.

Kevin gaped for another long moment, and then burst into a deep, hearty laugh. "Okay, ya got me. Very funny, Funny Man. Now the game's gonna be on in a sec—can you grab me another beer?" He turned back to the television, still chuckling, shaking his head. "You, a bachelor on the TV. Heh."

The promo for the show *Husband Material* presented a frenetically cut montage of highlights from previous seasons. The show's concept was the combination of a bachelorette contest and a survival competition. Bachelor contestants didn't just compete for the attention of the bachelorette; they competed against one another in tests both athletic and intellectual. This was the main reason Riley had chosen it to audition for; he had something to prove, and it went far beyond proving that he could look good in a tuxedo.

"I'm not kidding. I'm going to do it." Riley's voice was steady, despite the fact that the very idea of telling Kevin what he was planning had been making him anxious all week. But he was leaving for California on Monday, and he could delay no longer. He desperately wanted Kevin's support, but he knew full well what his friend's reaction would be.

Kevin turned back to Riley, who was sitting next to him on the couch in Kevin's basement TV room—his "man cave," as his wife had started calling it after watching too many home-renovation shows. He had stopped laughing. "Look, it was funny, but...." He trailed off as he looked at Riley's serious face.

"I leave tomorrow," Riley said quietly.

Kevin was silent for a moment, cocking his head as if struggling to make sense of what Riley had told him. "Dude... no way... really? Nah, you can't be... really?" He squinted at Riley, hard.

"Really."

"Swear?" Kevin asked, his voice low and urgent.

"On a stack of *Playboys*." This had been their absolute test of truth since the age of twelve, their sacred vow.

"Holy shit." Kevin shook his head. "She really did a number on you, didn't she?"

"This isn't about her," Riley replied. Then, since he could only tell Kevin the truth, he added, "At least, not all about her. It's about me trying to find my way back from the place she left me in. It's something I need to do."

"Couldn't you just go win a triathlon or something? I mean, look at you—since she ripped out your heart and used it to wipe her ass, you've worked yourself into the best shape of your life. There are a lot of things you could do to prove you're back on top, and none of them involve being on a stupid reality show about fake true love."

"I never thought I'd do something like this either. But I was kind of at a low point back in the depths of winter when I read in the Sunday paper they were casting the next season, so I sent in my video clip. Then I started busting my ass at the gym double-time so if I made it onto the show I wouldn't look like a depressed slob."

Kevin laughed. "So all of this"—he nodded at Riley's chest—"is because you wanted to get on TV?"

"Not entirely," Riley answered. He could hear the equivocation in his own voice—he knew that Kevin wouldn't let him walk.

"Bullshit. You're doing this to rub that bitch's face in it. You want her to see you on that show and eat her fucking heart out!" Kevin was laughing and nodding. "Payback's the real bitch," he said and raised his hands for a double high-five.

"Okay, so you got me," Riley said once their mutual laughter had died down. "It would be nice for her to see what she missed out on. But it's also a chance for me to get out of my usual life and try some new things, meet some new people. Chicago's great, but I could really use a change of pace, and weather, and people, and everything."

Kevin looked at his friend for a moment and then nodded. "If that's what you want, I think it's awesome. You go, and fucking play to win, my friend."

"Thanks, buddy. It means a lot to me."

"Anything I can do to help?" Kevin asked.

"Watch Biscuit for me?" He had inherited the dog from a niece who had quickly tired of the animal once it was no longer an adorable puppy. Biscuit loved Kevin, and Riley knew the feeling was mutual, if unspoken.

"No worries. He's got a home here for as long as you're out there chasing your dream."

"Thanks, man." Riley stared at the game on the silent TV for a moment. "Hey, you won't tell anyone that I'm—"

"Your secret's safe with me. But when you win, it's not exactly going to be a secret anymore, right?"

"I hope not. What I'm really hoping for is the cover of *People* magazine with me looking all shirtless and manly. You can frame that and hang it right over there." He gestured to the wall above the tacky old bar that Kevin had liberated from an abandoned tavern a couple of years before.

"I'd be proud to," Kevin replied, lifting his beer in a toast to Riley's imagined star turn as a cover boy.

Riley chuckled. "Might make your better half wonder, don't ya think?"

"Nah. First, she never comes down here if she can help it. Second, she knows that the bond we share goes beyond mere friendship," Kevin intoned breathily, leaning close to Riley. He topped off the act by blowing a kiss.

"Shut up, ya nerd," Riley replied with a sock on Kevin's arm and a grin.

Kevin laughed and took another swig of beer. "Now can we focus on the game, please? Honestly, you and your drama."

RILEY SMILED at the memory and closed his eyes. Whatever tomorrow brought, he wanted to be rested and ready. He had come to win.

CHAPTER THREE

SHINING ARMOR

THIS WASN'T exactly the Olympics.

The ostensible purpose of the competition at the heart of the show was to allow the bachelorette to find her champion, the man who was strongest, fastest, most capable. She would, in theory, see the men at their best, and be able then to choose the one who excelled in those manly arts most dear to her.

The real purpose of the ridiculous weekly challenges was to display the bachelors—or rather, their bodies—to the audience, who tuned in to discover how the contestants would be rendered soaking wet, shirtless, or both.

Riley knew this going in, of course, which was one of the reasons he had been hitting the gym so hard over the last several months. He knew that his survival, particularly in the early weeks, was more a measure of how he seduced the camera rather than the bachelorette.

The bachelors were bused to the site of their first challenge less than twenty-four hours after their arrival at the house. They had been given no clue as to the exercise the producers had contrived for them to battle through, and the chatter on the bus was filled with idle, and increasingly silly, speculation. Riley sat at the front of the bus and stared out the window, glad that the seat next to him was occupied by one of the show's handlers rather than one of the brainless bachelor herd. He had hoped to get a glimpse of the clipboard on the young man's lap, but it was covered securely by a bright-red plastic sheet with "TOP SECRET" emblazoned across it. He had to chuckle to himself at how seriously they all took this charade of "reality."

The bus arrived at an imposing block of a building, completely without identifying marks, and waited while a large door rolled up so that the bus could enter. It came to a stop just inside the building and shuddered to a halt. Eager to get going, the men stood and nudged into the aisle, and then fell quiet when the bachelor wrangler next to Riley stood and called for their attention.

"Welcome to the first challenge, gentlemen. Follow me, please." He led the way down the steps, with Riley right behind.

They were in a cavernous, warehouse-like space. The only structure Riley could see was a scaffolded cube about the size of a basketball court and some bleachers. He was unable to discern enough through the slats of the scaffold to get a sense of what was in the middle. Off to the side of the structure was a brightly lit area where some staffers awaited their arrival. The handler, reaching this point, turned and waited for the men to gather.

"Gentlemen, this is where you will face your first challenge. Or rather, this is where you will first challenge one another."

Riley looked instinctively side to side—all the men did, which was probably what the producers intended. Aggressive glances played well on the teasers for the episode.

"Our theme this season will be 'Ages of Romance,' and each week's challenge will take place in a different time and place. Today, you will compete to be our bachelorette's knight in shining armor. It's the age of chivalry, gentlemen, so get ready to joust for the hand of your lady fair."

"Wait, we're going to be wearing armor?" Riley heard one of the others ask.

"Glad you asked," rejoined the handler. "You'll be shining all right, but you won't be wearing armor. To tell you about that part is Alana—she and her team will get you ready for the contest. Alana?"

The towering Amazon of a makeup artist stepped forward. "All right, listen up." The bachelors fell silent. "My team is going to turn you into silver-plated knights for the competition. This," she said as she pulled a parcel out from behind her back, "is what you will be wearing." She held up a pair of boy-shorts in gleaming silver.

"That's it?" came a worried voice from somewhere in the rear of the pack.

"Oh, no, of course not!" Alana assured him. "You'll also be wearing silver body paint. Now, each of you will go with one of my artists, and we'll get you sorted." Conjured by her words, a team of rail-thin minions swept into view from behind her. They were exactly what Riley expected—tall, willowy girls with razor-sharp multi-colored hair and throat tattoos, and fast-walking, fast-talking boys with frenetic hand gestures. Each bachelor was claimed by a makeup artist. Riley had hoped for one of several of the friendlier-looking cosmetistas as they hurried toward him, but each veered at the last second and laid claim to his competition. He started to wonder whether he really presented so much of a makeup challenge that no one wanted to be saddled with him.

Finally, when the voluble flock had flown by, he was approached by one of the production crew—at least that was what he assumed, given the young man's appearance. He was wearing worn jeans, a tight baseball jersey, and a cap that sat backward on his head. Riley looked at him expectantly, eager to find out what would happen while he waited for a makeup artist to arrive.

"So, you belong to me," the young man said, his voice a Jersey-tinged growl, his mouth twisted with either a snarl or a wry grin—Riley wasn't certain. "C'mon." He turned and walked toward the last of the makeup stations.

"Who is…. I mean, where…?" Riley, confused, gave up trying to formulate the right question and just followed along.

They reached the last makeup mirror in the row and came to a stop.

"Name's Wilbur," the young man said, extending his hand. "Pleased to meet you."

"I'm Riley." The men shook hands. "So this is where I'll wait?"

"Wait? For what?"

"For someone to come do… whatever makeup thing needs to be… done?" Riley grew tentative when he saw no glimmer of understanding on Wilbur's face.

"I'm your guy," Wilbur said with a professional smile. "Now, here's what we're going to do—"

"I'm sorry, did you say that you're the makeup artist?"

"Yeah. Problem?"

"Um, no, no problem. You're just not—"

"Not the makeup artist type, right? Yeah, I get that a lot. Now, here's what you need to wear. Get into that, and then we'll start on the body makeup." Wilbur handed Riley a pair of silver shorts that looked somehow even smaller than the ones Alana had brandished moments ago.

Riley studied the thin, shiny shorts. "Where do I change?"

Wilbur laughed. "How about right here, right now, so we can get you ready? They aren't going to hold the show while you try to find a changing room in the junior miss department." He shook his head and started opening his makeup cases.

A quick glance around the area proved Wilbur correct—all around him Riley could see his competition stripping off and donning the tiny silver briefs. Realizing that he was gazing out over a half-dozen pale mooning asses, he turned abruptly back to Wilbur, who gave an impatient shake of his head at the delay in wardrobe.

Riley began unbuttoning his shirt, but it was brand-new and rather stiff of placket, which caused his nervous fingers considerable difficulty.

"Lemme," Wilbur grunted, slapping Riley's hands away. "You're gettin' nowhere with those sausage fingers."

Shocked, Riley looked down at his hands. His fingers bore no objective resemblance to sausages. He mulled this insult for a moment, and then was distracted from his mulling by the feel of Wilbur's agile progress in unbuttoning. He had reached the lowest button he could without—and then Riley felt a yank as Wilbur pulled his shirt out of his pants and finished the job.

"There. Can you take it from here, chief, or should I continue?" Only the briefest twitch in the corner of Wilbur's mouth telegraphed that he was having a bit of fun with his awkward bachelor.

"No, I've got it," Riley managed to mumble, and he proceeded with his undressing while Wilbur opened a distressingly large jar of sparkling silver paste.

Riley carefully draped his shirt, and then his pants, over the back of a chair that sat next to the makeup station. He slipped off his socks and then, ashamed at his blushing, slid off his boxer briefs as well. He grabbed up the silver boy-shorts, not so quickly as to come across as ashamed of his body, but not so leisurely as to seem immodest. He was overthinking this, he knew, but he couldn't stop himself.

He slid the paper-thin, stretchy briefs into place.

"Nice job there, chief," said Wilbur. "Wasn't sure you were gonna be able to park a limo in that one-car garage."

Riley gaped, wordless.

"Hey, lighten up! Most guys don't mind a compliment on the junk." Wilbur's smile was undaunted by Riley's fishlike speechlessness. "Let's get the glitter party started," he said, motioning Riley to step closer.

Riley took two small strides and found himself in front of the mirror. A quick scan up and down proved two things: his hard work in the gym had paid off, and Wilbur kind of had a point about the logistics of these silver briefs. They looked to be at capacity or beyond.

Wilbur dipped his sponge into the jar of silver and approached Riley with it. He stopped short, however. "Hey, mind if we clean up a little here before we silver-plate you?"

"What? I took a shower this morning," protested Riley.

"No, you're fine. It's just that you have some fine hair on your chest— you can hardly see it, but it's going to look clumpy when the makeup goes on. Can we just…?" Wilbur made a rapid downward stroking motion across Riley's chest.

"You want to shave my chest?"

"Trust me, chief. It'll look much better."

"Uh, okay," stumbled Riley. This was getting really weird really quickly.

"Awesome." Wilbur turned and grabbed up a can of shaving cream and squirted some into his palm. He rubbed the foam onto both hands and stepped directly in front of Riley. "Have you ever shaved your chest?"

Riley shook his head.

"Nothing to worry about, I do this all the time," Wilbur said as he began to smooth the cream onto Riley's chest.

"It's… warm," Riley said, surprised.

"Yep. It's my own formula," he replied as he spread the warm foam across Riley's pectorals and in between. "It works really well for location shoots where you don't have hot water."

"It feels amazing," Riley was shocked to hear himself say. The unexpected warmth on his chest was like being wrapped in a soft blanket.

"It's a pretty basic exothermic reaction," Wilbur replied modestly. "I like to put my chemistry degree to good use once in a while." He spread the warm foam down to Riley's abs, then stepped back to survey his work. "Now, if we do the chest, we should probably do your trail as well," he mused, cocking his head to one side.

"My… trail?"

Wilbur's head snapped back upright. "Your treasure trail, chief. The line of hair that runs between your navel and the top of your pubes? It's going to get gummed up with silver if we leave it. You okay for me to keep going down?"

"Uh, sure, I guess…." Riley's voice trailed off. He was so far out of his comfort zone that he hardly felt he was in his body at all.

"Great. Here we go." Wilbur squirted another dollop of cream into his hands and ran them down Riley's lower belly. "Let's make sure we get it all," he said, looking Riley right in the eye as he tugged down on the silver briefs, lowering them an inch or so.

Riley's disembodied confusion abruptly gave way to a feeling of being very much in his body, a body that was now being touched quite intimately by another man.

"And... done!" Wilbur said suddenly, as if he had sensed Riley's panic. He wiped his hands on a towel, and reached for his razor.

"You use a straight razor?" Riley asked, his voice quavering. He cleared his throat, attempting to cough the girlishness out of it. "I mean, I've never used one of those."

"I prefer my tools straight," Wilbur said, winking.

Riley laughed in confusion. What the hell was that supposed to mean? But he had no time to analyze as Wilbur was approaching with the gleaming instrument.

"Now, shaving with a straight razor is a little different from using one of those pussy safety things. As long as we keep the tension on your skin, you'll get a much smoother shave, and there's really no danger." He looked into Riley's eyes again, with that strong, clear gaze. "I've never had a client bleed out—never even nicked one." He must have read Riley's uncertainty. "Trust me?"

Riley's mind was a whirl. Not knowing what else to do, he nodded. And then he closed his eyes.

The first thing he felt was Wilbur's hand, pressing on the top of his right pectoral. He jolted, eyes wide, startled by the firm pressure on his chest.

"Dude, I haven't even started yet," Wilbur said softly.

"Sorry. I guess I'm just a little nervous."

"I know. This whole TV thing has got to be stressful. But just take a deep breath and relax. You're in good hands," he murmured with a smile.

Riley nodded and then took the recommended deep breath and closed his eyes.

"I'm going in," Wilbur said in a hearty voice, clearly meant to buck up his agitated subject.

Then the razor made contact, just below the spot where the hand maintained its firm pressure, and it glided down smoothly, just to one side of Riley's nipple. The touch of the blade was so light that he hardly felt it. Then

Wilbur's hand slid over a bit, and the blade swept down again, this time to the other side of his nipple. He looked down, and saw, to his mortification, that his nipple was standing erect—the light sweeping motion of the blade had excited it somehow.

"You're doing great," Wilbur murmured, his eyes locking on Riley's for a moment and then returning to his work.

Riley closed his eyes again, wishing for this to just be over.

Wilbur, having slicked Riley's right pectoral, moved to the left and repeated his gentle swipes with the razor. Then he worked down the valley between them, a cleft made deeper by Riley's weight-lifting regimen of the last six months. He gently denuded the abs as well, tensioning the skin as he glided the razor over the ridges of stomach muscle. He paused when he reached Riley's navel.

"You good?" he asked.

Riley opened his eyes, having—despite his anxiety—been caught up in the feeling of Wilbur's gentle touch. He was immediately embarrassed, if not precisely sure why. "Yeah, I'm good. Actually, you're good—you're amazing with that blade."

"Damn right. Now we're going to take care of the south forty. Almost done, chief." Wilbur knelt down in front of Riley, a posture that instantly doubled Riley's anxiety. As intensely personal as the shaving had been, having the other man kneel before him was beyond anything Riley had ever imagined.

Wilbur laid his hand over Riley's navel and pressed gently to tension the skin below it. Riley felt a flush of warmth, which flummoxed him so that he welcomed the distracting terror of seeing the blade approach his vulnerable lower belly. He sucked in a breath, causing Wilbur to look up at him, his blue eyes framed by kind wrinkles at the corners as he grinned conspiratorially.

"Ready?" Wilbur asked, his voice low and soft.

Riley tried to respond, but his mouth was dry. He gave up and just nodded.

Wilbur winked at him and then looked to the job at hand.

Riley felt the warm breath brush across his skin as the other man laid his blade onto the taut lower abdomen and then slid, slowly and gently, down and down and down. The blade stopped only an inch from the base of Riley's manhood, close enough that Riley was suddenly aware of nothing else in the world other than his cock and this man's proximity to it.

Wilbur repeated the motion twice, completely clearing the trail of fine hair that had connected Riley's navel to the root of his penis. He then reached for a towel to finish up.

"Now we'll just wipe up, and we can get to turning you into the Tin Man," cracked Wilbur as he touched the towel to Riley's lower abs.

"Oh, that's—warm," exhaled Riley, in a voice that was almost a moan.

"The portable towel warmer is one of the greatest inventions known to man," Wilbur replied, gently swabbing the remains of the shaving cream off Riley's smooth skin.

In spite of himself, Riley closed his eyes and let the warm, gently massaging touch of Wilbur's careful ministrations wash over him. Some part of him knew he was enjoying this far too much, but he couldn't help it—or just didn't care anymore.

"And then a light soother to keep the makeup from irritating your skin," Wilbur said, in a voice so soft that it didn't disrupt Riley's relaxed state. Then Wilbur's hands were back, and there was no thick cream this time, no warm towel—nothing between the two men but a fine slick lotion. His hands swept over Riley's muscled chest, down the cleft between his abs, down to the border marked by the silver fabric, and then—just for an instant—beyond. Wilbur's fingertips breached the elastic waistband, only for a fraction of a second, but the touch—the warmth of it, the violation of it—shot through Riley like an electric current.

Riley felt the surge of blood to his cock, a feeling that was a part of his essential manhood, of every man's identity, but one that had never—never in his life—been invoked by the touch of another man. He stood in breathless panic, willing his erection to halt its progress, knowing that he was powerless to stop it.

Wilbur seemed not to have noticed. He finished his last sweep of Riley's shaved region, and turned back to his case to wipe his hands and pick up the silver makeup. But when he turned back, his eyes immediately darted to Riley's distended briefs. He looked up at Riley's face, at Riley's mortified, breathless expression.

"Damn, it's not enough that you are handsome and built like a brick shithouse. Ya gotta have a lady-killer down there too, huh? Shit, man, I'd give anything to be you, just for a day." Wilbur's eyes crinkled with good-natured laughter, and he shook his head. "Now, hold still, chief. This is gonna be painless but tedious." He stepped behind Riley and began daubing the metallic paste on his back.

Riley looked up and saw them in the mirror: himself with the recently denuded chest, and behind him the artist at work, who seemed to care not a bit about the tent at Riley's crotch. He closed his eyes and tried to think of the most boring thing he could imagine, desperate to interrupt his penis in its inflation.

"So, what do you do, when you're not putting yourself out on the meat market like this?" Wilbur asked, his eyes focused on the canvas of Riley's back, but glancing up every few moments to make eye contact in the mirror.

"Boring stuff. I work for an insurance company. It's not as glamorous as what you do, obviously."

Wilbur snorted. "Yeah, right. Look at me, I'm a frickin' rock star!" He laughed and shook his head.

"But it must be interesting work," Riley continued, desperate to keep the conversation going, hoping to bore his erection into submission. He thought he could feel its pulse slackening already.

"I thought it would be—that's why I dropped chemistry. Went into special effects makeup—thought aliens and monsters were my calling. Heh." He snorted again. "That dream lasted about a week—not a job to be had in that. I consoled myself by taking gigs doing fashion makeup. I figured I could work the Victoria's Secret show, that kind of thing. So I did that for a while."

"That must have been exciting, right?"

"Again, for about a week. Then I found out two things: first, lingerie models only know about a dozen words, and all of them have to do with themselves. Second, they don't date the makeup guy." Wilbur stood back from Riley for a moment, cocking his head. "All right, I'm gonna move to your side now—can you lift your left arm? Thanks." He resumed daubing in this new terrain.

"So the supermodels turned you down, huh?" Riley had finally felt the constriction in his shiny briefs relenting, and he wanted to keep Wilbur talking as long as he could.

"Oh yeah. At first I thought it was because they'd never met a straight makeup artist before, but the novelty apparently never wore off. Blue balls every frickin' night, my friend. Let me set the scene for you: the models have about thirty seconds to change between looks, and to get touched up. They would come running toward me in those ridiculous heels, melons bouncing"—here he hopped up and down, miming wildly heaving breasts—"throwing off negligées, and demanding that I blot the sweat from their cleavage while they changed panties. Holy hell, man, how was I supposed to deal with that?" He stepped back again, appraising his work. "Okay, done with the left—lift your right for me?" Wilbur moved over and began daubing again.

The mention of the naked and demanding Victoria's Secret models had instantly put Riley's erection elimination plan off track—he was on the rise again, dammit.

"There was this one model—every time I patched her up between outfits, her nipples would brush against my arm. You know, like this?" He ran his hand down Riley's arm, barely touching his skin. "I thought she was sending me a message, right? So at the end of the show I ask her out, and she hauls back and slaps me. A good clean hit, right on the jaw. That was my last fashion show, and I didn't really have any other job opportunities. I heard about Alana from a buddy and hit her up for a job. She gets the weirdest gigs, but they pay well. And just look at this glamour—right?" He was chuckling as he finished Riley's right side.

"Yeah, it sure feels glamorous." Riley could not yet see the silvering of his body, as Wilbur hadn't started on his chest. But he was about to, and no matter how decorous he had been to this point, he could hardly ignore Riley's still-growing erection, which threatened to emerge from its silvery confines any second.

"You're tellin' me. Now I'm gonna do your chest, okay? We'll cover the big areas, then come back for the detail work." He started energetically stroking Riley's chest with the makeup sponge, making big loopy swirls of silver. The pasty pancake substance was cool on his skin, and his nipples responded by perking up again, pointing directly at Wilbur. Ever the professional, he simply daubed a little extra on each point of flesh and kept moving.

Soon Riley's chest was as silver as the rest of his upper body.

"All right, now the legs," Wilbur said jauntily.

"You aren't going to take the blade to my legs, are you?"

"No! First, your legs are pretty uniform in terms of hair, unlike your chest. Second, with muscles like these—what are you, a cyclist?—shaving them will leave you looking more Angelina Jolie than shining armor knight."

"Gee, thanks," Riley muttered.

"Hey, if I had legs like yours, I'd be wearing a silver bikini every frickin' day!" He knelt down again in front of Riley, his face mere inches from the now hard and throbbing manhood obscured by the silver fabric.

Riley was in agony. His tumescence would have been awkward enough in front of a gay makeup artist, but knowing that Wilbur was straight made it creepy as well as embarrassing. He tried to think about anything other than being here, but when he closed his eyes he was backstage at the Victoria's Secret show and bouncing melons filled his mental vision. He held his breath and willed the blood to flow out of his loins. After a couple of minutes of concentration, he had made—or at least convinced himself he had made—some progress.

"All right, now we're going to do the edges, give you a nice finish." Wilbur stood, took up a small makeup brush, and dabbed it into the jar of silver. "Right hand," he ordered.

Riley held out his right hand, as instructed. He was so relieved that Wilbur was off his knees that he would do anything he was asked.

With the steady hand of a surgeon, Wilbur traced a line around Riley's wrist, neatly bordering the silver body paint. When he had finished, it looked uncannily like the hem of a sleeve.

"And the left," Wilbur said, his brow still furrowed with concentration. Riley complied. Soon the left matched the right, and the cuffs were finished. "Okay, now we can do the neck. I'll start in the back."

Wilbur disappeared behind Riley, but the slow, steady sweep of his brush made his presence known.

"I made the neck opening pretty wide," he said, appraising his work. "It really shows off those broad shoulders of yours."

Riley could see himself blushing in the mirror.

Wilbur came around to the front again, and started work on the neckline.

Riley could smell Wilbur's minty breath as he exhaled slowly, evenly. His hand traced along Riley's upper chest, the brush tickling a little, leaving goose bumps in its wake as it swept over the top of his chest. Riley closed his eyes, trying to imagine himself somewhere—anywhere—else.

"And... good," Wilber announced, stepping back to check his work. He closed one eye, tipped his head. "You know," he mused, "they said we're just supposed to paint you silver, but I don't think it would really be against the rules if we...."

"What? If we what?" Riley blurted, panic creeping into his voice.

"Hang on. Just let me...." Wilbur picked up a second jar of silver paint, then what looked like a tube of oil paint. He squeezed a dollop of purest black into the silver, and stirred it briskly with a wooden stick. The silver tinged ever so slightly darker. "There," he announced.

"Where... what?" Riley's agitated voice grew a little louder.

Wilbur looked him in the eye. "Silver paint looks shiny, but it covers over everything—all the detail of your body is lost. Now, that's great if you have moles or freckles, which you don't, but not so good if the detail that's lost is, for example, your super-ripped ab muscles." He tipped his head toward Riley's belly.

Riley looked in the mirror and saw immediately what Wilbur meant. His belly was flat. Most men, of course, would be happy to have a flat abdomen, but Riley had worked really hard to carve out six hard plates of muscle—none of which could be seen through the paint. He nodded.

"Now, if we had time, I would do this with an airbrush, but since we've got about five minutes, I'm just going to wing it, okay?"

Riley nodded again. He wasn't sure what Wilbur meant by "winging it," but he had come to trust the other man and decided to let him do what he wanted.

Wilbur knelt in front of Riley again. Riley immediately felt the heat rising in his chest. He started to consider the possibility that he was getting sick or that something at breakfast had disagreed with him.

"I'm just going to shade underneath each muscle—a little shadow to make your abs pop." He swirled his finger in the jar of dark silver paint and then swept it, ever so lightly, across Riley's belly. He then blended the streak he had made with his other fingers, a soft flurry of touch that softened and smoothed the line into the appearance of shadow.

Riley was in agony. Every touch brought a new wave of chills crashing over his body. He was beyond goose bumps now—he was starting to quiver. It had been nearly a year since he had been touched, by anyone, and now he was being tickled by another man, in public, while covered in silver paint.

A flashback popped up in his mind: once he had gone to a massage appointment and his usual therapist, a taciturn Swedish woman with hands that could snap tree branches, was out for the day. There was another therapist—a man Riley's age—but he had cancelled his appointment rather than spend an hour getting a rubdown from a man. He wanted nothing to do with that kind of intimacy. Now he was boning up at Wilbur's touch. The fucked-upness of his life was becoming painfully clear to him.

"Done." Wilbur stepped back and smiled broadly. "Fuck," he huffed, smiling broadly, "I'd do you right now, and no shit." He gave a deep, rumbling laugh and stowed his brush. Just a guy being a guy.

Riley tried to reply, but no words would come and he could only croak.

"Ten minutes, artists!" boomed a voice on a PA system. It echoed through the cavernous space. "Ten minutes!"

Wilbur grabbed up the jar of silver paint and the sponge, and hurried back to Riley. "Just need to tuck the silver into your shorts," he said. "I saved this for last so that we didn't get smearing while I worked on the other parts." He knelt at Riley's side, and began daubing the silver high on his thighs. "Hey, can you hike up your shorts a bit so I can get the paint up under?"

Riley hooked his fingers under the elastic around the leg holes, and pulled up.

"Excellent." Daub daub daub. Wilbur scooted quickly from one side to the other, and repeated his daubing flurry. "Now, I'm gonna get your back," he said, now short of breath from his scurrying.

Riley felt the waistband of his briefs tugged forcefully down, and felt cool air on the top of his buttocks.

"Jesus, man, you have got it goin' on back here too," cracked Wilbur as he worked silver paint into the rounded muscle and down in between. "These things don't give a millimeter, even when I'm pushin' on 'em!"

Riley was relieved when the waistband slipped back into place. Finally, he would be able to get away from this bizarre thing they were doing.

"One more spot, and you're good to gladiate!" Wilbur shuffled around Riley to the front, where he did the same as he had done at the back. He gave a good yank and the waistband pulled down, right to the root of Riley's cock.

Panic shot through Riley, as time came to a sudden and sickening halt. With Wilbur's every touch Riley felt his cock surge, until it was throbbing in time with the makeup artist's frantic motions. He could feel the thin fabric tightening as his penis stretched farther toward his hip.

"And we're just about—Oh, shit! Dude!" Wilbur exclaimed as Riley's cock sprang free of the silvery confines it had been wedged into.

"Oh, fuck—I don't know what—" Riley blurted. He could hardly catch his breath—the room was starting to spin around him. "I'm sorry," he managed to mutter, the taste of breakfast surging into his mouth.

Wilbur looked up at him. "Dude, chill. You don't need to apologize. It happens. But I don't know how we're going to get you back into this very tight package." He stood up but stayed just inches from Riley, blocking the sight of the rogue erection from the rest of the room.

"Maybe they have a larger size?"

"They do, but that doesn't do us any good right now. Taking these off would smear the paint right off your legs—it'd be a mess."

"Oh, fuck! I'm going to have to drop out. I can't go out there with this—"

"Hold on there, chief. My momma didn't raise a quitter. We just gotta get rid of this thing."

"How am I going to do that?"

"Can you think about baseball or something? Car crashes? The stock market?"

"I was doing that the whole time you've been working on me. This is how much it's helped," Riley snapped, with a head-tip down to his crotch.

A grin tugged at the corner of Wilbur's mouth. "I did that?"

Riley sighed. "Well, I'm probably just anxious about this competition thing, but having your hands all over me didn't exactly help matters."

Wilbur chuckled. "Awesome." He suddenly regained his serious composure when he saw Riley's stern expression. "I think there's only one thing that's going to help."

"What's that—you have some ice or something?"

"No, that would be a drippy mess." He looked right into Riley's eyes. "You're going to have to tug one out, chief. It's the only way."

"What the fuck?"

Wilbur reached back and grabbed a towel. He held it up around the front and sides of Riley's body, not touching his skin but close enough to keep anyone from seeing what was going on under it. "You're covered. Now go!" he said urgently, looking from side to side.

The other silvery bachelors were starting to drift over to the edge of the structure, where the competition would shortly begin.

"I can't. This is too weird."

"Look, do you want to win this thing, or flame out before it starts?" Wilbur's voice was gruff and low. "Get to it, man!"

Riley couldn't think straight anymore, and in the absence of any other notion of what to do, he did what Wilbur told him to. He reached down into the towel and wrapped his hand around his inexplicably still rock-hard cock. But the insanity of what he was doing stopped him there. He couldn't move.

"What, you doing some kind of tantric isometric thing?" Wilbur said with a glance down into the towel. "Get moving!" He looked quickly around the room, then back to Riley. "Don't make me come in there!" he said, the sly grin reappearing on his stubbled face.

"Shit," Riley grunted, and willed his hand to start moving. It slid tentatively along his penis, which responded by producing a drop of fluid from its tip. Riley may have felt completely lost, but his cock was sure of what it wanted.

Riley had never in his life done this with another person watching him, and he had certainly never done it in a room with a hundred other people. As he quickened his pace, though, he began to hope that his problem would soon be behind him, and he could still compete.

Wilbur, seeming to sense how he might help, turned back to Riley after completing another sweep of the room. "You know that model I was telling you about earlier—the one who always brushed her nipples on my arm? Well, that wasn't all she did. This one time, during a break in the runway show, she disappears. Just disappears. Supposed to be in my chair so I can switch to evening makeup, and she's gone. So I go look for her—high and low, everywhere—and finally when I opened the janitor's closet, there she is with another of the models. They are going at it—hard. All of that work I did on her lips, and she's got them locked on this other woman's tits, her fingers rubbing away between her legs. Moaning and groaning like there's no tomorrow. Then they see me looking, so they start kissing and pressing their boobs together and sliding up and down on each other's thighs. They start shaking like they're having a month's worth of orgasms, and I just close the door and walk away."

Riley closed his eyes to better focus on the writhing super-lesbians. Another drop of precum slid from his cock, allowing his hand to slide more smoothly along its length.

"Then I head for the bathroom, because now I can't even walk straight I'm so hard. I close the door, whip it out, and just stand there, not caring who can hear me, not caring who's in the next stall or what they think I'm doing, and I start beating my cock. Like it owes me money. It was so fucked up, so dirty, I just about shot as soon as I started."

"Yeah?" breathed Riley, his pulse quickening.

"I was hard as a fuckin' pipe, and it took about thirty seconds before I could feel it."

"Feel... what...?" Riley's voice was a ragged whisper, his eyes wide.

"Feel my fuckin' balls start to hitch up, gettin' ready...."

"Ohh...," Riley moaned.

"Gettin' ready to shoot, man, shoot my shit all over the place." Wilbur was looking right into Riley's eyes. "Fuckin' pump it out. Stroke it... stroke it... stroke it," Wilbur huffed out his filthy chant, urging Riley on.

Riley couldn't speak, but neither could he look away. His hand was a blur of slippery motion.

"I came harder than I ever had in my life." He was leaning into Riley now, his lips against Riley's ear. "I just fuckin' blew that load all over the place, rubbed it until I was dry, emptied out. I came and came and came." Wilbur's words were hot and moist in Riley's ear.

Riley took a sharp breath, and froze. Then he felt it tear through him, this unwanted but desperately needed release, and his cock began wildly spurting. Riley was swept away, out of the bizarre competition—he was wrapped in the serene glow of orgasm.

"Got it!" Wilbur said, jarring Riley out of his ecstatic suspension.

Riley felt the other man's hand grasp the head of his cock and squeeze. Wilbur had gathered up a handful of the towel fabric, and was holding it firmly around the tip of Riley's penis as semen blasted out of it. He held on, his grip strong, until the flow of semen trailed off.

Riley was shocked. He had never been touched by a man in any of the ways that Wilbur had been touching him this morning, and certainly never as he was being touched now. His eyes wide with mortification, he turned to look at the other man's face, and saw his eyebrows were peaked, his mouth was open, and he was drawing a ragged breath as if he were the one in the throes of this unwanted but undeniable storm of pleasure. Riley closed his eyes and looked away.

"Just protecting the paint job," Wilbur whispered into Riley's ear. "No homo," he added, and Riley could see a grin as he pulled back.

With shaking hands Riley tucked his penis back into the silvery briefs, and Wilbur tossed the towel, now bearing Riley's semen, off to the side of the makeup station. In the mirror Riley could see that his briefs, though still tightly packed, were no longer obscenely stretched.

"Looks good to go, big guy," Wilbur said, a broad smile on his face.

"Yeah. Uh... thanks." Riley was trying hard to catch his breath. "I really... owe you one," he fumbled.

"No worries. Just go win this thing, okay?"

Riley nodded, and turned to go. He stopped and turned back.

"And just for the record," he said to Wilbur, "I'm not... you know."

A wry grin spread across Wilbur's face, lit by a genuine warmth. "I know you're not gay—you're just a guy with a superhero cock who is man enough to deal with it."

Riley surprised himself with a laugh, a release of tension in the face of how fucked up the whole thing was. Maybe it was going to be okay. He nodded his thanks to Wilbur and turned to face the competition.

IN THE lineup with all of the other bachelors, Riley got his first view of the arena where the competition would take place. There was a large apparatus in the middle, made up of what looked like huge gymnastic balance beams that had been wrapped in several feet of protective foam. Four of these beams, each brightly colored, converged in the center of the arena in an X-pattern. The beams stood about four feet above the surface of what appeared to be a pond of some kind—anyone falling off a beam would find himself splashing down into several feet of water. This is where the bachelors would do battle.

In the stands on the far side of the arena, Riley could see a small group of people chatting—the bachelorette was there, surrounded by her ladies-in-waiting. This was another innovation this season on the show: the bachelorette had been allowed to invite four of her BFFs to accompany her to some of the competitions and advise her on the journey to true love. This morning they were all dressed in their Renaissance Faire finest: flowing gowns, ridiculous headdresses, and push-up bras that were working double time to heave those bosoms skyward.

The men were broken up into four groups, each placed at the outside end of one of the four beams leading to the intersection at the center of the arena. Riley found himself with several bachelors he had not yet met; at this point he was uncertain whether the men next to him were to be his competitors or his team. He took a moment to size them up.

They were all silvered, of course, but a quick scan of the knights was testimony to Wilbur's skill. None of the other bodies were as smoothly colored, and certainly none were decked out with tidy cuffs or shadowed ab muscles.

"Listen up, gentlemen," drawled the handler standing at the head of the group. "Today you will be contesting for the favor of your lady fair," he read off the clipboard. He rolled his eyes. "Who writes this shit?" he asked no one in particular. With a world-weary sigh, he forged ahead. "You will use this jousting lance," he said, holding aloft a four-foot-long foam weapon, "to smite your opponents. The last man standing at the end of the jousting wins a kiss from the lady."

He looked up from his script. "Now line up by the numbers I give you, and let's get this hoo-hah over with." He pointed at Riley. "You, one." Then to the rest of the crowd. "Two, three, four, and you, there—five. Remember your numbers, meat puppets."

He reached into a crate next to him and pulled out a bag. "In this bag you will find your helmet, gloves, and boots. That's the uniform. Put them on and wait for the signal to...." He consulted his clipboard. "Vanquish your foes," he read in a deadpan voice. He threw a bag at each man and then shuffled through the other papers on his clipboard, muttering, "For this I got a masters in journalism...."

Riley opened his bag and found a lightweight plastic helmet that looked convincingly like the forged steel he remembered from some long-ago book on medieval times. It had a blue plastic feather sticking out of the top of it. The gloves had a chain-mail texture, but were made of a flexible rubbery material. Riley slipped them on and squeezed and relaxed his fists several times. At the bottom of the bag were two booties made of a slightly stiffer material than the briefs he wore. They weren't exactly boots—not even shoes, really, more like slippers—but they matched the outfit and their rubbery soles might be helpful in gripping the foam structure he would soon be fighting atop.

He pulled the boots on and then settled the helmet on his head. The visor blocked a good part of his field of vision, but he could still see well enough to make his way to the head of the group and watch for a signal—of what kind he had no idea. Behind him the other bachelors jostled.

The signal, it turned out, was a rough shove on the back of his head from the handler with the clipboard. Across the arena Riley could see three other faux gladiators being similarly thrust onto the field of battle. He stepped out onto the bright-blue beam, testing the consistency of the surface before putting his entire weight on it. It seemed stable enough, so he brought his other foot up and then balanced his lance next to him.

"Wait," a voice commanded behind him. He stood still, looking around at his competitors, at the bachelorette and her entourage, at the cameras that were simply everywhere. A silence fell over the entire scene, and then the bachelorette stood. She stepped to the railing of the balcony from which she looked down on the arena and pulled a handkerchief from her pushed-up cleavage. She waved it in the direction of all four men in turn, and then flicked it into the air.

"Let the jousting begin!" boomed a highly amplified voice.

"Go!" growled the handler behind Riley, and he took what he hoped looked like confident steps forward. He knew he needed to get to the intersection of the four beams before the others, and he beat them handily—the others seemed disoriented and took only faltering steps forward. Finally, the man on the red beam realized that Riley had claimed the central ground, and he lunged forward. Unfortunately for him, the sudden movement unbalanced him sufficiently to cause him to list to one side as he approached, and Riley was able with a nudge of his foam lance to tip him off the beam. He flailed wildly, looking not very much like a sturdy knight of the realm, Riley thought. He hit the pool of water face first, and then quickly stood—the water came up to his knees—and swore mightily at Riley.

But Riley had already turned to face the other two men. The knight on the yellow beam seemed to steady himself momentarily, and then he too lunged toward Riley with his lance straight out in front of him, closing the ten feet between them in a fraction of a second. Riley couldn't judge any off-center momentum this time, so he simply swung his lance as hard as he could at the man, slamming it into his shoulder with a loud smack. As he fell, the yellow knight grappled on the beam, trying to climb back on, but he could get no purchase on the glossy foam. He fell backward into the pool, completely submerging before springing back onto his knees. Riley could hear the deposed knight's frustrated growl as he turned to face the green knight.

So far the competition had gone just like an old martial-arts movie, in which the villains approach one by one to be felled by the hero. Riley knew this wouldn't last, so he took the initiative this time and sprang at the third man, swinging his lance back over his shoulder, winding up for a solid blow. The other man stopped dead, and even took a step back.

"Come on, you coward!" bellowed Riley. He had to take an extra step toward the man, but he channeled his frustrated adrenaline into swinging his lance even harder. The green knight fairly flew off the beam into the pool. Riley turned, panting, and looked at the stands, where the bachelorette and her crew cheered him delightedly. Though shocked by the brutal energy that surged through his chest, he waved in what he hoped was a chivalrous manner. The bachelorette giggled and waved back.

A bell sounded. "Let the jousting begin!" echoed the voice again.

Riley, startled, spun around and saw four more competitors mounting the beams. He rushed back to the place where the beams met and prepared to meet the onslaught. The red and blue knights ran toward him, and he tracked them both in his peripheral vision. They raised their lances to swing, and Riley jumped back, hoping he had calculated their trajectories accurately. They reached the center at the same moment, and swung their lances into each other with a simultaneous heavy thudding sound. They toppled backward in unison, splashing down into the pool on either side of the central point. Riley spun around again to face the other two. The green and yellow knights approached more cautiously, creeping along their beams. Riley backed into the center again and crouched low, waiting for the attack.

The yellow knight, apparently coming to the conclusion that a frontal assault would go no better for him than for the previous knights, all of whom had found themselves in the drink, hesitated for a moment about six feet from Riley. He turned to his right and, without warning, lunged at the green knight, knocking the lance out of his hand and tipping him dangerously over the side of his beam. But the green knight struggled back to his center of balance, and lacking a weapon, he had no recourse but to grapple with the yellow knight hand to hand. The yellow knight flung his own lance down and wrapped the green knight in a bear hug. For a moment their struggle was an immobile one, their flexing muscles the only sign of effort.

Riley was happy to have a breather while the other two men writhed and grunted. He checked the other beams every couple of seconds to be sure that no one was sneaking up on him, but apparently new combatants would only appear once the current ones had been dealt with.

The yellow knight gave a roar and pushed hard against the other man, who looked close to losing his balance. But as he tipped backward, he flailed, and one of his hands latched on to the waistband of his opponent's shorts. With a crackling rip, the briefs gave way, and back he fell into the pool holding the shredded garment in his hands.

Riley and the stunned, naked yellow knight stood and faced each other. Would the competition be halted due to unexpected nudity, Riley wondered? But the other man didn't hesitate. Ignoring the catcalls of the bachelorette's crew, he advanced on Riley—with no weapon and no silver shorts, all he had was an obvious determination. He looked ridiculous, silver from head to toe except for a narrow swath of flesh-colored flesh at the middle of his body.

Riley pondered this turn of events for a moment. He had just started to learn how to fight the other men effectively, and now he had to figure out how to dispose of a naked one. What the hell had he been thinking, getting himself into this mess?

The man was almost upon him now. *Think!*

"Dude," Riley said through the helmet's visor. "What's wrong with your dick?"

There was nothing wrong with it, at least that Riley could see. But he knew that the intense embarrassment of exposure would make him flinch at the very suggestion.

It worked. He looked down, and Riley's lance was already in motion when he did. Riley saw the whole thing in slow motion: the impact of his foam lance on the side of the man's head, his arms coming up in a vain attempt to recapture his balance, the wild flopping of his not-inconsiderable manhood as he flew off the beam.

The bachelorette cheered. "Now take yours off, stud!" shrieked the least ladylike of her ladies.

He waved and then stepped wearily back to the center to await the next wave of knighthood. When they would come he had no idea—at least until he spied the hourglass. During the first round, he had been too panicked to notice it. This time he saw its sands run out, and then the bachelorette turned it over. The bell sounded, and the booming voice announced that the jousting was to begin again.

This time the red, blue, and yellow knights came sprinting along their respective beams; only the green knight hung back. Riley made up his mind in a split second—he crab-walked sideways down the green beam, keeping an eye on the reluctant green knight as he did so. The other three men collided in the center, and after a few seconds filled with slashing foam lances, they all fell into the pool.

Riley turned to face the green knight and backed toward the center. The green knight advanced slowly, in no rush to join the battle with the apparently invincible Sir Riley.

Riley took stock of the man as he approached. He was a head shorter, but built like a jungle cat—the silver paint glittered over mounded pectorals and deeply cut biceps. The man's legs were an anatomical model—every muscle stood out in relief, sinews and tendons working smoothly under the silver skin. Riley knew that if he were to have a chance at knocking the man off the beam, he would have to come in low and by surprise. He counted down the steps until the man would be in reach.

"Three, two, one," he counted to himself and then he lunged. He threw himself at the green knight, his right shoulder aimed squarely at the man's kneecaps. He closed his eyes and braced for impact, hoping that he would be able to steady himself on the beam when the other man toppled.

Riley sprawled out on the beam, having hit—nothing.

He heard the other man land on the beam behind him, and he scrabbled back to his feet and turned around. The green knight must have jumped right over him and landed at the dead center of the arena. He was waving at the bachelorette, who was cackling with glee. Riley's status as the hero of the moment had faded as quickly as it had come. He rushed at the other man, caught him in the back, and shoved hard. The man flew forward, but tucked himself into a neat somersault and landed upright once again, as if he were a court jester doing little flips for the enjoyment of the princess.

It was working—the bachelorette jumped up and down and waved her handkerchief wildly.

"Shit," Riley muttered to himself. He cast about for a strategy to take out this circus acrobat of an opponent, but could come up with nothing. The green knight, though, took the initiative. He bounced toward Riley, his feet sure on the beam, and he leapt at Riley's chest, clearly hoping to overbalance the taller man. Riley saw the silver blur streaking toward him, and he knew that the impact was going to put him right over.

He dropped flat to the beam and held on. It was a less dignified posture than he had been hoping for, but it was effective. The green knight flew over him once again, but this time he didn't stick the landing. He caught the beam with one foot, and his arms and other leg waggled crazily as he struggled to stay atop the beam. Riley rose and stood back, waiting for him to topple. He could at least catch his breath while his opponent splashed down.

But he didn't splash down. He somehow managed to straighten up, and then he bowed graciously to Riley. The spectators erupted into wild laughter and applause. Then the acrobat drew his lance. He thrust it out, arched his other arm behind him in an Errol Flynn pose, and capered forward, slashing the air before him like Zorro practicing his signature.

Riley stopped short. Was he serious with this? He looked ridiculous. But the bachelorette and her crew thought otherwise—they were laughing and clapping delightedly. Really?

Riley shrugged and adopted a mirror pose. He advanced on the acrobat, and they were soon joined in swordplay. Back and forth along the beam they jostled, lances swatting ineffectually against each other. The other man seemed to understand that a bit of showmanship was in order, and that they would gain more from this silly bit of prancing than from actually trying to finish each other off. Riley went along—for the moment. He was too exhausted to push the issue.

And then the hourglass ran out. The bachelorette, still laughing, wiped her eyes, and turned it over. The bell sounded.

"Let the jousting begin!"

The two men took up their positions at the center of the arena. Riley was shocked to feel the smaller man's scapulae pressing up against the middle of his back, and he was pretty sure that his silver-clad buttocks were tucked under Riley's own. He considered for a second shoving backward and sending his compatriot into the drink, but he quickly reconsidered—having a teammate meant that he had only to face half of the onslaught. He stood his ground.

Four more knights appeared. Riley had now survived into the fourth round of the game, and all four of the men seemed to draw a bead on him from the first moment they were in the arena. Red and blue rushed at him instantly, and they collided into him like football players trying to take out the opposing quarterback. The blow knocked the air out of him and sent him crashing backward. This was the end, he knew—and he had come so far.

But it wasn't the end.

Instead of falling back through space and into the water, he thudded into something solid. Something immovable. Something that wrapped its arms around him to steady him, to keep him from going over the edge.

It was the acrobat.

Riley caught his breath, shook his head to clear the bewildered fog that enveloped it, and found his footing. The red and blue knights, as surprised as he was to find him still on the beam, charged at Riley with eyes blazing. With the smaller man behind him, now back-to-back, shoring him up, he shoved hard against the two other men and managed to push them off opposite sides of the apparatus. With a splash they went down. Riley spun around, intending to return the favor he had been granted by the other man.

His mistake was clear instantly. The green and yellow knights blasted in, smashing the acrobat into Riley. But where before the men had been back-to-back, now they were facing the same direction. This resulted in two untoward developments: first, Riley had little traction or leverage; second, his groin was pressed vigorously into the small of the other man's back. Riley ignored the intimate pressure, and he pushed back hard and reached around to get some hits in. Finally the men were able to summon their collective strength and wallop their opponents off the beam.

Both men were breathing hard, and the acrobat leaned back against him. They rested for a moment, and then Riley realized that his penis was still pressed tightly just above the buttocks of the other man. He jumped back, and the acrobat took an awkward, halting step toward him.

This was the moment Riley had been waiting for. By his count, they had just one wave of opponents left; he could drop the acrobat now, and then face the final two by himself. He stepped forward to shove the man off the beam—and then caught him by the arm and steadied him instead.

He had no idea why he did it—it was simply, suddenly, the right thing to do.

Applause from the bachelorette's box, and the bell rang again.

The smaller man nodded his thanks, and they turned to face their final foes.

The beam apparatus shook as the knights approached, one along the blue beam, one on the yellow. Riley remembered a video he'd seen on the news recently about a supercollider that smashed particles together to try to make new ones. He felt like he was at the center of a device specifically designed to smash silver muscle together in an attempt to make what—more muscle? He shook his head to clear it of ridiculous thoughts.

"Grab my elbows with yours!" the other man blurted.

"What?"

"My elbows—grab 'em with yours!"

Riley turned to look over his shoulder, and saw the elbows of the other man thrust out to his side.

"Why?" Riley demanded.

"You lift me, and I'll kick this guy off. Then I'll lift you and you kick the crap out of yours!"

"You're going to lift me?" Riley scoffed.

"Got a better plan?"

Riley didn't. He looped his arms through the other man's.

"He's here—lift!" the other man ordered.

Riley leaned forward and braced himself as best he could. He felt the impact, and heard the sudden expulsion of air from the rapidly compressed lungs of the other man. A splash let him know that the stratagem had been successful. He stood upright and let the other man back down to his feet.

"Now!" he yelled, and he felt his feet lift up off the beam. He planted his silver-slippered feet onto the chest of the last blue knight and kicked as hard as he could. He fully expected to tumble backward with the recoil, but the acrobat held steady. He was lowered back to his feet.

The two men unlaced their arms, and turned to face each other. The smaller man extended his hand.

"Well played, good sir," he said, a chuckle in his voice.

"And you," Riley replied with a bow.

The other man took a step back, and then drew his lance. "En garde!" he shouted.

Riley drew his lance as well, and struck a fencing pose. He lunged forward and made contact with his lance against the other man's chest, who took a faltering step back. As he fell, he turned toward the bachelorette and made a graceful gesture of retirement from the field of battle. He then held both arms straight out to the side and fell backward into the pool.

The bachelorette's box erupted in cheers and whistles as Riley removed his helmet and waved gallantly. He took a deep bow. Out of the corner of his eye he could see the acrobat, his mysterious partner in chivalry, wading over to the edge of the pool. He wondered if he would be the last man standing if that man hadn't stood with him.

TWO DAYS later, back at the house, the contestants gathered for the live, televised ceremony that would mark the end of each round of the competition.

Riley knew from reviewing previous seasons that the bachelor who won the contest would automatically be chosen by the bachelorette for a special date of some kind. Riley felt vindicated as he led the line of bachelors into the glass room at the top of the house—that horrible prequel with the makeup and the hard-on and the straight makeup artist willing to lend a hand could all be put behind him now, turned from the most embarrassing thing that had ever happened to him into a bizarre, but tangential, side note to his ultimate victory.

Of course, it was a side note he wouldn't share with anyone. Ever. But still, it was a whole lot better to look back on as a winner than as a mortified loser.

The men assembled in the glass room, and the bachelorette—with entourage—swept in through the double doors leading from the patio. They took up their positions on the dais before the windows looking out over the canyon.

"Bachelors," breathed the mistress of ceremonies. "Two days ago you contested for the hand of your lady fair on the field of battle."

Riley had to hand it to her—she managed to deliver the purple prose of mock medieval enthusiasm without the eye-rolling cynicism of the bachelor wrangler Riley had met at the competition.

"We will be saying good-bye this evening to one of our bachelors, who gave his all during the battle but was voted out by our loyal viewers. He fought heroically, and showed himself—"

Here the room broke out into titters. One of the contestants had certainly shown himself on the field of battle.

"—showed himself to be a worthy competitor," she continued once the giggles had died down. "But the vote of the viewers is final, and so tonight we will be sending home…." She paused for dramatic effect, and the show went to commercial. During this time the cameras captured all of the angles as everyone in the room stood with bated breath, coached by the production staff to remain statues of fervent anticipation.

Once they were live again, the host took a breath and finished her sentence. "Marshall."

A groan was heard from the back of the room. Marshall made his way to the dais, and stepped up onto the platform to stand next to the mistress of ceremonies.

"Now, Marshall," she began, "your appearance in the battle was one of the most talked about of the entire competition. The internet was abuzz with talk about your wardrobe malfunction, which," she continued as she turned to speak directly to the camera, "was edited by our production staff to preserve your privacy." A laugh washed across the room, and finally even Marshall was laughing, a blush rising on his cheeks. She turned back to him. "What was that moment like?"

"Bloody embarrassing," he said in a jovial British accent. The room erupted into laughter and cheers.

"How does it feel to be the first bachelor to leave the show by the vote of the viewers?"

"Well," he said with a shrug. "I gave everything I have, obviously." He paused for more laughter. "But if I was too much for the audience, I guess it's time for me to go."

"You are taking this like a gentleman, sir. Very appropriate for our challenge of chivalry." She embraced him, and then led him over to the bachelorette.

She embraced him as well, and as she did so murmured so only he and the bachelors nearest the dais could hear, "I liked what I saw—you wouldn't have been going if I had my way."

He smiled. "Thank you," he said, and kissed her on the cheek.

"Time to Say Goodbye" swelled on the sound system, and Marshall walked out the doors with a wave to the bachelors and the cameras.

"As you know, the winner of each competition scores a special date with the bachelorette. But this season, there's a twist!"

Riley's blood ran cold at the very idea. An unanticipated twist could derail his whole strategy.

"This season the voters will not only choose the bachelor who will leave after each competition, but will also choose another bachelor to share in the special date with the bachelorette. It will be a second chance at love for one of you!"

Riley blinked, trying to figure out how this changed things—would his strategy have to be adjusted to account for this new wrinkle?

"So, first," she continued. "The clear winner of our competition was…. Riley." She beamed at him, and clapped in that soundless way peculiar to the elderly and those who wear lapel mikes and don't want to blow the levels with sharp sounds. The bachelorette and her crew clapped loudly, however—their mics must have been turned down after Marshall's exit.

Riley made his way up the stairs and took his place between the mistress of ceremonies and the bachelorette. But instead of a congratulatory embrace from the bachelorette, he was left standing while the ceremony continued.

"And tonight the people's choice is…." And again she paused, television-style, this time for more than two minutes while the cameras recorded the anticipation from all angles. Finally, she was given the signal to continue. "Asher."

The men looked side to side—they'd not yet learned everyone's name. The crowd in front of the platform parted, and a man that Riley hadn't even been able to see came forward. He was half a head shorter than everyone else in the group and so had been completely invisible until now. But he walked confidently up the steps to his mark, midway between Riley and the mistress of ceremonies.

"Now, Asher," she said very seriously. "Your performance at the jousting challenge has quickly become the stuff of legend. Let's take a look and remind everyone of your prowess." She turned to face the large screen that smoothly slid down from the ceiling, and onto which a projected image of the jousting arena came into focus.

The video clip was of the moment in the third round when Riley had first attempted to dispatch the acrobatic green knight. He watched himself charge desperately at the smaller man, crouch down low, and lunge. Asher timed it perfectly, waiting until Riley's head was down to spring effortlessly into the air. But the most startling part was after he had flown over the prone Riley—he executed a perfect somersault as he landed on the beam and then shot upright when he reached the center of the arena. He had stuck the landing perfectly.

It was a breathtaking performance.

"But that wasn't the most amazing thing we saw at the tournament," she enthused at the end of the clip. "No, that was when the two of you teamed up to lay waste to your foes. Let's watch."

The screen jumped ahead to the final round of the competition, and Riley watched himself, in slow motion, lean forward and lift Asher off his feet. After the first knight went into the pool, it was his turn. He had to admit, it was kind of amazing to watch the smaller man lift him without any visible effort. He turned to appraise him now, standing next to him on the stage, but the suit he was wearing betrayed nothing of the musculature that Riley knew to lurk beneath.

"So, tell us now," she said conspiratorially. "Did you two plan this strategy in advance?"

Riley hadn't considered that he might be asked this question, and he stood pondering how to respond. Luckily, Asher seemed to have a response ready to hand.

"No, it just sort of happened," he said, with a shrug. "I knew from watching this guy lay waste to every other competitor that I didn't really stand a chance against him. So I figured I could at least make it to second place if I stuck close. I guess it paid off." He smiled charmingly for her, and for the camera, and for America.

Riley had to hand it to him—he knew how to work it. No wonder he had been voted up by the viewers.

"I'm going to ask our bachelorette to join us now.... Daphne, can you step over here?" She extricated herself from her entourage and came to stand next to the woman with the microphone.

"As you know, Riley was the winner of the jousting tournament, and he has therefore earned the honor of your company on a special date tomorrow night."

Daphne nodded and smiled sweetly at her champion. Riley smiled back, reminding himself to look strong yet emotionally available. He had practiced that look in his bathroom mirror several times a day for the last few months, and he apparently had it down—Daphne giggled and blushed when he unleashed it on her.

"And our viewers have decided that Asher will join you for the date." She turned to the men. "You two managed to work together during the tournament, but now you'll be competing for the real prize—the affections of your bachelorette!"

Riley looked at Asher and decided on the spur of the moment to be the gracious victor. He extended his hand. "Good luck," he said in what he hoped was a confident voice.

"I'll need it," Asher said, beaming at him at they shook hands.

Riley wasn't sure what to make of him—the video clip showed him to be a fierce competitor, but he seemed so genuine and friendly that Riley had a hard time seeing him as a threat.

"Now, Daphne, we've come up with a special event for you to share with Riley and Asher that will be the fulfillment of the chivalrous challenge they won. We'll be sending the three of you to a medieval-themed restaurant, where you will watch real jousting during dinner! Should be an exciting time for everyone!"

Daphne giggled and bounced excitedly. Riley wasn't sure whether to admire her for her convincing show of enthusiasm or to think less of her because she might actually be that excited about what sounded to him like a perfectly dreary date.

Asher, however, was smiling placidly at Daphne as if all he desired in the world was to be near her. Reproached, Riley also screwed his smile to the sticking point and beamed at the bachelorette, the mistress of ceremonies, the cameras, the world.

The grudging applause of the other bachelors died down, and a couple of model types in tuxedos arrived to lead the trio to their dream date of medieval awkwardness. They walked in smiling silence across the stone terrace and down the steps to the waiting stretch limousine. Daphne hitched up her glittery gown and slipped in first, placing herself in the center of the rear seat. Riley gestured for Asher to go next, hoping that the camera would capture his chivalry extending to both genders—and, somewhat cynically, that Asher would come off looking a bit feminized because of it. There was strategy in every moment of this game, Riley thought as he lowered himself into the car.

ASHER HAD taken a seat on the far side of Daphne, and Riley slid in next to her on the near side. The limo was large, but the three of them certainly filled the one seat across.

"You look lovely this evening," Asher said as the car headed down the long, steep driveway.

Dammit, thought Riley, he got that in first. Riley was about to offer his own appraisal of her beauty when she turned to Asher to reply.

"Thanks! They filled my closet with the most amazing clothes. I figured I would spend half my time trying them on and working out what to wear when, but then someone comes and lays out what they want me to wear, and I just put them on. It's not as much fun," she said with a shrug, "but at least I never have to worry about being dressed appropriately for whatever they have planned for me. For us," she added, casting a look at Riley and then back to Asher.

This was not going well.

"What would you have chosen for this evening, if it were up to you?" Riley asked.

Daphne smiled at him, seeming enchanted by the question.

"Well, there's this lovely gown with a beaded bodice that I thought looked old-fashioned, which seemed perfect for the theme, but then this was laying out for me, so...."

"Yeah," Asher chimed in, "because nothing says medieval like a sweetheart neckline and princess-length pearls."

"I know, right?" Daphne laughed and put her hand on Asher's knee. Riley had no idea what they were talking about, and now they were acting like they were on a date—alone.

He worked hard to keep the conversation going during the drive to the restaurant, but every word that Asher spoke was like the score spiraling up in a game Riley was losing. This wasn't how he imagined his first date going— he was generally a team player, but not when it came to romance.

Riley was at his wit's end when they finally pulled up in front of the faux castle that would be the venue for their date. As he stepped from the limo and reached back to take Daphne's hand, camera flashes popped all around them, momentarily stunning him.

"Are they taking pictures of us?" Daphne asked as she straightened the hem of her dress.

"This is LA," Asher said with a laugh as he too stepped from the limo. "Anyone showing up in a town car and a ball gown could be a celebrity." He turned to her with a graceful bow. "Which you are, as of this evening's broadcast."

"I'm just glad I have two strapping men to keep the paparazzi away," Daphne replied with a giggle. She wrapped her arms around theirs, and they walked briskly up the red carpet toward the crenelated towers and drawbridge.

Throughout the evening, Riley did his level best to be charming, but he could tell that Asher was keeping pace with him all along. Every time he tried to make real conversation with Daphne, something would happen to nip it in the bud—a dramatic (though certainly choreographed) clattering fall of a knight from horseback, or a passerby gawking and taking photos of the three of them with annoying strobes of light. Riley had hoped to use this time to learn about the bachelorette, to find out something about her that he could use in subsequent rounds of the game, but he was getting nothing. Nothing, that is, that Asher didn't seem to also be getting, as Daphne divided her attention between the two men equally.

They returned to the house and said goodnight to her, Asher again going first—Riley hoped it looked like he and Daphne were sending her little brother to bed. Then he turned to her and cranked up the suave charm he had practiced.

"I hope you enjoyed yourself this evening," he murmured to her, his arm around her waist. "I loved getting to know you better."

"Yeah, me too. And Asher. He's fun." She smiled at him in a way he could only interpret as "friendly."

"He seems like a nice little guy," Riley said, somewhat stiffly. Trash-talk had never come naturally to him, neither on the athletic field nor the field of competitive dating, apparently. "I hope that we—"

"Ooh, I'm exhausted," she interrupted. "I gotta get to bed. Well, I'll see ya!" She smiled again and tottered off atop her impossibly tall heels, glittering away into the darkness of the lower level of the house.

Date #1 was a draw.

CHAPTER FOUR
BACHELORX

"#HusbandMaterial makeup gal gets groped during shining armor challenge. No film at 11. Only @BachelorX has the story!"

KAITLYN STARED at the screen. "What am I looking at?"

"Twitter," Omar replied.

"Look, I may be older than you, but I'm not a dinosaur. I know what Twitter is. But why are you showing me this?"

"Read the top tweet."

Kaitlyn scanned the first tweet in a long line that ran down the screen of Omar's tablet—and for many screens below.

"Who sent this?" Her voice was taut, deadly.

"We don't know."

"Who knew about it? I thought you said the other bachelors didn't even know it happened."

"The location crew told me no one saw it—they all heard her yell, but she calmed down once he explained that he had lost his balance and only put his hand on her to keep from falling over. He felt really bad about it."

"And we believe him?" she asked skeptically.

"There was a crew shooting over the shoulder of the makeup artist at the next station, and they caught it in the background. I looked at the video, and he's telling the truth."

"But no one who sees this is going to know—or believe—that." She sighed. "So who is BachelorX?"

"I'm sorry, we just have no idea." His voice was small, shaky.

Kaitlyn gave a mighty exhale and clutched her hand to her brow. She conferred with the floor for a moment. When she looked up a moment later she was calm and even.

"We checked all of the bachelors for phones, right?"

Omar nodded.

"Then how did this get out?"

Omar stood stock still, perhaps hoping the snake wouldn't strike a stationary target.

Kaitlyn took another deep breath. "All right. Here's what we're going to do. Get the security team together, all of them, at the house. Evacuate the whole house—tell them it's a gas leak or something—and then toss the place. Search it top to bottom. When they find it, we'll figure out who it belongs to, and that lucky bachelor will get a free trip to Siberia for the duration."

Omar nodded and reached for the phone. Kaitlyn had a call of her own to make—to the network. She hoped they would have a sense of humor about this.

CHAPTER FIVE

AN ALLIANCE

IT WAS 3:00 a.m. when Riley's watch, tucked under his pillow, began to vibrate. He had set the alarm for this hour because as the winner of the first round of the game, he was the least popular guy in the house, and he wanted some time to work out alone.

He slipped silently out of bed and pulled his workout clothes from where he'd tucked them under the nightstand. He pulled on a pair of nylon shorts and a tightly fitted T-shirt, and carried his shoes and socks out with him as he noiselessly slunk out of the room. He padded down the hall to the workout room and paused outside its door to put on his socks and shoes. Having done that, he quietly opened the door and slipped inside.

The lights were already on, which startled him, but a quick scan of the room showed no signs of life, so he walked over to a weight bench and loaded up a hundred pounds on each end. He then sat down on the bench, ducked under the bar, and lay down; he placed his hand on the grips and pushed up.

He pressed the weights to the full extension of his arms and huffed out a breath—the first was always the hardest for him for some reason—and it was then that he realized there was a problem. The last person to use the bar had left some kind of slick coating on the grips, and his hands were slipping. He tried to get the bar mounted back on the brackets, but they were set up differently than the ones at his gym, and he couldn't get the angle right.

His arms began to shake with the effort of keeping the bar aloft as it slid through his grip.

"Fuck!" he managed to grunt through gritted teeth as he struggled. The bar was going to come down—the question was whether it would crush him immediately or strangle him slowly. His eyes were squeezed shut with the effort of holding the bar off of him for a few seconds more; that's why he didn't see the other hands grasp it. It wasn't until the weight began to lift that he opened his eyes and realized what was happening.

It was Asher. He was lifting the bar and placing it on the brackets. The guy who had saved him in the jousting was saving him again.

"You okay?" Asher asked, looking down at Riley.

"Yeah, man—thanks," Riley replied, panting from exertion and poorly concealed panic. "I don't know what happened there—I was fine, and then my grip went to shit and I thought I was gonna.... Well, let's just say I'm glad you showed up."

Asher sniffed his hands. "That surfer guy must have left a hemp oil slick on the bar." His nose wrinkled sympathetically.

Riley sat up, still breathing heavily, and then turned to face the other man. "Thank you, Asher," he said, having regained his composure.

"Don't mention it. Happy to help a brother out on the vampire shift." He chuckled and looked around the room, empty except for the two of them. "Do you always work out this late? Or, I guess, this early?"

Riley shook his head. "No, I'm a pretty regular after-work guy in normal life. But I kind of wanted to lay low after last night. I thought I'd sleep while everyone worked out their aggressions, and then come back when it was empty." He grinned at Asher. "Or mostly empty."

"My thoughts exactly. I was over there getting a drink of water when you came in. It was actually a little lonely, so I'm glad you're here."

"And I'm really glad you were here, obviously," Riley said, laughing ruefully.

"Well, I'll let you get back to it, then," Asher said, turning back to his own workout.

"Sounds good. Thanks again, man. You saved my ass."

"It was my pleasure," Asher replied, smiling.

The men worked out on parallel tracks for more than an hour, doing no more than nodding at each other when they crossed paths. Riley was finishing up when he noticed Asher walking toward a door at the back of the room.

Asher poked his head back around the door and called to Riley. "Hey, I found a sauna back here!"

"Wow, they've set us up pretty well here." He glanced at the clock on the wall, saw that it was almost 5:00 a.m. "Well, good night. I mean... good morning, I guess." He turned to leave.

"Don't you want to try it?" Asher asked, tipping his head back toward the sauna.

"Nah, maybe next time," Riley replied. "I kind of need a shower. Thanks, though."

"Suit yourself," Asher tsked. "I don't think I'm going to risk waking the others by turning on the shower this early. Who knows what they might do if I ruin their beauty sleep?"

Riley had to admit that Asher kind of had a point. The more time he had free from the drama of his fellow contestants the better.

"What the hell. Let's give 'er a go." He walked back across the workout room to join Asher at the sauna. By the time he got there, Asher was filling the water pitcher that sat on the floor next to the hot rocks.

"There are towels over there." Asher nodded toward a stack folded neatly next to the door. With Asher occupied in the sauna, Riley had a moment of privacy to slip off his damp workout gear and wrap a towel around his waist.

"There, that should be good," Asher said, coming back out of the sauna and holding the door open for Riley to enter. He did, and sat down on the broad cedar bench opposite the hot rocks. A moment later, Asher came back into the sauna, a towel wrapped around his waist.

The men sat in silence for some time, watching heat waves rise from the rocks. Riley realized that even though they had spent the evening together, he really knew nothing about the other man. He was about to try his hand at some small talk when Asher beat him to it.

"So, what do you do?" Asher ventured. "I mean, when you're not getting medieval on your reality show enemies?"

Riley laughed. "I have the most boring job in the world. I'm an insurance underwriter. In the exceptional policies office."

"What does that mean?" Asher asked.

"Well, exceptional policies is the very proper term my very proper British insurance firm uses to refer to insurance on completely bizarre things. Stuff that doesn't fit normal underwriting, but that people want to cover. Like record companies that want a policy on the voice of a singer, or tourist insurance for space travel, that kind of thing."

"It sounds fascinating," Asher said. "Like it would be something new every day."

"Yeah, but at the end of the day underwriting is basically just actuarial accounting. It can only be so exciting. And once you've had to determine the exact monetary value of a porn star's... well, equipment? After that the glamour kind of goes out of it."

"You wrote a policy on a porn star's junk?" Asher laughed, shaking his head. "Well, I guess somebody's got to do it. I mean, if it needs doing at all—which I didn't know it did, until just now. Wow."

"So that's how I pass my time at work. What about you?"

"Pssh," Asher replied. "It's nothing compared to that. I teach art at an elementary school."

"Now there's a job that makes a difference," Riley replied, nodding respectfully. "Insuring a walrus at the Omaha Zoo against tusk loss is nothing compared to helping kids appreciate art."

"Most days it's awesome, and then every once in a while it sucks—mostly when I have to deal with philistine parents or clueless administrators. Ugh. But overall, it's a great gig. Doesn't pay a lot, but I love it."

Riley sat silent for a moment. Then, he turned to Asher. "This may sound like a strange question, but how does an art teacher build up a form like that?" he asked, nodding to Asher's considerable shoulders and biceps.

Asher laughed. "I could ask the same thing. You're sure not built like an accountant," he replied, gesturing to Riley's own prominent musculature.

"That's just stress made visible," Riley replied. "I just imagine the chief underwriter's face on every weight, and suddenly lifting them and dropping them back down seems like a piece of cake."

"Well, my workouts are mostly habit. I went to college on a gymnastics scholarship, and so hitting the gym every day is just part of who I am now. I don't even think about it."

"God, I wish it were that way for me. I have to force myself to do it every time."

"Why do you do it, then? If you don't enjoy it…."

"I do it because after my fickle fiancée left me, I was suddenly back on the singles scene. It's a hell of a lot easier to get girls to notice you if you're built like Ryan Gosling rather than the fat version of Jonah Hill."

"Right you are." Asher chuckled.

They sat for a few silent minutes, soaking in the heat of the sauna.

"So, there's something I don't get," Riley said, his eyes still closed.

"What's that? I mean, unless you're talking about theoretical physics or something, because there's a lot of that I don't get either."

Riley laughed. The guy was a huge competitor—his deadly acrobatics during the joust proved that—but there was nothing even remotely aggressive about him.

"Yeah, let's leave string theory aside for now," Riley replied with a chuckle. "What I wanted to know is why you did it."

Asher turned to look at him, his eyebrows up. "Why I did what?"

"Helped me in the jousting. You really had no reason to cover my back when all four of those guys rushed me. You could have just jumped over all of them and pirouetted to victory once I'd been splashed."

Asher fixed Riley with a wry grin. "You really have no idea what you were doing out there, do you?"

Riley's brow furrowed. "What do you mean?"

Asher gave a good-natured sigh. "Dude, you were some kind of ninja linebacker assassin out there. You should have heard the other guys in line watching you on the monitor—they were practically shitting themselves as you sent wave after wave off the beams."

"But you had plenty of opportunities to just bump me right off—you're a gymnast, for God's sake—and you didn't. What the hell was up with that?"

"Think about it from my point of view. You were the Terminator out there, and all I had to do was help when needed and then stay out of your way until the next wave came."

Riley squinted a critical eye at him.

"Okay, and I took the occasional opportunity to ham it up a bit for m'lady. So sue me." Asher grinned with genuine glee.

"Yeah, that swordplay stuff was ridiculous."

"But she loved it! And all I had to do was make a decent showing—and coming in second to Iron Man certainly counts as decent—and hope for the viewers' votes."

Riley pondered this for a second. "Okay, so I guess there are two things I don't get. The second one is how you knew about the whole viewers' vote thing. I researched this show pretty thoroughly, and I never saw a mention of that."

Asher smiled, somewhat mysteriously. "Ah, I have my sources," he said. Then his habitually open personality seemed to win out, and he continued. "I have a buddy who is totally obsessed with reality shows, and with this one in particular. He read something in *Variety* a couple of weeks ago that they were planning something like this, and he rooted out more info from some discussion boards where folks in the business post things. But it wasn't until last night that I was sure we were right. That was a relief— otherwise, I'd have looked pretty stupid."

"Well, you did look kind of stupid when you went all melodrama at the end, falling back into the water." Riley laughed at the memory. "But it worked out just like you thought it would, I'll give you that."

"Thank you, sir," Asher rejoined. "That means a lot coming from you."

"As long as you're content to be number two, I'll remain a fan."

Asher was silent for a moment. "Actually, that's kind of my—hang on," he interrupted himself, and then he rose and picked up the pitcher of water that he had filled earlier. He poured a good amount on the hot rocks in the corner of the sauna. Steam immediately issued forth from the rocks, filling the small wooden room with a dense, hot fog. Asher sat back down on the bench, but slightly closer to Riley than he had been previously.

"Kind of your what?" Riley asked. If Asher had been about to talk strategy, he wanted to stay on him until he got the goods. But he got no further. Asher held up a finger to his pursed lips and shook his head. He tipped his head toward a camera mounted above the hot rocks. Its light glowed red in the dim swelter of the sauna.

The lens of the camera, specifically designed for low-light conditions such as one might find in a sauna, was as wide as a silver dollar. And it was now dotted with drops of moisture from the steam surge that Asher had created just below it. If anyone was watching the feed from this camera, their view just got a whole lot worse.

Asher leaned his head back against the wall of the sauna, and nudged Riley until he did the same. The two men were no more than an inch apart. Asher turned his head slowly toward Riley, until his lips brushed Riley's ear.

A shiver shot down Riley's spine.

"Even with the camera fogged, the mic is still live," Asher whispered into his ear. The shocking rush of warm air made Riley's ear tingle. "What I was going to say is that my strategy is to be the best damn runner-up I can be." Asher's husky whisper poured directly into Riley's ear.

Asher turned his head so that he was once again looking straight ahead. Riley swiveled his head to the side, took a deep breath, and found Asher's ear.

"I don't get it," Riley whispered, his lips brushing against Asher. "Why are you here if you don't want to win it?" He turned to face front again.

"Second place is enough for me. The money is good, but without all of the pressure of being the winner and having to be perfect in front of the world."

Riley knew that the bachelor who walked away with second place in the competition had, in previous seasons of the show, collected a substantial consolation prize: several hundred thousand dollars and a chance to present himself on a tour of daytime talk shows, where his purgatory would be answering the same "what could have been" question every single time. He always figured it would be an annoying also-ran hassle—it never occurred to him that anyone would want to go through that.

"I think you're better than that," Riley whispered.

Asher turned so suddenly that for a moment Riley thought their noses would touch as he swiveled his head back to the front.

"Thanks, but second works for me. I don't mean to sound mercenary, but I need the money a lot more than I need a wife right now."

"What does an art teacher need a couple hundred grand for? Gambling debts?" Riley chuckled, but then realized that he was basically breathing heavily into another guy's ear, and he quickly stopped and turned to face front.

Asher turned and Riley felt his lips brush his ear again. Asher took a breath, sighed, and then took another. "It's my sister, Meg. She's sick, and she needs treatment that her insurance won't cover. So I could either give her my entire salary for the next fifteen years, or I could do this. It's a long shot, I know, and it probably seems like a stupid way to get money for medical treatment, but I was kind of out of ideas." He sighed again and leaned his head back against the wall.

Riley licked his lips, which were suddenly dry. He put them next to Asher's ear. "I think it's a great thing you're doing." He paused, considering how much he felt he could trust the other man. He nodded, and continued. "If we can work together like we did at the jousting, we can do this. We just have to be a little more subtle—if people see us working together, they might get suspicious."

"What, is there something about whispering into each other's ears in the sauna that looks suspicious?" Asher grinned widely and giggled. He seemed genuinely happy that the two men had come to an understanding.

Riley extended his hand. "Partners?" he asked, in a deep and serious voice.

Asher shook his hand. "Partners," he said, just as solemnly.

"Now let's go kick some ass," Riley said, standing. His towel had become wedged between the planks of the wooden bench he'd been sitting on, and as he rose it pulled off from around his waist. He managed to catch it and gather it to his crotch, which preserved most of his modesty but left his buttocks bare.

"Yes, ass," Asher said, rising as well. "Let's go kick some."

They made their way back to their respective dorms, as silently as they could so as not to wake the competition.

CHAPTER SIX

HELEN OF TROY

"Which two #HusbandMaterial bachelors only have eyes for each other?
@BachelorX knows, and so will you!"

"DAMMIT, WHO the hell is he talking about? And why am I still reading tweets from this fucking BachelorX?" Kaitlyn was on fire, and the rest of the production staff was giving her wide berth. Only Omar seemed brave—or naive—enough to venture within range of her fury. "Didn't we search the house? How is this still happening?"

"They didn't find anything when they searched the house," Omar said gently.

"Well, then they didn't do it right, did they?" Kaitlyn slammed her fist on her desk. Then she remembered the advice of the stress management coach the network had insisted she see two seasons ago, and she focused on her breathing for a full minute, willing herself to calm down. She opened her eyes and saw Omar standing bravely in front of her desk, despite the fact that he was obviously scared to death. "Sit," she said in an even tone, pointing to a chair. "Now, what do you think of our little situation?"

Omar, despite being peppered only moments ago with questions he had no way of answering, had clearly not expected to be asked anything substantive at all. He took a deep breath. "We have two problems. First, we have a mole who has managed to hide a phone or some other device, and we've been unable to find it. Second, he was right about the first thing he tweeted, so we have to admit at least the possibility that he's right about this one."

"Very good," Kaitlyn replied. "It's very bad for us, of course, but you're very good at this. Now, given these two problems, what do you think we should do?"

"Searching the house didn't uncover the device he's using to communicate, which means either he's hidden it somewhere that security didn't look, or he's carrying it with him. But where could he have hidden it

goggling was a strong contrast to the scene in the work area to his right, where Asher was tearing through his workspace, sorting and arranging according to a system that Riley could not fathom.

Suddenly, Asher bolted for the center of the room and began gathering up power tools, spools of wire, and what looked like a welding outfit. Riley rushed in as well, not at all sure what to grasp but determined to lay claim to the best tools before the others got them. They returned to their adjacent workbenches, heavily laden with hardware, and set to work. The poet, to the other side of Riley, seemed finally to become aware of his surroundings and drifted toward the pile of tools and materials, now buzzing with the frenzied activity of the bachelors.

Riley looked about his workbench and tried to visualize what he was doing. He had no fucking clue. He looked over at Asher, and discovered that he had found a large piece of paper and a pencil, and was sketching with a calm energy that Riley found a little hypnotic. He watched him work for several minutes, as his arm swept gracefully across the sheet of paper, shadows and lines starting to merge into a form that was as ethereal as it was unmistakably equine.

Riley was jarred out of his contemplation by Asher looking up at him and flashing his broad, white smile.

"Yea, one for the art major!" he practically chirped, his voice jaunty with good cheer. He returned to his sketch, not seeming to care whether Riley saw what he was up to.

Knowing that his workstation must be similarly equipped with drawing implements, Riley rummaged through the drawers until he found them. It wasn't until he had laid out a sheet of paper and took a pencil in hand to render his ideas into visual form that he remembered: he didn't know how to draw. At all. No mark he could make on this paper would remotely look like a horse, so what was the point of even starting down that path? He set down the pencil.

Think.

He turned and leaned back against the workbench, and tried to breathe deeply. He looked over the pile of tools and lumber and bits of hardware that he had gathered, willing them to coalesce into some horsey form that he could work toward. It wasn't happening.

He looked up, just as Asher jumped up from his sketch. He was a blur of motion as he gathered up wire and a pair of pliers, and began forming loops of wire—a graceful spiral of shining metal spun out of the frenetic precision of his capable hands. He was smiling, and Riley heard a cheerful humming waft across the workspace to him. Asher looked up and smiled more broadly when he saw Riley looking at him. He nodded cheerfully and returned to his work. Which didn't seem at all like work to Riley—it looked like Asher had become one of his third-grade students, playing at art rather than working at it.

Riley tried to hate him, but he couldn't—Asher's entire being seemed to glow with the joy of creating. He knew he was going to lose to him this time, but he still couldn't be mad about it. Dammit.

He knew that beauty wasn't on the program for him—he couldn't be an artist all of a sudden under this kind of pressure. He needed to play to his own strengths. But what strengths did he have when it came to art? He wasn't the kind of free spirit that Asher was—he was much more analytical, much more structured. How could he use that to create something that would at least keep him in the game?

He looked to the other side and took a perverse joy in the utter confusion that embroiled the poet. Just how far poetry was from sculpture was impressed upon Riley as the other man cast his despairing gaze across the workbench, his brows knit into a fatalistic peak.

"I can do this," Riley said under his breath, not believing it. "I can do this." He would repeat this until he believed it, or at least until the day was over. He knew the latter was far more likely.

The idea came to him—from where he did not know—in a flash. He had spent several weeks last year at a large private museum in California, working out how their outdoor installations of abstract sculpture could be insured against the kinds of damage that traditional galleries didn't normally face: earthquake, vandalism, and—in the case of a particularly edgy work of site-specific postminimalism—termites. He had learned a lot about how artists try to evoke, rather than represent, the subject of their work. Of course, knowing that in theory was very different than actually putting it into action. Still, it gave him a way to start. He picked up some pieces of wood and began to arrange them on the floor in the middle of his workspace.

Evoke, dammit.

Once begun, he didn't look to either side, or even up from his work, for several hours. When his structure had risen to the height of his shoulder, he stepped back to take a look, and to slam down another coffee from the cart that kept circulating around the warehouse. His "horse" was composed of a series of DNA-like double-helix twists of wooden dowels, strips of leather, and springs wound from brass wire. From a distance of twenty feet or so, from a certain angle, it definitely looked horse-ish. But from a slightly different angle it looked like the aftermath of a tornado hitting a lumberyard.

Riley looked over to Asher's workspace. His mouth dropped open as he took in the gleaming, ethereal shape of his creation. The spirals of wire seemed to dance around the thoroughbred form that existed only in the intersections of the loops and swirls of shining metal. It was beautiful, already perfect, and yet Asher was still working. He was at the vise, the muscles of his upper body corded with effort as he wrought more metal with pliers and snips and a mallet.

A crashing noise caused both men to snap their heads to the left. There they saw the aftermath of the collapse of the poet's labors of the entire morning. "Shit," he said, with what Riley considered a complete lack of poetry. Like his sculpture, the poet crashed to the ground, and knelt next to the wreckage, a look of utter bereavement on his face. No fewer than three cameras swarmed around him, capturing his devastation from every angle.

"Sorry, man. Tough break," Asher offered.

As always, Riley thought, Asher was the bigger man. Of course, he was also clearly so far beyond the competitive reach of every other bachelor that he could afford to be generous with his empathy.

Riley took a deep breath and got back to work.

By the time the one-hour warning was given, most of the men were shuffling about in stupefied exhaustion. Riley's horse now looked horsey from most angles rather than just the one, and he was working on some of the finer details that he hoped would impress Daphne when the work was presented tomorrow. He glanced over at Asher, and saw him working on a tiny, intricate task with the relentless focus of an owl disassembling a field mouse. But when he noticed he was being stared at, he looked up, and that sunny smile flashed into view as always. Riley was exhausted, but smiled back in an effort to advertise his own tireless devotion to art. He didn't feel it, but he hoped he looked like he did.

He spent the last hour placing the final touches on his sculpture, and as the clock counted down the final minutes, he was standing at his customary twenty-foot distance, cocking his head to the side as he had seen the curators do last summer in California. He was still no artist. But he had created something that he could be proud of. He took another step back, and ran into something solid.

It was Asher.

"Sorry, buddy!" the smaller man said, cheerful as always. "Just trying to get a sense of how bad it is from this angle."

Riley looked at Asher's gleaming metal monument to equine beauty. It looked like the more graceful and delicate little brother to the Calder installations that Riley knew from around Chicago.

"Shit, man. You're an amazing artist," Riley murmured. "That's just fucking beautiful."

Asher turned to him, his mouth falling open. He blinked twice, and then his mouth slowly closed. "Um, thanks. I... thanks."

Riley was so surprised to hear anything other than chipper pleasantries come out of Asher's mouth that he turned to look at the other man. "Seriously. What you've done here is incredible. You rock."

Asher blushed and remained silent. He blinked again, hard, then cleared his throat mightily and stepped over to Riley's construction. "Now, this is not the work of an insurance accountant. This is... elegant. It has everything it needs, and nothing it doesn't—you couldn't take a single piece away and have it work so well. That's the test of sculpture, sir, and you have done it. Congratulations!" He held out his hand and beamed at Riley.

The men shook hands as the final bell rang, and crew members bustled about the echoing space throwing canvas tarps over all of the artworks to obscure them in preparation for their revelation tomorrow. The bachelors staggered out of the space, back to the bus and much needed rest.

THE NEXT morning Riley found his mind rested but his body wracked with aches and stiffness. He recognized each one from the movements he had performed hundreds of time over in the tense marathon of yesterday. He lurched to the workout room, laid out a yoga mat, and stretched out his angry tendons for half an hour before getting into a hot shower.

Yogurt, a banana, and some granola completed his recovery, and as he boarded the bus, he allowed himself to hope that the day would turn out for the best. Clearly, Asher would run away with the competition, but he could at least wish for a respectable second place. He hadn't gotten a good look at the other bachelors' work, but Asher's opinion carried significant weight with him. He stared out the window at nothing in particular, waiting for the bus to fill so that they could get back to the warehouse and get the competition underway.

"Morning!" chirruped Riley's new seatmate, plopping himself down with a bounce. It was Asher, of course.

"Good morning, Picasso," replied Riley. He found himself genuinely pleased to see Asher. Despite their agreement to work together, he realized he had still been viewing the other man as a competitor. But this competition, which was so clearly designed to Asher's strengths, had made Riley start to see him as a powerful ally instead.

"Haha. Good one." He took a swig of the coffee he had brought along from the catering table.

The bus lurched to life, and they were on their way back to the warehouse, swaying and rumbling through the increasingly seedy streets of the city that surrounded it. The bachelor horde didn't talk much—this challenge had so baffled them that they couldn't even seem to work up any convincing trash talk. They sat in restive silence, the tension building but lacking any satisfactory outlet.

"God, that looks good," Riley said, looking wistfully at Asher's coffee. "I completely forgot to grab a cup this morning. Had some kinks to work out on the yoga mat. Artisting is hard work!"

Asher giggled. "Here, I'll share," he said brightly, holding out the cup to Riley.

Riley looked at the cup. It had a sipping lid on it, so there was no way for him to take a drink without placing his mouth exactly where Asher's had been. He couldn't take the lid off without risking spilling the entire thing as the bus dipped and swayed along.

"That's all right, thanks," he said, shaking his head.

"Oh, come on," Asher retorted. "You need the caffeine, and this is more than I usually drink in the morning anyway."

It did smell awfully good, Riley had to admit. But putting that cup to his mouth would be far more intimate than he was comfortable with, and he wasn't sure he needed caffeine that badly. But Asher kept pushing it over to him, and his hesitation faded when the aroma hit him. "Well, if you insist," he finally said, giving in. He took the cup to his lips, and for some perverse reason he found himself looking right into Asher's eyes as he took a chug of the burning liquid. It was both disturbingly erotic and completely satisfying. The caffeine surge wiped away any reserve he'd felt, and he took another swig.

Asher beamed at him.

Riley handed the cup back. "Thanks, man. That's exactly what I needed."

"Me too," Asher agreed as he put the cup to his own lips again. He closed his eyes as he drank in the hot liquid.

Riley felt warm—warmer than two swigs of (admittedly hot) coffee should have made him. He nodded at Asher and quickly turned to look out the window.

"You're going to win this, you know," Riley said to Asher during a lull in the roaring distemper of the bus's diesel engine.

"No way. It was a good idea on paper, but it ended up being too airy once I'd started winding the wire. But by the time I saw that, it was too late." He sighed and took another sip of coffee. He held the cup out to Riley, his eyebrows up.

Riley took the cup, a move complicated by the lurching of the bus back into motion. He ended up grabbing Asher's entire hand, and then letting go suddenly when he realized what he had done.

"Sorry," he blurted.

"No worries," Asher said in a low voice.

Riley noticed that a bit of color had come into the other man's cheek, but he figured that it was a reaction to his own clumsiness. He took the cup more carefully and raised it to his mouth.

"It's almost gone," he said, handing it back to Asher.

"Go ahead and kill it," Asher replied. "I'm over my morning dosage as it is."

"No, you take it—you're the one smart enough to bring it along in the first place."

"No, seriously, you do it. I'm done."

"Drink it!" blurted Riley in a drill-sergeant tone he meant to be a joke. But Asher startled, and sat back a bit, away from Riley.

"Okay, man, just chill! Don't do something we'll both regret." His delivery was a spot-on impression of a surfer-dude drug dealer talking a renegade cop out of blasting away with a shotgun. He smiled that bright sunrise of a smile and took the cup from Riley. He winked as he brought it to his lips, and tried to swallow the last mouthful while stifling a giggle.

Riley burst out laughing as well. The rest of the bachelors cast angry glances their way, which delighted him—nothing better to psyche out the competition than to go into the challenge laughing.

The bus pulled up to the warehouse shortly thereafter, and the men filed out and stood in the staging area, just as they had the day before. At the front of the group, on the raised platform from which the host had given her instructions yesterday, stood a Stonehenge-like grouping of shrouded monoliths—their creations had been moved here in preparation for the unveiling today.

"Bachelors," the host said as she walked out onto the platform, "welcome to day two of the Helen of Troy challenge." The bachelors met this greeting with a stony silence befitting their frustration with how this artsy-fartsy challenge was going. "Shortly, these creations will be unveiled to your Helen. But we have a new wrinkle to add to the challenge," she continued.

A chorus of muted groans worked its way through the crowd. Wrinkles were clearly not welcome.

"As you know, the Greek warriors were carried into the city of Troy inside their wooden horse. So this morning, you will pay homage to their cunning by riding your creations into the arena. Daphne will judge the success of your artistry once you have been rolled in atop your sculpture!"

Riley stood stunned.

"You will have one hour to prepare your horses for this part of the challenge." She nodded to one side and then the other, and crew members pulled the tarps off of the horse sculptures. "Your one hour starts now." The host strode off the platform, and a large LED clock began the countdown from sixty minutes.

"Fuck me," Riley heard Asher sigh next to him.

"I think we're well and truly screwed, buddy," Riley agreed. His and Asher's creations were astonishingly beautiful in their own right, especially so against this crowd of crudely designed and heavily built monuments to clumsiness. But that was the problem right there: this part of the challenge would reward the crudely designed and heavily built. Riley's delicate helixes would shatter like toothpicks were he to place even a tenth of his weight on them; Asher's spun-metal horse would bend and twist until it looked like the place tangled Slinkys go to die.

Their creations had been placed next to each other, just as they had been neighbors during their making, and the men walked resignedly up to the platform to see what could be done. There were some tools and basic materials available for creating a place to sit, which is what most of the other bachelors were busily rigging up. Nothing here would be of any help to Riley and Asher, certainly not within an hour.

"Well, Trigger old boy," Asher said as he patted his steed on its gracefully arching neck, "looks like this is the end of the road for ya."

"Don't look too smug, Mr. Ed," Riley warned his own horse. "You have a date with the toothpick factory."

They laughed. Given the fact that they had just seen their chances of winning this challenge ride off into the sunset, what else could they do?

Riley stepped over and extended his hand. "You played it well, sir. In my mind, you ran away with this thing."

"I think that's debatable, given what you fashioned," Asher replied. "But since you're here, would you like to see the part I'm proudest of?"

"Of course! Since Helen won't get a chance to."

"Come over here and look," he said.

Riley walked around to the other side of the horse, and saw for the first time that it was, in fact, half of a horse. The other side was completely open, showing the structure from the inside. It made the work of Asher's fine artisanal hand even more impressive. "Here," Asher pointed to the chest of his metallic beast. Nestled in the fine swirls of wire was a more densely crafted piece, so perfectly integrated into the whole that though one could look right through the sculpture, Riley hadn't even noticed it was there.

Asher placed his hand around the object, and with a soft click he removed it from its hidden mount. "It's his heart," he said, softly. "I spent more time on it than on the entire rest of him." He sighed. "I had it all ready to give to her, if I won. Here," he said, handing the heart to Riley. Then, wrapping his own hand around Riley's, he pressed a heart-shaped button on the surface of the metal organ, and a thumping noise began to resonate within it. "It's beating."

Riley was stunned. The metal heart, no bigger than the palm of his hand, was gently but surely tapping out a pulse. He looked up at Asher, his mouth hanging open. "You?.... How did...?"

"I apprenticed with a watchmaker one year during art school—I was thinking of majoring in metals. He showed me how to make a basic clockwork out of pretty much anything I had at hand. So that's what I did. I found this box full of gears, and I was able to wind a pretty good spring out of some spooled metal strands." He fell silent as he watched the clockwork heart beat in Riley's hand.

"How long will it run?"

"I think about a minute. It's probably about finished," Asher said, with a shrug.

"Can you stop it? She should see this—she should have a chance to hold your heart in her hand."

"It can't be stopped, once it starts. You're the only one who will get to feel it beat."

Riley looked at the heart, aghast at the new meaning it had suddenly assumed. "But, why…?"

Asher shrugged again. "I wanted someone to feel it. You're the only friend I have here, so…."

Riley drew in a confused breath, began to say something—he knew not what—and then he felt the clockwork heart start to wind down. He gasped. "It's starting to—"

Asher nodded. "It's time." He smiled at Riley.

Riley could only shake his head slowly as he felt the last beats of the heart slow and then fade away. He stared at the now still organ, which was suddenly heavier than it had seemed to be just a moment ago. When he could bear to look at it no longer, he raised his eyes to the horse that was its home.

A shattering realization dawned upon him.

"Oh, God," he said, so softly that Asher didn't seem to hear him. "Oh my God."

Asher leaned closer. "What?" he whispered. "What is it?" His voice was full of concern.

"I have to show you," Riley replied. He walked around the metal sculpture, still holding Asher's heart in his hand, and then around his own to the far side—the side Asher had never seen.

"Oh, God." Asher repeated Riley's words without seeming to be aware he was doing so.

The men were standing in front of Riley's sculpture, which was, like Asher's, only half a horse. Riley's opened to show the intricate complications of his double-helix structure, but there was a place where there were no complications at all—where the heart would be. There was a space there, as if the animal were waiting for its animating force.

"I was going to tell her that the Trojan horse was missing its heart—Helen—and that only if she returned with Menelaus to Greece would it live."

He held up Asher's heart, and asked the question with his eyes that he had no words for—had no idea, actually, how to express it even to himself. Asher nodded. Riley placed the clockwork heart into the space in his own creation, where it fit, perfectly. The two men stood, shaken into silence by whatever strange magic had made this happen.

"Now we just have to finish it," said Asher, finally.

"What?" asked Riley, still staring at how perfectly Asher's heart fit the space in his design.

"Watch," was all Asher said. The sculptures had been mounted onto rolling sleds to facilitate their being moved into the arena for judging. Asher knelt down and pushed the sled on which Riley's horse stood, and the sculpture neatly spun around to face the other direction. Now its open side faced Asher's creation. He walked over to it, and spun it around as well. "Ready?" he said to Riley.

Riley nodded, his head swimming at the very prospect of what he knew he was about to see.

Asher pushed his horse toward Riley's, and when the sleds met, a single horse was formed. The two halves didn't meet precisely, of course—the head of the wooden horse stood taller, as if it were at rest, while Asher's leaned forward as if racing toward the horizon—but they did form an amazing study in metal and wood, in wire and leather. And in the center was a single heart.

The two men stood before their unified creation, silent. Riley was suddenly breathless—he couldn't believe this was happening, and had no idea what it meant. He turned to Asher, and saw the other man's unblinking stare that seemed completely unaware that he, or anyone else, existed in the world. Then Riley saw a tear edge its way from the corner of Asher's eye, and roll down his cheek.

"Can we forfeit?" Asher whispered. It was not really a question, the way he asked it. It seemed to Riley that he was simply stating what would have to happen if he were to be able to continue living. That's all.

"Yes," Riley answered. "This will only make sense to us," he said, but even as he said it he knew that it didn't—probably wouldn't ever—make sense to him either. They stood in silence another long moment.

"Thank you," Asher said at last. He was finally able to turn and look at Riley. "Thank you for this."

"It wasn't me," Riley said. "Sometimes things like this just happen, I guess." He paused for a moment, startled anew by this conglomeration of their individual efforts. "To other people, I mean. Nothing like this ever happens to me."

"Me neither," said Asher, his grin finally returning, though not as sunnily as before. "Me neither." And with that he turned, walked back down the steps, and sat on one of the black equipment trunks that were scattered around the warehouse.

Riley took in the strange sight one more time, then shook his head and followed Asher. The two men sat and watched the others hard at their clumsy work. They chuckled to each other, without malice, when one of the bachelors dropped a tool or crafted an ingenious solution to a particularly challenging saddle-construction quandary.

After a quarter hour of this, Kaitlyn walked over to them.

"Sitting this one out, gentlemen?" she asked.

"Discretion is the better part of sculpture, as they say," Riley offered, smiling.

She looked puzzled.

"What he means is that as soon as anyone sat on either of our horses, the shrapnel would fly," Asher offered.

"And that would be a mess, from a liability insurance standpoint," Riley concluded, with a laugh.

Kaitlyn turned and took in the sight of the two horses that had become one. She paused for a moment, cocked her head to one side, then turned back to them. "This wasn't a team competition, you know. Oh, I get it—were you two trying to repeat your jousting performance?"

"Actually, no," Riley said. "Just like last time, our cooperation was unplanned. We didn't even know until a few minutes ago that they fit together at all."

"Well, even together they're not going to support much weight," she said.

"That's why we've decided to send them directly to the glue factory," Asher said. "Can we bow graciously out of this round?"

"You two have immunity this time because you won the last competition," Kaitlyn replied. "But I really want Daphne to see what you've created...." She paused here, as if trying to work out the logistics. "We'll do a behind-the-scenes bit with the three of you before the final judging. I want to make sure we get the look on her face when she sees your sculpture. Hang out here, and I'll send for you when we're ready." She bustled off to make arrangements.

"Damn," Asher said once she was out of earshot. "Even when we lose, we win. This is going to make us look pretty good."

Riley, though, didn't completely share Asher's excitement. "You don't think it'll look funny that the horses, you know… fit together like that?"

Asher looked him in the eye, unblinking. "I think they're beautiful, and I'm proud to have my work joined with yours."

Riley smiled—Asher's calm was contagious, and he could feel himself relax. "You're right. I'm overthinking it." But there was still a small voice, somewhere deep inside, that fretted over their horses sharing a heart.

THE BUS ride back to the house was the same lurching affair that the ride to the competition had been. Riley and Asher, who had already been in the bus for a couple of hours by the time that filming had concluded, stared out the window and watched the city roll by.

The bachelors were still abuzz with the excitement of the Trojan Horse finale. Riley and Asher had filmed their little scene with Daphne (who was enchanted with their sculpture, and seemed sorry that it had to be disqualified) and then returned to the bus where they had chatted for a little while, then napped until the competition was over.

Late that evening Riley again met up with Asher in the fitness room. The hour was quite advanced, but since they had managed to catch a nap on the bus, they were up later than the rest. They performed their parallel workouts and then, without speaking of it, headed to the sauna together.

They sat for a long moment, soaking in the heat.

"So that guy Gavin won," Riley said finally. Daphne had chosen his entry from among the competing designs—the viewers' choice would be determined tomorrow when the episode aired and the vote was held. "Did you see what his horse looked like?"

Asher chuckled. "It looked a lot like him, actually," he replied. "Overbuilt."

Riley shared his laughter. "Yeah, he's kind of built like a horse, isn't he?"

Asher laughed even harder. "You haven't seen him in the shower!"

Riley shot a scandalized look at the man next to him. Asher, looking like he'd said too much, stopped laughing. But then Riley burst out a mighty guffaw, and both men had a good long laugh. Riley figured they both needed it after having this competition go so badly. They sat quietly again for a time, listening to the soft hiss of the sauna.

"I have just one question for you," Riley said, once again breaking the silence.

Asher's eyes remained closed, his head leaned back against the wall. "Yeah, what's that?"

"Why didn't you show her the heart?"

Asher took a sudden breath and didn't answer immediately.

Riley had been pondering this all day. When Daphne came to see their twinned artwork, she walked around and around the conjoined horse, emitting oohs and ahhs of appreciation, pointing out particularly elegant turns of steel or delicate twists of wood. Once she had bent close to look into the internal structure, and Riley assumed that Asher would pull the two halves of the horse apart to reveal what lay inside, but he didn't. Riley couldn't puzzle out why he didn't want to show his clockwork heart.

"It wouldn't have worked for her, so I didn't think it was worth showing it off." His voice, though low and soft, didn't have the tone of regret that Riley expected to hear.

"It was wasted on me," Riley replied, his own voice heavy with the regret that Asher's lacked.

Asher shook his head slowly. "No," he said definitively. "It wasn't wasted on you."

The look of intensity in Asher's eyes startled Riley. He opened his mouth, but as he currently had no clue how to respond, he simply closed it again.

"You know I'm not here for her. I mean, she seems nice and all, but I don't have any illusions about a storybook romance blossoming between us." He paused, took a breath. "I'm glad you were the one to hold it," he said, slowly and with a quiver in his voice that Riley could just detect.

"It was an amazing piece of work," he replied. "But I think she would have been able to see the amount of effort you put into it, and that could help you in the long run."

"Yeah, but...," Asher began, then trailed off.

"What?" Riley asked. He was struck by the change in the other man's demeanor.

Asher was silent, his eyes darting back and forth between Riley's.

"Hey, buddy, what is it? You look like you've seen a ghost."

"It's just that.... I think you should know that...."

Riley leaned closer. "You can tell me anything. We're in this thing together, right?"

Asher looked somewhat relieved but still hesitant. "Riley, you should know that I—"

The siren that cut Asher off was deafening, even in the sauna. The men bolted up and out of the sauna and followed the flashing fire alarm lights out of the building. They stood on the driveway in their towels for nearly an hour with the other bachelors—strangely, no cameras were visible.

As Riley settled into bed well after midnight, he realized that Asher had never finished saying whatever it was that was causing him such anxiety. He would have to ask about that next time they found some time alone.

CHAPTER SEVEN

ZERO TOLERANCE

OMAR HAD volunteered once again to take the overnight shift watching the feeds from the house. He sat at one end of the control room, idly tossing a stress ball from hand to hand, while Kaitlyn went over her notes from her earlier meeting with the executive producers. There was not much action on any of the cameras as the bachelors were getting caught up on beauty sleep after the exertions of the week, including the fire drill two nights ago. Camera after camera, some in night-vision green-gray, showed heads on pillows. As Omar scanned the displays, the most interesting detail was that one of the bachelors was drooling. The infrared light made the small pool of liquid glare brilliantly in the dark.

Kaitlyn was startled by his sharp intake of breath. He had bolted upright, and was staring intently at a pair of monitors at the end of the long row of bedroom cams.

"Omar, something wrong?" she asked, then dropped her head back to her work when he didn't immediately respond.

"We're missing two bachelors," he said slowly, almost under his breath. "3-8 and 4-7 are showing empty beds."

Kaitlyn looked across the room to where Omar was transfixed, his eyes glued to the images of the pillows that held only the impression left by the head of a now-departed bachelor.

"They're gone," he said simply, with a helpless gesture of his hands.

Kaitlyn's hand found her phone before she realized what she was doing. "Security!" she barked into it as she raced along the rows of monitors, looking for motion of any kind that might indicate where the bachelors had gotten to. She turned back to Omar, who was still rooted in place. "Who are they?"

Omar shook his head, and joined here on her transits across the room, searching. "I can't tell yet—I have to pan over and zoom in on each bed before I can tell who's missing."

"Control, this is Security," a somewhat drowsy voice emerged from the phone.

"Doors!" she nearly shouted into the device. This had an immediate effect on the voice of the security chief.

"Checking doors!" came the sharp reply.

She waited, fruitlessly scanning the displays. Bachelors on the loose were never a good thing—a couple of seasons ago three runaways had turned up at a strip club, having given away key plot details to their lap dancers. It had cost Kaitlyn a pretty penny to buy the silence of the bimbos. It was not an adventure she would gladly repeat.

"System shows doors are secure. Repeat, doors are secure. No unauthorized egress. We're scanning the door footage now to be sure."

"We have two empty beds and no sign of life on the monitors. Can you send someone through the house?"

"Patrol is out on the perimeter. We won't be able to get anyone in the house for about ten minutes."

"Shit," Kaitlyn muttered.

"Wait! What's that?" Omar said, pointing toward a couple of monitors at the edge of the room.

Kaitlyn strode over to join him and squinted at the images on the screens. These were the cameras trained on the shower room in the number two dorm. One of the two bachelors had entered the shower room, and for a moment the picture flared as it adjusted to the light being switched on. Once the levels had reset and the image resolved she recognized Liam, mostly by his height and build—he was facing away from the cameras, adjusting the water.

"One down, one to go," Kaitlyn muttered. "Security, Control. One of them is in bathroom two. We're still looking for the other one."

"Hold on," Omar said, pointing. "Is that...?"

On the monitor, the second escapee—Gavin—entered the bathroom as well. He seemed not to take notice of Liam, but busied himself taking off his robe and placing it neatly on the hook in his cubby next to the shower. Then he entered the shower, where Liam was already soaking himself under the spray. They seemed to exchange words of some kind. The two men stood under adjacent showerheads, talking without looking at each other.

"Is this normal?" Omar asked, turning to Kaitlyn. "Do they often take showers together in the middle of the night?"

"No… no, they don't. Something must be up. Turn up the audio and let's hear what they're saying." The possibility that she might salvage something interesting out of this midnight kerfuffle was appealing indeed.

The sound of rushing water filled the control room, completely obscuring the voices of the men in the shower.

"We're not going to get much in the way of scintillating dialogue with that water running," Omar said, his brow furrowed.

"See that button that says 'Active Filter'?"

Omar nodded.

"Press it, and see what happens."

He did, and instantly the sound of water began to fade into the background. Within a few seconds, it had diminished into a gentle whoosh just at the edge of hearing. Omar blinked at Kaitlyn, clearly amazed at what he was hearing—and not hearing.

"It's a new dynamic filter algorithm that we're trying out this season. It takes anything that's not in the range of normal human speech and levels it down—it's like noise cancellation, but it's selective based on the environment. Luckily, the sound of water in the shower doesn't have much variation, so fuzzy logic built into the filter has learned to take it down almost immediately."

"Very impressive," Omar said.

"All in the service of reality television," Kaitlyn replied with a roll of her eyes. "Now, let's hear what they're up to."

They fell silent, and in unspoken unison leaned in toward the monitors.

"But what if they can read lips?" Liam was asking Gavin.

"Do you really think they'll have a lip-reader sitting up all night just in case someone says something in the shower? Seriously? Now calm down— they can't hear us."

Omar and Kaitlyn exchanged a look and a shrug. They turned back to the monitor.

"We've totally got this," Gavin was saying. "We stick to the plan, we're golden."

Kaitlyn's ears perked up at this. A midnight shower was nothing, narratively speaking, and if suds and trash talk were all that it offered, she may as well return to her paperwork. But strategy—that was a development that could really give this slow cycle in the show some kick. She turned up the volume a bit and listened carefully.

"And I'm telling you, she has no idea. None at all," Gavin concluded.

This was good—very good, Kaitlyn thought.

"Maybe we can fool her," Liam replied. "But that lunkhead weight lifter is starting to pick up on us. Did you see him watching us during that picnic thing in the park? I think he knows."

Gavin chuckled and shook his head dismissively. "No one's on to us, mister. Just relax." He turned and faced the camera, letting the water run down his back.

"Oh, my," Omar whispered.

"What is it?" Kaitlyn asked.

"I think your blurring specialist will have his work cut out for him," Omar murmured.

Kaitlyn's head swiveled back to the monitor, which presented her a clear image of the reason for Omar's alarm.

Gavin was hung. He would need to be blurred well down his thighs— even if the actual flesh were obscured, the sheer length of it would be scandalous enough to keep it off the air. Kaitlyn struggled to regain her composure.

"Turns out our Gavin is quite a specimen." She pondered for a moment, head tipped to one side. "We'll just do a zoom-and-pan on the frame," she said, authoritatively. She turned back to Omar. "We'll cut them off at the waist."

He nodded, with a shrug that indicated he thought that would probably work.

"Now, tell me"—Gavin's voice was picked up again on the monitor— "what you are going to do with all of that money?"

"Mmm," Liam growled. Kaitlyn noticed the flexing of his buttocks as he smoothly shifted his weight from one leg to the other. Gavin may be hung like a racehorse, but Liam's body was a work of art. "I'm thinking the south of France. During the spring and summer months, of course. Then, I'd buy that huge stone pile of a mansion I used to walk past on my way to school every day. I'd go back to my hometown and move into the castle. There's no place like New England for the fall." He heaved a sigh. "Oh, and a little place in Tahiti for the winter. I'd spend all of the cold months lying naked on the beach—in between getting coconut oil rubdowns from a sweet young local practitioner of the happy-ending massage."

Omar sucked in a breath.

"What?" Kaitlyn asked, seeing his confused expression.

"He's not planning to marry the bachelorette? But isn't that the point?"

Kaitlyn chuckled. "Actually, the number of contestants who have ever come here—in twelve seasons—intending to leave blissfully wed you can probably count on the fingers of one hand," she explained. "But it doesn't really matter for our purposes. All we care about is that they are strongly motivated to compete—if visions of a native girl with strong hands and weak morals gets our Liam going, then that's fine with me. Whatever keeps him keen to win."

They both turned back to the monitor when they heard one of the men make a groaning noise.

"Ohhh, fuck," Gavin uttered. His eyes were closed and his head tipped back as if he were already under the spell of the nymph masseuse Liam had described.

"Okay, so we're going to have to do some bleeping as well as blurring," Kaitlyn muttered. She hoped the strategic insight this pair would deliver would be worth the production headaches this shower scene would entail.

"I tell ya what I'm going to do," Gavin continued. "I'm going to follow fashion week—Paris, New York, London, Milan—so I can nail a limo-full of supermodels every night."

"If you're going to regale me once again with the charming tale of the threesome you had with a couple of Versace's finest, I'm going to drop this soap somewhere you'll never find it."

Gavin laughed off the threat, and Liam joined in—this was good-natured ribbing, not the kind of trash talking that Kaitlyn knew made for good television.

"You know when you said you would crop them at the waist?" Omar said suddenly.

"Yeah?" Kaitlyn said, somewhat absently. She was running scenarios in her head about how she would use this footage.

"I'm not actually sure that's going to help," Omar whispered, eyes still glued to the monitor.

Kaitlyn blinked at the monitor, immediately seeing the problem. Gavin's hefty endowment was no longer hanging halfway to his knees—it was rising. And it was, impossibly, getting even larger as it did so. It jutted rudely in front of him—way out in front of him.

"I don't have a lot of experience with showers in this country," Omar said, his tone one of forced evenness. "But I have to assume that this would be considered bad form in most cultures."

Kaitlyn knew as little as Omar about the locker room etiquette of the American male, but she had to agree that a boner in the shower was probably not going to be well received.

"Hmm," she grunted. "I guess that talk about models and three-ways got him going." She squinted at the monitor, which documented the hefty member's continued rise. It was pushing up past horizontal, and showing no signs of slowing. "Good man," she whispered.

"Indeed," agreed Omar.

Kaitlyn turned to him in surprise. "Really?"

He startled, and turned from the monitor. "Really what?"

"I didn't expect you to be so calm when there's a tremendous wang bouncing before you," she giggled. "You just keep surprising me."

"When faced with a situation such as this, I fall back on the training I received as a boy in one of the most ancient of spiritual arts."

"What ancient spiritual art prepared you to deal with an enormous schlong being waved at you on video?" Kaitlyn was unable to finish this sentence without giggling.

"The ancient spiritual art of denial," he said flatly. "It allows my inner eye to turn the 'schlong,' as you so poetically put it, into a peaceful tree, standing over a spring meadow."

"I'll have to try that myself! There are some guys I've dated who would make better trees than people." Kaitlyn laughed hard enough to bring tears to her eyes, which she was finally able to wipe away some moments later. "We really should see what our night owls are up to in the shower," she said, turning back to the monitors.

"Those models are always so starved," Gavin continued, embroidering his fashion week orgy, "I'll rub butter all over my body and invite a dozen of them to lick me clean."

"Ugh—men," Kaitlyn muttered.

Gavin's peaceful tree continued its growth, apparently spurred on by his vision of models' tongues, and now reached nearly to his navel—it would dominate any spring meadow. Luckily, Liam did not seem to have noticed it. His back was still to the cameras, and he was soaping up.

"Perhaps he should turn the shower all the way to 'cold,'" opined Omar.

"You may have a point there," Kaitlyn agreed. "Though it might make a fine dramatic moment, especially if Liam takes offense. If he sees Gavin's wood, he might lash out. Shower fights kept 'Oz' on HBO for years. Then again, I don't think that the network would allow us to even hint at why they're suddenly fighting."

"And your blur specialist would really have a challenge if they make like antelope and cougar in the shower."

"Right you are," Kaitlyn replied, giggling. She liked Omar more and more.

"Uh-oh. Looks like we're about to find out," he said, pointing at the monitor.

Liam, working himself into a lather, was slowly turning around. He didn't seem rushed—just rotating idly under the water.

"He's almost there," Kaitlyn whispered. Neither of them was breathing now—the suspense was too delicious. She just had to find a way to be able to use this on next week's show. Of course, it all depended on what the men did next.

Liam completed his turn, and once he did so, he could hardly avoid seeing Gavin's prominent member, standing as it did eight or so inches, proudly arching out in front of him. Liam's eyes bugged out for a split second, then he looked away.

"Dude! Really? What the fuck?"

"What? You never seen a real man before?" Gavin said with a swagger in his voice.

Kaitlyn liked the way this was going. She could use some of this—especially if Gavin continued to be macho and cocky and egged Liam on. This could be good.

"There are cameras right over there," Liam said angrily, tipping his head (through the magic of video) directly at Kaitlyn and Omar. "They could be watching you right now."

"No way, dude. Why would they have the cameras running in the middle of the night in the fucking shower? Besides, they can't use anything when we're naked. This ain't HBO, you know. Even if they do see it on tape, they'll never show it. Relax."

"You sure?" Liam asked, with a skeptical but wishful tone.

"Sure I'm sure. Look, I don't want to screw up this chance any more than you do. Trust me, I got this figured out."

"Great. But there's still the issue of your dick pointing at me."

"What are you going to do about it, huh, tough guy?" Gavin challenged.

Kaitlyn and Omar leaned in close. What Liam chose to do about it could be the centerpiece of the show. Please, please, please, do something stupid and dramatic, she thought.

"You leave me no choice," he said, warning in his voice. He turned to fully face Gavin, and he reached out his long, muscled arm.

And he wrapped his hand around Gavin's cock.

Kaitlyn jumped and shrieked, knocking Omar to the ground with the force of her recoil. He curled into a defensive fetal position under the desk, his glasses having skittered across the floor to the other end of the control room. Kaitlyn knelt down to check on him.

"You okay? Sorry about that. That was kind of a shock." She reached her hand out to him to help him to his feet, then darted over to the other side of the room to pick up his glasses. Once she had sorted him out, she turned back to the monitor.

Liam still had his hand wrapped around Gavin's penis and was sliding his fist along the considerable length of it, from base to tip. Gavin, meanwhile, leaned back against the shower wall and closed his eyes.

"Ohhh, fuck," he murmured.

"Holy shit, they're really doing this," Kaitlyn exclaimed, a hand clamping over her mouth to keep her jaw from hanging open.

"Doing what?" Omar asked, still trying to settle his glasses back in place and straighten his shirt.

"Each other! They're the ones BachelorX was talking—err, tweeting—about!"

Omar glanced at the monitor and then looked quickly away. "Oh, dear," he whispered.

"It's been so hard," Liam was saying to Gavin, "to be so close to you and not be able to touch you."

At this Gavin opened his eyes and straightened up. He brought his hands up to Liam's face, and cradled his jaw gently. "It will all be worth it," he said, quietly and seriously, and then he kissed Liam—slowly at first, but then with more force. Their bodies drew closer together. Liam released his hold on Gavin's cock and brought his arms around to Gavin's muscular buttocks. He gripped them so tightly that he left marks, and then his fingers began to tease their way into the cleft between.

Gavin broke their manic kissing. "Fucker," he said, chuckling with a throaty rumble. "You can't imagine how much I want you in me."

Liam's response was to put his hands on Gavin's shoulders and turn him around so that he faced the wall of the shower. Gavin leaned against the tile and arched his back, thrusting his ass out.

"Can we turn it off now?" Omar squeaked, hands over his eyes.

"Wait," Kaitlyn said. "I want to see what happens next."

"Even I know what's going to happen next," Omar moaned. "I would just rather not see it."

But Kaitlyn's mind was spinning too fast to pay any attention to Omar's delicate sensibilities. What was going on in that shower was unexpected, to be sure, but it didn't have to be a disaster, as long as she managed it well. She would need to pull Liam and Gavin off to the side tomorrow, tell them that she knew what they were doing, and figure out how to get them off the show without causing a scandal. The question was, would they cooperate?

Back on the screen, she saw Liam kneel behind Gavin and press his face energetically between the wet, round buttocks before him. Gavin appeared to be holding on to the wall with his fingernails under the onslaught of Liam's mouth on his ass. He spread his legs farther apart to afford greater access, and if his increased moaning was any indication, he got what he wanted.

"Is it over yet?" Omar asked from the chair he had stumbled into. He was looking at the ceiling, breathing in measured huffs like a woman in labor.

"Honey, I think they're just getting started."

Omar's response was to swivel the other direction and shake his head as if trying to dislodge the sights and sounds that had already been inflicted upon him.

"Hurry," Gavin gasped. "What if someone else gets up?"

"Oh, thank God," Omar whispered. "Yes, please hurry."

Liam reached over for a bottle of something—conditioner, perhaps, or oil of some kind, Kaitlyn couldn't tell—and appeared to pour out some onto his erect penis. His was, in contrast to Gavin's, of average size, but seemed to be as thick as Kaitlyn's wrist.

"Good Lord, is he really going to take that thing?" she muttered.

"Two of your contestants are going at each other like depraved rabbits, and all you are concerned about is technique?" Omar asked incredulously.

"Look, if they finish and get cleaned up before anyone sees them, we're in the clear. So, yeah, I'm kind of rooting for them to get it done."

Omar groaned again and swiveled back around to face the wall.

"I'm going to give you something that your precious Versace models never could," Liam growled as he pressed the head of his cock into the cleft between Gavin's buttocks. The muscles in Gavin's legs stood out in stark relief as he readied himself for the invasion.

"Oh, hell no!" Kaitlyn suddenly yelled at the monitor. "No no no no no!"

"What? What is it?" blurted Omar.

"He's not using a condom! Oh, this is bad."

"Oh, *now* you think it's bad?" Omar asked with a shiver.

"Yes, it's bad! They shouldn't be doing that!"

"That's the point I was trying to make earlier."

She turned to face him. "There's a difference between shocking and deadly, Omar. What these guys are up to is a problem for us, but unsafe sex is a real problem—for them." She turned back to the screen and gasped as Liam slid the full length of his bare cock into Gavin.

"Oh, fuck!" Gavin groaned into the wall. Then he turned his face to the side. "Every time feels like the first time," he growled.

"After all these years? You don't have to flatter me, babe. Unlike those Versace models, I'm in love with you."

Kaitlyn, hearing this, stopped hyperventilating and stared at the monitor. Suddenly, their words were no longer swagger or strategizing—now they were flirting, sweet nothings between lovers. Though she had watched with rapt attention until now, in defense of her show, now it felt like an invasion of their privacy—a privacy that long preceded their arrival in the bachelor house. She was reaching for what the production staff called the "kill switch," the button that would cut off the video feed and stop the recording, when her phone rang. It was the security chief.

"We finally got someone in the house," his brusque voice announced. "He'll be in the number two dorm right about... now."

"No! Call him back," Kaitlyn shouted into the phone. "It's okay, we don't need him to—"

"Kaitlyn! Kaitlyn, look!" Omar said, pointing frantically at the monitor.

Liam's thrusting had reached a fever pitch, and both men seemed to be thrashing in the grips of a passion that encompassed just the two of them—which likely explained why they didn't appear to hear the heavy footsteps of the approaching security guard. The monitor blinked white for a split second as all of the lights were switched on at once (including those used to illuminate the men for the cameras during their morning grooming—muscular men with towels wrapped around their waists shaving was a guaranteed ratings-getter), and then the image normalized. Liam and Gavin froze midthrust.

"Who's in here?" shouted the security guard as he strode toward the shower.

Still the two men stood motionless, not even daring to separate. Move! thought Kaitlyn, but of course the men didn't know what she did—that the security guard was going to come into the shower whether he thought anyone was in there or not. She could see the dark form of the guard looming through the glass blocks that formed the side wall of the shower. By the time the men seemed to notice, though, the guard was in the shower with them.

"What the fuck!" he shouted, as he rounded the corner and caught sight of the men, still connected by Liam's cock.

Liam pulled back abruptly, causing Gavin to lunge forward against the wall. The men turned toward the guard, who glared back at them with a look of pure, enraged shock. Then he blinked twice, bent forward, and threw up vigorously onto the floor of the shower.

"Did not see that coming," Omar mused.

Kaitlyn collapsed into a chair and buried her head in her hands. This just kept getting worse.

"What's going on?" a new voice echoed through the control room, causing Kaitlyn and Omar to freeze and glance with some trepidation at the monitors. The cameras in other parts of the bathroom showed every other resident of #2 dorm streaming into the bathroom, apparently awakened by the shouting of the guard and spurred on by the awful sound of his retching. The first new voice was followed by several others as all of the men rushed into the bathroom. Liam and Gavin were trapped.

If the other bachelors were slow to pick up on exactly what Liam and Gavin had been up to in the shower, Liam's indefatigable woody gave conclusive evidence. He tried to hide it, but he had begun to shiver with either shock or cold, and it kept poking back out from behind his cupped hands.

"Holy fucking shit!" yelled the largest of the men, who, in his rush to deliver this exclamation, stepped directly into the security guard's dinner. Though Kaitlyn couldn't see the floor from the angle of the camera, she could tell from the look on the man's face that his foot had come into contact with something unsavory. "What the fuck are you two faggots doing?"

Liam and Gavin, Kaitlyn was surprised to see, remained silent. Though they were wet and naked, there was a certain dignity in their bearing as they stood their ground against the half-dozen men who had suddenly invaded their privacy.

"They were f-f-f-fucking!" shouted the security guard. He took an uncertain step back and slipped (whether on some soap or his own sick was uncertain as well) and fell back against the glass-block wall. He slid down to the floor and pointed at Liam and Gavin as if accusing them of being witches.

"And that made you throw up?" a calm voice from the back of the crowd intoned. "Dude."

The men who had crowded into the shower turned, and Kaitlyn could see that the speaker was Asher. She had to admire his humanity in this moment of crisis.

Asher turned to one of the other men. "And put that thing away. What the hell are you going to do with that video anyway?"

Kaitlyn, not for the first time this evening, felt ice water in her veins. She leaned in close to the monitor and saw that one of the men—Harris—was holding up a phone. Shit. She picked up her own.

"Security, there's a phone in the number two dorm shower. Get your guy to grab it!"

"On it!" came the quick reply.

Almost immediately she heard the security guard's walkie-talkie crackle, though she couldn't understand the words being spoken to him. He straightened up and looked around the shower room with a new urgency. He caught sight of Harris, but before he could get to his feet, the man lowered it himself.

"There," he said. "Done."

"What's done?" one of the other bachelors asked.

"I posted the video."

"Where? Facebook? You want your friends to see you're hanging out in shower rooms?" Asher asked.

"No, idiot. Twitter. This feed is going to make me famous, whatever happens in the stupid competition."

Kaitlyn gasped and held the desk with white knuckles. They had found BachelorX.

"I don't think so, asshole," the security guard growled. He yanked the phone out of Harris's hand and threw it against the wall in an explosion of anger and plastic. He then stomped on the pieces until Kaitlyn was certain there must be no shard larger than a kidney bean.

Kaitlyn ran across the room to her laptop, and pulled up the BachelorX Twitter feed. Nothing new had been posted since the afternoon's competition—perhaps the phone had been smashed before it finished transmitting the video. She began to think that she might have caught a break for the first time today.

It was at that moment that her laptop gave a little "ding," an innocent tone announcing her doom. A new tweet from BachelorX had arrived.

"Which #HusbandMaterial bachelors are soaping up together? See them having a gay old time in @BachelorX video exclusive!"

KAITLYN KNEW what she would find when she clicked the link—and find it she did. Seventeen seconds of confusion and jostling, during which Liam's and Gavin's faces (and all the rest of them) were clearly visible.

She sat staring, unfocused, at the video for no more than a minute, during which time the "views" counter spun up into the mid-four digits. At two in the morning, thousands of people apparently had nothing better to do than monitor the tweets of an anonymous reality show contestant. On principle she clicked the "Flag this video" button, but she knew it would do little good. The cats were out of the bag.

And they were gay cats at that.

"THEY'RE HERE," Omar said softly as he nudged at Kaitlyn's shoulder. She had dozed off an hour ago over her laptop, having collapsed in the wake of the shower drama and the frenetic e-mail traffic she had exchanged with the network's public relations and legal staff. She wiped her cheek absently, and despite a fleeting hope that the whole thing had just been a nightmare, she recalled what she was now facing.

The three bachelors at the heart of the scandal—Liam, Gavin, and now Harris—were waiting for her in the conference room. About their fates she was certain, even if she had no inkling of her own—or the show's. They could be canceled by midmorning if the publicity around the BachelorX Twitter feed broke the wrong way. The best thing about the age of Internet PR was that even the most dire train wreck could result in positive buzz. The worst thing about it was that often the train, having left the rails, then crashed into a crowded shopping mall and exploded.

The three men stood as she entered the room, as if chivalry mattered now.

"Sit," she commanded and took her seat at the head of the table. Omar retreated from the room as if he sensed a bloodbath was coming.

"First, I'd like to say—"

"Shut up. Just shut the fuck up." Her unblinking stare conveyed how seriously she meant this. Harris sat back in his chair, chastened. "I'll get to you. First, though, Gavin and Liam."

The two men, who had been studying the grain of the tabletop since they sat down, looked up. They'd both been crying, that was clear.

"I've got nothing against you. People try all kinds of strategies to win this show, and yours was no worse than what I've seen in past seasons."

Harris snorted and rolled his eyes.

"What part of shutting the fuck up do you not get?" she growled at him. Seeing him wilt under her glare, she turned back to the other two men.

"That being said, you've put me in a really bad spot. You will not meet a more pro-gay-rights person than this girl—I've marched in my share of pride parades—but right now I don't have the luxury of behaving like a human being. I have to be a television producer. And what you have done is fucked me six ways to Sunday, and now I have to try to fix it before my show is cancelled out from under me. Which"—she glanced at her watch—"is probably happening right now in New York. Fuck." She sighed and slumped a bit.

All three men around the table sat, silent, waiting. They seemed to know better than to utter a sound right now. After a moment, she took a deep breath and sat upright again.

"So, right now, thanks to Bachelor-fucking-X here, everyone knows that two of our bachelors are gay, and are so sex-crazed that they decided to get frisky in the shower in the middle of the night and have generally turned out to be the scheming, sexed-up, cynical queens that every homophobe in the country still thinks all gay people are and thank you very much for setting back the cause like twenty years!" She was shouting now and didn't particularly care.

At this outburst, Gavin wiped his eyes and Liam stifled a sob.

Kaitlyn took three deep breaths in succession, rubbed her eyes with the backs of her hands, and started again. "I think it goes without saying that you are off the show, should there still be a show by the end of the day. I will not comment, nor will anyone associated with the show, about what happened in the shower. That's your business. Well, yours and BachelorX's here. And then he made it everyone's business, fuck you very much," she spat at him.

Another deep breath, and she turned back to Gavin and Liam.

"There's a car outside waiting to take you to the airport. Pursuant to the terms of the contract you signed with the production company, the network, and, to hear our lawyers tell it, God himself, you will be taken to an undisclosed location for the duration of the show's production schedule. Depending on what New York decides, that may be the next twelve weeks, or it may be a matter of hours. In any event, you will not make any statement or public appearance of any kind. Our only hope is to strangle this thing and hope that the tabloids move on out of boredom. Do you understand me?"

Both men nodded, clearly relieved.

"Good. Now, as for you, BachelorX—"

"Harris, please, Kaitlyn. Call me Harris." He flashed a smile that Kaitlyn immediately recognized. It was the smile that said "I'm a pretty big deal, sweetheart."

She seethed.

"I will call you whatever the hell I want to call you. Right now I'm leaning toward That Asshole Who Got My Show Cancelled, but I'll probably experiment with a few others before I settle on one—I think there needs to be more swear words in it. Until then, I'll call you whatever I damn well feel like at the moment. Understood?"

He nodded and remained silent, the smile wiped completely away.

"You are in violation of several clauses of your contract with the production company. There's a team of lawyers on their way over here who will spell out for you exactly how screwed you are. Let me just say that what they have in store for you will make what Liam was doing to Gavin in the shower seem like a peck on the cheek." She turned to the two men. "Sorry, no offense."

Gavin gave a wry smile. "None taken."

Omar poked his head in. "Lawyers are here."

"Great." She turned to Gavin and Liam. "You two grab your duffels and get in the town car that's parked out front. A rep from the company will escort you to your new home. They won't be giving you back your phones, in case you were wondering. You'll be incommunicado for the duration. Enjoy prison, gentlemen."

She stood, and the two men stood, seemed to debate for a moment whether to shake her hand, decided against it, and left the room. Harris also stood.

"Sit down. The sharks will come to you, chum." She turned to Omar. "Let's go meet our fate." She led the way out the door.

"I see what you did there," Omar said after they passed the triumvirate of lawyers coming down the hall. "Sharks. Chum. Funny." His deadpan delivery was belied by the laughter that followed.

Kaitlyn found herself laughing along. Dark humor was better than none at all.

KAITLYN RETURNED with Omar to her office to await the phone call from New York. Knowing that these may well be her last moments as a producer, she sat looking at the wall of her office, where she had tacked up the scattered memorabilia from her tenure. A few covers of celebrity magazines from the show's early seasons, a joke Pulitzer from a colleague who worked on "serious" television, a bobble-head doll of the show's first winner. Not much to show for the show that had consumed her life over the last twelve years.

She was jarred from her reverie by the ringing of the phone. She saw the 212 area code and hit the Speaker button.

"This is Kaitlyn," she announced glumly.

"Katy, it's Peter. How're you holding up, hon?"

"I've had better days, Pete. What's it look like for us?"

"It's bad. Not gonna sugarcoat it."

Kaitlyn sighed, and her forehead contacted the desk with a clunk. She counted to ten, then lifted her head toward the phone. "Let me guess. Their hands are tied, we've done great work in the past, this one is too big to get in front of, we're cancelled, and they're sending someone to salt the earth so that nothing ever grows here again, right?"

Peter apparently thought this was funny—all Kaitlyn could hear on the speaker was chuckling.

"Laughing at my suffering is not very attractive, Peter. After the spy games and shower sexy-time I've been dealing with instead of sleeping, I'm not really in the mood to go to the gallows with a smile."

"Calm down, hon. It's not a complete cluster. The BachelorX thing looks like it's trending the right way for us this morning—he's set a record for reality-television-related retweeting among women eighteen to thirty-four, and every one of those damn things has our hashtag. You can't buy viral velocity like that. Our current thinking is that we black-hole him for a week to get back in front of the narrative and then bring him on the morning show to do color commentary on the remaining bachelors."

"Wait, so we're not being cancelled?"

"No, sweetie. Not yet, anyway."

"But the guy who caused the scandal gets a gig out of it?"

"Now, hold on a minute. BachelorX didn't cause the scandal—it wasn't his dick. All he did was get it on video."

"And post it online in direct violation of his contract."

"Which has made your little show the second-most-searched term on Google today. If there hadn't been that bombing last night in... well, wherever that was, we would have been first. As for the video itself, we got the legitimate sites to take it down, but that only makes people look harder for it. Win/win!"

"Great," muttered Kaitlyn with a roll of her eyes that she was glad Peter couldn't see. "So we can keep going?"

"Hold on a minute. We're still concerned about how the whole 'soap and sodomy' thing makes us look. I'm sure you won't be surprised when I say that this kind of thing can't—can-fucking-not—happen again."

"I hate to break it to you, but this kind of thing has happened more times than you might think."

"I'm sure it has. All of those alpha males in a house, only one woman, I'm sure it gets.... Well, I imagine...."

"I'm sure you do imagine it, Pete. That's why we broke up."

"Very funny. But in seasons past, you could fix all of this in editing, and there was no one live-tweeting it. This time, well, we simply cannot have another gay panic, Katy. If you get any inkling about any of the remaining bachelors—if any one of them makes your gaydar ping at all—you cut them loose immediately. No questions, no second chances. They all signed the contract, including the hetero addendum."

"The what?"

"The hetero addendum. We added it to the contract after that hot-tub incident in season seven."

"Wait, you knew about that?"

"Of course. I reviewed the video very carefully."

"I'll just bet you did," Kaitlyn retorted with a sarcastic snicker.

Season seven had been her worst of the series, in no small part because of what four of the disgruntled bachelors got up to with a large bottle of smuggled tequila and an hour by themselves in the whirlpool. But that had been in simpler times, when all they'd had to do was send the offenders home, clean the semen out of the pool filter, and disinfect everything. The four randy contestants were then edited out of the entire show—it was as if they'd never existed. That was an option she simply didn't have this time around.

"So here's what you're going to do. Go ahead with the show, and make sure no one says squat about the dearly departed. The bachelor brain trust you've assembled should run out of attention span in about forty-eight hours. Then, going forward… you know I love you, Katy, but I swear to God, if word leaks that any one of those remaining bachelors has so much as winked at another, we will pull the plug and pull it hard. Is that clear?"

"Perfectly clear. I'll make sure the bachelors keep to the straight and narrow, and you keep your hands off your plug. Got it."

"Don't ever change, love. TTFN." And Peter was gone with a click.

Kaitlyn could hardly believe her good luck. At least she thought it was good luck. She couldn't really tell anymore. She turned to Omar.

"I need to get some rest, and I think you slept less than I did. Let's take a few hours while the buzz runs through the bachelors—we're not going to be able to use any of today's footage anyway, while the gossip works its way along—and we'll have a production meeting at two. Figure out how we're going to get past this. Sound good?"

Omar nodded. "I'll get an e-mail out to the rest of the staff now. See you at two." He turned to leave Kaitlyn's office. "It was an honor to watch you work," he said softly, and then closed the door behind him.

CHAPTER EIGHT
CAVEMAN CHICKEN

KAITLYN STUDIED the monitors showing the progress of the day's competition, which was being held in a remote canyon a couple of hours outside the city. Remote shooting always made her a bit nervous—she didn't like being so far from where filming was taking place, but then again, if she were in a mobile production studio, it would be a tenth the size of the control room she was now sitting in, and much hotter and noisier. Gazing up at the screens, she was glad she was here rather than there.

"Kaitlyn?"

"Yeah, Omar? What is it?"

"I have a question about this concept."

She turned to her assistant. "It's a caveman thing. They're supposed to show their hunting and gathering prowess."

He looked at her quizzically. "Yes, I get that part. What I don't get is why."

"Why what?"

"Why the bachelorette would fall in love with the best caveman. They don't exactly have a great reputation when it comes to romance. There are two dominant cultural models that I'm aware of—the hairy, stinking brute who drags a mate home by the hair—"

Kaitlyn shrugged, smiling.

"—and Fred Flintstone."

Kaitlyn laughed out loud at that image. She hadn't imagined that Omar would be conversant with cultural touchstones produced on the cheap several decades ago.

"You have to remember that the point is to dress up the boys like that." She pointed at the monitors, which showed the group of bachelors preparing for their competition. Each was dressed in a faux fur loincloth—and nothing else. What the wardrobe lacked in sartorial innovation was more than compensated for, at least in the typical viewer's eye, by its relentless brevity. Each challenge found the bachelors wearing crotch-covers skimpier than the silver briefs back in the jousting arena.

Kaitlyn turned back to Omar. "As long as they keep showing that much skin, no one cares about the details of the silly challenges."

Omar gazed at the monitors. "God, I love this country. This deeply, deeply disturbed country."

They laughed and then settled in to watch as the competition got underway.

THE MEN had their instructions—this was to be a sort of Neanderthal scavenger hunt, with the men seeking out such treasures as a certain quantity of berries, nuts, and other edibles, and having to perform such tasks as starting a fire and securing a supply of fresh water. What would have made for a mildly diverting day for a Boy Scout troop was fascinating—at least by reality television standards—because it was all done by strapping men in tiny furry loincloths.

Kaitlyn and Omar had their choice of prime moments to collect for the montage scenes of the episode—bachelors trying to climb trees to gather fruit, which made their loincloths ride up teasingly, and others scratching through the underbrush, which often resulted in their loincloths snagging and being yanked almost off. It was quality television indeed.

About midday the camera crew monitoring the stream that was the only source of fresh water in the area picked up the first bachelor to find it. It was a well-tanned denizen of the Jersey Shore whom the crew had nicknamed Vinny; he was now standing knee-deep in the water trying to figure out how to bring some water back to the cave he had chosen to be his base.

A rustling of the shrubbery on the side of the stream signaled the approach of another bachelor. The camera panned over and caught Asher as he emerged into the bright sun shining on the water. He squinted and held up a hand to shield his eyes while they adjusted to the brightness.

Vinny, meanwhile, stood stock still in the water, blocked from Asher's view by a large tree trunk that protruded from the bank of the stream. He craned his neck, watching Asher negotiate the steep bank. The camera pulled back to a wide view, reminiscent of *National Geographic* specials in which the unsuspecting antelope approaches the river's edge for a drink, unaware of the ravenous crocodile that lies in wait.

"What's he doing?" Omar asked, watching the feed back at the control room.

"I have no—oh shit, look," Kaitlyn replied.

Vinny, careful not to make a ripple in the water, slipped his loincloth down and off and tossed it onto a low-hanging branch that jutted out over the water. He now stood buck naked in the stream, his tightly-clenched buttocks pale white in the bright sun. Still he waited—but for what?

Kaitlyn's phone rang. She glanced and saw that it was the assistant producer on this competition.

"Let me guess," she said into the phone once she had pressed the button to answer. "There's something down at the creek I should keep an eye on?"

"Glad you're on it," the AP replied, relief in her voice. "So, do you want me to send in the troops?"

"What, because we're getting mooned? No, hold tight, and we'll see what happens next."

What happened next is that once Asher reached the edge of the water, Vinny stepped out from behind the tree. He made a show of not noticing that the other man was there, and he instead was entirely focused on splashing water on himself.

"Uh, hey," Asher said, startled. "Didn't see anyone else was down here." And then he seemed to notice that he was addressing a naked man, and he stepped back, nearly falling backward onto the bank of the stream. "Dude, what are you—?"

"Oh, I'm so embarrassed!" simpered Vinny. "It was just so hot! I thought I'd just slip off that tacky little loin thingie and get... nice and... wet."

"Oh good God," Kaitlyn muttered. "He sounds like a drag version of Marilyn Monroe."

Asher continued his backward ascent of the stream bank, crab walking when his footing was unsure. "That's nice—looks... uh... refreshing...."

"It is!" hooted Vinny. "You should try it. You look hot. Really hot. I mean, like, really really hot!" All the while he was advancing toward the water's edge, the parts of his body that didn't normally see the sun glistening.

"Yeah, great... um, enjoy that, okay?" Asher had reached the top of the rise, and quickly scrambled to his feet. He spun around and disappeared at a brisk pace.

"Shit," expectorated Vinny. He turned and waded back into deeper water.

Kaitlyn speed-dialed her assistant producer. "Okay, so what the hell was that?"

"Either Vinny has been bitten by a mosquito carrying the gay virus, or he was working some kind of strategy."

Kaitlyn set her phone down and watched. Vinny resumed his original position around the other side of the tree trunk. His loincloth still hung limply from the branch nearby, so he clearly wasn't going to give up the game yet.

"Okay, now it's just getting creepy," Omar said. "It's like he's a big naked spider waiting for a bug to stumble into his web."

Kaitlyn jolted. "That's it! That's what he's doing!"

"I was kind of joking about the spider thing."

"No, he's—wait, here comes someone else." Her attention turned back to the scene at the stream.

There was more rustling, this time at the top of the bank a little farther down the stream, and Vinny froze. From the shrubs another bachelor emerged. He started down the bank, scanning the scene for competitors. He had just reached the water and bent down to get a drink when Vinny emerged from behind the tree.

"Oh, how embarrassing," Vinny announced, a little more definitely this time. "I didn't know anyone else would stumble upon my little watering… hole." He clutched his hands to his cheeks in dinner-theatre shock-horror. This almost Victorian display of modesty, however, left his genitals completely uncovered—a state of affairs clearly not lost on the other man.

"The fuck you doin'?" barked the other man, a fireman from Houston whom the other bachelors had nicknamed Tex.

"I just needed to cool off a bit, and thought I would just slip out of that horrid fake-fur thing and enjoy the feel of the cool water all over my body."

"Uh-huh," replied Tex. He seemed unimpressed by Vinny's display, but at least he wasn't backing his way up the bank in panic.

"I'm just too well endowed for a loincloth, is all…." Vinny slipped a hand down to his crotch, handled his cock roughly. "Don't you think I'm just too big for it?"

All the way back in the control room, Kaitlyn could see the exaggerated wink that accompanied his fondling and insipid come-on. Something really wasn't right with this guy.

"Omar, you're a guy," she said, not taking her eye from the monitors.

"Yes, I believe so," he answered.

"Is Vinny… well, is he flirting?"

Omar frowned at the screens. "Have you ever seen anyone flirt like that?" he asked, slowly and seriously.

"But what if he's doing it for the first time?"

"Who gets to be in their twenties without flirting at least once?"

"What if it's his first time flirting with a guy?"

"Why would he come on this show and suddenly start flirting with guys?"

"Do you two realize you communicate entirely in questions?" the assistant producer's voice crackled from Kaitlyn's phone.

"Oh, sorry! Forgot you were still there," Kaitlyn said.

"No worries. But I think you're going in the right direction, Kaitlyn. He's definitely awkward."

Back at the stream, Tex had finally found his voice. "Uh, yeah," he said, woodenly. "You are a bit big for it." His eyes jerked up from Vinny's crotch, and he looked him right in the face. "It's, uh… it's nice, though…. Heh. Maybe I'll join you," he said, his voice halting and uneven. "Would you like that?" He tugged at his loincloth, and it slid down his legs.

"Oh God," Kaitlyn muttered. Again. She knew a fair bit about these men, of course, having watched them in various unguarded moments for some time now. But nothing she had seen had given any hint that these two would find themselves standing in the woods, naked, flirting with each other so clumsily that it was painful to watch.

"Oh my God, it's so big," Vinny opined, sounding very much like a dim-witted porn starlet seeing the business end of a professional penis for the first time.

"I'll give him that," Kaitlyn cracked. "Tex is packing some serious heat there."

"It'll get bigger if you treat it right," Tex growled.

"Would you like that, if I treated it right? Is that what you want?"

"If it's what you want. Do you?" Tex's intonation clearly conveyed that every word he spoke caused him pain. But he plowed ahead. "Do you want this?" He laid hold of the monstrous cock that hung in front of him, and he wagged it at Vinny.

"Holy shit. He's doing it too," Kaitlyn whispered.

"What did you say?" the assistant producer asked over the phone. "Should I send in the muscle to pack them off the show?"

"No," Kaitlyn answered. "What I said was Tex is doing it too. He's playing the same game Vinny is—he's trying to get Vinny to hit on him so we'll send him home." She turned to Omar and, through the phone, to the assistant producer. "What we have here, people, is the world's first game of caveman gay chicken."

"Um, Kaitlyn, what the hell is gay chicken?" the voice on the phone asked.

Kaitlyn raised her eyebrows at Omar, inviting him to chime in with an answer. He held his palms up and shook his head helplessly.

"Gay chicken is when two straight guys pretend like they're going to kiss, but as they get close one of the guys pulls back at the last second—he's the chicken. It's like when two high school idiots drive at each other—the loser swerves."

"Let me understand," Omar said, his brow furrowed in concentration. "When played with cars, people could get killed. But when played with kissing, people could get... kissed." He mused on this for a second. "It seems like the better option."

"You'd think," replied Kaitlyn. "But if you were to survey one hundred high school boys, ninety-eight of them would tell you that they'd rather die in a fiery crash than be caught kissing another guy."

"What about the other two?"

"Statistically, they're already kissing each other."

"So, back to the issue at hand," interrupted the assistant producer. "We have two straight guys at the stream who are basically trying to seduce each other so each can get the other thrown off the show."

"That's my read of it, anyway. Let's see what happens," Kaitlyn said, then turned her attention back to the monitors.

Tex stepped toward Vinny. Vinny also stepped forward, as if trying to show just how much he wanted to be closer to the other man. Finally, they stood about a foot apart.

"Well," Tex said, breaking the silence. "Here I am."

"Here we are," mused Vinny. "Aren't you going to...?"

"Aren't you?" asked Tex, a bit defensively.

"I thought you were going to make the first move," Vinny replied, a real edge in his voice now.

Tex looked around, scanning the area for cameras. He spotted it, and looked directly at it—and through it, directly at Kaitlyn. He seemed satisfied that they were being watched. He looked back at Vinny. "A first move like this?" he said and stepped closer, bringing the two men only inches apart.

"That's a good start," Vinny replied, his voice low. Then he too stepped forward, closing most of the remaining distance.

Tex jolted when he felt their penises touch. He looked at Vinny, wide-eyed, but he swallowed hard, blinked, and kept his calm. The two men stood, eye to eye, cock to cock, motionless.

"Um, I think we'd be doing them a favor if we went in now—put them out of their misery," said the assistant producer over the phone.

"No! No, this is too good! Look at them—they're practically shaking, but they're sticking with it. Best gay chicken ever!" She giggled and clapped her hands with glee.

Vinny licked his lips. "What are you going to do now?"

Tex's stare was unflinching. "What are you going to do?"

They leaned closer. Closer. Tex heaved a breath, closed his eyes, and pushed forward the last half inch. Their lips met, reluctant and awkward, and then, as if an electric current had blasted through their bodies, they threw themselves back.

"Faggot!" yelled Tex, at precisely the same instant that Vinny bellowed, "Queer!"

Mutually stunned by their outbursts, the men stared slack-jawed at each other, panting as if kissing each other had been the hardest physical labor they'd ever performed.

"What did you call me?" they demanded of each other, almost in unison.

Tex lunged at Vinny, but this time kissing was evidently not on his mind. Swearing furiously, he swung hard at the other man's head, but Vinny was agile enough to duck out of the way and drive his shoulder into Tex's ribcage. Down the men went, splashing and grunting and writhing, two naked warriors dead set on defending their masculine honor.

"Oh, hot," breathed the assistant producer.

"Let's be professionals about this—" Kaitlyn began, then stopped short when the men launched in a ball of fury onto the muddy bank of the stream.

Smeared with mud and glistening with sweat, the men wriggled and ground against each other. "Okay, that's a little hot," she murmured.

Neither man could gain effective purchase on the other to effect anything like a dominant position, and so they rolled and slipped and grappled along the bank of the stream, alternately grunting with exertion and howling in frustration. Kaitlyn would never be able to use most of the footage—no amount of blurring could make broadcast-ready a view of Tex's wide-spread legs as he struggled to flip the other man, his buttocks flexing open and closed as he brought to bear all of the leverage he could summon.

Throughout, the men continued to accuse each other of being homosexual. Their vocabulary was that of high school bullies whose phobic anger far exceeded their wit.

"You fucking want this, fucking faggot?" demanded Vinny as he delivered a series of punishing slams to Tex's torso.

"I'm gonna fucking fuck you up!" rejoined Tex, rolling over Vinny to force his face into the mud.

"You'd fucking love that, wouldn't you?" Vinny sputtered, mostly to the mud.

"Shut up, faggot!" Tex screamed as he smashed the wriggling Vinny into the squelching mud, their hips pressed tightly together.

It was at this moment that Vinny seemed to realize the position he was in—face down, spread-eagled, with a larger man's pelvis pressed against his buttocks. The realization did not sit well.

"Help!" he screamed, his voice a full octave higher than it had been. "Help! He's trying to buttfuck me! Help! Someone help! He's gonna fuck me!"

Vinny's screams, which continued in this vein, though in progressively higher registers, seemed to jar Tex out of his frenzy. He looked down and saw just how intimately he was joined to the other man, and he pushed himself up and off as if he had been attempting to mount a campfire. He staggered back and fell into the water with a flailing splash. He quickly righted himself, stood, and glared at the prone man on the bank, panting.

"Get up!" Tex screamed. "Get the fuck up!"

"Fuck you!" Vinny choked out, his voice broken.

Tex charged at him again, shoved his foot under the sprawled man, and rolled him over. He shrieked and staggered back when he saw Vinny's penis jabbing the air, semierect, pointing at him. "Fuck! Fuck!" he repeated in a strangled voice, his eyes riveted on his opponent's penis, as if the shock of its increased size was now hitting him.

"Oh, party foul," the assistant producer cracked. "Offsides boner—that'll be a penalty!"

Omar and Kaitlyn gaped at the monitor, silent.

"Shut the fuck up!" Vinny screamed, rolling back over onto his stomach. His words were angry, but his face wore an expression of shattered mortification. His eyes welled and his cheeks burned in mute, roiling horror.

Tex realized he had won. "You're fucking going home, asshole! You're done!" He burst out with a horrible, cutting laugh. "At least you enjoyed it," he spat.

Vinny seemed to snap at this last aspersion cast on his heterosexuality. Every muscle tensed with menace as he slowly got to his feet. "I am not the faggot here," he said slowly, with a chilling snarl. "And if you tell anyone about this, I will tell them how you tried to bone me in the ass."

"Fuck you. You enjoyed it, obviously," Tex barked. Vinny's deflating member was still larger than it had been before the commencement of hostilities.

"No, fuck you. If you hadn't been grinding on me—you pushed me into the mud! What did you think was going to happen? I'm a man, damn it, and my dick gets pushed into something soft and wet it fucking responds. Or don't you have that problem?"

Tex stood silently for a moment, as if turning over in his head what Vinny had said. "Yeah. I guess."

"And for the record I'm completely 100 percent straight," Vinny said, recovering a little more of his dignity now.

"Me too," Tex said, and though his words were defensive, his manner was less so.

"I'm thinking we look pretty stupid here," Vinny said, with a half-hearted chuckle.

Tex took up the joke. "We're just two guys rolling around in the mud, naked. Perfectly normal. Nothin' to see here, folks, move right along."

Vinny laughed with something more like real feeling. "Damn, man. You really had me pinned there. If you had really wanted to put it to me, I couldn't have done anything about it, and no shit."

"Like I'd want to bone your raggedy ass!" Tex guffawed, then spat amiably into the stream. "Well, shit. We both took our best shot here, didn't we?" He fished his loincloth out of the stream where it had drifted up against a rock, and slipped it back on. "What say we keep this just between us?"

"I like that a whole lot better than what was between us a few minutes ago, which was nothin' at all," Vinny joked, pulling his own loincloth back into place.

The two men began to climb the steep bank, and then Tex froze. He turned around and looked right at the camera. He opened his mouth as if he were about to say something and then seemed to think better of it. He followed Vinny up the rise and out of sight.

"And that is how it's done, people," Kaitlyn laughed, her fist pumping in victory. She was already planning how to splice together some wild wrestling footage, while carefully excising the surreal romance that led up to it. It would be a highlight of this week's show.

CHAPTER NINE

LONG WALKS ON THE BEACH

KAITLYN WAS relieved to find that after the failure of the gay chicken gambit during the caveman challenge no one else tried it—word must have spread among the bachelors that the producers were not as quick on the eject button as some of them had hoped. It helped that no one got sent home afterward; with the previous week's departure of Liam and Gavin and Harris, the show needed to keep its bachelor count up. A sort of calm settled over the bachelors, who now focused more on winning competitions than on strategizing against one another.

The next three weeks passed without significant incident, providing Kaitlyn and Omar solid material for each show. The bachelors competed in a Vaudeville-style talent show, a ballroom dance competition, and a cooking challenge; each week one unlucky suitor was sent home by the vote of the viewers. The show had settled into such a predictable rhythm that Kaitlyn found her interest waning—she began to hope that someone would do something outrageous so that she could liven up the weekly show.

The following week the bachelors were sent to the beach for what looked to be another sleepy episode. But Kaitlyn wanted to recreate some of the creativity of the Helen of Troy challenge, so she threw in a twist: the bachelors would have two hours to search the beach for items to make into an artistic gift for Daphne; while each had a few minutes to walk on the beach with her, the others would be at work creating. At the end of the day on the beach, the creations would be presented to her, and she (and the viewing audience) would choose the winners and the loser.

FROM THE crates of tools arrayed under the shade of a tent, Riley snatched up the only metal detector. While he felt (and no doubt looked) like a complete tool wandering the beach with it, he hoped it would yield some useful trinkets for his creation. In this he was not disappointed. At the end of the search period, he had gathered a spectacular array of coins—it seemed as though someone had returned from world travels and then had their pockets explode while walking the beach—and some hopelessly twisted wire. He would have thrown the wire back, but having unearthed it he didn't want to throw it down where someone might step on it and get tetanus. He brought his treasures back to the tented area to pick up some tools to work with.

The producers had told them that there would be a bonfire on the beach at the end of the day, and that they would each have a chance to tell about how what they had found captured something about Daphne. This stilted, treacly romance plot seemed to nauseate most of the bachelors, judging from the reactions that Riley had noted during the briefing; but he was happy with the idea—it gave him a chance to look thoughtful and intelligent, even if all he had to show for his beachcombing was a handful of colorful coins with alien markings. He began to arrange them by size, by color, and then by nationality, spinning tales in his head to tell during the bonfire.

Motion in the corner of his eye distracted him, and he turned to see Asher fiddling with a pile of tiny shells that he had apparently gathered from the beach. They were shining and white, and they clicked elegantly as Asher ran them through his fingers.

"Those are beautiful," Riley observed.

Asher looked up and smiled. "Thanks, but I'm kind of stuck."

"What's wrong?"

"I have these shells, but there's nothing here to string them on. I can't very well present her with a pile of discarded exoskeletons and call it romantic."

Riley chuckled at Asher's casual intelligence—not just a gymnast and an artist, but smart to boot. Then, he realized that he could help. "I picked this up," he said to Asher, reaching into his pocket. "It's kind of a tangled mess, but you're pretty good with wire." He handed over the knot of metal.

Asher beamed at him. "This is perfect. Thank you, Riley. I really appreciate it."

"Just be sure you make something second-rate with it," Riley joked.

"Fear not—it'd take a miracle for me to get second place this week."

"Don't sell yourself short. You're pretty good on romantic gestures."

"Thanks," Asher said, and then turned abruptly away, like there was something he didn't want Riley to see.

Riley shrugged and returned to his coins, idly flipping through them while he waited for his chance to walk on the beach with Daphne.

LATER, WHILE the bonfire raged, bathing the entire cast in the warm flicker of firelight, the bachelors presented their gifts. It was a largely painful exercise; most of the men had found nothing very special in the sand, and what they said about it to Daphne was even less so. It wasn't until Shane that anything interesting developed.

He held out a smoothly polished piece of wood in the shape of a boomerang, and as he handed it to Daphne he talked about it representing his mission in the competition—to take his best shot and return home with a great prize. He closed with some nonsense that Riley couldn't bear to listen to about how she would be the loveliest woman in the hemisphere when he brought her home to meet his loving family.

It was kind of sickening, but it would probably make for good television, what with the flickering light and all. Then it was Riley's turn.

He held up one of the coins: it was gold and silver and inscribed with the beautiful script of a far-off land. "People come from all over the world to walk this beach," Riley began, looking at the coin. "They bring with them the trappings of everyday life." He held up several more exotic coins, which glimmered in the firelight. "But once they see the beauty of this place, what seemed important before falls away, like grains of sand." He turned to Daphne. "That's what this experience with you means to me—I hope to be transformed by the beauty that is inside you. Today when we walked you told me about your brother Charlie, and how much he means to you, and how he will always need someone to take care of him. And that you have promised him you will be that someone. The goodness that is inside you is what makes you special, and what makes me want to leave the world behind to be with you." He dropped the coins, one by one, into the sand.

Daphne had clasped her hands to her mouth as Riley spoke. "Thank you, Riley. That was beautiful."

The next three bachelors didn't share this opinion, obviously—they seemed incensed that they had to follow such a sappy speech. The last person to talk was Asher.

He stood, and walked around the ring of people surrounding the fire until he reached Daphne. "I found the most beautiful things on the beach—after you, of course—and as I was sorting them, and polishing them up, I realized that each of these"—he held up the bracelet he had fashioned using the wire Riley had given him—"was a home to some creature. They lived their lives inside these shells, and then when that life was over, they left behind these beautiful traces of themselves, of the homes they made. I want you to have this, to remind you that the best home, our true home, is always with us." He fastened the bracelet around the wrist she extended to him.

She turned the bracelet around her wrist, looking at all of the shells. "It's lovely, Asher, thank you. I'm a really long way from home, so I appreciate the thought so much."

IT WAS clear to Kaitlyn that the beachcomber challenge belonged to Shane, Riley, and Asher. Daphne chose Asher, saying during the results show how much she loved the bracelet and that it reminded her of home despite the fact that her hometown was more than a thousand miles from a beach. The viewers weighed in heavily for Riley and Shane, but in spite of Shane's entertaining Aussie accent, Riley edged him out for viewers' choice.

Once again, Daphne would be going on a date with Asher and Riley. This time Kaitlyn had arranged a much more elegant setting than the medieval restaurant: the three would be flown by helicopter to a dramatic cliff top retreat, where they would have massages, eat gourmet food, and watch the sun set over the ocean far below. It promised to be the most romantic scene of the show so far, and had the bonus of also being photogenic as hell. Kaitlyn was looking forward to this one.

ASHER, RILEY, and Daphne boarded the helicopter exactly as they had done the limousine after the first challenge: Daphne first, then Asher, then Riley. This time, though, Riley was more focused on looking out the window and holding on—he had never been in a helicopter before and was not expecting the buffeting caused by the afternoon winds rising up the sides of the valley. The ride smoothed out as they gained altitude, and he turned back to Daphne. She had an anxious look on her face, and her hand was white-knuckled in its grip on Asher's.

He recalled how frustrated he felt during their first date, after the jousting competition. He should have been relieved that this time he didn't have to worry about Asher upstaging him, but there was something about watching him gaze placidly into Daphne's eyes that made that old competitive instinct rise up inside him.

The helicopter put down near a cliff overlooking the ocean. Riley could see a gazebo of some kind, complete with white sheer curtains blowing gently in the sea breeze, looking like something out of an ad in a high-end travel magazine.

The door swung open, and Riley stepped out of the helicopter, and then turned and held out his hand for Daphne. She smiled—a dazzling brightness in the afternoon glare—and for a moment he was struck by her beauty and the thrill of having her direct the full force of it at him, but then he remembered that there were cameras behind him, and it was at them that she was beaming. The heaviness he felt in his chest was a reminder that he was here to do a job.

Asher followed Daphne down the steps of the helicopter's air stairs, and the three of them made their way toward the pavilion at the cliff's edge. They must make a dazzling ensemble, Riley thought as they walked, with the breeze and the bright golden sun and the excitement of this carefully choreographed and yet completely unknown event ahead of them.

They arrived at the cliffside patio, and there they were directed by Bernie, the location producer, to a table set with three places. Champagne was chilling in a silver bucket on a stand, and three flutes stood nearby. There was a plate on a silver stand at the center of the table, holding something no doubt delicious and fattening.

"Oh, chocolate-covered strawberries! My favorite!" gushed Daphne, as she scooted giddily toward the table. Asher reached the table before she did, and he picked up the largest strawberry from the plate and lifted it to her lips. She took a dainty nibble, but the chocolate covering the strawberry shattered and she had to stuff the entire thing into her mouth. It was inelegant, but she didn't seem to care—she made happy noises as she tried to chew without losing any of the juicy strawberry out the sides of her mouth.

Exactly when the noises she was making stopped being happy and starting being desperate Riley was unsure. But Daphne made some truly desperate noises as she doubled over, retching. She reached out and grabbed the table to steady herself, and then suddenly both hands clutched at her throat.

Why would someone poison the bachelorette? was all Riley could think. "Daphne? Daphne, are you choking?" he asked, kneeling in front of her. She shook her head, but when she tried to speak, nothing would come out. Riley studied her face, trying to tell what was going on, but all he could see was that her face was starting to swell.

Finally, she got out one word: "'Lergic."

Riley was stumped. But Asher leapt into action.

"Do you have an epi?" he shouted as he grabbed for the clutch purse she had brought with her. "You—call 911!" he shouted to the caterers who were setting up the dinner that the three of them were to have shared. "Tell them she's anaphylacting!"

He ripped the purse open and dug through its contents for a plastic tube. In a blur he yanked the top off of it with his teeth, and spat it across the patio. He shook the contents of the tube out, threw the empty tube aside, and flipped what looked like a cap off the smaller plastic tube that he now held in his hand like a dagger.

"Ready?" he asked, and she nodded. Her eyes were now almost swollen shut.

With a thump he stabbed the device into her leg, and he counted the seconds while holding it firmly. "One... two... three...." He looked at Daphne, right into her eyes. "It's going to be okay. You're going to be fine. Help is coming, and I'm right here." He continued to nod his head, as if counting silently.

Riley noticed that Daphne's breathing was less labored, and despite the fact that she had just been stabbed in the leg, she seemed to be calming down.

"... nine... ten," Asher concluded and pulled the plastic tube away from her thigh. "How are you doing, Daphne? Is it getting better?"

"Yes," she was able to say, finally. She took some deeper breaths, recovering. "Thank you. I don't know what happened—the only thing I'm allergic to is hazelnuts, and I didn't see any."

"There might have been some in the kitchen when they made the chocolate for the strawberries," Asher said. The swelling was going down more noticeably now.

Bernie rushed over, a phone clutched to his ear. "It's going to take an ambulance twenty minutes to get here. They want us to put her on the helicopter, and it will take her to the hospital. Let's go!"

The three of them bundled Daphne along to the helipad, where three other crew members dressed in white were waiting to accompany her to the hospital. Asher stepped up the ladder to join them, but Bernie grabbed his arm and tugged for him to come back down. Before he did, he handed the expended syringe to Daphne. Riley thought this was a strange thing to do— did she really want a souvenir of having nearly been killed by a chocolate-covered strawberry? But she seemed to appreciate it, and she held the plastic tube in her lap.

The three men stepped back from the helipad.

Asher gestured back to the helicopter as the rotors began to turn. "Why couldn't I go with—"

"We need to do at least some shooting here," Bernie shouted over the fury of the craft's engines starting up. "She'll be fine."

Both men waved to Daphne, and she waved back confidently, more color back in her face with every passing minute. They watched the helicopter take off and zoom away toward the city.

"Nice work there, saving her life and all," Bernie said to Asher. "The paramedics said that if the shot got her breathing to ease up and brought the swelling down, she should be fine." He led the men back to the pavilion at the cliff's edge.

"Wow," Riley said to Asher as they walked. "You were like some kind of superhero there."

"These days you don't get put in charge of a roomful of third graders without being trained on allergic reactions," he said modestly. "I've never had to stick one of them, though. That part was pretty intense."

"You handled it like a champ," Riley said, clapping Asher on the back.

"Thanks, man," he said as they reached the pavilion. "I wonder what they're going to want us to do here—it's not really a dream date by the ocean without Daphne."

"All right, gentlemen," Bernie announced, his clipboard in front of him like a shield against anything else going horribly wrong. "I've talked with the producer, and she really needs us to continue today's shoot—the light is perfect, and we really can't afford the delay of coming back and trying again. Plus, the forecast is for this little cliff top paradise to be completely socked in with fog this time tomorrow. So, can we forge ahead?"

The men looked at each other, then back at the staffer.

"I hesitate to point out the obvious," Riley said, cautiously. "But how can we film a date with Daphne, without Daphne?"

"You let me worry about the magic of television."

"I'm with Riley," Asher spoke up. "I don't see how the 'magic of television' is going to conjure up someone who is, as we speak, I hope, getting medical attention."

Bernie sighed, as if he were faced with the task of teaching calculus in a kindergarten. "We are going to film the dinner, and the other activities, to get your shots—conversation, reactions, that kind of thing—and then we're going to film her once she's back from the hospital. We'll get her in a studio, put the location shots behind her on a green screen, and she'll film her part of the evening. We'll compose it overnight and have it ready to air on schedule." He looked from one man to the other, and apparently saw they were skeptical. "Ta-dah," he summed up, hand waving in the air, "the magic of television. Now let's get to work."

Riley and Asher shared a shrug and followed behind the magician with the clipboard.

"We were to begin with the chocolate-covered strawberries and champagne," he read from his clipboard. "We're going to cut that part, given the circumstances, and move right to the second act. Here"—he pointed to his right—"are massage tables where the three of you will receive relaxing shiatsu while listening to the waves pound on the surf below." He looked up, and a realization seemed to dawn on him. "Of course, the massage therapists were in the helicopter with Daphne, so they're...." He trailed off as he looked out over the cliff to the distant emergency room to which everyone he needed to complete this shoot had fled. "Shit."

"We could do it," offered Asher.

"Do what?" Riley and Bernie said in startled unison.

"The massage thing. One of us can get on the table, and the other will do the massage, and you can get the shots you need without showing the other's face. Then we'll switch. That'd work, right?" He smiled brightly at the other two men.

"Whoa whoa whoa—" Riley began, but he was cut off by Bernie.

"That's a great idea! Here, let's get you"—he pointed to Riley—"into one of the caterer's shirt and pants, so you don't get your suit mussed, and you"—Asher—"get into a bathrobe." He took a breath. "I think this is going to work!"

"Well, I don't think so," Riley said, to no one in particular, since Bernie had hustled off to denude a caterer, and Asher was sprinting off to the wardrobe rack to grab a bathrobe. Riley did what had become a habit lately—closed his eyes, counted to ten, and reminded himself of what his goal was in being on this fucking ridiculous show. Come to think of it, having a mantra with an F-bomb in it probably wasn't kosher in a meditation sense, but it worked for him, so he wasn't going to look into it too closely.

When Bernie returned with the caterer's clothes, Riley simply sighed and started unbuttoning his dress shirt. Might as well get this over with.

Soon he was standing by as the camera crew filmed Asher slipping off his robe and settling onto the massage table. He was wearing only his underwear, so Riley knelt down and pulled a large white towel from the stack under the table. He laid that over Asher's midsection, and then stood awkwardly waiting for directions.

"Have you done this before?" asked Bernie.

"What, given another dude a massage on a romantic cliff top retreat?" Riley asked, voice dripping with sarcasm. "All the damn time. Keeps the spark alive, you know."

"Very funny. Now, take the massage oil, pour some on, and get to it!"

Riley took a brief moment to repeat his mantra before carrying out the orders he'd been given. When he opened his eyes, he was resolved to just get this thing done. He squeezed out some of the sweet-smelling oil from the bottle he'd found hanging on the corner of the massage table, and Asher shivered when the liquid hit him.

"Ooh, chilly," he said. "Sorry—didn't mean to jump."

"My fault. Should have thought of that. Sorry!" Riley stood for a moment, regarding the broad back of the man on the table. He knew gymnasts had to be in good shape, but there was seriously not an ounce of fat on this guy's frame. Riley knew that admiration wouldn't get the job done, so he took a deep breath and placed his hands on Asher's shoulders. He felt the slickness of the oil, the smooth softness of the skin, and just below that he felt absolutely iron muscle. It didn't budge when he squeezed it, so he simply moved his hands along the surface as the camera crew came closer to capture Asher's blissful reaction to the massage. Riley figured that his hands would simply be seen moving in the background, and that would be convincing enough.

This continued for about fifteen minutes, the camera crew getting different angles and having Asher turn his head one way and then the other to get the best light. All the while Riley moved his hands on Asher's back, trying to seem professional. At one point his hands traced along Asher's ribs, and he felt a twitching that immediately turned into giggles.

"Oh, I am so ticklish there!" Asher practically shouted, gasping for breath.

"Sorry! I just was trying something different—I was getting kind of bored just squeezing your shoulders."

Asher turned and looked back at Riley. "It wasn't boring for me. You're kind of a natural at this." He turned back to the cameras, wearing an expression of contentment that, surprisingly, made Riley quite proud.

"All right, let's switch it up," announced Bernie. Riley wiped his hands with the towel that had been draped over Asher.

Asher sat up, and picked up the bathrobe that he had tossed over the other massage table. He put it on and tied it tightly around him before turning around to face Riley.

"Ready when you are," he said.

Riley slipped off the shirt and tossed it over to Asher, then untied the drawstring on the chef's pants—they pooled around his ankles, leaving him standing in just his boxer briefs (he had chosen a bright-blue pair for the date, a choice he now regretted). Asher pulled the pants on and tied the drawstring and then opened the robe and tossed it across the table to Riley. The men finished their costume change at the same moment.

"Okay, same deal. Riley, you come up to the table, slip off the robe, and lie down. Asher, stay in the background until Riley gets settled. Then we shoot the massage, and we're golden. Go!"

Riley attempted to project an air of relaxed anticipation as he untied his robe and climbed onto the table. He stretched out, and though the face he showed the cameras was placid, he was anxious in the extreme. He felt a towel settle over his bright-blue underwear, and that helped a little, but he was still not looking forward to—

"Ready?" Asher asked. Riley could hear him working the massage lotion between his hands.

"Good to go," Riley answered in confident tones. He closed his eyes, worried that if he was looking into the camera lens at the moment that Asher made contact his discomfort would be visible.

Asher's hands were so gentle that at first Riley thought they were a breeze coming off the ocean. There was no cold jolt of liquid—only smooth touch that grew a little more vigorous with each pass over the muscles of his back. He began to think he could handle this.

"Perfect," breathed Bernie, watching the footage coming from the cameras trained on Riley's face.

Riley breathed deeply and focused on providing several different expressions for the benefit of the cameras—contentment, relief of tension, dreamy relaxation—while Asher's strong hands roamed over his back.

Soon, though, Asher began to concentrate on several areas of tightness in Riley's back—places where the stress of the last several weeks had created knots in his muscles—and he brought his considerable strength to bear in breaking them up. Suddenly, Riley was giving the cameras expressions not of dreamy relaxation, but of surprised pleasure.

And then, it all became too much. The heat of the sun was suddenly oppressive, and Asher's hands seemed to be everywhere at once. Riley had no idea why the tears came, welling up in his eyes, but come they did. He blinked hard to force them back, but they defied him and ran down his cheeks. He felt the woman holding the camera startle and then draw back from him. He turned his head so that he was face down in the towel on the massage table, hiding the hot tears that continued to flow from his eyes.

"A—All right," stumbled Bernie. "That's, um... great. Let's get you guys dressed and move on to dinner, okay? Asher, why don't you come with me and we'll get you all set." He hustled everyone away from the massage table.

Riley was left alone in his confusion—he was both relieved and completely mortified. He sat up, took a deep breath, shook his head to clear whatever dismal fog had settled over it. The tears faded away as mysteriously as they had emerged. What the hell had that been about? He slid off the table, stretched, and headed over to get dressed as well.

His back felt more relaxed than it had in ages.

A half hour later, as the sun sank closer to the surface of the ocean, the men sat down to dinner. An empty seat was between them, arranged so that the camera angles would allow Daphne's contribution to the conversation to be spliced in later. An unopened bottle of fine champagne chilled in a silver bucket next to the table, and the delicate frisée of an endive salad sat in front of each man. They awaited their cue to begin eating and stared at the ocean while the crew prepared.

Riley took a sip of his champagne in an effort to force down the lump in his throat—it was treacly sweet, clearly chosen for its telegenic sparkle rather than taste; the expensive stuff in the silver bucket was just for show. The two men hadn't spoken to each other since the massage—not that he would have any idea what to say. He didn't think Asher knew about the whole breakdown thing on the table, and he wasn't about to bring it up himself, of course. But what else he should say at this moment he had no idea.

"We're ready to begin," announced Bernie, bringing Riley out of his distracted reverie. "Let's top up those champagne flutes and get a toast to kick off the meal." An assistant rushed over with an open bottle of bubbly to replace the swallow that Riley had taken. One of the female crew sat in "Daphne's chair" and held a flute aloft at an awkward but effective angle that obscured rough, unpolished fingernails. They brought their flutes together no fewer than seven times—each requiring a slightly different arrangement of cameras and microphones—until Bernie had the shot he needed.

"Great. Now salad, and let's have some sparkling conversation. Go!"

As instructed, both men picked up their salad forks and stabbed bits of greenery from their plates.

"It's a beautiful view," Asher offered, then took his bite.

Dammit, he always gets there before me, thought Riley. Then, luckily, inspiration struck.

"The sunset is amazing, but it's nothing compared to the light in your eyes," he said suavely and took another sip of champagne.

Asher was stunned. "What?" he was finally able to say.

"I was talking to Daphne," Riley replied, grinning slyly. His ability to play along with the charade was certain to place him in a positive light when this bizarre episode was edited up.

"Wow. You are a pro. Kudos to you, sir," Asher said, raising his glass.

Riley accepted the compliment with a gracious nod and a rakishly raised eyebrow. The expression would be perfect, he imagined, for a reaction shot to some of the sparkling conversation that Daphne would be coached to provide.

The men delicately picked at their salads—Riley suspected that voraciousness would not play well on the romantic cliff top—and gazed out over the ocean. The light ambered slowly as the sun dipped lower toward the sea, and their conversation relaxed into an easy banter, as if there weren't a camera crew around them and an empty seat between. As they were polishing off the lobster that constituted their main course, the light off the ocean deepened into a glowing crimson. They had cast off their reserve and finished three flutes each of the sweet bubbly, which despite its sugary taste delivered the requisite alcohol content.

Dessert arrived just as the sun disappeared, and the torches that the crew had lit around the cliff's edge bathed them in their flickering light. Slices of a dense chocolate torte were placed before them, surrounded by swirls of chocolate sauce and a glossy dollop of whipped cream. Riley pulled the bottle of good champagne out of the silver ice bucket and began to open it. Bernie stepped forward as if to object, but Riley fixed him with a warning glare and he backed off. He poured as Asher leaned forward and examined the dessert.

"Hazelnuts," he said as he poked at the caramelized chopped nuts atop the torte. He turned to Bernie, who turned to the caterer, who held his hands up.

"They tell me she allergic to filbert, so no make with filbert," he said in a thick accent that Riley couldn't quite place. Italy? Croatia?

Bernie growled in frustration. "Hazelnuts *are* filberts, you moron!"

The chef was dumbfounded, clearly betrayed by the English language. He stormed off, probably to beat a sous chef into somehow taking responsibility for endangering the star of the show.

"You're not allergic, are you?" Asher asked Riley. "I don't think I could handle stabbing you too."

Riley laughed and shook his head. "I actually love a good filbert," he said with a laugh. "It's a well-known fact that no jar of Nutella is safe anywhere near me."

The next several minutes were given over to the tasting and retasting and then wholesale demolition of the aforementioned torte.

"Oh my God, that was amazing," Riley said with a sigh. "That was like every dessert I've been denying myself for six months all in one."

Asher sighed and set his fork down onto his now-spotless plate. "Woof. You got that right. He may have tried to kill Daphne, but he makes a mean torte."

Riley laughed and was about to lift the flute to his lips when he saw Asher pick up his napkin and reach over with it. He pulled back a bit, uncertain.

"You have just a bit—right there," Asher said as he dabbed at the corner of Riley's mouth. "There. Now you're perfect again."

Riley could not recall ever having been dabbed at by anyone other than his mother. Perhaps it was the two bottles of bubbly that they had managed to put away, but he didn't really mind. It just seemed like the kind of thing that a friend would do.

Didn't it?

"Um, thanks? But I don't think 'perfect' is the word I would use. And, come to think of it, I'm not all that crazy about you using it either." Riley's lilting inflection clearly conveyed his steadily rising inebriation.

"I'm an artist," Asher replied, his own voice a little uncertain. "I am completely qualified to offer aesthetical judgments of all varieties. And you, sir, are a specimen without equal. I speak solely of your value as a subject of sculpture. Of course." He tossed back the last of the wine in his flute and set it a little too hard on the table.

Riley giggled. "Did I tell you about the time I actually was a subject of sculpture?"

Asher drew in a shocked breath. "Really? Oh, do tell."

Riley hadn't meant to tell this story—hadn't told it to anyone in years, in fact—but the combination of tipsiness and Asher's silly statement about aesthetics had brought it to mind, and the competitor in him was apparently able to overpower the drunkard and still work out strategy. He figured that the producers might like something a little more interesting to have Daphne react to.

"I was a junior in college, and I'd just moved out of the dorms into an apartment with a couple of buddies. I was working at the law library to make rent money—just reshelving books, that kind of thing—but then my hours got cut and I wasn't earning enough to pay my share. I was on my way to sign up to sell plasma when I saw a flyer asking for models for an art class. The pay was decent, and standing still has always been one of my core competencies—"

Asher burst out laughing.

"Shut up! It's true—I used to freak my parents out by saying I wanted to be a mannequin when I grew up, and then I'd stand in the window for like an hour, not moving." He saw Asher's face contort with even more violent spasms of laughter. "Hey, I was a teenager then, and I didn't have much else to freak them out with on account of being a boring Goody Two-shoes."

"Sorry, I'll try to keep it under control."

"Thank you. Now, where was I? Right, the flyer. So I tore off the little tab thing at the bottom and called the number when I got home. They needed somebody for a class that evening, so I said I was up for it. Turned out to be a sculpture class run by this kind of crazy German guy who made his class spend weeks on a single figure. I had to go back twice a week for a month, each time trying to get into the exact same pose while he shuffled around the lights and stuff to 'eeluminate new rrrrrealities.' Dude was nuts, but he paid well."

"And what was your specialty, pose wise? Can you strike one for me here, let me see your professionalism in action? Or, rather, inaction?" He laughed again.

"I'm pretty versatile," Riley said with a bit of swagger in his voice. "This was my go-to though," he said and stood—a bit uncertainly, at first.

He shook his head to clear it, then slowly and deliberately shifted his weight to his right leg. His right arm dropped to his side, his hand coming to rest with the fingers gathered against his thigh. He brought his left arm up, with his fingertips just touching his shoulder. He looked to his left, out over the ocean.

"Oh my God, you're David," breathed Asher. He clapped his hands to his mouth in wonder.

Riley stayed frozen for a long moment before finally responding. "It's better when I'm naked," he said in a casual tone.

Asher's hands dropped from his mouth. He seemed not to breathe for a long while and then took several breaths in succession. "I'll... umm... take your word for that."

Riley relaxed his pose and resumed his seat. "So that's how I paid the rent. And that's also a story I've not told anyone in a long time."

"It's a gripping tale, and you tell it well," Asher replied, with a giggle that sounded a little strained to Riley. "But since we're going for full disclosure here, can I ask you something?"

"I think we're well on our way to having no secrets from each other. Shoot."

"When we were doing the massage thing," Asher began slowly, his voice lower than when he was speaking for the benefit of the microphones. "I was kind of wondering what happened there at the end. Was I hurting you?"

Riley froze. He had so effectively convinced himself that the other man had not even noticed his strange tears that to find out they had been observed completely threw him.

"Oh, I'm sorry," Asher blurted. "If you don't want to—"

"No, no. It's fine." It wasn't, but there wasn't much he could do about it now. "It's stupid, really." He half expected Asher to talk him out of calling his emotions "stupid"—his fiancée always had, at least until she decided he really was stupid and she was leaving. But Asher just waited patiently, his eyebrows up, the torchlight dancing in his kind, wide eyes. It was a response that Riley had never expected, and it disarmed him completely.

He took a deep, stabilizing breath. When he began speaking, his voice was barely above a whisper.

"This is going to sound kind of...." His voice drifted off, and he cleared his throat before continuing. "Anyway. It's been a year since my fiancée left me, and it had been a long time before that since she had touched me. It's been a damn long time since anyone's laid a hand on me out of anything other than a fiancée's grudging obligation—" He halted here as the memory of Wilbur's makeup debacle flashed back in his mind, but he beat it back and forged ahead. "At first I was okay with the massage idea, but then suddenly, for some reason, I wasn't."

Asher's brow had steadily been knitting into a more concerned expression as he listened. "I feel awful that I did that to you," he was finally able to say.

"No, it wasn't a bad thing. It was really good. It felt really good. But then it all broke over me—that this was happening to me, and it was going to be on this fucked-up television show, and it was another guy who was making me feel this way—the way I hadn't felt in so long...." He sighed. "It was just too much for me, I guess." As if on cue, Riley felt his eyes burn, and they filled with tears again. "Shit," he said and wiped his eyes roughly with his hand.

"I don't know what to say," Asher whispered back. There were tears in his eyes as well, something that made Riley's eyes burn even more.

"Say what you're really thinking—that I'm a basket case loser who needs therapy and testosterone injections." Riley's lips lifted in a miserable half smirk.

"Riley, no!" Asher somehow managed to make his whisper as emphatic as a shout. He looked quickly side to side and then lowered his voice again. "What happened just means you're starting to deal with the crap you've been through. That's a good thing."

Riley shook his head. "You just don't stop, do you?"

"What does that mean?"

"You see the best in everyone, and in every situation."

Asher chuckled. "*You* spend five days a week with third graders, and see if it doesn't make you start to see the brighter side of everything."

Riley heaved a great sigh and gave his eyes a final wipe. "Okay, that's enough sappy introspection from me. Your turn."

"What, I'm just supposed to come up with deep dark emotional turmoil on command?"

"No, I'll help you. Remember back after we crashed and burned on the Trojan horse competition?"

"Vividly," Asher replied with a roll of his eyes.

"We were in the sauna that night, and just before the fire alarm went off you were about to tell me something."

"I was?"

"Yes, you were. And don't try to fool me with that innocent look. We get special training in the underwriting office to deal with perjurers like you."

Asher laughed. "Okay, you got me."

"Now, we had been talking about the clockwork heart, and you said you needed to tell me something. So, emote away."

Asher turned serious again, the light no longer dancing in his eyes. "I can't."

"Weren't you the guy who told me that dealing with things was the best way to get through them?"

Asher looked at Riley, right into his eyes. "I want to, but I can't. Not now."

Riley looked around them. "You're perched here on a cliff top over the ocean, waves crashing below, torchlight and champagne, on a dream date with a former model"—he placed his hand immodestly on his chest—"and this is not the right time? Come on now."

Riley meant this to lighten the mood, but as he spoke Asher's face had fallen further and further, as if he were seeing the life stamped out of him word by word.

"Oh God, Riley, I wish I could," he said, his voice weak and reedy. Then he took a deep breath and reached out his hand to place it atop Riley's. "Thank you. Thank you for asking. And I will be able to tell you—tell you everything—once this is over. But not now."

Riley would normally have continued pressing Asher for information—it wasn't in his nature to suffer deflections like this—but something in the other man's manner made him take him at his word. If this wasn't the right time to talk about whatever it was he was hiding, then Riley would have to trust him.

"Right, then. We'll talk about it later. Now, how about we head back to the house and find out how Daphne is?"

"Excellent idea," Asher said. "You go see if you can scare up a helicopter—I need a sec. I'd hate to have the cameras catch me all soppy like this."

"Sounds good. And, Asher," Riley said, clapping a hand on Asher's shoulder, "I love you, man." He strode away to find Bernie and see if they had performed well enough to be released for the evening.

IN THE control room, the large monitor was zoomed in on Asher, frozen in the moment after Riley had patted him on the shoulder and left him at the table. He had put his own hand on the shoulder that Riley had touched, and he sat for a long moment with tears running freely down his face—even in the freeze-frame they glittered in the torchlight. It would be a touching scene for the show.

"We can't use any of this for the show," Kaitlyn said to Omar.

They were working late, as usual, and the rest of the production staff had long since left them to it. They had begun creating this cut-and-paste date hours and hours ago, as soon as the footage of the (fully recovered) Daphne in front of the green screen had been shot. They worked through the massage and the dinner, elegantly splicing in the absent bachelorette and making convincing conversation out of miscellaneous bits and parts. They had been able to easily skip over an awkward moment on the massage table—they weren't sure, but it seemed like Riley teared up there for some reason—but this final conversation at the table was too intense for them to simply recast as bachelorette-centric banter.

"Can we play that again?" Kaitlyn asked, her voice steady—though it cost her a lot of effort to make it seem so.

"Which part?" Omar replied, his fingers already twiddling the shuttle dial.

"The whole thing after dessert," she responded, again keeping her voice devoid of obvious emotion. She wanted desperately not to see what she thought she saw the first time through.

"Here it is," Omar said immediately. He really was a whiz with the shuttle.

They watched in silence as Asher dabbed at Riley's mouth and as Riley described his stint as a sculpture model and struck the David pose.

"There. Can you move Asher's reaction shot to the big monitor?"

Omar froze the image, and Asher's face filled the big screen in the center of the control room's panel.

"All right, forward slow." Kaitlyn stood and leaned closer to the image. She studied his expression—his eyes, the hand covering his mouth, his inability to draw breath when Riley mentioned posing nude. "Shit," she whispered.

"Something wrong?" Omar asked.

"I don't know. Let's keep going."

Omar started the playback again. They watched as Riley and Asher talked about Riley's breakdown on the massage table and as both men teared up again.

"Shit," she repeated.

"I'm sorry, I must be missing it," Omar said.

"Let it play through the end again," she said, avoiding the question implicit in his statement.

They watched the conversation conclude—Kaitlyn had Omar bring both men up on the big screen in turn—and then sat in silence while the frozen image of Asher's tears flickered above them. Then Kaitlyn stared at the screen, not really seeing it, for several long minutes. Omar seemed to know better than to ask her what she was thinking. Finally, she shook her head a little and came back to the present moment.

She turned to the side and looked Omar right in the eyes. "Close the door," she said, too exhausted to keep the weariness out of her voice.

Omar rose and gently closed the door. There wasn't anyone else in the building, so far as Kaitlyn knew, but she wanted to be sure. Omar came back to his seat next to hers and waited.

"Omar," she began, "I need to know that I can trust you."

He nodded his head gravely. "Of course you can."

"No, I mean with something really big. Like get-us-both-fired big."

If he was shaken by this dramatic statement, it didn't show. He simply nodded. "I have this job because of you. If I lose this job for the same reason, I haven't really lost anything."

Kaitlyn was touched by Omar's loyalty, but she did not relish the conversation that she was about to have. "Did you notice anything about our two bachelors just now?"

"They saved us from a potentially disastrous production problem."

"That they did," Kaitlyn agreed. "They were real troopers. But after dessert they seemed less concerned with the scene we had planned and more interested in talking about themselves."

"I don't think we can blame them for that—they did really well up to that point."

"Oh, I don't blame them for that at all. They deserved to relax after giving us what we needed to cover for Daphne's emergency. But what did you observe happening between them?"

Omar thought for a moment. "They are becoming friends as well as allies in the competitions. But that's not against the rules, is it?"

Kaitlyn shook her head. "Let me tell you what I see. I see that our Asher is smitten with his fellow bachelor."

Omar's mouth hung open. When he closed it, he had some difficulty forming words. "But... if they're... then we have to...."

"We're not going to do anything yet."

He looked shocked at her. "But New York said if we even suspected—"

She held up a hand to stop him. Then, once he had fallen silent she asked, "Do you have any gay or lesbian folks in your family?"

Omar blinked—this was not a turn he'd been expecting, apparently.

"Sorry, is this too personal?" Kaitlyn asked. She was pretty sure all of their late nights together had established a rapport that allowed for such questions, but she had to admit she didn't know much about the culture Omar had grown up in—she worried that it was a drastically conservative one, judging from his reaction.

"No, not at all. I have an uncle who is gay, but the rest of the family doesn't have much to do with him."

"And how do you feel about him?"

"I live with him, actually. He moved to LA about ten years ago, and when he found out I wanted to go to film school here, he offered to give me a place to live. The very thought sent my mother to her bed for a week, but she's come around now that it's been a few years and nothing untoward has resulted." He shrugged and waited for the next question.

Kaitlyn looked down at the desk for a moment. "My brother," she finally said softly. She heaved a great sigh and sat silently for another full minute. "It was twenty years ago," she resumed, her voice gravelly. "He knew from the time he was eight years old—he didn't tell anyone but me for the longest time. I was two years younger than he was, but we were so close. In high school he started to get bullied in the worst way. He would come home with blood on his face, and I would help him get cleaned up before our parents got home, but I think he was really hurt on the inside. Not that he wanted them to like him or anything—they were mostly athletes and stuff—but facing that much hate every day...." She huffed out a breath, wiped her nose with the back of her hand. "That last day he seemed so much happier, like he had finally found a calm place inside and they weren't able to hurt him anymore. Turns out he had already decided that he would do it. I found him that night, in the garage. He was already cold, but I tried to lift him anyway, tried to keep him from dangling by that rope, while I screamed and screamed for my parents." She was crying now, her voice thick, the memory still shocking after all these years.

Omar reached out and put his hand on Kaitlyn's arm. She covered it with her own hand, and pressed it hard. She sat, hunched over, until the shaking slowed and she could breathe again.

"After the shock wore off—not that it ever does, but it gets less oppressive over time—I became quite the little activist. I started a gay-straight alliance at the high school when I got there the next year, and I've always been the best advocate I can be. That's why the situation that Liam and Gavin left us in makes me crazy."

Omar nodded. "So you're not going to say anything?"

"Did you see the look on his face? He knows exactly what would happen if he told Riley how he feels."

Omar paused for a second. "Are you sure you know what he's feeling?"

"I know. I've seen this before—my brother used to look at boys that way. There's the light in his eyes that's all about crushing on the guy, but then there's the fear of being found out. You can see that in the way he looks down whenever Riley looks at him. It's textbook gaydar stealth mode."

"So he's worried about Riley's gaydar? Do you think Riley's gay too?"

"I don't know," she said, carefully. "The whole being left at the altar thing makes a pretty strong case for straight. But the way he is with Asher kind of argues the other way. When your average straight guy talks about strong emotions, he gets angry. Doesn't matter what the emotion is—if there's a chance he's going to reveal something about himself, he protects himself with anger. If this was just two guys talking, we would have been hearing about how his ex was a bitch, how much he wanted to strangle her for jilting him." She saw his skeptical expression. "I'm kind of an expert in this area, having been engaged to a gay man myself, back in my checkered past."

Omar sat back, a look of surprise on his face. "Peter?"

She nodded. "You're a pretty quick study."

He thought for a moment. "Even if we assume that your impression is correct—"

"And it is," she interjected.

"Then can we really let them continue to head down this path? It was kind of a disaster last time two of the bachelors let their... um, feelings... develop."

"I'm pretty confident they're not going to pull a Liam and Gavin in the shower—they're shrewd enough competitors to know where that would get them. And with those two, it was mutual; my best guess is that Riley may well have feelings for Asher, but he's been too emotionally destroyed by his breakup to access those feelings. Though he may just need more time."

"So, we do nothing?"

Kaitlyn tried to look serious, but a grin twitched to life and betrayed her.

"Is this the part where we get fired?" Omar asked, a smile emerging on his face.

"Maybe," Kaitlyn responded with a conspiratorial giggle.

"What do you have in mind?" He asked this in the manner of Ricky Ricardo asking Lucy her plans for the evening while he performs at the Tropicana Club for a Hollywood agent.

"Nothing yet."

Omar squinted at her.

"I mean, nothing too much until we know for sure where things stand between them," she said innocently.

The skeptical squinting continued.

"Stop that!" she yelped, then giggled. "Okay, here's what I'm thinking. Riley and Asher really helped us out with this oceanside date disaster, so in order to show our appreciation, let's send them out on their own for a thank-you experience. We'll tell them that we want to show our appreciation for their help last night, and we'll see what happens between them."

"You know I'm behind you 100 percent, right?" Omar asked. Kaitlyn nodded. "But I don't get why we're sending them on a date when New York was so clear that nothing even remotely gay would be tolerated? That seems like entrapment. Why not just send them home and let them sort it out for themselves?"

Kaitlyn stared at him crossly. "Do you know why I do this show?" she asked, bluntly.

"I assume it's for the relaxed work schedule," he replied, with a glance at the clock. It read 3:24 a.m.

"Very funny," she deadpanned. "The reason I work on this show is that I'm a romantic. Always have been. Now, I know that there's very little actual romance to be had on this show, with all of its artifice and posing, but I'm just a diehard when it comes to love. I still want to believe that when two people find each other, it's magic."

"And you think that our bachelors might be finding each other?"

"You saw the way they were together! You can't fake that kind of connection. They're falling all right—I'm just not sure if they're falling in love, or just into friendship."

"But you mean to find out," he said, smiling.

"I do. And you're going to help me, because you're a romantic at heart too. We didn't see the thing with Liam and Gavin coming, so we couldn't manage it. This one we can get out in front of, and if Asher and Riley end up together, we will have increased the net happiness in the world just a little bit."

He shook his head at her, smiling. Then the shaking turned into a nod. He was in.

"Excellent," she said. "Now, let's get this date set up. We've got to find something that will not seem like a romance setup, but will actually be romantic once they get there. And we'll film it with hidden cameras—we'll tell them that their evening won't be recorded, but I have to see how they are together." She cut off his attempt to object. "We won't keep the recording—we'll just monitor it. No camera crews, no location producer. Just the two of them and us. Okay?"

He nodded. "You are truly terrifying when you set your sights, you know that?"

"I've been told it's one of my best qualities," she said with her best debutante's decorous smile.

"By those who live in terror that you might bring your 'best qualities' to bear on them someday," he replied. "But what you're doing here is noble. Crazy, but noble."

"Thank you. Now, let's get some rest. I think my eyelids are permanently stuck to my eyeballs."

THEY WERE back in Kaitlyn's office by ten in the morning.

Kaitlyn took a deep drink of her coffee and settled behind her desk. "We need a setting that will allow us to hide cameras and will provide them the privacy they need but not make them suspicious that we're setting them up...."

"Why not send them back to the warehouse—we have all of the cameras there already, we could just leave them running."

"Practical, but not really romantic. We need something that will encourage them to be honest with each other, but not look overly precious." She pondered this for a long moment, and then it came to her. She picked up her phone and flipped through her contacts until she found the one she needed. She punched the numbers on the speakerphone and waited.

"Beverly Palace, this is Marc" came the clipped British tones of the hotel's general manager.

"Marc, it's Kaitlyn, from—"

"From BachelorX's show! How's it feel to be Twitter famous, Kaitlyn?"

Luckily, Kaitlyn's scowl wasn't visible by phone. "It's a slice of heaven every day, thanks for asking. Now, you've mentioned to me on more than one occasion that your little motel might be interested in hosting the show."

"Indeed I have. And by 'little motel' I know you mean 'exquisite boutique destination hotel,' hmm?"

"Precisely. So here's the deal. I'd like to send two people from the show tomorrow for a little break from shooting. Things have been kind of intense here, and they need a respite."

"I have just the thing... hang on, let me make sure we can... yes, yes we can. The courtyard villa is available tomorrow. It's private, and it's beautiful."

"That sounds perfect."

"Now, how many crew are you sending? If it's more than five we may need to arrange for more space."

"No, it'll just be the two cast members. But we would like to get a couple of techs in there in advance to rig some hidden cameras. Think we can do that?"

"Of course. It'll be available after eleven tomorrow morning. We'll need an hour to clean, and then you can have your crew come in at noon. What time will our guests be arriving?"

"We'll get them there around four?"

"Got it. Here's what I'm thinking: your bachelorette and her lucky beau can take a dip in the villa's private swimming pool. Then we'll serve them an elegant dinner poolside, and what comes after that will be up to them."

"That sounds great. Just one thing—the bachelorette won't be on this outing."

There was a pause on the other end of the phone line.

"Umm, you are clear on the whole point of the show you're producing, right?"

"Yes, I'm well aware. Here's the thing," she said as she leaned in closer to the speakerphone. "Can you keep a little secret?"

Marc laughed. "Honey, you don't have any secrets, thanks to BachelorX."

Kaitlyn sighed, a wry smile on her face. "Yeah, he's made it a joy to come to work. What I need is kind of related, as a matter of fact. I've got two bachelors who may be kind of sweet on each other, and I need to know for sure. If my gaydar is malfunctioning, then we don't need to do anything. But if there's a spark there, I've got to manage it better than last time."

"Wait—so if love blossoms, you're going to kick them off the show? I'm not sure I can go along with that. It might result in the revocation of my membership in Gay club."

"No, I'm not going to kick them off. Not unless they get unruly about it, anyway. I just need to be sure we don't get another BachelorX blowup."

"All right, I think I see what you're going for. We'll give them the honeymoon treatment and see what happens."

"Fantastic, Marc, thank you so much. And—I'm sure I don't need to say this, but—can you keep a lid on this?"

"My lips are sealed, love."

"You're the best!" Kaitlyn breathed a sigh of relief.

"I know, I know," Marc said with a laugh. "*À demain*, dear." The phone clicked.

Kaitlyn stabbed a button on her phone, then a second one.

"Security."

"This is Kaitlyn. Can you tell Riley and Asher that I'll be at the house at two this afternoon and I'd like to meet with them, please?"

"Will do."

Kaitlyn punched the button to end the call and then sat back in her chair.

Omar smiled as he shook his head. "What a tangled web we weave, Kaitlyn."

"I know, isn't it fun?"

They shared a conspiratorial cackle and then got to work putting the plan into action.

CHAPTER TEN

THE VILLA

"THIS IS really weird, isn't it?" Asher asked as the limousine carried them down the hill from the house.

"Well, I've never seen this kind of thing on the show, but then again, she said it wasn't going to be taped, so it makes sense that it wouldn't have been part of the show…. Yeah, it's weird." Riley sighed and looked out the window.

"It's nice that she appreciated how we tried to help out. And it will be really nice to be away from the rest of them for a while."

"I hear ya. As people get sent home, the tension level keeps rising. This morning one of the muscleheads threatened to beat the crap out of a guy for eating the last of the Cheerios. I think he would have done it, too—he's going through steroid withdrawal or something."

They rode in silence for a few minutes.

"So, where do you think we're going?" Asher asked as the limousine merged onto the freeway.

"I hope it's not back to that damn cliff top."

They both laughed at the idea and gave up trying to guess. It was easier just to go along and let it happen, Riley decided.

The limo eventually pulled up under the porte cochere of a hotel and came to a stop. The car was opened by a hotel doorman in a snappy uniform, who greeted them as if they were celebrities. They were met in the sleek marble-and-metal lobby by a man in a suit and tie, who escorted them to an elevator that he summoned with a swipe of a card. Above the elevator doors in elegant script appeared the words "The Palace Villa." Inside the elevator there were no buttons, as if its only job was to convey people to the Palace Villa, whatever that was. They rose the entire height of the building, it seemed, and then the doors opened.

It was as if they had been transported to the Mediterranean, to a courtyard grotto where a fountain splashed and marble columns surrounded a sparkling blue pool. Trellises covered with the bright fuchsia blossoms of bougainvillea shaded the area around the pool. To the right of the water was a dining table with two chairs, and to the left, through a line of open french doors, was a bedroom.

What struck Riley immediately was that this setting would be far more appropriate for a date with Daphne in a far later stage of the show; why he and Asher were here was a complete mystery.

The suit from the hotel—his name tag said "Marc"—pointed out the features of the villa and told them that dinner would be served at their leisure.

"So what, exactly, are we going to do here?" Riley asked, a bit annoyed at having been shipped around without any idea of what the point of all of this was.

"Relax, gentlemen. Kaitlyn told me that we were to ensure you had a chance to simply take a day and de-stress." He turned and walked back to the elevator. He pointed to a small panel next to the doors. "Should you require anything—food, drink, anything at all—simply press the appropriate button on any of the touchpads you will find throughout the villa. Until you do so, you will not be disturbed." He leaned toward them and repeated, "Unless you call, no one will enter the villa." He smiled broadly. "Anything I can get you right away, or would you like to settle in?"

Riley looked from Asher to the hotel manager and back in disbelief. "We weren't told we would be staying overnight, or that there would be a pool, or anything. We didn't bring anything with us."

"Not to worry, gentlemen. You will find toiletries and robes and pretty much anything else you need in the bathroom. When you are ready to retire, simply set your clothes by the elevator in the laundry bags you will find in the closet, and they will be washed and pressed for you in the morning. Now"— he beamed at them with glowing good cheer—"will there be anything else?"

"Nope, I think we're good," chirped Asher, and he extended a hand to the hotel manager. They shook hands, and with a nod to both men (and what Riley would later recall as a hint of a smirk), he opened the elevator and stepped inside. With a gentle whoosh he was gone.

Riley stood looking in disbelief at the elevator doors. He was trying to figure out exactly why the producers would think this was a good idea, and whether they could really trust that they would not be filmed during whatever it was they were doing here. Strategy made his head pound lately, and it was certainly doing that now.

Asher, however, apparently had no such qualms. He was walking around the pool in gaping awe at the luxuries offered by the villa. After making his circuit, he returned to Riley, who still stood in the elevator foyer.

"This is pretty amazing," Asher offered.

"I just can't figure out why they are doing this for us," Riley replied, his voice one of professional distrust.

"Because you did such an incredible job back on the cliff. You saved the show, man."

Riley snorted. "I think you're remembering it wrong. You're the one who saved Daphne's life—I'm the one who broke down crying for no discernible reason."

Asher stepped closer to him, his voice low. "Look, we've been through a lot already, and the show's probably not even half over. This is something nice that's come our way, and I think we should stop looking the gift horse in the mouth and just enjoy it."

Riley was unable to overcome Asher's native good spirits, and he relented. They walked into the pool courtyard together. The pool was a sharp rectangle of midnight blue, and at the far end a smaller pool poured water into the larger with a soothing plash. There were a couple of teak loungers covered with impossibly plush white toweling, and on the table was a silver tray bearing an assortment of drinks in exotic bottles, as well as a silver ice bucket.

They walked to the other side of the courtyard and discovered that the bedroom contained only a single large bed. Riley stopped short and shook his head.

"What is it?" Asher asked.

"One bed? What the hell?"

"They probably had lined this up as a date spot for the show, and no one thought about it when they decided to send us here instead. Do you really think this is some plot to get us into bed together?"

Riley looked at him for a moment, then back at the bed. He chuckled at how ridiculous it seemed, once Asher had said it aloud. "You're right, sorry. I'll lighten up, I promise. If I start asking X-Files conspiracy questions, you just tell me to shut up."

"Check," Asher replied buoyantly.

Riley nodded and willed himself to give up his worrying. He needed a distraction, and the pool provided a perfect one. "I'm gonna hit the pool. You coming?"

"Let's see if they left us some swim trunks," Asher said, opening the doors of the considerable closets that lay between the bedroom and the palatial bathroom. "Bathrobes, but nothing else," he announced from deep within.

Riley screwed his positive attitude to the sticking place. If Asher could be relentlessly upbeat, so could he—if he worked really hard at it. "Well, then, I'll just have to make do." He walked over to the chaise lounges at poolside and started removing his clothes.

"What are you doing?" Asher asked, his voice devoid of the sunshiny good cheer it had evidenced moments ago.

"Getting in the pool, my good man," Riley replied in his most practiced devil-may-care inflection. "I'm taking your advice and just going with it." His shirt was off, and he was unbuttoning his pants. "Are you going to join me?"

Asher stood and watched Riley disrobe with an expression Riley couldn't figure out—his smile seemed forced, but he never looked away. Riley folded his pants over the back of the lounger and then turned to face Asher.

"Your loss," he said cheerfully as he slipped his boxer briefs down and off and then leapt naked into the pool. This sent a wall of water right at Asher, who narrowly avoided getting drenched by stepping off to the side just as the wave hit. The shock of water flowing over his nude body liberated Riley. Suddenly this seemed like the best idea in the world. "It's perfect, man. Come on in!"

Asher swallowed hard and walked over to the lounger next to Riley's. As Riley paddled around the pool, he could see Asher very slowly unbuttoning his shirt.

"Come on, slowpoke!" Riley called. He emphasized his command by sending several splashes of water toward the other man. Finally, something seemed to snap inside of Asher, and he threw off the rest of his clothes. It was Riley's turn to jump away from the splash as Asher's cannonball blasted toward him.

The two men paddled around the pool for a few minutes, soaking in the sun that filtered through the trellises. Then Asher made his way over to the end of the pool where the waterfall burbled. "Hey, it's a hot tub!" he called.

Riley turned, just in time to see Asher lift himself up out of the water and onto the ledge that separated the two pools. Water ran down his back, across the solid muscle of his buttocks, and down his strong legs. "Shit,"

Riley muttered when he realized what he was staring at. He turned away and studied the plants growing alongside the pool.

"Oh, man, this is nice," Asher said from the hot tub. "Come on and check this out!"

"I've been in hot tubs before," replied Riley, who was treading water in the deeper end of the pool, far from the naked Asher.

"But this one makes the most amazing bubbles—it's like being in a big glass of champagne!"

Riley shrugged and swam smoothly over to the other end of the pool. He attempted the same lift that Asher had executed but found that gravity had other ideas. He dropped back into the water and then climbed out of the pool before stepping up to the hot tub. "Oof—how'd you just leap up here?"

Asher's eyes snapped up to meet Riley's as if they had been looking somewhere they shouldn't have been. "Still got the gymnastic moves, I guess," he said with a shrug. "Now get in—it's amazing."

Riley lowered himself into the water, which, as Asher had promised, was bubbling not from jets in the walls of the tub but from somewhere deep under the water. Little bubbles crawled up every part of his body, most notably those parts that had never before been exposed in a hot tub. The effect was like being tickled all over—in the most relaxing way.

"Wow," Riley said, stretching out and laying his head back on the ledge surrounding the tub. "That's pretty awesome."

"I know, right?" agreed Asher, who mirrored his repose and breathed a sigh of contentment.

They lay back and reveled in the hot, bubbly water for a time, until Riley felt something brush against his foot. He was too relaxed to yank his foot back, so he just left it there, in casual contact with Asher's. The other man didn't seem to notice, or to mind if he did notice, so Riley decided to ignore it.

"I had no idea this would feel so good," Riley finally said, his voice heavy with drowsy warmth.

"I thought you said you've been in hot tubs before," Asher replied with a chuckle.

"Yeah, but not like this. And not naked. And not alone with another dude." His eyes opened, and he looked across at Asher. "You have to admit, this seems kind of gay."

Asher's head rose, and his eyes drilled right through the steam rising from the water and into Riley's. "What?"

"Nothing." Riley leaned back.

"It wasn't nothing," Asher replied, his voice strained.

Riley sat back up, pulling his feet back from the middle of the pool. "I just meant that this would seem like the perfect romantic getaway if we were, you know, romantically involved."

"Oh," Asher said. "Sorry. It's just that we've been through so much training at school about bullying that whenever I hear someone say that something seems 'gay,' I tense up."

"Didn't mean anything by it. Just an observation."

"Understood," Asher said, but he didn't lie back this time. "Hey, do you want something to drink?"

"That would be great," Riley replied. "I think I saw some iced tea there?"

"One iced tea coming up," Asher said as he lifted himself out of the water.

Riley didn't realize he had neglected to look away until Asher was already walking across the courtyard to the table to get the drinks.

He had again seen the water running down Asher's body—but down the front this time. Down it had run, over his rounded pectorals, down it had trickled between the slabs of his abdominal muscles, and it had flowed in a rivulet off the end of his penis, surrounded by carefully trimmed hair slicked down to his body. Riley had seen it all, and more—the flexing of Asher's powerful legs as he walked away from the hot tub. It was only when Asher turned and asked if he wanted sugar that he realized he had been unable to tear his eyes away.

"Sugar?" he asked, looking down at the water.

"Yes, sugar. Do you want some in your tea?"

"No, thanks," Riley said, perhaps a little too loudly. "No, I take it straight."

Well that was an odd turn of phrase, he thought.

Asher walked back over to the hot tub, during which transit Riley had the presence of mind to look away.

"Here you go," the other man said as he handed the glass of tea over to Riley. He had placed a mint leaf atop the glass in a decorative flourish that Riley would never have thought of.

Riley sipped. "Thanks, that's great."

"You're welcome. Though I guess we should have pressed the 'drinks' button on the touchpad and had someone in a tuxedo bring it to us."

"Which wouldn't be awkward at all, given that we're naked."

"Oh, come on. They probably see worse every single day up here. Yesterday it was an aging diva whose breasts could be tucked into her girdle, and tomorrow it'll be an old Hollywood couple recovering from his-and-hers face- and butt-lifts."

"Well, then, it would be a treat to come up here and find you," Riley said with a wink.

"I don't care how you flatter me, I'm not putting out," Asher replied archly.

"Damn. Thought I was going to get lucky."

"Naked in a hot tub with me? That's luckier than most people will ever be," Asher said with an imperious nod of his head.

Riley watched the intricate swirls of bubbles roil the surface of the water. He was silent for some time.

"I guess I am pretty lucky," he said, quietly, finally.

"Why is that?" Asher asked.

"Because I've gone all day without thinking about my ex. Not until this moment, and only because you made that comment about being lucky. Might have gone even longer. Hmm."

"She really did you in, didn't she?"

"Yeah, she did. People joke about being left at the altar, but unless you've experienced it…."

"Did you have any idea? That she wasn't going to show?"

"At the time, no," Riley said with a sad shake of his head. "But after, when I thought about it, I could see all kinds of signs. Like how she never touched me unless she wanted something. And how I was never good enough for her friends, or her family."

"That's rough, man."

"I spent the last year we were together learning all of the ways that I had failed her. I kept hoping that I wouldn't be a failure as a husband, but she apparently didn't want to find out."

"I can't believe she could make you feel that way about yourself," Asher said.

Riley scoffed. "In the end, I made myself feel that way more than she did. I tried so hard to make things work, but I couldn't do it, and then I'd beat myself up for it. But, you know what I've learned?"

"What?"

"That if it's that much work, it's not really a relationship. I shouldn't have to be worried all the time that I'm not giving her what she needs, or be anxious that she's not going to like the same things I like. Next time I'm going to find a woman I can just be myself with. Like you."

Asher blinked hard. "Like... me?"

"Hell yeah. I mean, look at us—we're closer than I am to anyone else in my life, except for my friend Kevin, and we started hanging out in grade school. Stuff we've been through just in the last month? Fucked up, man. But we've gotten through it, and we're lookin' pretty good for the win, and now we're kicking back in the fanciest hotel I'll ever see the inside of. It's easy with you."

"I guess...," Asher managed to mumble.

"Now I just have to find a woman I get along with as well as I do with you, and I'm golden." He knocked back the last of his tea. "Look, I'm going to get out—it's kind of hot in here."

"Yes, it is," agreed Asher, though he made no move to get up.

Riley lifted himself onto the edge of the hot tub and sat for a second, not wanting to risk a head rush from standing too quickly after the hot soak. He looked down and saw ribbons of steam rising from his body, from his thighs and his chest and his genitals, and he realized all modesty was gone—he really did feel comfortable with Asher, and he let himself feel it without the need for his usual obsessive analysis. He got up, walked over to the bedroom, and pulled a bathrobe out of the closet. He wrapped it loosely around himself and walked back to the courtyard. He poured himself another tea and lay down on the chaise.

"I could get used to this," he said, his eyes closed.

"So could I," Asher replied, though his voice was noticeably less relaxed than Riley's.

THEY ATE dinner in their bathrobes, having summoned the waitstaff at sunset. A flurry of tuxedoes arrived to light the torches around the pool, set the table with fresh linen and silver, and lay out course after course of intricate food.

"This is completely ridiculous," Riley said as the main course dishes were cleared. "Eating what has to be a thousand-dollar dinner in bathrobes."

"If it's any consolation, the bathrobes are probably worth several hundred on their own," Asher replied, brushing a hand casually along the thick white cloth of his lapel.

A final set of trays was brought in and laid on the table—a selection of dessert plates, coffee, teas, and digestif spirits. "Will there be anything else?" asked the headwaiter.

"No, thank you," Riley replied with a smile. "This is really amazing."

"Thank you, sir. Should you require anything further, please touch for us. Otherwise, we shall not disturb you," said the waiter as he retreated with his cohorts to the elevator.

Once the doors slid shut, Riley turned to Asher. "They always say that with a leer in their voices, don't they?"

"You're just being sensitive—I didn't hear any leering at all," Asher replied. "Of course, that may have been because I couldn't hear it over this apple crisp calling my name." He picked up the plate and held it so he could take in its aroma.

They rotated through the desserts, taking a bite of each and passing them back and forth until all six were at least half-eaten. Riley picked up the silver coffee pot. He poured himself a cup and held it questioningly toward Asher.

"Don't know if I should," he said in answer. "It's kind of late for coffee."

"It's going to have to get a lot later before I'm ready to slip between the sheets with you—no offense," Riley said with a smile.

Asher grinned in response and flipped his cup over. Riley filled it with steaming black liquid. They touched their cups together and sat back to sip. A few quiet minutes passed before Riley broke the silence.

"You know, I've talked a lot about my breakup, and my emotions about my breakup, and my feelings about my emotions about my breakup, but I've gotten nothing out of you at all."

"What do you want to get out of me?"

"Surely you must have some heartache or, preferably, joy in your love life that you can share."

Asher tipped his head to one side, then took another sip before answering. "Nope, not much to tell on that front, I'm afraid."

"Bullshit."

"Excuse me?"

"I said bullshit. There's no way that the guy who makes a clockwork heart to impress a girl has 'not much to tell.'"

"That didn't impress a girl," Asher replied, somewhat dismally.

"It impressed me," Riley said. "I know that wasn't the point, but it was amazing."

"Great. Let's say that's the story of my love life. Always managing to impress the wrong person."

Riley nodded. "I hear ya. We've all been there."

Asher chuckled, but in a kind of bleak way. "I'm not sure we've been in the same place. At all."

"But we are now," said Riley. Asher's opening up—even a tiny bit—made him feel such warmth for his new friend that he continued, speaking from the heart without allowing his mind to censor it. "I was completely alone in my woeful state, picking the scabs of a relationship gone to crap, but I'm feeling better every day. And that happened right at the moment I met you. You really were a knight in shining armor for me. And I can be that for you, if you'll open up a little." Riley noticed that Asher had set his coffee cup down, was looking a little pale. "You can tell me anything, Ash. Anything."

Asher blinked twice and stared at Riley for a long moment. "Did you just call me Ash?" he finally managed to say.

"I guess I did. I'm sorry—you don't like it?"

Asher was silent for a moment.

"It's fine... it's just that...." He cleared his throat and looked past Riley, as if he could see far into the distance. "No one's called me that in a long time."

"I won't do it if—"

"No, it's fine. I like that you called me that. It makes perfect sense that you would," Asher said, looking back at Riley from wherever his gaze had gone.

They finished their coffee and sat for a while looking at the stars above them. Then Asher took two formidable crystal tumblers from the tray and dropped several ice cubes in each. He opened the oldest of the three single malts that the waiters had arranged for them and poured a healthy amount into each glass. He slid one of the glasses over to Riley's side of the table.

"Join me for a drink?" he asked.

"Isn't that what we've been doing already?" Riley replied, taking the Scotch nonetheless.

"Not here," Asher replied, standing. He untied his robe and opened it, never looking away from Riley's eyes. He slid it down and stood naked before Riley, bathed in flickering torchlight. He picked up his glass and nodded toward the hot tub. Riley nodded, then stood and slipped his robe off as well. They strode together to the pool and stepped into the hot, bubbling water, resuming their previous positions facing each other. Gentle light filtered through the bubbles from below them. Spontaneously, they touched their glasses together with a melodious ringing of fine crystal and settled in to sip the smooth amber spirit.

"Fuck me, this is a lovely thing," Riley growled in a passable Scottish brogue.

Asher laughed giddily. "Great. Now I'm going to be picturing you in a kilt."

"That'd be a fair bit more than I'm a-wearin' at the moment, laddie," continued Riley in his highland best. Asher's peals of laughter filled the courtyard.

"This is the best night of my life," Asher said, once he could catch his breath.

"Oh God, I hope that's not true," replied Riley. "I'm certain you've had better."

"What could possibly be better than this?" Asher asked, gesturing around them.

"Oh, I don't know, perhaps if I had breasts?"

Asher wrinkled up his nose. "I don't think I'd like you with breasts."

"Very funny. I just meant that as nice as this is, all of this romantic ambiance might be put to better use."

"We'll agree to disagree on that one," Asher said, putting the subject to rest.

They soaked in the tub and sipped their Scotch and spoke of nothing of consequence—refilling their glasses twice—until the hour was quite late.

"I guess I'm gonna rinse off and get to bed," said Riley, as he stood up somewhat uncertainly. The advanced hour, the Scotch, and the sapping heat of the tub had nearly done him in.

"I'll come with you," said Asher, even more unsteadily. "If you leave me out here I'll probably get lost."

Riley grabbed a towel from a shelf next to the hot tub and tossed one to Asher. They dried off haphazardly, and instead of wrapping the towel around his waist Asher tossed it around his neck. Riley, without thinking, simply did the same. They walked into the bedroom, naked and completely without reservation about their nudity.

The shower was in keeping with the scale of the rest of the bathroom. There were showerheads on opposite walls of the glassed-in marble expanse, and so each man took one. They rinsed and soaped and rinsed again, distracted only once by Asher flicking water at Riley accidentally when he shook his head to get the water out of his hair. Riley splashed back, and they spent the next five minutes playing in the water like kids at a hydrant in the summer. Returning eventually to their adult bearing, they toweled off and availed themselves of the toothbrushes that the hotel had provided for them.

Washed and brushed and ready for bed, they stood staring at the king-size showpiece of Egyptian cotton and goose down that was theirs for the night. Riley's mouth was suddenly dry, and he had no idea why.

"Well, I guess we just get in," Asher said, pulling the towel off from around his waist and tossing it into the hamper next to the closet. He walked around the bed and got in on the far side. "See?" he said, as he swept his hand across the wide duvet, "plenty of room. You won't even know I'm here."

Riley smiled as he unwrapped the towel he was wearing. He slipped under the covers on the near side of the bed. He reached out and turned off the lights, leaving them in the dark save for the flicker of torches out on the courtyard. "I'll know you're here," he said softly.

Asher turned toward him. "Is that a problem? Do you want me to see if that couch over there pulls out?"

"No" came Riley's answer, almost before Asher had finished his question. "No, it's just that…." His voice drifted off in the dark.

"It's just what?" Asher asked, after at least a full minute had passed.

"It's just that…. I haven't slept with anyone—I mean gone to sleep in the same bed with—since my breakup."

"Is it too weird? I can find some other place to—"

"No, it's fine. I mean, it's good. It's actually really nice to have someone there. I mean, here. With me. In bed."

"Are you sure?"

"Yes. I know this is going to sound completely gay, and I'm sorry, but it's just been so long, and after the hot tub and the Scotch and everything…. I guess I'm just a sloppy mess is all. I just didn't realize how lonely I'd been until you came along."

"That's… awesome, Riley. I'm glad I could do that for you."

"I just wish I could tell you what it means to me. What… what you… mean to me…."

Riley wasn't sure where he was going with this, wasn't even aware of where these words came from or what would come out of his mouth next. But there was a heaviness in his chest that he knew would only be lightened if he could find a way to tell Asher what he was feeling.

He took a halting breath and continued. "Ash, I just want you to know… now, please, don't take this the wrong way…. I need you to know that I—"

Riley was stopped in his meandering disclosure by Asher's fingers touching his lips. In shock, he stopped talking—stopped breathing.

"Shhhh." Asher was closer to him now.

"But… but what—"

"I know," Asher said, his voice right next to him, his breath brushing Riley's cheek. "You don't need to say anything. I know it all. I know."

Riley took in another breath as if getting ready to speak again, but fell silent. In that moment he knew that Asher spoke the truth. That Asher knew him—really knew him—and that knowledge went beyond any need he might have had to explain.

And then he felt it. He felt Asher's lips on his.

They only touched for a second, for a fraction of a second, but the jolt that shot through Riley was instantaneous and electric. His whole body shook, and he gasped as if there were not enough oxygen in the room for him to draw into his lungs.

Asher threw himself backward, back over to his side of the bed. "Oh God, Riley, I'm sorry. I don't know what—"

"Did you... just... *kiss* me?" Riley asked, each word bitten off brutally.

"I'm so sorry. It was just that—"

"Fuck."

Asher let that word linger in the air. Then, in a tentative voice he repeated, "I'm sorr—"

"No!" Riley interrupted. He lay silent for a moment, hearing the breeze in the trees outside but not a single breath from Asher. He could feel the bed trembling, though. "Look, we've both had a lot to drink, and I'll admit I was getting a little sappy there. But I just want to be clear that nothing like that is on, okay?"

"Okay" came Asher's response from the darkness, his voice torn with emotion. "I really didn't mean—"

"No. No apologies. We've been through too much to have something like this end our friendship. Okay?"

"Okay," Asher answered, after a long pause in which Riley was certain he heard a sniffle.

He knew he was at fault—he had gotten drunk, and that always brought out his sad and lonely side. He certainly hadn't intended to draw Asher into something they would both regret. But lashing out wasn't the right thing to do, either.

Riley reached out a hand and found Asher's cheek. He patted it awkwardly—it was damp, which made things even worse—and then pulled his hand back and rolled over. It took him a long time to finally drift off to sleep.

HIS EYES opened slowly, blinking in the light of the morning sun streaming through the skylight that had escaped his notice previously. The room came into focus gradually, and he became aware of his situation only once it did.

He was alone.

He sat up in the bed and felt over on the other side—Asher's side—and found it cold.

He reached for the bathrobe he had thrown aside last night and wrapped it around himself, tying it tightly. Then he walked out of the bedroom area into the courtyard and looked around for a sign of life. On the other side of the trickling fountain he saw Asher, fully clothed, sitting at the table. He seemed lost in thought, staring blankly at the ground, a coffee mug cradled in his hands.

Riley walked around the pool to the table. Asher glanced up as he heard Riley approach but then looked quickly away.

"Morning," Riley said, with a chipper note in his voice that he certainly didn't feel.

"Good morning," Asher replied, his tone cool and formal. "I asked them to bring coffee first. Breakfast will be here soon."

Riley sat down, poured himself a cup of coffee. He sipped—it was strong and hot and everything he needed it to be—and looked into the distance opposite from the one that Asher was staring into.

They sat that way for a long while, as long as Riley could stand it.

"Nice morning," he said, lamely.

"Yes, it is," replied Asher, still in the detached manner of a dental office receptionist.

The water lapped softly at the edge of the pool. A bird chirruped in the distance.

Riley's patience gave out. "So, are we going to—?"

"I called to see if the car would come get me before you woke up. They said that they needed us to come back together. So I'm kind of stuck here. Sorry."

"No, I'm glad you stayed. We need to talk."

"Do we have to? You made it pretty clear last night. I don't know what else we need to say."

"Well, then, you can just listen while I apologize. I was in a bad state last night, and I said some things that led you to believe that I wanted you to... well, that I wanted you. I'm sorry—that was all my fault." He paused here and chuckled at the situation he had gotten himself into last night. "You must have thought I was putting the moves on you, looking for pity or something. The whole thing was just a mistake."

"That's not what—"

"No, let me finish. In the light of day, we just have to take a step back and say that this whole experience has fucked with our heads something awful, and that when all is said and done we're just two guys who ended up having an awkward moment. It's done, and over, and we can put it behind us."

Asher looked at Riley—really looked at him—for the first time since he had gotten out of bed. "I can't do that."

Riley wasn't expecting this. He had been relying on Asher to keep up his end of the bargain and block out what had happened last night. "Why the hell not?" His words were tough, but his voice was soft.

"Because it wasn't a mistake," Asher said, in a voice Riley could just barely hear. "Not for me."

"I… I don't understand," Riley faltered.

"What happened last night—"

Asher was cut off by the soft whoosh of the elevator doors opening. A trio of waiters appeared, one pushing a cart and the other two bearing silver trays draped with crisp white linen. They set breakfast on the table between the men and quickly retreated to the elevator.

Riley cast his gaze across the laden table and found that breakfast consisted of all of his favorite foods: an omelet with bell peppers and red onion, bacon that was cooked to a caramelized crispness, a mélange of melon and mango. Sourdough toast with butter on the side and a pitcher of mimosas completed the spread.

"Whoa. I guess I won the lottery on this one. They seem to have known exactly what I like."

"I ordered it for you," Asher replied, under his breath.

Riley looked up from the table at the man opposite him, gaping in surprise. "How did you know?"

Asher answered, but he spoke to the coffee cup in his hands, not meeting Riley's eye. "I've seen what you have for breakfast. Most days you limit yourself to a greek yogurt, granola, and a banana, but once in a while, when you allow yourself to indulge, you have this. It makes you happy, though I can tell you have to talk yourself into it, and then you work out twice as long afterward." He looked up at Riley when he had finished saying this, his face devoid of expression.

Riley didn't know what to say. He looked at the breakfast plates, and then back to Asher, and then around again two or three more times. "I can't believe this."

"Like I said, I'm sorry." Asher stood suddenly, setting his coffee cup on the table. "I should just go. I'll wait in the lobby." He strode toward the elevator, but Riley grabbed his hand as he walked past.

"No, stay. Stay!" He held on, and while Asher could no doubt have yanked his hand back and continued on his way, he seemed to wilt under the pressure of Riley's grip. He stopped.

"Please. Sit," Riley urged, and Asher complied.

Riley took a deep breath, tried to compose himself. But he was still unsure what to say. He fell back on a safe topic—perhaps the only safe one between them right now. "Are you going to have anything to eat?" he asked.

Asher shook his head.

"Well, this is far too much for me. Here," Riley said, and began scooping food onto a plate. When it was full, he pushed it across the table. "Please. Eat something."

Asher took up a fork, and though he did no more than pick at the food, it was enough to satisfy Riley, and he tucked in.

"Wow, this is really good," he said, halfway through his omelet. "It still amazes me that you knew what I like for breakfast."

"I'm not a super sleuth or anything. I just observe."

"Well, what you were able to observe in a couple of weeks is more than my ex was able to in four years. She never could have ordered this, even though we had breakfast together all the time."

He returned to his meal and made short work of it. Asher had only managed a couple of bites.

Riley poured two mimosas, handed one to Asher, who set it down without a sip.

"Okay, so we need to talk," Riley said finally. Asher shrugged, but Riley pushed ahead. "You said that what happened last night wasn't a mistake. That's the part I don't get—if two straight guys end up in bed, and they kiss, then that's a big fucking mistake."

"That's not what happened," Asher said with a note of grim finality in his voice.

"So you're saying I imagined it? You didn't really kiss me?"

"No, that's not what I meant," Asher said, his voice still quietly determined. "What I meant was that it wasn't two straight guys in bed last night." As if this declaration had cost him dearly, he grabbed up the flute of mimosa in front of him and took a long drink of it.

Riley shook his head. He must be mistaken—he couldn't have heard what he thought Asher had said. No.

"Riley, I'm gay," Asher said.

So he hadn't been mistaken. What the fuck? "Look, one kiss doesn't make you gay. That's all I've been trying to say this morning. What happened last night doesn't change anything about us—about who we are."

Asher squinted at Riley. "Last night didn't change me. Last night I was foolish enough to think for once, just maybe—"

"No, you definitely are not," Riley interrupted conclusively. "Not that it's a bad thing—I have gay friends, I like them a lot—but you aren't."

"I'm going to have to beg to differ with you on that." Asher poured himself another mimosa, downed it in one go.

"No way," Riley said, laughing and shaking his head. "You don't act like any gay man I've ever met."

Asher stared at Riley, speechless.

"Some of those makeup artists from the first challenge—the ones who acted all, you know, gay?" Riley's mortification from the encounter with Wilbur came flooding back to him. He swallowed hard and continued. "But you—you're an athlete, you're a regular guy, and you're on a fucking reality show so you can, they keep saying over and over again, 'compete for the love of a woman'!"

Asher opened his mouth to speak, but Riley forged ahead.

"Two guys, under the kind of stress we are, sometimes things just get weird and intense and it doesn't mean we're suddenly gay or anything. It's like being in prison—you know, no other outlet, things happen."

"This?" Asher said, gesturing to their posh surroundings. "This is prison?"

"That's not what I meant. I'm just saying that we're—that I'm in a kind of a bad spot emotionally, and then the stress of being in this competition, and all of that together…. I'm not making very good decisions right now, and last night was one of my worst."

"Huh. Thanks."

Riley sighed. "This isn't about you. I'm sure you have women all over you in real life, and once you're back there with the sacks of cash you're going to win you'll be beating them off with a stick."

"Sounds awesome," Asher replied as he sat back in his chair and folded his arms over his chest. "What with the stick and all."

"Look, I'm just saying I'm sorry about last night. I made things weird, and I apologize. I'll stop explaining, since I seem to make it worse every time I try."

Asher nodded in agreement. "Can I talk now?"

Riley smiled and nodded. "Sure. Sorry."

"Stop apologizing."

"Sorry."

Asher scowled. Riley shrugged, helpless to control his native urge to smooth things over.

"What happened last night wasn't a mistake. Or, at least it wasn't your mistake. It was mine."

Riley took a breath as if to interject, but Asher raised a warning hand. "Your turn is over."

Riley nodded and sat back.

"Last night was not your fault. It was... well, it was no one's fault, really. I misunderstood you, and I saw what I wanted to see, not what was really there, apparently. When you said you'd been so lonely, and that it was nice to have someone in bed with you, I just thought that maybe I had a shot. So I took a chance." He looked at the glass in his hands, fidgety. "I've wanted to do that since I met you and saw what an amazing guy you are."

Riley was stunned. "Wait, you really are...?"

"Yep. I am."

Riley shook his head in disbelief. "And you thought I was?"

"No, I didn't. At least, not consciously."

"What does that mean?"

"I thought that with your recent unfortunate experience with heterosexuality, you might be open to something... else."

Riley's eyes narrowed. He stared at Asher, long enough that the silence obviously made him uncomfortable.

"I was wrong," Asher finally blurted. "Clearly."

"I don't get why you thought I might be willing to—"

"Because I read you wrong. All wrong, obviously. Here you are, this perfect guy—charming, and whip-smart, and beautiful to boot—and you were happy to be hanging out with me. You confided in me, you told me that I made you feel better, you said you were glad I was there for you. All of that added up to 'maybe I have a shot.' Again, I was wrong." He stood suddenly and walked away from the table.

Riley bolted to his feet and stomped after him. He grabbed Asher's arm and spun him around. "No fucking way! Oh hell no!" he bellowed.

Asher shrunk back, terror in his eyes.

Riley grabbed his other arm, pulled him close. "There is no fucking way," he growled into Asher's recoiling countenance, "that the only person on the face of the fucking planet who thinks I'm 'charming and whip-smart and beautiful' turns out to be a dude."

The confusion on Asher's face was manic. His eyes darted side to side, and then he simply stared at Riley, dumbfounded.

Riley couldn't control himself any longer. He burst out laughing. He clapped his hands on Asher's shoulders, and he simply roared with laughter, until tears filled his eyes, until he had trouble catching his breath. He doubled over and clutched his sides.

It was a full minute later when he was finally able to stand up straight and wipe the tears from his eyes. Throughout this demonstration, Asher had stood frozen.

Riley, mostly recovered, cleared his throat and found his voice. "It's not you, it's me. This is just the last in the long, long line of blows to my ego that I've enjoyed over the last couple of years." He huffed out an anguished breath. "Fuck," he said, shaking his head.

"Wait—I take the biggest risk of my life and all you see is a blow to your ego?" Asher's voice was high and angry. "Pardon my indelicacy, but what kind of fucked-up macho bullshit is that?"

"What is that supposed to mean?"

"I admit I took a calculated risk, and I lost. But for you to tell me that I'm some kind of natural disaster that hit your life—that's just mean."

Riley drooped, at a loss. "Look, I've never been in this situation before, okay? So I freely admit that I may be doing it wrong."

Asher squinted at him. "You've never had anyone kiss you when you weren't expecting it? I find that hard to believe."

"Maybe once, in college, when I was drunk. But even then it was a girl. A not very pleasant-smelling girl, who still had braces at the age of twenty, but I'm pretty sure she was a girl."

Asher turned away, making an exasperated noise.

"What? I'm not comparing you to her, okay? You smell a lot nicer, and your teeth are perfect."

Asher froze for a moment, then turned around slowly. "Seriously? This is seriously the line you're going to take on our little drama here? That I may not be as horrifying as some drunken, stinky chick who mashed on you in college, but almost? Thanks, buddy. That's great." He stomped over to the table and picked up the touchpad. "I'm done. I'm going to call for a cab and get back to the house. If they cut me loose because of that, at least I'll be able to salvage whatever shreds of dignity you've left me."

Riley yanked the touchpad out of his hand. "Stop. Don't do this."

"Why the hell not? I told you I fucked up, and I'm sorry. All you've done since then is tell me how my kiss is a cross you have to bear. I'm getting kind of tired of hearing how Hurricane Asher demolished the tattered remains of your life."

"I just need to know… why…?" Suddenly words weren't coming easily to Riley. His brain was as thick as his tongue. What was he trying to say? "What made you… try to…."

"I've already told you. I've spent weeks hoping that something like last night might happen, and then it did, and I jumped to the conclusion I wanted."

"I get that—I guess. I see why you did it. What I'm trying to figure out is what it says about me."

Asher, clearly unable to fathom what Riley was asking, simply shook his head and shrugged.

Riley knew he needed to take a new tack. "Can we at least sit down? Talk about this?"

Asher sighed, then nodded, and they resumed their seats at the table.

Riley poured out the last of the mimosas into their flutes. He set the empty pitcher down and stared at it as if it somehow contained the answers he sought. When the pitcher turned out to be less than forthcoming, he looked at Asher. "I told you before that I have gay friends, and I'm fine with it."

Asher nodded curtly—Riley thought he detected a hint of an eye roll.

"My company makes me go to this nondiscrimination training every year, and the whole point of it is to accept people as they are because they were born that way or whatever."

"An admirable goal," Asher said noncommittally.

"But that's the thing. If I'm supposed to accept that gay people are born that way—and I do—then…." He paused for a moment, reluctant to cause offense. "Why didn't you accept that about me? Are straight people not born that way?"

Asher's eyebrows shot up. He clearly wasn't expecting this turn of the conversation. He took a moment to compose his thoughts, his lips moving as if trying out various ways to answer. "It's more complicated than that," he said finally.

"Why? That's the part I don't get."

Asher took in a big breath, his cheeks puffing as he let it out. "I wasn't always an art teacher," he said, quietly.

Riley shook his head at this non sequitur.

"When I graduated from college, I had an art degree whose primary purpose was to annoy my father. I didn't know what I was going to do with it, and so I spent the summer after graduation volunteering at a group home for gay youth near the university. I didn't have any formal training in counseling or anything, but I could help out with keeping things running and making posters for events and stuff. But after a while I started to sit in on group sessions for guys who were suicide risks—the psychologist said he wanted them to see a well-adjusted gay man who was close to their age. I'd never thought of myself as a role model, and I hardly felt qualified. I'd been an athlete all my life, and I had never been bullied or even looked at funny. What did I have in common with a kid who was thrown out of his house for coming home after curfew—in drag? But here's what I learned: most of the kids who fit the gay stereotype are going to be fine. They find strength in drag, or in fashion, or in theater, or just being the sassy best friend of some cheerleader whose popularity will protect them. But the ones who seem straight—the jocks, the nerds, the student government movers and shakers—they're the ones who are going to hit the rocks hard when they are finally too exhausted to deny who they are. They're the ones who are going to consider killing themselves rather than admit they have a crush on another guy." Asher fell silent and stared at the table. He sniffed and seemed to pull himself together. "The ones who are 'born that way' have Lady Gaga on their side. It's the ones who have no idea which way they were born that we have to worry about."

Riley thought about this for a moment. "How can someone not know?"

Asher nodded. "I used to wonder that. I had the most wonderful, accepting parents in the world—they totally didn't deserve my passive-aggressive art major, but then again, that's worked out for me, so they get the last laugh there. I only ever remember knowing that I was attracted to men, and that was okay. But the kids in this group—well, they had a different experience. Think about all of the subtle ways that people get told how to behave, and what is acceptable for people of their gender. A five-year-old boy who puts on a dress during playtime can sense the disapproval in a grandmother's frown. At twelve kids are hearing jokes about fags from friends and family. We are told in a million little ways how to behave, and that's enough to make anyone bury the parts of themselves that don't fit. By the time these kids were in high school, they were so good at hiding that they'd hidden from themselves. When they couldn't lock it up any longer, they tried to off themselves rather than deal with it."

"Oh, man, that sucks," Riley said, his voice heavy with empathy.

"Yeah, it does. There was this one guy in the group who had been the total jock in school—football team star, knockout girlfriend, the works—and he had probably stuffed a few gay kids into trash cans along the way. But one day his best friend borrowed his laptop and found some gay sites in his browser history. The friend mass mailed a screenshot to every single one of the kid's friends—even his girlfriend. He took a shower, got dressed, said goodbye to his parents, and drove his car into the side of a Walmart at sixty miles an hour. No skid marks, just straight in—but he survived. He ended up in the group home because his parents wanted nothing to do with him. I met him when he was trying to come to terms with how his entire life had been a lie, one that he had told himself before he told it to anyone else. And everyone in his life had believed it—until he couldn't tell it anymore."

"I don't want to speak ill of anyone," ventured Riley. "But if he was looking at gay websites, he must have had some inkling."

"You'd think so, but it's amazing what people can rationalize. He said he did it out of curiosity, or because he thought his cousin might be gay and he wanted to find out about what he was going through, or because he wanted to see how his body stacked up against those workout models—there was a different rationalization every time he talked about it. He had a lot of reasons, none of which stood up in the light of day, but they kept him from thinking about himself as anything other than straight and narrow."

"Wow. I can't imagine going through anything like that," Riley said, once Asher had finished relating this sad story.

"Me either," Asher replied, "but people go through it all the time—that and worse."

"So, is this what you think of me? That I'm in denial about who I really am?"

Asher snapped upright, as if Riley's question had startled him. "It's not about denial. People use that word all the time, as if they assume people like that kid know who they are and simply don't want to deal with it. Lots of guys in our stupid macho culture are so beaten up by all of the rules and prejudices they see around them that they honestly don't have access to that kind of truth about themselves. It's like a protective layer gets built up around their sexuality, from before they even know what sex is, to the point that they have no idea which way they were born. It's not denial—it's much deeper than that." He sighed at the memory. "They offered me a job. I worked there for a year, helping out with groups and stuff until I was kind of overwhelmed with it all. They just kept coming, these kids who were at the end of their rope. I thought long and hard about the kind of difference I could make in the world, and I decided that if I could be an influence earlier in their lives, maybe some of them would keep from ending up there. So I went back for a teaching certificate in art, and a year later I was in the classroom. I make sure that kids have a chance to explore and be creative and not be judged. When a boy paints ponies dancing under a rainbow, or a girl draws football players crashing into each other, they know that I'm not going to make them feel bad about it. I know I've helped a few, at least. A couple of them have come back to me in middle school—middle school!—to tell me that they're gay and they're okay with it. I like to think I helped keep them from burying that part of themselves, and I know that they're not going to end up at a group home for suicidal teens."

Riley fell silent. While he admired Asher's commitment to helping people, he found the whole thing terrifying. What if he was like that kid in group therapy? What if there was some deeply buried secret about him that even he didn't have access to? How could he be sure of... well, anything?

Asher must have seen the rising panic in his eyes. "Hang on. You're a nice guy who's had some unbelievably bad luck when it comes to women, and you are sensitive enough to know at least the rough outline of what's going on inside you. I thought I saw something that obviously wasn't there. Don't freak out thinking you might have a sex time bomb ticking away somewhere deep inside."

Riley sighed in confusion and knocked back the last of his mimosa. "Well, this has been angst inducing," he said cheerily as he set his flute back on the table. "How about we talk about how I have unresolved sexual feelings for my mom? Just to finish off the morning?"

Asher chuckled. "I'm just going to say one more thing. Sex is supposed to be fun, not make you crazy. If it does that, then you're probably doing it wrong."

"You sound like my ex," Riley cracked and then broke out laughing.

"So, I have to ask," Asher said once they had cleared the air and their laughter had quieted. "Are we okay?"

"Yes, of course we are. I said too much last night, you did too much—let's just call it even."

"Okay, but there was also some stuff this morning that you're leaving out."

Riley blushed. "You mean your delusion that I'm charming and whip-smart and beautiful? It's already forgotten."

Asher grinned. "I see you've forgotten my exact words, in the exact order I used them. That's an impressive memory you're not using there."

Riley mirrored Asher's grin back at him. "Those are the nicest things anyone's ever said about me, much less to me. I'm never forgetting those, just so you know."

"And you're okay with me still feeling that way about you, given I'm a 'dude' and all?"

"Nobody's perfect," Riley said with a laugh. "But I'm flattered, and honored, and again, it's all been forgotten already. Movin' on."

"A toast to denial!" Asher cried, holding his empty flute aloft. They touched glasses and pretended to drink—at least until their laughter forced them to put the glasses down lest they drop them.

"I guess we should get going for real, huh?" Riley asked, seeing the sun peek through the trellises above them. "I'm going to get dressed. You'll call for the car?"

"I'm on it. Oh, and prepare for a treat—I don't know what fabric softener they use here, but they left my boxer briefs in a miraculous state."

"Well, then, you'd better tell the car to take its time. I'll be in the dressing room introducing the boys to heaven." He cackled with delight and strode off to the bedroom. Once there, he discovered that Asher was right—the drawers that he had chosen primarily for looks (reality television does love to show skivvies) were softer than he ever imagined they could be. He pulled on the rest of his clothes and took a moment to brush his teeth and look at himself in the mirror. Beautiful? Asher had called him beautiful. That's not what he saw, of course, and doubted he ever would. It was not something he could ever imagine seeing in the mirror—and he was pretty sure his ex had never seen it either. But isn't that what love is supposed to be about? Seeing something that no one else sees? Well, whatever she saw, it wasn't enough. He shook his head and turned out the light.

"The car will be along in twenty," Asher said as Riley emerged back into the sunlight. "They'll let us know when it's here."

Riley sat on a teak bench next to the pool, bathed in a shaft of sunlight. He looked over at Asher and patted the seat next to him. Asher walked over and sat, gingerly, next to him. They looked at the light glinting on the water and listened to the splash of the fountain.

"Thank you," Riley said, softly, not turning to look at Asher.

"For what?" Asher asked, mystification in his voice. He studied Riley's face, as if trying to divine his meaning.

"For saying I was beautiful," Riley answered, still looking at the surface of the water. "No one's ever told me that before. I had no idea how much I needed to hear it."

Asher took in a deep breath, but no sound issued from his throat.

Riley suddenly turned at looked him in the eye. "Yesterday it would have freaked me out to be told that by another guy. Hell, an hour ago it would have freaked me out. But now I'm good with it. Because it's you. You make it okay. So, thank you."

"I don't know what to say," Asher was finally able to eke out.

"We've done enough talking. We're guys, after all. We've talked more in the last day than most guys do in a month."

They shared a laugh and spent the next few minutes just sitting, each enjoying the setting and the friendship of the one next to him.

The elevator doors eventually slid open, and Marc once again stepped into the villa. "Gentlemen! I trust you enjoyed your stay with us?"

"We did," Riley answered. He shot a quick glance at Asher. "Very much."

Asher blushed and refrained from offering his evaluation.

They swept through the hotel and out to the waiting limousine and were soon on their way back to the house. It was a longish drive through relentlessly uninteresting terrain, urban and sprawling.

"I never did ask you," Riley blurted suddenly.

Asher jumped a little, as if surprised that their agreed-upon silence was once again being broken by the person who had insisted upon it in the first place. He looked at Riley with raised eyebrows, allowing the question.

"When I called you Ash, and you said it made perfect sense that I would call you that. What did you mean by that?"

Asher paled—visibly, there was no mistaking it—and took three breaths in quick succession. He looked somewhat crazily around the limo, as if searching for a distraction dramatic enough to put Riley off this particular scent. But finally, whether out of friendship or lack of any other option, he attempted to answer the question.

"There are only two people in the world who have—ever—called me that," he said, slowly. "My parents never would, because Asher is a family name going back umpteen generations. None of my friends ever has either, first because they knew how my parents felt about it, and later because I introduced myself with my full name and never gave anyone permission to shorten it. And then...." he trailed off.

Riley waited a minute, then two. "And then...?" he prompted when his impatience got the better of him.

"And then I met Kofi. He came to the university from Ghana on an exchange program in his—and my—junior year. Most of the students from Africa came to study engineering, but he came to make art." Asher looked out the window, but his eyes were unfocused. "I needed a roommate, and he needed a place to stay, so he moved in. He had the most amazing voice—it was like music to hear him speak, even if he was just giving directions to the pizza delivery guy. He had trouble with the 'r' at the end of my name, so he quickly decided to shorten it to Ash. When he said it, it was like a prayer—how could I object to that? I let him call me what he wanted. But only when no one else was around."

Riley looked at Asher, his eyebrow raised. "Did you two spend a lot of time alone?"

A grin started to twitch to life at the corner of Asher's mouth. "We spent some."

Riley nudged Asher with his elbow—"you dog" was the message he sent. Asher's laugh let him know he received it.

"So?" Riley asked.

Asher looked at him and shrugged. "So, what?"

"What happened to Kofi?"

Asher laughter was long gone now. He looked down and sighed. "He went back to Ghana at the end of the school year. We exchanged some emails, but once he was back home, it was pretty clear that what happened in the US stayed in the US. I got a final e-mail from him six months later—he was getting married."

"Ouch," Riley replied. "That sucks."

"Yeah, it wasn't great. I don't know that I expected anything else, really. He came from a very traditional family, but in patriarchal cultures men are often forgiven their indiscretions before marriage."

Riley saw the pain on Asher's face. "That's what he considered you? An indiscretion?"

Asher nodded.

Riley could see that the memory was excruciating for Asher, and he felt terrible for bringing up the subject. "I'm sorry, I didn't—"

"I loved him," Asher said, quietly. "He was the first man I really loved completely. But all I was to him was a fling before marriage, some wild oats that he sowed in foreign soil. He broke my heart when he left, just ripped it out and stomped on it. Looking back on it, I think he must have figured I was on the same page—that we were spending a year wrapped up in art and creativity and physical abandon, and of course it had to come to an end. But I didn't want it to end."

"I'm sorry I reminded you of him. I'm so sorry I called you that name."

"No, don't be sorry. I'm actually relieved that you called me that. And you can keep calling me that—it reminds me of how happy I was then, and also of how I have a tendency to make bad choices under the influence."

"Under the influence of what?"

"Straight men."

Riley grinned. "I don't think your Kofi sounds all that straight."

"He might have said the same thing about you," Asher replied, with a chuckle. Riley's pantomimed offense at this remark caused Asher to laugh harder.

"We keep discovering things we have in common," Riley said. "We can add 'bad breakups' to the list, I guess."

"If by 'bad breakup' you mean 'abandonment that resulted in the complete destruction of self-esteem, both emotional and sexual,' then hell yeah!" He held out his fist to Riley, and they bumped in solidarity.

They were still laughing as the limousine pulled into the driveway of the house.

"I CAN'T believe it," Kaitlyn said as she watched the two men bump fists in the limo on the monitors she'd had set up in her office; using the control room for her secret project would have raised too many questions.

"That you were wrong about them?" Omar asked, a note of respectful sympathy in his voice.

"Are you kidding? I was completely right!" Kaitlyn objected. She fixed him with a withering glare. "My gaydar is functioning perfectly, thank you very much. I was about to say that I can't believe how perfectly this has all turned out."

Omar squinted at her, clearly baffled. "But Riley not only pushed Asher away, he says he's straight. And Asher seems like he believes him. So our job here is kind of over, isn't it?"

Kaitlyn gave him a knowing smirk. "Our job is just beginning."

"What can we possibly do? Asher made his move, got rebuffed, they're still friends—which I find completely baffling, by the way—and so didn't we already get what we wanted? Unless you think they're still at risk of ending up like Liam and Gavin, I don't see why we... have to... do...." His voice trailed off under Kaitlyn's renewed glare.

"We didn't get what we wanted at all. What we wanted was for romance to blossom in the arid fucking soil of this fucking show. Okay, so the first seedling was stomped on. That happens. But it's a poor gardener who gives up when the first sprout wilts."

"I'm sure people tell you all the time that your metaphors are delightful."

"Actually, no one's ever said that to me."

"Hmm. That's a puzzler, that is," Omar replied, dead serious.

"As charming as I find your sarcasm, can we stay focused, please? Now, it is true that Asher put the move on suddenly, and it didn't go well. But Riley didn't go all gay-panic on him, and in fact he seemed quite flattered by Asher saying he was beautiful. He's just got to realize the way Asher makes him feel about himself is the important thing, and that Asher happens to be a man is no big deal."

"Um, it's kind of a big deal," Omar said.

"That's the kind of thinking that is holding you back, my friend," Kaitlyn pronounced. "Now, the question is how do we make Riley see Asher for the great guy he is?"

"While making sure that no one—especially New York—finds out about them? Why can't you just let them finish the show and then do your Cupid bit when it won't matter?"

"Because we have them here, now, and we can control the situations they're in. We can make this happen, Omar. We can increase the happiness in the world by making sure these two guys have the best possible shot at love." She looked excitedly at him. "C'mon, we can do this!"

Omar shook his head slowly. It was a look that Kaitlyn by now had come to understand meant "I'll do it—I won't like it, but I'll do it."

"Awesome!" she shouted and held up her hand for a high five. He brought his palm up to hers, all the while continuing to shake his head.

CHAPTER ELEVEN

WILDERNESS

"GENTLEMEN, WELCOME to the National Forest," said the host. "Today you will be competing not against all of the remaining bachelors, but against just one. As we are now down to ten contestants, each of you will be paired off with one other bachelor. You will face a series of challenges today, and you will weather a difficult evening in the wilderness. Tomorrow your performance will be reviewed by our bachelorette, and she will choose the competitor she deems to be the champion. Of course, our viewers will also choose a champion from among you."

Riley cast a glance across the crowd at Asher. For once they would not spend an entire challenge joined at the hip, and he had to admit he was kind of looking forward to that. Better to compete separately for now—once they were in the final rounds they would need to manage the perception of their competitiveness carefully.

"An assistant is walking among you now, carrying a bag that contains ten tokens. Once you have drawn a token, you will find the person who drew the other half, and he shall be your partner in competition for the day. The member of each pair who loses the most challenges is vulnerable—one of the losers will be sent home."

Just at that moment, an attractive young woman walked up to Riley and held the black velvet bag open for him to reach in and draw out his token. Feeling very much like a magician's assistant, he smiled warmly at her as he slipped his hand into the pouch. He pulled out a gold coin—it looked like something people threw during Mardi Gras—that had been broken in two, leaving a jagged edge. He watched as the other men pulled out their coins and began to see which ones fit together. Riley tried to match his coin up with the men around him but did not find its mate. He walked to the other side of the group and tried them all. No match. He caught Asher's eye.

"What are the odds?" he murmured to Asher as they each held out their coins. Riley watched in disbelief as their coin halves nestled together perfectly, united in golden perfection.

"You can't argue with the luck of the draw," Asher replied with a shrug.

It wasn't that Riley didn't want to be paired up with Asher again; he was concerned that the more they were seen as a team, the harder it would be for them to manage the endgame of Riley winning and Asher coming in second. Would the audience really want to see the same pair who'd been working alongside each other throughout the competition end up in the final round? That outcome would lack the choreographed drama reality television worked so hard to deliver.

Riley leaned close to Asher, after checking to be sure no cameras were on them. "Look, you're going to win whatever we end up doing today, okay?"

Asher looked at him in surprise but said nothing.

"It's better for our plan in the long run, right?" Riley whispered.

The other man nodded, and they separated without looking at each other again.

"You will now be given a map showing the path you must take. Each pair will face the challenges in a different sequence. The order in which you arrive at the finish line will determine where you spend the evening; there you will also find refreshments. A rustic cabin awaits the first pair across the finish line, complete with a blazing wood stove and hot food. As an added incentive, both members of that first pair will get automatic immunity in the next round of the competition—the race is to the swift, gentlemen! The second pair will complete their trials at a tent that has been provisioned with down-filled sleeping bags and a warm campfire. Pair number three, there is a cave set on the rock face of the mountain that will provide you shelter for the evening. It's a rocky place, but you will find a small fire and some blankets. Pair number four, you will ascend to a tree-top platform just large enough for the two of you. It will be cold, but you should at least be safe from cougars."

The crowd rippled with the obvious cougar joke and then settled down again.

"And the last team to arrive will spend their evening in a hammock." The host paused for dramatic effect. "That has been suspended from a sheer rock cliff." More dramatic effect. "One hundred feet in the air." There was actual gasping this time. "As I said, the accommodations reward the earliest finishers. Now, please make your way to the starting line, where you will be issued a compass and an emergency transponder. Should you be injured, or become lost, simply activate the transponder and help will come to you. Alas, victory will not." The host stepped to one side to gesture grandly at the starting line. "Gentlemen, your challenges await!"

The crowd surged forward—the description of the various accommodations awaiting them at the end of the course was obviously a strong motivator. Asher grabbed up a compass and Riley a transponder.

"You good with a compass?" Riley asked as they jostled against the other bachelors at the starting line.

"Eagle Scout," Asher replied, proudly.

Riley raised an eyebrow.

"Yeah, I know. But the troop leaders were friends of my parents, and they were really liberal. Plus, I can make this baby sing," he said, brandishing the compass. He held up the map and studied it, then watched the needle's movement as he swayed gently side to side. Then he froze, and his gaze narrowed as if he was working complex sums in his head. This lasted only a moment, and then his head snapped up and he scanned the landscape all around, seeming to map what he could see against the mathematical model he had worked up in his head.

"You are a man of many talents," Riley replied, admiringly. He snapped the transponder around his wrist and shook his arm to make sure it would remain affixed.

"We're good to go, champ," Asher said brightly.

"You're the champ, remember?" Riley replied under his breath. Asher winked at him—an intimacy he hoped no one else noticed.

"There are five challenges on the map—what say we just split them? I'll win two, you win two, and then I'll take the last one?"

"Excellent strategy! You take the first two."

"Got it." Asher nodded.

"The challenge begins in three… two… one!" called out the host, and the starting line dropped. All ten men charged down the path, kicking up dirt and twigs as they stampeded.

About fifty yards from the starting line Asher touched Riley on the arm and nodded to the side. He then bolted suddenly off the trail, through a gap in the trees Riley hadn't even noticed was there. Suddenly they were charging through brush and brambles, dappled sunlight flashing on their arms and legs as they ran.

"You sure about this?" Riley called ahead to Asher. They were running in tight formation, Riley focused like a hawk on the heels of Asher's trail shoes.

"Just another little bit... right around this ridge here...." Asher called back as he leapt over a log that lay across the deer path they were running on.

Riley jumped over the log after Asher and followed him around the bend to the left and over a small rise in the forest floor. Suddenly, the trees opened onto a meadow, where there was sunshine and a cool breeze... and a camera crew. They had found their first challenge.

"Holy shit, they here already?" Riley heard a familiar voice gruffly exclaim. It was Bernie, and he clearly thought he would have a few more minutes to finish his latte before any competitors arrived. "Riley! Asher! Good to see ya!" he called to them, waving his clipboard over his head.

"Bernie! How you been, buddy?" Asher called out in response.

"Can't complain," Bernie said, his voice lowering to a conversational volume now that the men had jogged to a stop next to him. "You guys primed to battle it out?"

"Ready to rumble," Riley assured him, feinting a boxer's stance at Asher, who simply stared at him with a critical knit in his brow. He dropped his fists and shrugged.

"All right, here's the deal. Running along the other end of the meadow is a creek. It forks into two streams right about... there." He gestured into the distance. "Your challenge is to build a dam using the rocks and whatever else you can find. The winner is the one who can force the creek to overflow the other man's dam. That clear?"

Both men nodded.

"All right then, go!" Bernie crowed, reaching for the latte he had clearly been missing while he gave instructions.

Asher and Riley took off across the meadow at a run, knowing the cameras were on them as they dashed away with the look of fierce competitors on their faces.

They quickly located the fork in the stream, and Riley began to pile rocks energetically into the water. He didn't hear any splashing on Asher's side, and when he looked over, he saw the other man standing in the water, his hand on his chin. The cameras were trained on him, standing there like a statue.

"Trying to move the rocks with the power of your mind?" Riley called.

Asher shot him a withering glare in response, and then he returned to contemplating his fork of the stream. Riley shook his head and continued piling rocks. Finally, when his dam had risen nearly a foot above the water, he stopped again and looked over. What he saw stopped him cold. Asher had quietly arranged several rows of rocks into a convex arc across the mouth of his branch of the creek. The rocks fit together like bricks, and a pool of calm water was rising slowly behind them. Asher coolly added another layer of rocks and the water rose higher. Barely a trickle was getting through.

Riley looked back at his effort, his monument to impulse and brute force. It was quickly being overwhelmed by the water backing up against Asher's dam, and though he tried to reinforce it, he couldn't keep up. Within a few minutes it was breached in the middle, and the stream found its new course running right through the remains.

Riley's complete lack of engineering prowess was captured by all three cameras, and he held his arms out and shrugged in a manner he hoped spoke of good sportsmanship. Then all three cameras panned over to Asher's homage to Hoover Dam, which was holding strong. A placid pool rippled gently behind it.

"Well played, sir," Riley said grandly. "You clearly have what it takes to make any beaver happy."

Asher's eyes widened in shock, and then he burst out laughing. "Thank you, my good man," he said, bowing deeply. Then, the performance of good sportsmanship accomplished, he retrieved the map and compass from the pocket where he had tucked them and did some quick figuring.

"All right, gentlemen, off to your next challenge," Bernie said, having joined the crew at the stream once he had finished his latte. "And best of luck to you!"

"Thanks, Bernie," they said in unison as they jogged off in the direction Asher had pointed.

They were back running through dense forest before Riley came alongside Asher. "That was pretty amazing work back there," he said.

"Thanks. Or, rather, thank the Scouts for all of those survival weekends."

"You should really thank me for coming up with the plan for you to win this challenge," Riley replied. "I mean, if I wanted to win...."

"Yeah, I'm thinking you would have lost anyway," Asher answered with a chuckle. "But I'm sure you'll lose less badly on the next one."

"Thanks, man. You're a real sport." Riley couldn't help but laugh along with Asher, though. His high spirits were simply contagious.

"Next challenge is just over here," Asher said, motioning off to the right where the path ascended steeply.

They ran uphill through several hundred yards of trees and brush before emerging, panting, into the sunshine at the edge of a valley. A platform crowned with camera crews and two zip lines stood before them. They climbed the ladders that led to the top of the structure.

"You guys done zip lines before?" asked the assistant producer who waited for them at the top.

Both men nodded. Riley had reluctantly allowed himself to be strapped to one atop the cruise ship on which his ex had insisted they spend their vacation one winter. It had been expensive and less than thrilling, but at least he knew what to expect.

"Excellent. Now, put on these helmets, and we'll get you ready for the competition."

"What kind of competition?" Riley asked. "Seems like gravity does all the work here."

"Along the zip line there are targets for you to grab—six tennis balls that have been suspended within arm's reach. But in order to gather them all, you will have to let go of the harness that holds you up, and that can be hard to do when you are dangling from a wire several hundred feet in the air."

"Step in," ordered a man Riley hadn't even noticed before. He was dressed like a park ranger and was kneeling at Riley's ankles holding a harness. Riley put his feet through the large openings in the harness, and the man pulled it smartly into place. The cargo shorts Riley was wearing bunched up in his crotch, making his package protrude grotesquely between the straps. He looked like he was smuggling a mango in his underwear.

"You next," said the humorless ranger to Asher. He snapped the harness in place, where it framed Asher's jutting crotch as luridly as Riley's. "We're ready," the ranger said into his walkie-talkie, and crackling responses from each of the camera operators along the zip line signified that they were good to go. "Now, normally I tell people to hold tight to their harness so they don't touch anything they're not supposed to, but special rules apply to you TV folks," the ranger intoned, disdain for "TV folks" clear in this voice as he snapped them onto the zip line trolleys. "I'll just say that when you reach for those balls, you make sure you stay upright and facing forward. Otherwise we'll all be on the valley floor looking for *your* balls. Good luck," he humphed and stepped aside from the spectacle.

"All right, ready?" asked the producer. The men nodded their assent. "Go!"

Asher and Riley pushed off from the platform at the same moment. The line was steep, much more so than the one Riley had experienced on the cruise ship, and the speed built up quickly. He was glad the helmet's visor provided some protection for his eyes as the wind was whipping at him during the descent into the valley. The line dipped down below the tree line, and as they glided among the branches Riley spied a tennis ball floating next to the line. He reached out a hand and snagged it—it snapped smartly off of what appeared to be light fishing line—and quickly tucked it up under his shirt for safekeeping. He looked over at Asher just in time to see him grasp a ball on his side. Riley figured he would simply have to drop the last ball to be sure that Asher won this event as well.

They continued their descent, picking up tennis balls along the way, until each man had five in his grasp. They approached the final ones, and Riley made a great show of almost keeping hold of his until it slipped from his grip and fell into the forest below. "Damn!" he yelled, with what he hoped would sound like real anguish. Asher neatly completed his collection and dangled the rest of the way in, content to watch the scenery whiz by. Riley had to admit he admired the guy's ability to enjoy whatever moments of joy life offered him.

There was no warning before the owl, startled by Riley's shout, flew across Asher's path. A wing smacked into his face, catching him completely by surprise. Startled, he waved his hands about frantically, and though he was never really in danger, all six of his collected tennis balls exploded from his grasp and arced gracefully through the trees and down to the rocky floor of the valley.

"Shit," he muttered as he hung limply in the harness and watched them, and his chance of winning this challenge, fall away.

The brake cables kicked in as they neared the end of the line, and they slowed dramatically before arriving at the platform where they would dismount. "Tough break there," offered a crew member who had unhooked Asher from the trolley and was helping him out of his harness.

"Thanks. That thing came out of nowhere," he said, sounding a little shaken. "I hope it's okay—I hope I didn't hurt it. I was just so surprised!"

Typical, thought Riley. Guy almost gets sent to his death by a stupid bird and he's only concerned about whether it came through their collision okay. Once again, being more like Asher was moved to the top of Riley's to-do list.

"Nice job, man," Asher said, with a quick glance at the five tennis balls Riley was still holding.

"Thanks," Riley replied with a camera-ready smile. "I'm considering going pro—that's where the real money is."

As soon as the cameras were lowered, Riley mouthed "Sorry!" to Asher. Asher shook his head as if to dismiss the very idea that Riley might apologize.

They climbed down from the platform where they had landed and walked back toward the woods.

"You okay?" Riley asked. "That was pretty scary back there."

Asher snorted. "You should have seen it from my angle. One minute enjoying the scenery, the next minute my mouth is full of owl feathers. The taste was… unpleasant." He smiled, probably just to let Riley know he was fine.

"So it looks like we're tied," Riley said as Asher took his bearings and pointed the way to the next event. "How about this—we'll split the next two, however it works out best, and then you'll take the last one in a triumphant victory lap. Sound good?"

"If you are determined to lose, I'm happy to get the benefit," Asher replied. Then he set off into the woods at a jog.

Riley fell into formation behind him and went over their strategy in his head. They hadn't seen any of the other pairs of competitors this entire time, and he was starting to wonder if they were so far out ahead that they had left the rest of them behind. He hoped so, but he also knew not to get too cocky, especially when they had only completed two of the five challenges.

Asher guided them through the woods, back toward the edge of the meadow where they had built the dams. This time they arrived at the downhill end, where the stream had become a river. There were two river kayaks propped against the bank, and as they jogged up, members of the production crew began readying them for departure into the rapids that roiled a little farther downstream.

"Pretty straightforward, gentlemen," the crew leader explained. "You'll head downriver through the rapids, and the one with the best time across the finish line is the winner. Any questions?"

The two men shook their heads.

"Excellent. Here are your helmets. Have you used a kayak before?"

Both men again shook their heads.

"Excellent. Makes for much better television," he added, smiling grimly. "Here's your paddle." He handed each man a double-ended paddle. "Try not to get jammed between rocks—we'll have people on the river to get you unstuck, but it'll cost you in terms of time. Keep to the clear water as much as you can. These are designed not to roll, but they will if you get sideways in the current and hit a rock. Any questions?"

Riley could think of no question he could ask that would help in any conceivable way, so he simply shook his head again. Asher seemed to have come to the same conclusion.

They stepped into their kayaks, which seemed to Riley significantly less stable than they should have been. But he hefted the paddle around in a simulation of how he had seen it done on television during the Olympics, and he was shortly thereafter given a hearty shove in a downstream direction. The race was on.

The current picked up as the men floated down the stream. Riley looked back to see Asher's face lifted to the sky, tracing the path of a hawk as it lazily wheeled about, hunting or just sightseeing. Riley shook his head, constantly amazed at Asher's almost childlike wonder at the world. But he needed to win this challenge, and so he began to paddle purposefully into the rapids. Only when the water around his kayak began to froth did it occur to him that he had no idea what he was doing. In this challenge, as with the zip line, he hoped that gravity would simply do its work.

He slipped past a large boulder on his right, then another on his left, then between two even larger boulders that bestrode the river. Scylla and Charybdis, he thought—would echoes of the Trojan War and its mythical accoutrements never cease? He skinned between the rocks, holding his paddle straight up, and found himself hoping Asher would make it through safely as well. But the current continued to build, and the river ahead was studded with smaller rocks that just broke the surface of the water—it looked like warped glass flowing over the tops of them. But when the kayak struck them it rocked mightily to one side and then the other; Riley hoped that kayak was more tip-resistant than it felt.

As he rounded another bend in the river, he could see a finish line ahead—or, rather, he was looking down on a finish line that was rising slowly above the horizon. The last part of the course was a steep, rocky sluice of broken water and elephantine boulder formations. The sound of the water crashing down was deafening, and Riley was frozen for what seemed to him like a full minute. It couldn't have been more than a few seconds, but during that time the kayak doubled in speed, caught in the flume that would soon fling him—or the surviving pieces of him—across the finish line. He took a deep breath and simply tried to keep the little boat pointed downstream. The kayak attempted to buck him off, rising and falling in random lurches, dipping to the left and right as it buffeted around rocks, and several times threatening to roll over. But he held on and kept his balance, and he floated, exhausted, across the finish line. He was soaking wet, and his arms ached. His legs he couldn't even feel, so rigidly had they been locked in desperate, pointless exertion. But he managed to lift his paddle above his head in a pose of victory for the cameras, and smile in what he hoped looked like a champion's glowing exuberance.

He was holding this pose when he felt something bump his kayak from behind. He turned to see Asher, beaming, waving his congratulations. "Did you see that colony of egrets back there?" Asher said. "It was amazing! There must have been a dozen nests. What beautiful birds."

"I was kind of busy trying to keep from being beaten to death by rocks, so I must have missed those," Riley replied, shaking his head.

"Yeah, you did make it pretty easy on me. All I had to do was follow you, so I could kick back and watch the scenery. So, thanks for that!" Asher smiled warmly.

Riley had to admit that Asher's sportsmanship would make for good television. That would help them both, of course, as their strategy depended on both of them getting into the final round.

"Happy to help, as long as I win in the end," he replied, his championship smile still in place. They shook hands (the producers had mentioned several times that they liked to be able to capture such moments at the end of competitions, and the cameras were well positioned to do so now), and then they coasted over to the edge of the river and were helped out of their kayaks by the crew.

Asher retrieved the map from his pocket, did a quick read on his compass, checked for landmarks, and then pointed off into the woods once again.

"Man, how much did that suck?" Riley asked as they left the cameras behind.

"I thought it was fun," replied Asher, not breaking his rapid stride along the path he was picking out of the thick forest undergrowth. "But then again, I didn't have the pressure to win." He turned back and flashed Riley a grin.

"I just hope the next one's on dry land. My feet are squishing. I sound like an octopus out for a jog."

"We'll know in a sec—next one should be over to the left in about another couple hundred—"

"If we end up in the fucking river one more fucking time I'm going to fucking…!" interrupted another bachelor, stomping angrily down the path toward Riley and Asher. "Oh, hey," he said in a more controlled voice when he noticed them. He stopped, panting, dripping wet. "You guys just coming from the one down on the lower part of the river?"

"Yep," said Riley, who had at least had a chance to dry out a bit on the walk. "You coming from the one up this way?"

"Yeah. Have fun with that—it's a real hoot." The other bachelor's partner/opponent caught up with him, and they continued down the path with a grunt.

"Nice folks. Perhaps we should have them over for brunch or something," Asher said as they too resumed their course.

Riley stopped short. "Was that sarcasm? I wasn't sure you were capable of sarcasm. I'm impressed!"

"You have no idea what I'm capable of," Asher said with a wink, and he turned to continue up the path. Riley could hear him chuckling.

Before Riley could make a reply, they once again emerged from the woods at the precise spot where the next challenge was set up. That Asher could so consistently navigate these unfamiliar woods was deeply impressive to Riley—but he couldn't really compliment him on it in front of the cameras.

"Welcome, guys!" called the producer waiting for them—on the bank of that damn river, Riley noticed.

They jogged over to him and stood to catch their breath.

"Second to last event, right?" he asked, consulting the tablet in his hand.

"That's right," Asher replied, a bit of pride in his voice.

"You're making great time. All right, here's the deal on this one. Across the river there's a big log that serves as a kind of squirrel and raccoon highway. You're going to go across."

"Well, that sounds easy enough," Riley said, relieved.

"There's one catch" came the reply—with a grin. "Hanging from the middle of the log is a wire basket. Inside that basket are several fish: live fish, caught on the river this morning. Your job is to cross halfway on the log, pull the basket up out of the water, open it, grab out a fish, drop the basket back into the water, and finish crossing the log without dropping the fish—or yourself—in the water along the way. The one who gets the fish to the other side of the river in the shortest time wins."

Riley could now understand the frustration of the cursing bachelor they had encountered on the path.

"Now, since you lost the last challenge," the producer said with a head nod to Asher, "you'll go first in this one." He stood aside and made a sweeping gesture with his hand in the direction of the riverbank. Asher nodded and strode down the path to where the fallen tree's roots still held on to the riverbank. There were two cameras on each bank, one on each side of the log bridge, and they were all trained on Asher as he assumed his position at the root end of the log.

"And… go!" called the producer, clicking a stopwatch.

Asher walked confidently out onto the log, expending no visible effort toward maintaining his perfect balance. He stopped halfway across and executed a graceful crouch from which he leaned down, grasped the bucket's chain, and pulled it up neatly, hand-over-hand. The basket contained at least a half-dozen writhing trout, all of which were spurred into furious motion by the insult of air. Asher flipped open the wire lid, thrust his hand into the squirming mass of fish, and pulled out a healthy specimen. Holding it firmly just behind its head, he closed the basket and lowered it gently back into the water. He then rose to his feet and quick-stepped to the far riverbank.

"Excellent!" called the producer, clicking his stopwatch.

Asher hurried down to the water and gently lowered his captive trout back into the water. Once it thrashed in his hand, he let it go. He watched it swim away and then looked up with a smile on his face.

Another camera-perfect moment, Riley thought. He was increasingly glad Asher was a partner and not a competitor—the guy knew how to work the camera.

"All right, Bachelor Number Two! Head on down."

Riley picked his way along the top of the riverbank and stepped onto the log much more tentatively than had Asher. He hadn't noticed before that it was covered with moss and that the bark had been broken away in layers by years of wear by claws, hoofs, and boots. As usual, Asher had made the difficult look effortless.

"And… go!" shouted the producer.

Riley's heart pounded as he stepped out over the river, but then he reminded himself that his performance here didn't matter. As long as he was slower than Asher—and there was no way he would be faster—he could dawdle, he could waver, he could plunge headfirst into the river along with the fish. None of it mattered. That calmed him immediately, and he walked out across the log with an easy swing in his stride. At least he thought it looked that way. He would probably view this later on the show and laugh at his tentative and staggering progress.

He reached the halfway point without tipping off the log, but he knelt without any of Asher's graceful elegance and almost pitched himself over. He waved his arms a couple of times and found his balance, then flattened himself down on the log so he could reach down without doing himself in. Hauling the wire basket up out of the water went more smoothly, but after he opened the lid he looked down into the roiling pile of fish without relish. He wasn't squeamish, really, but the days of fishing with his father—those family summers at Lake Geneva—were long gone, and he hadn't really missed the fish-handling part of it. The first few slithered from his grasp, but finally he was able to lay hands on a slow-moving one and pull it out. He clapped the lid down on the basket and let it splash back down into the water. He was up and scooting quickly along the log before he realized the fish in his hand was not just slow-moving—it was not moving. At all. He hurried across the remaining distance and, without pausing to hear that he had come in a distant second to Asher, he ran down the river and released the fish into the cold crystal water. It floated to the surface and drifted slowly away. Riley shook his head and trudged back up the bank, where Asher stood mournfully, hand over this mouth, watching the dead trout make its funereal way downstream.

"I think it was already dead when I picked it up," he said, somewhat lamely.

Asher clapped his hand consolingly on Riley's shoulder. "You did everything you could," he said, genuineness in his somber expression.

Riley waited as an appropriate moment of silence passed and then said, "Well, let's get to the last event and lock this thing up, huh?"

"Hell yeah," answered Asher, who had apparently worked out the route to the next challenge while Riley fumbled across the log—he shot off into the woods without a moment's hesitation. Riley followed.

The path they took now was steeper than any they had previously traversed. They seemed to be winding their way up a mountainside, crossing back and forth repeatedly, all the while ascending precipitously. They stopped twice on the way to catch their breath and take a drink of water, but knowing that the only thing between them and the finish line was this final challenge spurred them to keep moving. At last they crested the top of whatever it was they were climbing and emerged into sunlight. They jogged across a small patch of open ground and arrived at the spot they'd apparently been bound for: a small group of people standing together near a rock formation.

As they approached one of the people walked toward them, hand extended in greeting. "Gentlemen, congratulations! You are the first team to arrive at their final challenge. You have the added advantage that your final challenge is the one closest to the overall finish line. If you do well here—and I'm sure you will—you have an excellent chance at being the first team across the finish line. That means both of you would have immunity!"

"We're in first place—that's awesome!" said Asher excitedly.

"Of course, I'm still going to be first across that finish line," Riley chimed in. He hoped to throw off any suspicion that they were in cahoots by indulging in a trash-talking swagger line every once in a while. The producer's face beamed in response, so Riley felt validated in his strategy. The fact that he was about to lose hardly dimmed his pride.

"Now let's get to the challenge," the producer said, taking both men by the elbow and leading them over to where the cameras and other crew gathered. "We are standing atop the tallest, most forbidding rock face in the entire national park. It rises almost 400 feet straight up from the valley floor. Climbing it can take an entire day, sometimes two, depending on the difficulty of the particular route. But you won't be climbing it today—you'll be rappelling down it."

They reached the edge of the rock wall, and Riley peered over the precipice. It was a long way down, sure enough, but he was excited at the thought of gliding down toward the rocks at the bottom—it seemed to him far more refined than the other gravity mechanisms he'd experienced today.

It wasn't until he stepped back from the sheer drop that he noticed Asher standing stock-still about ten feet from the edge of the cliff, looking not down but straight ahead, an expression of blank, frozen terror on his face. He was saying something under his breath Riley couldn't make out—he stepped closer to him, and leaned in, and then he could make it out.

"No. No. No. No." Asher's head began to twitch side-to-side in little manic jerks.

"What's up, man?" Riley whispered.

"I can't do it. No. Can't—I just can't. No." Asher stepped farther back from the edge as if retreating from a house fire. "Just... no."

"What... why?" stumbled Riley. "You were fine on the zip line, right?"

Asher shook his head, as if clearing it of the horrors that had filled it. "We weren't dangling over open space. I got through that because the trees were right there, and I could focus on that. That owl just about made me shit myself, but it all happened so fast, and right before the end of the line, so I got through. But this? No way. Can't do it."

"Guys, give us a sec?" Riley asked the crew. They nodded, and he took Asher by the arm and led him away from the cliff's edge. They walked until they reached the woods.

"Okay, so take a deep breath," Riley said, once they were well out of earshot.

Asher heaved several breaths. The exercise did not seem to help him.

"So, tell me what's up," Riley urged, his voice calm.

"Heights. Can't do it. Never could." Asher's voice was dead level.

"And yet, you need to. Just this once. It's perfectly safe—they wouldn't do it if it weren't completely safe."

Asher looked at him intensely. "You're being perfectly rational about this. But there's nothing rational about it. I just can't do it."

Riley huffed in frustration, his cheeks ballooning as he shook his head. He took another deep breath and tried to push ahead gently. "Look, I get that this is going to be hard for you. And that you may need to just close your eyes, grit your teeth, and go to your happy place while you get down the damn rock. But down the damn rock is where we need to get, so let's get going!"

Asher closed his eyes—the life seemed to drain out of him. He paced in a little circle, his hands flopping side to side in random, desperate motions. Suddenly, he stopped. He opened his eyes and again looked Riley straight in the eye. "I can't do it."

Riley stepped forward, closing the gap between them in a single stride. He grabbed Asher by both shoulders, clamping his hands on tight. "You can do this. You *will* do this."

Asher, tears welling in his eyes, shook his head slightly, helplessly.

"This is what you need to do for your sister," Riley said, regretting the words as soon as they left his mouth.

The other man paled and seemed to shrink several inches in height. Tears edged out of the corners of his eyes.

"I'm sorry. That was... um...."

Asher wasn't looking at Riley anymore; his unfocused eyes were gazing at something in the distance, far beyond where they were and what they were doing. His head was shaking slightly, and then it stopped. Riley wasn't sure he was even breathing.

"You're right." Asher's voice was a raspy whisper, but it got stronger as he returned to the here and now from wherever he had gone seeking strength. "Meg's why I'm here, and she's facing something much worse than this." He took a deep breath and then snapped back to full height. "I can do this. I can." He wiped his eyes and turned to look over to the edge of the mountain where the crew awaited them. He nodded and then looked back to Riley. "Thank you," he said, solemnly. "Thank you for reminding me."

"It's all you, buddy. You just needed a nudge."

"That I did," Asher said with a smile, and he bumped Riley with his shoulder before taking off for the challenge at a jog.

Riley was hugely relieved. Without Asher competing—and winning—there was no way they were going to be able to stay in the game this time around. The competition was just too tight. He jogged after Asher, eager to get this done.

The climbing crew spent the next ten minutes swaddling them in safety gear: an even more restrictive harness than he had been encumbered with at the zip line (Riley felt as though he were wearing two jockstraps at once, and both were too small), a suspendery thing with attachment points both for the rope they would use to rappel and for the not one, but two, safety ropes they would be wearing, a helmet and gloves, and special shoes with soft, grippy soles for best purchase on the rock face. Riley felt like he should be hoisted into a tree and used as a piñata.

The safety lecture seemed to take as long as the installation of all the gear, but soon enough (and probably too soon for Asher's comfort), they were standing on the edge of the rock face, ready to step back into nearly four hundred feet of open space. Riley noticed that Asher had not once glanced down to the bottom of the descent; given the jumble of craggy boulders that awaited them, it was probably a good thing. There were two crew members at the top of the rock, connected to the men by a rope that had been fed through a braking device. If they needed to be rescued from the top part of the climb, they could be hoisted up. There were two more sturdy ranger-looking folks at the bottom of the rock, ready to belay the men down should they panic or lose their footing. Riley assured himself that the only way he could come to harm was for all three ropes to fail at once, which statistically was all but impossible.

Still, as he edged toward the precipice, "all but impossible" was not good enough to keep his heart from racing.

"Ready, gentlemen?"

Despite the fact that Riley now wished he could go the rest of his life without ever hearing that phrase again, he nodded, then added for the benefit of the cameras, "Hell yeah! Let's drop!"

"Yeah," Asher added gamely, but Riley could tell he was lockjawed with terror. He wanted to lean over and offer some words of reassurance, but the cameras were tightly focused on them now, and any signal he might try to give would surely be picked up and dissected endlessly by the production staff.

"On belay," the lead climbing crew member called into the walkie-talkie clipped to her shoulder strap.

"Belay on!" came the reply from one and then the other of the crew down at the base of the rock.

"Gentlemen, step back." They followed her command. "Climbing," she called into the walkie-talkie.

"Climb on!" the answer crackled back from the bottom of the cliff.

Riley tugged on the rope he was holding, just to assure himself one more time that it was taut, and then he carefully stepped backward. He was at the edge of the rock, and as he leaned back, he saw hundreds of feet of open space yawning beneath his foot. He swallowed hard and, clamping his eyes shut tightly for a moment, lifted his focus to the edge of the cliff from which he was gradually tipping backward. He planted a foot on the rock's vertical surface, twitched it to be sure it gripped firmly, and then brought his other foot down to join the first. And then he... stopped. He perched less than a yard into his descent, frozen. Then he reminded himself to let some rope through the metal descender at his waist, and he started moving downward again. Two more steps down and he was descending smoothly. Once he had the rhythm of it all, he looked to his left to check on Asher's progress.

Asher was nowhere to be found.

The safety ropes dangled about ten feet from him, but there was no one making use of them. Riley stopped; he was only about twenty feet from the cliff edge but didn't want to go farther until he knew that Asher—who, after all, had to win this thing—was at least on his way.

"Hey, slowpoke! I'm runnin' away with this thing!"

Nothing. No motion at the top of the cliff.

"Come on—just a little, so you can at least watch me win!"

The safety ropes jumped a little next to him, and then he saw Asher fling himself backward out over the edge of the rock. He seemed to fly out about five feet from the wall, and then he released the rope so that he dropped all of the distance in one swoop that Riley had covered in his cautious unspooling of rope.

"Oof." Asher looked over at Riley, panting. "Well, that was about the worst thing ever." He grinned, not entirely convincingly.

"Only three hundred and some odd feet to go!" cheered Riley. Then, he whispered, "You okay?"

"Oh fuck no," Asher replied. Then that grin again. "Let's get this over with."

"Right." Riley pushed back from the rock face and let out some rope. He made slow, bouncing progress down the rock, and he checked to be sure Asher was doing the same. The top part of the rock wall was flat and smooth—hellish for climbing, easy for rappelling. But as the men descended past the first hundred feet, the wall began to roughen. Soon they were having to pick carefully along the face of the rock for good spots to plant their feet, and occasionally they had to creep down the rock one foot at a time. They were about halfway down when Riley stopped for a break, and Asher lowered himself alongside.

"You know, if you can set aside how utterly terrifying this is, the view is pretty amazing," Riley said looking around. They were above the tree line, and the view extended for what seemed like eternity all around them.

"Yeah, can't really set that aside." Asher was facing the rock, not looking anywhere but into a small knot of lichen that had attached itself to a crevice in the rock face.

"Sorry. You're right, we should keep going. Oh, hey—I can see the finish line from here! It's in a meadow at the bottom of the mountain. As soon as we get down, we can run there in, like, a minute!"

"As soon as we get down, I'm going to kiss the ground. Then we can go wherever you want."

"You know what—there's still no one else there. We're the first, buddy! We can win this thing!"

"Awesome," Asher said in an exasperated tone. "Let's get moving, okay?"

"Check." Riley let out some rope, and the two men resumed their descent. They rappelled in quiet concentration for another few minutes, until Asher came upon an overhang of rock directly in his path. He tried to shuffle around it, but it was a good ten feet wide.

"Shit," Asher said, holding on the edge of the outcropping. "What do I do now?"

"Just push off and run your rope out enough to get over it, then back to the wall below it. Easy, right?" Riley knew it wouldn't be easy—in Asher's place he would have been petrified, and he had never had any fears about heights.

"You say so," Asher said grimly and pushed back. He let out a good amount of rope, but it wasn't enough. He swung back in under the overhang and bounced off the rock wall awkwardly. He twisted slightly as he swung back out into open air, and by the time he came back to hit the wall he was facing out. His back hit the rock, knocking the wind out of him, and he gasped as he swung back out, twisting freely now.

"Let out a little more rope! Get past it!" Riley cried.

Asher seemed too panicked to do anything at the moment except hold on desperately to his rope and scrunch his eyes shut. He finally stopped swinging and dangled there, more than a hundred feet up from the boulders that lined the bottom of the rock, motionless.

"Asher?" Riley said, softly. "Asher, you okay?"

Asher opened his eyes warily and shook his head.

"Look, you've just got to let out a little more rope. Get yourself down to a level place on the rock. It flattens out about ten feet below you. You just need to get there."

"No. Can't."

Riley didn't know what to do. He was trying to think of how to coax Asher along when he heard voices. He looked out across the meadow at the bottom of the mountain and saw two other contestants walking toward the finish line. Their posture clearly showed their exhaustion—they had no energy to pick up the pace and get across the line quickly—but they were going to get there first if Riley and Asher didn't get moving.

"We can win this if you get moving now. If we don't move now, we're going to miss first place. So just slide down and win this, and then we'll cross the finish line first and we'll both be safe. Okay? Can you do that?"

"I can't. I just can't. I'm going to pull the cord and have them rescue me. I can't go on." Asher's voice was miserable, hopeless. His hand was on the red pull tab that would activate the emergency call. They would lower him to the bottom of the rock immediately. And he would lose the competition and risk being sent home.

"No! Don't pull it. You can do this! You can!"

Asher just shook his head and slumped miserably in his harness.

Riley was seeing his plan wither in front of him. If they didn't hurry, they would both be vulnerable. If Asher didn't win this challenge, their strategy would be in trouble. What happened in the next thirty seconds could determine their fate in the game. He took a deep breath and tried to make his voice calm and soothing. He imagined talking to Biscuit during a thunderstorm.

"Ash?" he said softly.

Asher startled. He opened his eyes and looked at Riley, eyebrows peaked in a sort of hungry, shocked expression.

"I want you to listen to me," Riley continued, keeping his voice soft and low. "I just want you to listen to my voice. Block out everything else and just hear me, okay?"

Asher nodded.

"I need you, Ash. I need you to look at me, and listen to me, and ignore everything else. You need to come down, and you need to do it now. Can you do that for me, Ash?"

Asher blinked hard. He hesitated, but his head slowly shook side to side. He couldn't. "You go. You'll win this, and then you can cross the finish line and be safe."

Riley stared at the other man for a long moment. His turn to shake his head. "No. I won't leave you here. I won't let you give up."

"I'm holding you back. You go. You deserve to win this. If I get sent home, then I get sent home. I don't want to drag you down with me."

Riley snorted. "I would love to drag you down with me," he muttered.

Then from the ground, still too far away, he heard a shout, followed by more shouts and clapping. The first pair had crossed the finish line.

"I'm sorry," Asher murmured. He turned and looked down at the source of the commotion and jolted at the vivid reminder of how high he was perched above it all. He spun back toward the rock wall, eyes crazed with fear.

"Don't look down!" Riley commanded. "Don't look down. Just look at me, Ash. Look at me!"

Asher turned and fixed his gaze on Riley's face.

"That's right. Look at me. Look in my eyes. I'm right here. You aren't alone, Ash. You're never alone. Just look at me, and let some rope out. We'll slide down slowly. We'll go together. I won't leave you here."

Asher nodded and, keeping his eyes locked on Riley's, he let the rope slip a little and began to drift downward. Riley matched his pace, and they floated down the rock face in perfect synchrony.

They heard another outburst of hooting and clapping. The second team had crossed the finish line. As they inched down the rock, they heard the cries go up two more times.

They would be last.

But they would be together. And that was more important to Riley than he had ever expected it to be. As they reached the bottom of the rock wall, he held back just enough that Asher's foot touched the craggy boulder before his. Asher had won.

The crew swarmed over them, releasing the safety gear and checking to be sure the men were uninjured by the descent. Once that flurry of activity was concluded, they stumbled away down the craggy path toward the meadow.

"I am so sorry," Asher said as they walked toward the finish line.

"No apologies. You did something you never thought you could do. That's amazing. Sure, it was hard, but you got through it. And that's awesome."

"You got me through it."

"Pssh. I just nudged you."

"You did more than that," Asher said, shaking his head. Then, the first hint that his brilliant smile was returning. "All that 'look into my eyes' stuff? Oh, man, that was... well, that was amazing."

"I did what I had to do," Riley said, his tone one that he hoped signaled the end to this line of conversation.

"It did the job, is all I'm saying," Asher said with a wink and a giggle.

The setting sun showered the meadow with brilliant oranges and pinks as they walked up to the finish line. The other pairs had already been escorted to their camps for the evening—only two khaki-clad rangers and some cameras awaited their arrival.

"Whoooo!" Asher called as the crossed the line, his arms raised high.

"And hoooooo!" rejoined Riley, holding his arms up as well. They did an exhausted high-ten and then turned to the rangers.

"Since you are the last to cross the finish line," the ranger said once their moment of ironic victory had passed, "you'll be spending the evening in a special place."

"Oh, shit," exhaled Asher. He seemed to have rather suddenly recalled the accommodations promised to the last-place finishers.

"Yep, back on the rock. They're setting up the hammock now. By the end of this night you two will have solved your rock-climbing issues," said the ranger, who added under his breath, "or died trying." He led them back up the path to the base of the rock wall.

"You should have just cut my rope and let me go splat," Asher said to Riley as they fell in behind the ranger.

"Shush. You've done the hard part. All we have to do tonight is sleep up there. And it's not like they're going to hoist us all the way to the top. We'll probably just be a few feet off the ground. No sweat."

"I hope you are as right in this as you always are," said Asher, his voice tinged with forced brightness.

"Don't worry. We'll get through this."

Asher smiled—genuinely, Riley knew. They were going to be okay.

THEIR DINNER was a spartan affair, served while they stood at the base of the rock whose face they had descended less than a half hour previously. Hissing propane lanterns lit the area, casting a light that was both harsh and insufficient against the rapidly approaching evening. They ate aggressively, as it had been a long day of exertion, soon to be followed by what was sure to be a sleepless night dangling from the face of a rock wall in the wilderness.

The crew began setting up the hammock that was to be their place of rest; there was very little to it, at least that Riley could see. It was made of bright-blue nylon fabric and was laced all around with ropes and grommets and other mysterious bits of hardware. It did not seem capable of holding two grown men.

"Now, normally when climbers bivouac on the ascent, they set for the night and then deploy the hammock and climb in. But since we're just doing this for show"—the ranger rolled his eyes in the manner Riley had come to expect from people who helped manage these stunts—"we'll get you settled in and then hoist you up. We'll use a belay rope to keep you from hitting the rock, and then once you're set, we'll slack that up and you'll end up alongside the rock, snug for the night. Sound good?"

"It sounds like hell, actually," groaned Asher. He grinned—whether because he had been joking or because he was worried he sounded too dismal Riley couldn't tell. But it was no surprise he wasn't thrilled about how they were going to be spending the evening.

"Can you make sure that I get the outside spot?" Riley asked. "My friend here would like to be next to the rock."

Asher smiled at Riley and nodded his thanks.

"Sure, mate," growled the ranger. "Your enjoyment is my number one priority." He stalked off to talk with the crew about the ridiculous ascent they were about to execute.

"You okay?" Riley asked once they were alone.

"I've had better days," Asher replied. "But we're still in the game, and that's the important thing." He looked up at the rock face, a looming darkness above them. "How bad can it be, really?"

As if in answer to this question, the ranger marched back into the glare of the lanterns. "All right, you're going to be stuck up there in pretty tight quarters, and it's going to be a long night. I suggest you answer the call of nature now, whether you need to or not. Once you're up there, you're staying up there until morning."

Riley and Asher exchanged a woeful glance and retreated separately into the woods.

A few minutes later they gathered with the crew at the base of the sheer wall and began the process of settling into their sleeping quarters. Asher stepped first into the hammock, stretching out on one side of the anchor points that attached in the middle. Riley stepped in and began to lie down the same way, when the ranger stopped him.

"Usually climbers sharing a double hammock will lie head to foot. Otherwise it can get rather... intimate." He looked significantly at Riley.

"Thanks for the advice," Riley said, nodding, and then he laid himself down so his head was right next to Asher's blushing face. "But I think this will be fine."

To the men's surprise, the ranger burst out with a creaky rattle of a laugh. "Well," he groaned, "I guess it can get lonely up there." He spat vigorously into the dirt and then grunted to the crew, "Let's get these men to their rest."

The crew buzzed around them, hooking and tying and tightening down carabiners until they were cocooned securely in the long nylon pouch.

"There's a rain fly here," the ranger said, pointing to a roll of nylon fabric at the middle of the hammock, "in case we get sprinkles tonight and you don't want to get your hairdos damp." He erupted into the same creaking, rude laughter as before.

"Thanks. You know how cruel the cameras can be," joked Asher in a starlet's lilting voice. The crew joined in the laughter and then began to hoist. They were a few feet off the ground when another crew member rushed up to the group.

"Almost forgot this!" he called and then clipped a wireless camera to the rigging above them.

Riley hadn't realized how much he had been looking forward to some time without a camera staring at him. But this was the kind of thing that reality television was built on—stressful situations, darkness, the possibility of a fight a hundred feet in the air. Wouldn't want to miss any of that.

The hoisting resumed and seemed to Riley to go on forever. Surely they must be at the top of the rock, he thought, and then the motion stopped. He felt a slight bump as they came to rest alongside the rock, and then all was still.

"Goodnight!" came the ranger's voice from far below, and then all was silent.

Riley and Asher lay still for some time, as if each were waiting for the other to say something, or perhaps to start snoring.

"I don't think I've ever seen so many stars," Riley finally said, breaking the silence. "It's amazing."

"Does that mean I should open my eyes?"

"You haven't opened your eyes? Yes, you should! Just pretend that you're lying on the ground at a campsite. You've got to see this sky."

Asher's sharp intake of breath let Riley know he had seen the sky. They stared up without talking for several minutes.

"Thank you." Asher's voice was no more than a whisper, but in the absence of any other sound, it was clear and distinct to Riley.

"For what?" Riley asked in response. "Surely you've had better accommodations. I've heard you're the kind of guy who stays at the Beverly Palace."

"I don't know who gave you that idea—a gentleman would never tell."

"Your secret's safe with me."

"Seriously, though. You got me through the worst thing ever today, and I really appreciate it."

"We're a team, remember?" Riley said, turning a little toward Asher's voice. The night was so dark that even as his eyes adjusted he could see absolutely nothing except the stars above them.

"It was more than that, and you know it." Asher's voice was low again, urgent.

"Why do you say that?"

"It was what you said to me. You knew the only thing that would make me shake off my fear and get moving again."

"And what was that?"

Asher was silent for a moment; all Riley could hear was his breathing.

"You." Asher's one-word answer hung in the air between them for a long moment. Above them, a meteor shot across the sky. Riley followed it as long as he could see its sparkling trail.

"I'm never going to get to sleep up here," Riley sighed. He didn't know how to respond to Asher's last word, so he did what men do—set it aside and moved on.

"I'll tell you a story," Asher offered. "It'll keep my mind off the fact that I'm hanging a hundred feet above death-by-blunt-trauma."

"You really don't have to—"

"Once upon a time there was a boy named Telemachus. He was the son of Odysseus, but his father had left for the Trojan War so long ago that he really didn't remember him at all. Just about everyone in Ithaca had given up on Odysseus ever returning, but not Telemachus, and not his mother, Penelope. They still hoped he would someday return."

"If you're going to tell me the *Odyssey,* I should mention I've read it before."

"Everyone's read it before, but I'm going to tell you this part of it, so shut up and listen." Asher cleared his throat, and continued. "Telemachus and his mom are holding things together as best they can, but there are a hundred or more suitors who want to marry Penelope and succeed Odysseus as king. She's putting them off any way she knows how, but it's been ten years since the Trojan War ended and Odysseus still isn't home. Meanwhile, the suitors and their entourages are eating and drinking them into poverty. Now, Athena knows that Odysseus is on his way home, and he's going to have to fight the suitors to reclaim his throne, so she wants Telemachus to man up. She decides to send him out into the world on his own to learn of his father's fate."

"Kind of like a reality TV challenge or something, huh?" Riley said, laughing.

"Yeah, just like that," Asher replied, laughing as well. "When I first heard this story, it was in my high school English class. We had this teacher, Mr. Neleus, who loved the classics, and so he read to us every day from Homer. This was my favorite part of the story—I so wanted to be Telemachus."

"So you could hunt down a hundred men with your dad?" Riley asked, deadpan.

Asher huffed in response. "Anyway, Telemachus gets a crew of rowers together and sets off for Pylos, to visit his dad's friend Nestor, who long ago returned from Troy. Nestor greets Telemachus like a prince—the first time he's ever felt like that, since at home he's been treated as an annoying remnant of his father. So there's a feast, and all of Nestor's sons and daughters and the rest of his court gather, and Nestor gives him all kinds of gifts. But then, at the end of the night, when it's time to go to bed, you know where Telemachus gets to sleep? Nestor has this huge palace, and he's the richest man Telemachus has ever met—and he tells Telemachus that he's going to bunk with Nestor's youngest son, Pisistratus."

"They have to share a room? That doesn't seem like how you treat a prince."

"Yeah, that's what I thought. So Telemachus and Pisistratus go upstairs, and they are bathed and anointed by the lovely maidens in the employ of the household and are given fresh robes to sleep in. Then they bring the young men to bed and cover them with furs and sheepskins and turn out the lights. In the morning they harness fresh horses to Telemachus's chariot and he heads off to see the next guy on the list, Menelaus. And Pisistratus goes with him on his journey."

"Well, as someone who was also once a high school boy, I can see the attraction of the whole bathing and anointing thing. That's pretty hot."

Asher chuckled in a manly way; Riley knew it was for the benefit of the camera. He glanced at it instinctively, but as he did so, something landed in his right eye—a raindrop. He noticed that the stars were gone, blotted out by a sudden rainstorm. He reached out and felt around until he found the rain fly. He pulled it up over them and fastened it to the clips he found on the upper end of the hammock, above their heads.

"There," Riley said. "All snug." The camera was on the outside of the rain fly, and the pattering of raindrops would keep its microphone from picking up their words.

Their cocooning was now complete, and Asher seemed to relax immediately. "Thank you," he murmured to Riley.

"You're welcome. Now, I believe you were telling me a story?"

"Right. What always struck me is that among all of the gifts Nestor gave Telemachus, the most precious thing was a friend. Nestor gave him his son to be his companion. That image stayed in my mind forever: Telemachus, made glowing and strong by Athena's power, bathing with Pisistratus, scrubbed clean and fragrant by the maidens, then covered up together with warm, soft blankets and left on their own all night. It was about the sexiest thing I had ever heard in my life. That was my dream—to find a friend who would come to me completely out of the blue, and be my companion, and my partner, and my love. And we would find ourselves swaddled together at night, under the stars, alone in the world but complete in each other."

"It's been a while since I've read the *Odyssey*," Riley said. "But I don't remember Telemachus and Pisistratus being an item."

"Well, they weren't, really—at least in the sense of ending up living happily ever after together. Telemachus makes his rounds of the area, talking with the warriors who had been at Troy, and then Athena makes sure he gets back to Ithaca in time to fight alongside his father when they take on the suitors. I kept hoping for the action-movie ending—you know, where one of the suitors has Telemachus backed up against the wall and is about to run him through with a sword, and suddenly he gasps and falls over, and there's Pisistratus standing behind him with a bloody dagger. And then he'd say something suave like 'We were joined at Pylos, and no man will keep me from you.' And then they'd make out. It's silly, but I was kind of lonely in high school."

"Well, they were Greeks," Riley offered. "That kind of opens the possibility that they were more than friends."

"In a way. But the Greek tradition was for adult men to take lovers who were still in puberty—their delicacy and immaturity was part of their attraction. So the Greeks replicated heterosexuality in a way, because once their lovers reached manhood, they were no longer fit to be lovers. Only love between older and younger was sanctioned. That's what made Telemachus different. He was clearly a man—he's the only one who can string his father's bow, which is symbolic of his passage into manhood. Before I read his story, the very concept of a masculine gay man seemed like an oxymoron. There were certainly no masculine gay characters on TV or in books, at least that I knew of. I grew up thinking that the only way to be gay was to be feminine and swishy, and that's certainly not what I was, so although I had always been attracted to men, it was hard for me to accept that I was actually gay. Telemachus showed me I was not the only masculine gay man in the history of the world."

Riley thought about this for a moment. "I'd never even considered that," he mused. "It's what kept me from taking you seriously when you told me that you're gay. You don't fit the stereotype, which I didn't even know was a stereotype."

"It was a dream that got me through some tough times," Asher continued, "because it was the first time I had ever seen love between men expressed so simply, and so powerfully. I lived in the hope that I would experience that very thing someday. Then I grew up and realized that life isn't just going to hand out miracles like that."

He was quiet again.

"I'm kind of hoping I was wrong." Asher's voice was low.

Riley felt Asher shifting around, and then the heat of the other man's breath was on his cheek.

"Thank you," Asher whispered. "For being my Pisistratus."

The heat on Riley's cheek seemed to burn through him. There was something in the urgency of Asher's voice that twinged in his stomach, and he felt a heat he had never experienced before.

"You're… welcome," Riley whispered. Asher made no response, so he set his native caution aside and continued. "That high school boy who heard that story and dreamed of it coming true—I can't believe that was you."

"Why not?"

"Because you're the eternal optimist. You see the good in everyone, and in every situation, even the fucked-up ones we find ourselves in during this stupid show. I just can't imagine you pining away."

"Do you remember falling in love for the first time?" Asher asked from across the mere inches that separated them in the dark.

"Like, as a kid?"

"Yeah, the very first time. When was it?"

Riley thought for a moment. "Fourth grade." He laughed. "Her name was Lindsey, and I thought she was the most beautiful girl in the world. Blonde hair, these big blue eyes, all of it. Man, I was stupid for her that whole year."

"Did you tell her?"

Riley chuckled. "Oh, man, I sure did. Every way I could think of. I sent her notes, I drew pictures of her, and then when she ignored me, I followed her around the playground being a general pest. You know how kids are—I threw dirt clods at her just to get her to notice me."

"Sounds like you were a real charmer." Asher laughed along with Riley. "So you fell madly in love, and you wanted to be sure she knew it, right?"

"Oh yeah. I was the Casanova of my fourth grade class, I was."

"And how did she respond?"

"She basically ignored me. One time, when I caught her alone at the end of recess, she actually talked to me like I was a human being, but aside from that she didn't seem to care that I even existed. But I was still stuck on her. Fourth grade boys can be stubborn."

"My first crush was in sixth grade."

"Late bloomer, huh?" Riley joshed good-naturedly.

"You could say that. I did all the things you did—playground stalking, cryptic notes, all of it—but at the end of the year I got up my nerve and made a move. Spilled my guts during the end-of-the-year camping trip."

"I'm sure you did better than I did."

"I wouldn't say that. I poured out my heart, just let it all go. By the end I was a mess—I was so scared. But I did it."

"What happened?"

"He punched me. Right in the face. And then before I could get myself up off the ground, he started kicking me. Must have hauled back and slammed his hiking boot into my guts a dozen times. I think I blacked out, because the next thing I remember is him spitting on me. Then he ran off so he could tell everyone in the class what happened. What *I* had done to *him*."

"Oh, fuck." Riley felt heat rising into his cheeks, as if he were the one to have suffered Asher's humiliation. "That's... that's just awful. No one should.... Oh, man, I'm so sorry."

"Just part of growing up. Well, part of growing up gay. This is the part that a lot of people don't get. When you're young and figuring out how love works, you do stupid things. And generally, you get ignored, or embarrassed, or just left twisting in the wind. But when you're young and gay, you can get beaten—or worse. After that day I figured I was going to be alone. I sure wasn't going to tell anyone ever again that I had feelings for them." He sighed and sniffed. Riley felt him move, as if he were wiping his eyes.

"So when you heard this story in high school...."

"I suddenly knew what I wanted—what I needed. Until that moment it had seemed like a freakish thing, like something that made me different, less of a person. You grow up never seeing any people like you on TV, or in movies, and you start to think that you're destined to live a life of loneliness. And then something comes along and shows you that friends can turn into more than friends just by opening themselves to it. That story kept me going when I was lonely because it allowed me to hope for something more. It seemed like the impossible dream. It was so easy for Telemachus: he was alone in the world, so a friend came to him, and they just climbed into bed. God, I cried myself to sleep every fucking night with those guys in my head. They got me through, but I've not exactly been lucky at love since then. I try hard not to give up hope that someday, maybe, I'll find—"

Riley interrupted him. With a kiss.

The last time their lips had met Riley had recoiled; this time he was insistent. Asher gasped, but Riley didn't release him and instead pressed their lips together ever more forcefully. He hadn't planned this, hadn't known he was going to do it until he was already doing it. He had never in his life kissed another man—though he had been kissed by Asher, he didn't count that because it had come as a surprise and ended so badly—but now it seemed like the most natural, and most important, thing he had ever done. He kissed Asher with a gentle intensity that was nothing like any kiss he had ever experienced. It was like his body knew how to do this thing he had never intended to do.

After a minute or more of slippery friction between their mouths, Riley finally released Asher from his grip.

Asher exhaled in shock. "What the...?"

"Hang on, let me—" Riley stumbled, trying to wrangle the words he needed to describe something he had never tried to say before. "Look, back at the hotel I freaked out because I didn't know what else to do. But now I... well, I just want you to know that you deserve better than life has seen fit to give you. You are an amazing person—an amazing man—and it just kills me that someone hasn't snapped you up. I know you will find someone who sees you the way I do. I have to believe that. But in the meantime, I want you to know that I see all the amazing things you are, and I just...." Words failed Riley again, and so he did the only thing he could think of to do: he kissed Asher again, holding nothing back.

"Back at the hotel," Riley said, once he had pulled back from their kiss, "you didn't deserve that. I freaked out, and I'm sorry. I shouldn't have pushed you away the way I did. I hope you can forgive me."

Asher was silent, breathing heavily in the darkness next to Riley. Finally, he said "Keep doing that and I'll forgive anything."

Riley laughed. "Look, I don't want to give you the wrong idea. I'm pretty pissed at the universe, because there's something deeply wrong with it if a guy like you is alone. This is the only way I could think of to show you how much... well, how much you mean to me, and how great I think you are. You deserve a great guy to stand up at the altar and make you an honest man—and I know you'll find him."

"I was kind of hoping I had."

"Pssh. Like you'd want me, with all my baggage. Heh." Riley was silent for a long moment. "Look, we should get some rest. Who knows what the hell they're going to have us doing tomorrow."

"Whatever it is, it can't be more disorienting than what we've just been doing," Asher replied, a rueful chuckle under his voice.

"You're telling me," Riley answered. The part of his brain responsible for sorting out emotional chaos was offline, and he did not relish the idea of processing the mess of conflicting feelings that were washing over him at the moment. So he simply rolled over as gently as he could and within a few minutes felt himself start to drift away.

RILEY WAS on a sailboat, rocking gently in the water, back and forth. He wondered how he had gotten here, when the last thing he remembered was something about a rock, and ropes, and—

A kiss.

Oh.

His eyes sprang open, and the world was blue—the rain fly still covered them, the two of them, as they swung lazily from side to side in their nylon cocoon. When he remembered where they were, dangling a hundred feet over a craggy nest of boulders, a surge of panic welled up in his chest, making the next two breaths exquisitely difficult to take.

But then he looked to the side and saw Asher's placid face, still wearing the peace of slumber. Riley smiled—an instinctive response to seeing his friend so innocently at rest. A hint of a smile played on the sleeping man's face.

And then Riley remembered what he himself might have done to cause that contented, sleepy grin.

He hadn't dreamed the kiss—it wasn't on the sailboat, it was here, here on the rock—and the panic again surged in his chest. He tried to keep his breathing calm, because the last thing he wanted was for Asher to wake up, for them to have to say anything about what happened last night.

"Oy up there! You sleepyheads ready to come down from the clouds?" The ropes holding the hammock pulled and swung again, this time a little more strongly.

The ranger's rude shout awakened Asher, and his eyes slowly blinked open. If Riley had come to consciousness in a haze of confusion, Asher's expression was one of instant, calm clarity. His grin, which had formed in his sleep, widened into a smile of such genuine joy that Riley couldn't help but mirror it back.

"Morning," Asher said, his voice low and—not sleepy, but rather luxuriant. It was the voice of someone who's spent the week at a spa and now was able to face the world refreshed and unreservedly happy.

"Morning." His voice surprised him; some unbidden instinct inside Riley made it match Asher's in pitch and timbre, like a tuning fork picking up a sympathetic vibration from another.

They looked at each other for a long moment, the blue cast of the morning light through the rain fly giving their intimate scene an otherworldly glow.

"We'd better answer him," Asher said, his smile still shining. "Who knows what they'll think is going on up here."

Riley paused for a second, debating whether he should ask what actually was going on up here, but he thought better of it. He reached up, unzipped the rain fly, and pulled it open. The bluish privacy of their snug lair gave way to the golden brilliance of the morning sky. Fresh air and bright light flooded over them and brought Riley back to his senses, such as they were. He looked again at Asher, trying to figure out what they had done, what needed to be said between them—to himself—to explain it. He shook his head, deciding he would think those thoughts later.

"Ready!" Riley called down to the crew at the base of the rock. Instantly the hammock began its descent, smoothly bringing the men back to the ground. Riley smiled at Asher, but it felt different now, forced. Something had happened to them up there, but now that they were nearing the reality of the ground, he wasn't at all sure what it was, nor whether he would ever feel it again.

With a bump they jostled to a halt a few feet off the ground and then gently slipped the rest of the way to the cushion that had been laid for them. Riley sprang up as soon as he felt his back come to rest on the pad, and he stepped out of the hammock with the look of a man who had never been so glad to have his feet on the ground. He turned back to Asher and extended a hand—the other man took it despite not needing it (he was, Riley reminded himself, a gymnast) and they stood there for a moment with their hands clasped.

"Right. Looks like you two are still friends. I guess we'll call this the Brokeback Ascent from now on," the grizzled ranger growled before erupting with a torrent of rasping laughter. Once his humor had exhausted itself, he continued. "They want you back at the starting line. Hurry along now while we hose out your love nest." He burst out a derisive chortle and pointed them away into the woods.

Asher led the way, as he had before. They didn't rush this time as they were no longer competing. What they would find at the end of this final trudge through the wilderness would determine whether they would continue in the game. Asher was probably safe, but Riley certainly was not. Once they were out of sight of the rock wall, Asher slowed and stepped to the side of the trail and then fell into step next to Riley.

"We need to talk," Riley said, looking at the trail ahead rather than at Asher.

Asher walked several more paces. "Do we? Really?" His tone wasn't snippy—he sounded as though he'd simply rather not, thanks very much.

"Um, yes, I think we do," answered Riley. "What happened up there was kind of—"

"Nice," Asher interrupted. "What happened up there was kind of nice. Can we just leave it there and carry on with our lives?"

Riley looked at him, studying his face for signs that he wasn't actually suggesting they not talk about what happened between them. "Are you serious?"

Asher stopped walking. He stood in the path, arms dropped to his sides. "Yes, I am serious. You don't need to explain anything to me."

"But I…."

"You kissed me. Twice. Yes, you did. And it was amazing. And then we went to sleep. And now we're exactly where we were before. You're still planning to win this thing, right?" He looked at Riley with his eyebrows up. "Did I miss anything?"

"Uh… no, I guess not…." stumbled Riley. There was so much in his head trying to force its way out his mouth that he couldn't find where to begin.

"Great. Done. Let's move." Asher's smile was stretched a bit tight as he said this. He lunged forward and strode purposefully down the path.

Riley followed because he didn't know what else to do.

They were the last to arrive at the starting line, just as they had been last at the finish line the night before. The competition winner was announced (the leader of the pair that finished first) and those who were in danger of being voted off were given a chance to record their own assessment of their performance for the episode that would air tonight. The viewers would vote on who should be sent home, and on Sunday they would broadcast the dismissal live.

The bus ride home was fairly dismal. With only ten bachelors still in the competition, the bus was less than half-full, and the men spread out on rows of seats. Riley boarded before Asher and chose a row that had several open rows around it. Asher, however, simply nodded at him and continued down the aisle, plopping down in a row toward the back of the bus. As the bus pulled out of the park and onto the highway, Riley mulled over what had happened between himself and Asher, and why he was feeling so… lonely? Was that the tug he felt in his chest? He watched the treetops glide by the window as he pondered, tried to make sense of it all. The ride back to the house was several hours long, and he was wrapped in restless slumber before the first ten minutes had passed.

"ALL RIGHT, all of you who doubted can now bow down before me and beg forgiveness," Kaitlyn announced as she finished reviewing the tapes of Riley and Asher in the woods. She had carefully watched the two men interact through all five challenges and had paid special attention to the footage recorded by the camera attached to the hammock rigging.

Omar answered her. "Kaitlyn, we're the only ones here. Again."

"Well then, you may bow down before me."

"How about I just agree not to file a grievance with the Department of Labor about the working conditions here and we call it even?"

She looked at him sternly, then burst out laughing. "Okay, we have a deal. But how about our boys on the mountain, huh?"

Omar squinted at her critically. "I guess I'm not sure what we're looking for. They didn't exactly fall into each other's arms."

"No, but they are getting closer. And some of that stuff they said to each other? 'Look into my eyes, listen to my voice, do it for me?' Come on, you gotta admit…."

"Yes, I will admit that they did share some intense moments. I guess we're just lucky that they drew each other in the drawing for pairs, right?"

"Lucky?"

"Yeah, lucky. They drew each other's tokens out of the bag. Almost like you planned it that way."

Kaitlyn stared at him and shook her head slowly.

"Wait," he said, "are you telling me that you rigged that?"

Kaitlyn smiled slyly and nodded.

"How? It looked completely legit."

"You did notice that the lovely young lady holding the velvet bag was new?"

"Yes, I did. She was gorgeous. I meant to ask you about her—what happened to Kendra? She usually does that kind of thing, and she hasn't missed a single challenge before this one."

"She had a little accident," Kaitlyn replied. "Twisted her ankle rather badly when she tripped down some stairs a couple of days ago."

Omar's mouth dropped open in horror. "You didn't!"

"No, of course not. It was just great timing. I was going to send her off to do a promo or something, but with the sprain I didn't have to. Then it was a simple matter of hiring a replacement. I happened to find one working nearby. In Vegas. For a magician."

Omar nodded. "Brilliant. As usual."

"She was able to ensure our love-struck bachelors drew each other from the velvet bag and make it look completely random."

Omar stopped nodding. "But you could have accomplished the same thing by simply pairing them up and saying that it was done randomly. We do things like that all the time."

"Yes, but we wanted them to believe that they had been paired up randomly. That way we keep them from being suspicious about why they keep ending up together."

"The people who call you an evil genius are absolutely right," Omar said admiringly.

"Give me names," Kaitlyn replied and then burst into villainous laughter.

"So, what's next for our two maybe-in-love bachelors?" Omar asked when they had stopped chortling over Kaitlyn's evil ways.

"They have a little downtime while the voting takes place and we prepare to send someone home. Let's just leave them to their own devices, and see what happens."

THE PUNISHING competition in the woods, followed by a restless night suspended in the air, capped off by a squirming nap on a bus seat, had left Riley's body feeling as though he'd been pushed down a flight of stairs. As soon as the bus arrived back at the house he showered, donned his swim trunks, and headed out to the hot tub. It had been cranked up to a nearly unbearably high temperature, which was exactly what he wanted—what his body needed.

He stretched out along one side of the tub and settled down into the water until the jets were hammering on the precise spot where the tension of the last two days had lodged in his spine. He looked skyward into the twilight, through the swirling clouds of steam and tried to sort out all of the things he was feeling. He didn't get very far—there were things in his head he didn't understand, in his heart he didn't recognize.

"This seat taken?"

It was Asher. Of course it was.

"Come on in. The water's blistering."

"Perfect," Asher replied as he lowered himself into the tub. He leaned back against the edge and closed his eyes.

Riley watched him through the mist between them, trying to see how he remained so calm after what had happened on the mountain. That kiss—those kisses, he reminded himself—had thrown Riley's entire being out of whack, but they didn't seem to have affected Asher in the slightest. Riley couldn't figure that out.

Riley wanted to talk with Asher about whatever this was between them, but he remembered their first serious conversation in the sauna and slid over to the other side of the hot tub first. Asher's eyes popped open as Riley settled in next to him, and his usual warm smile appeared as he closed his eyes again.

Riley took a deep breath and brought his lips to Asher's ear. "Hey," he murmured.

"Hey yourself," Asher said jovially. He opened his eyes and cast Riley a sideward glance.

Riley leaned in and spoke directly into the other man's ear again. "We need to talk."

Asher sighed, but his smile stayed in place. "All right. But you don't have to whisper out here—I've overheard the crew talking about the mics out here not being able to pick up anything when the jets are running. As long as we keep our voices down we should be fine."

Riley nodded and pulled back a bit from his perch right at Asher's ear. It was only then that the enormity of what he felt compelled to say hit him, and he struggled to find the words he needed.

"I'm listening," Asher prompted. If they had to have a conversation, he was at least being a good sport about it.

"In the hammock, last night...." Riley began, slowly, carefully. "I just want you to know... that I... um—"

"Stop," Asher interrupted, as if he wanted to put Riley out of his misery of stumbling and grasping. "I know what you're going to say. Or, rather, I know two things that you might say, but we both know which one you're trying to say. Option one is that you suddenly realized on the mountain after all of these years of loving women that you are gay, and in love with me, and we should run off together and leave this all behind. Spoiler alert—that's not what you're trying to say. Option two is that you got caught up in the exhaustion and emotion of the moment and did something crazy you would now very much like to have us both ignore completely. Which, I will once again point out, I've been perfectly willing to do, and in fact desperately trying to do, but you have thus far ignored my efforts. So, to sum up, we agree that what happened up there was a result of altitude sickness, or whatever, and it thus never actually happened." He smiled at Riley despite the desolate words he spoke. "So, are we good?"

"No." It was the most definite word Riley had spoken since the outdoors challenge ended, and he spoke it with a force that made Asher sit back against the edge of the hot tub.

"What?" Asher asked.

"No, I don't want to ignore what happened. I want to talk about it—I need to talk about it. With you. Because otherwise I'm going to drive myself crazy with it."

Asher again sighed, and shrugged, and finally nodded, while his expression was unchanged—the smile remained, and from it Riley drew his strength.

"Okay, so... first... yeah, it was a tough day, and I was pretty wiped out, but that isn't why I did it."

Asher's eyebrows lifted. "Oh?"

Riley shook his head while he tried to string together the next sentence. "I did it because... because I couldn't think of any other way to tell you... to show you—" He paused to catch his breath. "You've been through things that I can't imagine, and yet you manage to live every day as if it were a gift. I wish I were like you—hell, I wish I were you! And when you talked about Telemachus and how his story gave you hope that you would find a friend like that someday... I just wanted you to know that you have a friend, and he thinks you're amazing."

Asher's eyes widened, and his expression reflected Riley's overwhelming flattery.

"Wait. I needed to tell you that, but I need to tell you something more. I'm not ashamed of what I did, but I also don't want to give you the wrong idea. I—"

Asher silenced him by lifting a hand out of the water and holding it up between them. "I know. You're not gay. You let your emotions run away with you, but it doesn't mean to you what it means to me, and you want to let me down easy." He looked at Riley, as if he were gauging his reaction. "Would it break your heart if I told you that this isn't the first time I've heard that?"

Riley shook his head in confusion, not answer.

"A surprising number of straight men will, given half a bottle of tequila and half a chance, make a pass at a gay friend. It may be when they are really sad, or really happy, or just really too damn drunk, but later, once the dust settles, they have to find a way to break it to me that it didn't mean what they apparently think I thought it meant. Right. Put yourself in my place. A guy who's never shown any sign of being gay suddenly has his tongue down your throat. Does he really have to tell you once he sobers up that he didn't actually mean it? Yeah, thanks, I never would have figured that one out for myself." He stopped, took a breath, and when he resumed the subtle sarcasm that had crept into his voice was gone. "Look, it's fine that you're straight—most people are—but I just want you to consider that while you have your reasons for wanting me to understand that the kiss meant nothing, I might have my own reasons for wanting it to be forgotten."

Riley stared at Asher, his mouth hanging open. He had no idea what any of that meant, and he shrugged helplessly.

"Okay," Asher resumed, sidestepping Riley's complete befuddlement. "It's like this. You kissed me, and you want me to know things cannot develop between us, because you are just not that way. Fine. I get it. What I want you to know is that I was already very clear that things cannot develop between us. I thought we had established that at the hotel. I'll admit you surprised me last night, but two kisses on the side of a mountain can't change who we are, or what we are to each other. They didn't give me false hope, or start me planning a wedding." He reached out and put his hand on Riley's shoulder. "I am proud to call myself your friend, Riley. And I know that friends are what we will be to each other, forever, and that's fine with me. Okay?"

Riley took in a breath as if to say something, but he quickly realized two things: first, he had no idea what to say; second, he wasn't sure he could say anything without crying. What the hell was that about? He should be relieved Asher was handling this so well, but he couldn't deny that somewhere in him there was a small voice expressing its doubts about the whole thing. But that didn't make any sense, and so Riley nodded, and put his hand on Asher's and patted it a couple of times.

"Thanks," Riley said, but his voice, like the one in the back of his head, seemed small and uncertain.

Asher's face softened, as if he too had heard the underlying tone of reservation.

"Look, I...." Riley fumbled, desperately searching for the words that could express emotions that had no names.

"Riley. It's fine. Let's just let it go, okay?" Asher's smile returned, though now Riley had seen the more complex expression that hid behind it. "Whew, it really is hot in here. I'm going to go rinse off and get something to eat. I'll... see you... tomorrow."

He got up and strode, with water running off him and steam rising from him, into the house without looking back.

Riley flopped back against the edge of the hot tub and rubbed his eyes. What the fuck was going on inside him? He looked up into the sky, but the stars that had guided him last night were obliterated by the lights of the city, and they had no answers for him now. All he knew, the only thing that was clear to him, was that he felt better—felt himself to be truly himself—only when Asher was with him. He tried to understand this simple fact, to break it down and see what it was made of, but he could make no headway on it. He knew what falling in love felt like, or at least he thought he did, and this wasn't like that. It was more of a feeling that there was something inside him that only fully existed when it found resonance in another person. It needed the harmony of that other person nearby in order to come fully to life.

And that person was Asher.

Once he said this to himself, once he made it real in that way, two things happened. First, he felt a weight lift off of him, as if he'd been strangling under the load of not acknowledging this obvious reality. Second, a complementary rational faculty swung into motion and began to spit out a storm of counterarguments. The stress of being on the show, of being on display, of constantly competing. The devastation of being left at the altar, of never finding the right woman, of being alone every single night. The vast horizon of his loneliness yawned wide around him, and of course the first person who comes along who is sympathetic, who is compassionate, who seems to care about him—of course that person becomes his lifeline, his beacon in the darkness. Nothing gay about it.

These two forces battled inside Riley until he could take it no longer. He shook them out of his head and got up from the steaming tub and went inside. Perhaps a cold shower would help him think through it. Even as he thought this, he knew it wouldn't work. But he had nothing else to try.

CHAPTER TWELVE
SAINT ERASMUS

"OH MY God oh my God oh my God!" Kaitlyn chanted as she watched the camera feed from the hot tub deck. "This is awesome!"

"He looks miserable," rejoined Omar, watching the slumping figure of Riley walk into the house.

"Of course he's miserable. Denial is an ugly thing. He's fighting against it, but it means going against everything he's ever been taught, or thought about himself. But he's getting there!"

"He may be, but you heard Asher: he was letting him down easy. I think you have to face up to the fact that Asher just isn't into him."

"Really." She looked at him critically. "That's what you got out of that conversation?"

"Yes, especially when he said he just wanted them to be friends. What I got from that is he just wants them to be friends."

Kaitlyn just shook her head at her poor, benighted assistant. "Omar, I feel sorry for you."

"And why would that be, exactly?"

"Because you don't seem to have a romantic bone in your body."

"You keep talking about romance. What I see is two guys who can't seem to find their way to doing more than stress kissing and then freaking out about it."

"Or, looked at another way, we're talking about two guys who keep kissing each other, despite their repeated insistence that they are just friends and they're both fine with that. They're *not* both fine with that, in case you hadn't noticed. Asher looked miserable when he explained that he's perfectly happy to be good, platonic friends, and Riley just about withered away completely when Asher got up from the hot tub. They are so close!" She looked at Omar, a fire in her eyes. "You know what we have to do."

"Leave them to figure it out for themselves, like sane people would?" Omar's voice clearly telegraphed that he had absolutely no confidence this would be their course of action.

"Oh, you crack me up with your talk about sanity. Good one! No, what we're going to do is pull out all the stops and give them one last chance at romance." She looked brightly at him, willing him to get caught up in her enthusiasm.

He shook his head slowly but smiled and shrugged. His loyalty had never yet faltered. "What's the plan?"

"It's fucking brilliant, which I'm sure you will agree once you hear it. Now, we can't just keep throwing them together. They're going to get suspicious, and the show can't take that kind of repetition. But until the results show, the bachelors basically have free time. So how about we send them out into the real world and see what develops?"

"Didn't we try that? Not that the Beverly Palace is the real world, but—"

"No, the real real world. Here's what I'm thinking…."

As she described her plan, Omar's expression changed from one of confusion to surprise to admiration. He nodded as if he actually thought it might work.

"SO, WAIT. You're sending us out of the house? Why?" the bachelor with the expensive shoes that Riley had always thought of as The Banker—even after he had learned the man's name—asked the producer.

"It's for publicity, pure and simple. We want you to be seen around the city doing normal things: getting coffee, seeing a movie, walking in a park, that kind of thing. We'll drop hints that you're out on the town today, and people will, we hope, recognize you from the show."

"So anyone we randomly run into will see us. Who cares? We're talking about a dozen people, maybe two, total. Are the ratings really that bad?"

The producer sighed. "Think about it this way. How many people carry a camera around with them everywhere they go?"

"Just about all of them," answered Shane.

"Exactly. We'll get BachelorX to seed the cloud by tweeting some hints about your locations, but we're relying on the crowd to make this happen. Just be visible, and when someone comes up to you with a camera, be friendly and do what they want. Remember, these are the people who are voting as we speak on whether you stay on the show. There's no such thing as bad publicity, so get out there and get as much as you can. Just don't embarrass yourselves, or us. Questions?"

The ten remaining bachelors were silent. The Banker was trying to adopt an expression of "I knew that all along," while Shane had gone back to chugging his disturbingly green breakfast smoothie.

"Excellent. We'll be loading up into the van in an hour, and we'll drop you around town. You'll roam, be photogenic, work the crowd. You'll carry these," he said as he handed out tiny transponders—the kind used to locate skiers after avalanches. "We'll be tracking your location, and we'll come by and grab you midafternoon so we can get back here for the live show. If anything happens and you need help, just press the red button on the transponder. Got it?"

They nodded and headed off to get ready for their crowdsourced PR tour.

An hour later they were loading into the van. With the decreased number of bachelors, the belching diesel behemoth that had been their ride previously had been replaced by a sleek airport-shuttle-style Mercedes with deeply tinted windows. As they descended the hill from the house, the producer gave them some additional information.

"Because we want everyone to be safe, we're going to drop you off in groups. Try to stick together, okay? People will be much more likely to recognize you if they see more than one bachelor in the wild."

They rode the rest of the way into the city in silence.

"Where are you going to drop us?" one of them asked.

"Up to you, chief. Where do you want to go? You should pick something fun—maybe something that you haven't had a chance to do for a while because you've been, you know, on a TV show." They were stopped at a red light on the edge of downtown.

"How about right here?" Asher suddenly piped up, standing and pointing out the window. There was a soup kitchen on the opposite corner: a line composed of men, women, and a dispiriting number of children snaked out the door and down the block. This was one crowd for whom Sunday brunch was a decidedly downscale affair.

The other bachelors were aghast. Clearly not one of them wanted to be caught by a citizen camera ladling out soup to homeless people. The producer, perhaps wondering how many homeless people would have Twitter accounts, shook his head skeptically.

"If publicity is what you want, I think this one's a winner." Riley stood to join Asher. He had to admit to himself that he would pretty much follow Asher anywhere. What this meant, he would think about later.

Asher beamed and nodded his thanks for Riley's support.

The producer shrugged. "All right, you win. This is not a great part of town, so take care of yourselves, and keep the panic button handy." He nodded to the driver, who pulled over and opened the door.

They stepped out the van's side door, and took advantage of a break in traffic to jog across the street. The van pulled away, leaving them to make their way in one of the rougher parts of the city.

As they approached the door of the soup kitchen, Riley pondered how they would go about making themselves useful. The long line meant they couldn't easily make their way inside.

"We can't just barge in and announce 'We're bachelors and we're here to help,' can we?" Riley asked.

"Hang on," Asher replied, reading a notice posted in the dirty window of the establishment. "Says here that volunteers are always welcome. We're supposed to go around to the back of the building, to the door marked 'St. Erasmus.'" He turned to Riley. "Easy, right?"

Riley nodded, though things with Asher rarely turned out to be uncomplicated.

They walked down the side of the building, turning into an alley when they reached the back. There were three rusty, graffiti-besmirched doors set into the blank back wall of the building, and the middle one wore a crooked sign above it that read "St. Erasmus." They approached that door, and Asher knocked.

No one answered.

Asher knocked again, this time more loudly. Riley heard the shuffle and scrape of someone approaching, and then the door swung suddenly open with a tremendous creak. The woman who had shoved the door so energetically stood on the threshold; she was barely five feet of ebony-skinned, white-haired gumption, her nun's habit scarcely able to contain the energy that practically vibrated from her entire person.

"Well?" she demanded. She had clearly missed her calling as a drill sergeant, which had probably not been a career option in whatever distant decade she had come of age.

"We're here to help," Asher said, sounding both meek and capable at the same time.

A smile burst forth from the nun's lips. "God will provide," she said with a glance to the sky. "We are so short-handed today, I had me a little chat with the man upstairs not ten minutes ago. 'Lord,' I said, 'you want these people fed you better send me some backup 'cause I can't make with no loaves and fishes like your son done.' And here you are. You ever been the answer to anyone's prayers before?" She jabbed a calloused finger at Asher. "Because you is today. Come on in here, and bring your friend. He gotta answer some prayers too. Amen and amen!" She turned on her orthopedic heel and rocketed away into the building.

They followed, winding their way through a maze of shelves, storerooms, and piles of flour sacks and produce bins, all presided over by faded posters recommending hope and serenity and regular dental hygiene. The kitchen itself was full of massive pots of bubbling liquid, tended to by a whippet-thin, heavily tattooed man in his midtwenties who was in constant motion, stirring and pouring among the pots while simultaneously pulling trays of bread out of the huge wall oven that loomed through a mirage of superheated air on the far side of the kitchen.

The nun pointed out a pile of aprons and a box of disposable gloves, and they put them on. Then she charged through the kitchen and out to the larger room at the front of the building. It was typical of the kind of diner that once lined the streets of every American city, back in the '30s and '40s when downtown was the center of life. Riley had seen the old photos on the walls of Chicago restaurants: there would have been bright-red stools at the counter, a soda machine under the window through which food would be passed from the kitchen, and a sassy waitress in a bright white apron who probably called everyone "Hon." But now it was a dark, tattered box of a room, with gray light filtering through the windows that faced the grimy street, and far more tables crammed in than the fire marshal would ever have allowed, assuming he cared about such a place. It was clear no one did.

The nun approached the two people who were working behind the counter and laid her hand on their shoulders—this required quite a stretch on her part. She spoke into their ears when they leaned down to her, and both seemed to sag with relief when she nodded in the direction of Asher and Riley, who stood in the doorway from the kitchen. The young woman who had been serving soup laid down her ladle, and the older woman with the bread knife set it down on the counter. They smiled at the men and then slid past them into the kitchen.

"Now," said the nun, pulling herself up to her full five feet and beckoning Riley and Asher over to where she stood. "Each person gets a ladle of soup and two slices of bread. And a kind word, that's the most important part. We feed the body and the soul here." She nodded firmly, as if she were able to tell without even asking that the men were ready to take over. She walked back toward the kitchen. "Tell Mr. Gomez here when you need more soup or bread. And thank you, gentlemen. Thank you." She dashed away—her only speed seemed to be a righteous scurry.

For the first time Riley looked around at the bleak and hungry faces in the room. The tables were full, even though those who sat at them were rushing through their meals so quickly they hardly seemed to be swallowing. Riley recalled how far the line stretched down the block and how all of those people somehow had to squeeze into this room and be fed. He felt very small indeed in that moment.

Asher grabbed up the ladle and began to scoop up soup. He filled the first bowl and handed it across the counter to the first person in line, a man in his sixties who wore a camouflage jacket of the Vietnam era. He then held out the bowl to Riley, who set two slices of bread atop it. "Thank you," he said softly and began to shuffle away slowly.

"It's an honor, sir," Riley said, remembering the nun's instructions. The man stopped and looked at Riley, his face devoid of expression. But then he nodded with an unmistakable dignity, and he drew up a little taller before turning to find an empty seat.

Riley took a deep breath and began to slice bread as quickly as he could.

The line advanced on them for two full hours, until finally the soup, the bread, and, luckily, the line itself, all seemed to exhaust themselves at the same time. Asher scraped the bottom of the last pot of soup to give the young girl in front of him, the last to be fed today, a little extra. Her face was radiant as she looked up at him, and for a moment, Riley saw Asher through her eyes: a tall, handsome man who was smiling warmly down at her. Riley gave her three pieces of bread, hoping this second kindness would make today one of the best in her short memory.

"Thank you, thank you, and thank the Lord," the nun said cheerily as she approached the counter. "Now"—she settled her bony elbows on the counter—"why you here?" She burst out laughing. "Oh, I know why you here—the Lord put it in your heart to be here—but where y'all from, and where y'all goin'?"

Asher blushed. "We just set out today to do some good. Thank you so much for giving us the chance."

The nun held up her hands and shook her head. "The Lord brought you here. I just opened the door because that's what God wants us to do. Closed doors ain't never the way to help people." She laughed and shook her head. "We'd be pleased to have you back anytime you want to 'do some good.' We don't get so many volunteers down here. Not with the gangs so strong these days. People just don't want to come help ol' Saint E no more!"

Riley looked around the room. He doubted any one of the hundreds of people they had served today had a camera, much less a smartphone with a Twitter app. And that was just fine with him. He looked at Asher, his face animated with excitement as he walked around the room, cleaning up and talking with the nun about her work to try to keep "Saint E" open. He really felt as though he was the best person he could be when he was with Asher. It would never have occurred to him to simply walk into a soup kitchen and start ladling, but it had to Asher, and he answered prayers while doing it. He watched as the nun and Asher saw the last people out the exit door and locked it behind them. Riley shook his head in wonder, all the while debating whether his growing admiration for Asher was developing into something more—what that might be he hadn't let himself consider, but now it was a feeling too strong to ignore.

He might have actually made some headway on sorting out his feelings had he not been interrupted by the sound of gunfire. Not just the sound of gunfire, he quickly realized, but actual gunfire. The popping sound from outside the building was synchronized almost perfectly with holes blossoming in the paneled wall of the soup kitchen. Riley stood and watched the line of holes work across the wall toward where he stood.

"Get down!" roared the nun, her voice suddenly twice as deep and three times as loud as it had been before. She launched herself at Riley, tackled him around the middle, and threw him to the ground. Asher followed closely behind, and the three of them huddled behind the counter while the shooting continued. Then, suddenly, it stopped.

"It's them," the cook said under his breath as he peered out the crack in the kitchen window. The nun nodded in response.

"We been expecting a visit from them," she said to the men sprawled out on the floor behind the counter. "They're mad that we serve everyone who comes in. They only want us helpin' people they got under their 'protection.' I won't do it, because I serve a man greater than anyone out there with a gun." She sat up, straightened her habit, and got to her feet. "Now, I know how to deal with these boys—they're just boys, no matter what they say or how many guns they have—but I want you two to follow Mr. Gomez into the storeroom. Better they just have the two of us to deal with."

"We won't leave you here," Asher began, but she held up her hand so decisively that he fell silent.

"No arguments. I've dealt with them before. They scared of me because I remind them of their grannies. Ain't nobody going to hurt their granny. Now, you, you look like you got money, and we don't need them to get botherin' with you and doin' something that will get them in even more trouble."

"Come," Mr. Gomez whispered and beckoned to them. They crawled to the kitchen door and then got to their feet and followed him down a dark hallway off the kitchen. The cook opened a door after the hallway turned abruptly to the right, and he waved them in. "You stay quiet until I come for you. Got that?"

The men nodded, and he pulled the door shut. They could hear him lock it and then retreat down the hallway.

The room apparently served as a sort of community closet—there were piles of clothes stacked neatly all over the room, as if they had been carefully washed and folded before being donated. There was no furniture in the room, only the mounds of clothing, so Asher sat down on the floor and leaned back against a mountain of jeans and T-shirts: the young men's department.

"You should probably sit down," Asher said, conversationally, as if getting down on the floor so as to avoid a potential hail of bullets was an everyday activity.

Riley slumped to the floor, coming to rest atop the junior miss department's stacks of sundresses and hats. "Well, this turned out to be an adventure," he said, trying to keep an upbeat tone in his voice and mostly failing. "All in a day's work for us reality-show bachelors—"

He was cut off by the sound of a door being smashed in somewhere in the building. They could hear the nun's voice—Riley realized with shame that they had never even learned her name—rise to a terrifying volume. She wasn't screaming or scared, though; he could tell that much. She was probably lecturing them on their obligations to their fellow man, chapter and verse, Riley thought with a smile that half broke through his terror and then receded again almost immediately. Other voices joined the nun's, and tempers seemed to be calming.

"Can you hear what they're saying?" he asked Asher in a whisper. Asher shook his head.

Then the voices—the nun's, the cook's, and several others—started to move through the building. They became more and then less distinct as they moved along until Riley eventually recognized the creak of the back door as it swung open into the alley. Finally, as the group passed under the high window in the closet the men had been locked into, he could make out what they were saying.

"Child, why didn't you tell me you was Miss Ruby's niece's boy? We been family all along and here you shootin' up the place. Now, I can go with you to call on Miss Ruby, but I got to be back here in an hour to finish cleanin' the place up." This last part Riley was sure she spoke loudly and plainly toward the high window in the wall above them.

A car door opened in the alley. "No, that's all right, Mr. Gomez can drive me there."

They heard a couple of cars start and then the sound of engines fading away in the distance.

They were alone.

"Sounds like a family reunion out there," Asher said, his voice wishfully cheery.

"You know as well as I do it was nothing of the kind," Riley said, getting up to rattle the door handle. It spun freely, but the door didn't budge. "She found a way to get them out of here so we'd be safe—and to let us know she'd come back to let us out in an hour. She saved our lives."

Asher nodded gravely. "I'm sorry about this," he said, miserably.

Riley turned from the door to face him. "Are you serious?"

"Well, we did kind of end up getting shot at, and then locked in a closet in the worst neighborhood in the city."

Riley sat down next to Asher. "I wouldn't have missed it for the world."

Asher turned to him, dumbstruck.

"You answered someone's prayers today, just by being you. Just when I think I've seen the depths of the kindness and generosity that runs through you, you somehow find more." Riley shook his head in wonder. "I like myself more when I'm with you than at any other time in my life. You make me a better person just by being the person you are."

Asher blushed deeply. "Better be careful. You can turn a boy's head with talk like that." He grinned.

"I kind of hoped I could," Riley said in a low voice, and he reached out his hand. He placed it on Asher's shoulder and felt the strong sinews under the skin. He leaned in, tipping his head to the side, and drew his mouth close to Asher's. This time it was daylight. This time he knew what he was doing. And this time he knew what he wanted.

"Whoa, there!" Asher blurted, pulling back from Riley's approach and pulling his hand off his shoulder. "What are you doing?"

Riley sat back, confused. "I was going to kiss you. I'm sorry, I thought that was obvious?"

"Why? Why would you do that?"

Riley shook his head, surprised to be asked this question. "I thought I made it pretty clear. Weren't you listening?"

"I heard what you said, and if you were to read that at my funeral there wouldn't be a dry eye in the place. But I'm not sure how we get from effusive relief at not being shot to making out."

"This is all I've thought about since the night on the mountain. And after I finished being freaked out that I kissed another guy, I started to realize that you aren't just another guy. You're this amazing person I would follow anywhere, and do anything with, because of who you are and how you make me feel. And now, seeing you here today—and granted, being shot at probably sped things along—I know this is what I want." Here he paused to swallow hard. "Ash, you are what I want. Who I want. Sorry, this is the first time I've ever—"

Riley lost the use of his mouth at that moment, because Asher had commandeered it with his own. They kissed, and to Riley it was like he had never been kissed before. The lips on his were strong and sure and yet beckoning and soft—they were and could only be, he knew instantly, Asher's. They were everything he was, everything he had become to Riley: new and familiar, comfortable and revelatory.

Riley kissed him back with an energy that shocked him. Just as stars began to dance around the edges of his vision, he finally remembered to breathe. His sudden intake of breath seemed to urge Asher on. Suddenly, Asher surged forward, snaking his tongue into Riley's mouth.

Riley was dimly aware of the voice in his head that screamed, "You're kissing another man!" But it was drowned out almost immediately by the other voice, the one that murmured, "The man you're falling for." That second voice, though warm and sultry, perhaps overstated things, but Riley couldn't spare a single neuron to respond. They were all fully engaged in firing off endorphins and other delicious chemicals in response to Asher's insistent kiss.

Finally, when time had stopped completely, Asher pulled back from Riley's lips and caught his breath. He looked into Riley's eyes, darting from the left to the right and back again as if searching for something. Riley laughed.

"What are you doing?" Riley asked.

"Trying to see if this is okay—if this is what you want."

Riley stopped laughing. He opened his mouth, but then shrank back from what he had been about to say. He took a deep breath, then: "This is exactly what I want. I just never knew it before now—before you."

Asher closed one eye and regarded him critically. "Are you sure that's not the bullet holes on the wall talking? You might just be so relieved to still be alive that this seems like a good idea."

Riley grabbed both of Asher's hands in his own. "No. It's you. It's all you." He leaned in and kissed Asher again, and this time it was his tongue that found its way into their kiss. He was still working out more ways for their mouths to fit together when Asher pulled back again.

"This is amazing, but don't you think we should push the panic button on our transponders and get the cavalry to come pick us up?"

Riley shook his head. "First, they would drive by here a dozen times and never know that we were inside. Second—" He pounced on Asher, pushing him back onto a pile of onesies and knit booties, and crouched astride him. "—if being rescued means we have to stop doing this, I don't need to be rescued, thanks very much." He leaned down slowly, so slowly Asher had to thrust his head up to meet him halfway in a kiss that was noisy and passionate and nothing Riley had ever imagined and everything he now knew he needed.

"Ohh, fuck," Asher whispered after several minutes of their slow grind. "I know you're okay with the kissing, but dammit, there's some other side effects going on here, and I don't know if you're okay with that." Asher nodded down to where their bodies met at the hips.

Riley's eyes widened, and he thrust his pelvis from side to side, taking the measure of the man beneath him. "My good man, you are becoming an even better man by the minute!" He laughed and resumed kissing Asher's grinning mouth. He didn't think he'd ever want to stop doing that.

Within a few minutes, however, Riley's body began to respond as well. He couldn't really say it was the first time he had hardened to a man's touch—that had happened at the shining armor challenge when Wilbur plied his cosmetic trade on Riley's scandalously willing body. But this time there was no shame, no hesitation. The body wants what it wants, and right now Riley's body wanted more contact with Asher's. And, for what seemed like the first time in his life, the person he wanted, wanted him back in the same way—and palpably so. Their erections pressed against each other, slipping and grinding along their considerable lengths, realizing their purpose in the world.

"As first dates go," Asher said, somewhat breathlessly, "this one's fucking amazing." He looked around at the dismal gray closet with its piles of clothing, the locked door, the fading daylight through the grimy glass that looked onto an alley in the worst part of town.

Riley smiled. This was exactly where he wanted to be. "Well, it's not the Beverly Palace, if that's what you mean," he said, and then burst out laughing. "All of those amazing places, and we couldn't make it happen. Get locked up in this dump, and—bam! We're parked at Inspiration Point."

"It's not like I didn't try, remember," Asher scolded mildly. "I'm not the one who freaked out."

"I tried too," Riley scolded in kind. "But you wouldn't even talk about it afterward."

Asher grew serious all of a sudden. "I just couldn't believe—wouldn't let myself believe—that you really wanted this. Wanted me."

"Is it that hard to believe that someone would want to be with you?"

Asher fixed him with a questioning look. "Are you serious?"

"What?"

"Riley, you're straight."

Riley looked down at the place where their bodies met. "Not everyone agrees with you on that."

"I will admit that I have been impressed by the evidence," Asher replied, wiggling his hips a little so Riley's erection slid along his own. "But I don't know what it means."

"I thought a boner only meant one thing," Riley said, with a giggle.

"You know as well as I do that just about anything can get you going if you don't have any other outlets, and we've been out of circulation for weeks. Our poor neglected privates are probably ready to spring at anything that comes near."

Riley had to admit to himself that he had been on a hair trigger the entire time he'd been on the show, but his reaction to Asher's proximity was undeniable. "Don't sell yourself short," he murmured into Asher's ear as he once again rolled his pelvis from side to side. "You are doing this to me. Only you."

"Ohh, fuck, Riley," Asher murmured in response. He grasped Riley's neck with both hands and pulled him down, locking onto his lips with his own.

It was nearly an hour later that their rollicking abandon in the charity-clothes closet was brought to a rather sudden close by the approach of a car in the alley outside. The men, whose clothes were mussed but still covered them, stood reluctantly, stealing last kisses from each other as they attempted to straighten up. Riley heard the back door creak open and then approaching footsteps.

"Hurry, Mr. Gomez. Let's get our poor volunteers on their way home before any more trouble decides to show up on Saint E's doorstep today."

They heard rapid footsteps approaching. Riley glanced at Asher, nervous. He told himself it was because of what he and Asher had been doing, but deeper inside he knew his real fear: that what they had created together here might only exist here, that when they left this dingy room and entered the world again, the fragile magic that had passed between them could shatter. He tried to manage a smile to cover over the ache of dread in his stomach.

Asher smiled broadly and reached out to put a stray lock of Riley's hair back in place. This small gesture, the casual affection of it, filled Riley with a warmth he had never known. He turned and faced the door with Asher at his side.

They were going to be okay.

AFTER MR. Gomez opened the door to the clothes room and let them out, they hurried down the hallway toward the kitchen. There they met the nun who, as was her manner, stood beaming at them. She approached them with outstretched hands and took one each of theirs.

"Are you all right?" she asked, looking them over from head to toe in her bird-like way.

"We're just fine, Sister...?" replied Riley.

"Sister Angelica, child."

"Sister Angelica. I'm Riley, and this is Asher, the one who decided we should stop in and help today."

"Thank you, and thank you," she said to Asher, and then to Riley, a huge smile shining from her face. Then she looked at the two of them, and a new light seemed to come into her eyes. She nodded several times, as if confirming her suspicion with the man upstairs.

"You keep a hold of this one, you hear?" she said to Riley. "A good man is hard to find, and you done found yourself a real good one."

Riley's mouth dropped open.

"Sister Angelica, you are a gem," Asher said, clasping his other hand on top of the nun's small but steely one.

"Now you two better be on your way," she said, moving toward the alley once again. "It'll be gettin' dark soon, and you best be where you're goin' when it does."

They walked out into the alley and turned back to the diminutive sister on the top stair. "Thank you, Sister Angelica," Riley said.

"Whatever for, child?"

"For reminding me what's important."

She shook her head. "You already knew that. But it doesn't hurt to be reminded sometimes, does it? Now you two take care. And take care of each other—that's all God wants of you."

The two men looked at each other for a moment, in the fading light of day, and then headed out toward the street. Riley heard the door of the soup kitchen creak closed behind them.

They walked along the avenue, which was clogged with afternoon commuters taking a shortcut through the old downtown, probably avoiding a backup on the freeway. The neighborhood got a little better with each block, until they were in an upscale, somewhat artsy district that bore vanishingly little resemblance to the one from which they had just come.

"Dying for a coffee. You?" Asher asked.

"God yes. And maybe a bagel or something? We must have served three hundred people lunch today, and it didn't even occur to me that I hadn't eaten anything."

Asher nodded toward a cafe at the corner ahead, and as they stepped through the door, a wall of coffee aroma threatened to knock them back out onto the sidewalk.

"Perfect," Riley murmured, breathing deeply.

"You, sir, are an addict."

"It was your idea to stop for coffee. I'm just along for the ride."

"Right," Asher replied, rolling his eyes. They approached the counter. "Can I get an Americano with a splash of scalded milk?"

"Hey, that's what I drink," Riley said when he heard Asher order.

"That's why I ordered it," Asher replied, shaking his head.

The barista chuckled. "Now you do him," he prompted Riley, a sly grin on his face.

It took Riley a second to grasp what he was being asked to do, but he recovered quickly. "Half-caff skim latte, short," he said confidently.

The barista nodded and turned to make the drinks.

"What the hell did you order me?" Asher asked.

"You'll love it. Promise."

Sitting at a table by the window a few minutes later, Asher had to admit he did. "How did you know?"

"Elementary," Riley said, in a grand voice. "I remember you said that you don't drink much coffee except in the morning, so I figured half-caff would be best." Asher nodded. "You also like milk in your coffee in the morning, so I thought a latte would be nice. I made it short because otherwise they drown the coffee with too much milk, and I assumed since you stopped for coffee you'd want to taste it."

Asher beamed at him, clearly touched beyond words. He lifted his cup, tipped it toward Riley with a nod, and then sipped. He closed his eyes and visibly reveled in the strong, hot liquid. They spent a long moment drinking their coffee and watching the activity on the street through the window.

"So, what do we do now?" Riley asked, setting down his cup.

"I'm assuming that the van from the show is going to pull up in front of the cafe at some point, and we'll go back to being prisoners—this time in a mansion in the hills rather than a closet, but prisoners just the same."

"No, I mean about... you know... us." Riley's voice drifted lower as he spoke. The final word was barely audible.

Asher looked at him, silent, for a time. "Us?" he asked and then sipped his latte, eyebrows up in expectation of clarification as to precisely what Riley meant by that term.

Riley blushed and looked down at the table. "Yeah, us," he said quietly. "You and me. I kind of thought that, what with all of the"—he tipped his head side to side and his eyes widened insinuatingly—"that we were kind of... you know...."

Asher smiled. "I can't imagine what this is like for you. It must be very strange."

"Oh, you mean the part about everything I ever thought I knew about myself has to be thrown out the window? Yeah, that's going to take some getting used to."

Asher set down his cup. "You don't have to throw everything out," he said emphatically.

"Doesn't feel like it. I'm really at sea here, Ash. I never in my life imagined doing what we just did. And now that we've done that, I don't know who I am anymore."

"You are the same person now that you were yesterday. A good person. The best."

Riley winced a bit—he hadn't been fishing for a compliment. "I'm not the same. You changed me." Too blunt, Riley realized as Asher recoiled. "No," Riley hurried to add. "That's not a bad thing—not at all. I'm not blaming you. Well, maybe a little. I never imagined I'd meet a guy I wanted to make out with, and you certainly changed that."

"Oh my God oh my God oh my God!" shrieked a woman from across the cafe. She was looking directly at Riley and Asher, and she hurried over to them, phone at the ready. "Are you two…? You are. You are! Oh my God!" She raised her phone and began shooting pictures wildly, as if she expected to be tackled by bodyguards at any moment and wanted to get at least a blurry shot before being thrown to the ground. But, as there were no overprotective thugs in sight, she finished shooting pics and lowered her phone. "I can't believe I'm actually looking at you! I just saw you on the show last night—I totally voted for both of you! You're my favorites out of all of them. I love watching you guys. You are so awesome!"

Riley had no idea how to respond to this fusillade of admiration, and Asher looked equally at a loss. In the end, Asher smiled and nodded, so Riley followed his lead.

"Would you like a picture with us?" Asher asked, ever the gentleman.

This sent the fan into paroxysms of joy. "You are so thoughtful. That Daphne is a lucky lady!" She knelt next to the table and held her camera out in front of her. The men leaned in, placing their heads in the frame of the shot, and she clicked three times to be absolutely certain. "Thank you so much!" she blurted. "I'll be watching tonight. I just know you two are going to win this thing!" She smiled with an almost demented enthusiasm and then walked back to the table where her coffee was growing cold.

"She's right, you know," Riley said once her retreat was complete.

"About what?" Asher asked, still appearing a little shell shocked from the whirlwind that had descended so suddenly and left just as abruptly.

"You are thoughtful, and any woman would consider herself lucky to be with you."

Asher grinned. "Thank you, and I'm terribly sorry to have to let Daphne, and her entire gender, down."

"But that's just the thing—women always talk about how they want a man who will listen to them, and who thinks about their needs."

"And the men who fit that description are usually gay, right?"

Riley nodded. "It's ironic, isn't it? That the best straight men are the gay ones?"

Asher grew serious all of a sudden. "It's not, actually. I think if you listed all of the things that women say they want in a man, the vast majority of them would be traits gay men are known for. Not to say all gay men fit the model, but in terms of a lot of the things women want, most gay men have them in greater amount than most straight men."

"Well, except for one thing," Riley said with a chuckle.

"Yeah, the complete lack of sexual attraction is often a deal breaker."

Riley stopped laughing. "Huh," he said and turned to look out the window in an unfocused way.

"What?" Asher asked, sounding concerned.

"It's just that... well, I'm kinda...." He continued to stare out the window and then turned back to Asher. "I guess what I'm trying to say is that I'm still attracted to women."

Asher looked at him blankly. "Well, duh—you're straight."

This took Riley by surprise. "What? How can you even say that?"

"Easy. 'You are straight.' See?" He shook his head and shrugged.

Riley leaned in over the table between them. "I'm not sure how to break this to you, but I kissed a guy. I think that means I'm not straight."

"Hmm. Let's think that one through," Asher replied. "Would you say that a straight woman who kisses another woman immediately becomes a lesbian?"

Riley frowned—he wasn't sure what Asher was getting at. "No, I don't think so. That would mean half the girls I went to college with would be lesbians. Seems unlikely."

"Okay, then why does kissing me make you gay?"

Riley pondered this one for a moment, unsure whether it was a trick question Asher was asking. "Because you're a guy," he said, aware of how lame it sounded, but unable to come up with a more elegant way to state the obvious.

"Quite perceptive," Asher replied with a smile. "But why does it work that way for men and not for women?"

"Because," Riley said slowly, as if he were explaining to a simpleton, "men are different from women."

Asher fixed him with a scowl. "Seriously? How have I lived my life not knowing that?" He pounded his fist on the table. "If only someone had told me!" A sly grin emerged once his histrionics had been accomplished.

"Could you dial back the sarcasm a little? All I'm saying is that women are more.... I don't know, flexible? When it comes to this stuff."

"You're kind of being a typical man about this, you know?" Asher replied, more seriously now. "Women can fool around and that's sexy, because the assumption is they still really want a man. But two guys? Gotta be completely gay, from the first kiss. Or the first time they even think about kissing."

"Why does this get you so worked up? I never figured you for a gender warrior."

"Think for a minute about the double standard. In college, I met plenty of guys who were scared to death to even let themselves admit that they might be attracted to other men. Because if they ever kissed a guy—even once—they would be forever and irretrievably gay. Those stakes are just too high. It would be like as soon as you learned a word of French you had to move to France and never leave it. It keeps them from exploring that side of themselves."

Riley's mouth had dropped open during this exposition, and he only now thought to close it. "You've really thought this through," he said, finally.

"When you see it tearing your friends up, you start to think about how it all works. Meanwhile, my female friends could get drunk and make out with each other every weekend. In fact, they could get drunk for free if they made out with each other, because there were always crowds of guys who would buy them drinks if they said they would kiss. It was kind of a racket."

Riley wanted to object to this entire line of reasoning, but upon a moment's reflection, he could see the logic behind it. "Not to be selfish, but I'm trying to figure out what this all means—for me. After today, I'm going to have a hard time calling myself straight. And it's not because we kissed once. We kissed for like an hour." His eyes darted around and he leaned close again. "And it was fucking amazing," he whispered.

Asher blushed bright red but smiled so sweetly that Riley couldn't help but join him.

"So don't think of yourself as anything," Asher said. "Don't put a label on it. Just relax and see where it takes you."

"Where it's gonna take me is back to that camera-filled house where we won't be able to so much as be in the same room together. You remember what they said after the shower incident—any sign that there's something between us, and we can kiss the whole thing good-bye."

Asher looked down at the table suddenly, as if he didn't want Riley to see the expression on his face. "I would do it, if you would," he murmured.

Riley stopped cold. "What? No way. No. We've come too far to start thinking that way now. We can still win this thing—and you can still help your sister. We just need to be careful, and not do anything that will arouse suspicion. We play it cool, just for the next couple of weeks, and then we can see where this takes us."

Asher jolted upright. "Where it takes us? Are you serious?" There was panic in his voice, but something more—excitement?

Riley reached out his hand and laid it atop Asher's on the table. It stayed there for several seconds, until a passerby approached their table and he pulled it back with a protective glance at the intruder. "Yes, I'm serious. You're the best thing to happen to me in... well, ever. We need to see this competition through because it's what we came to do, but once we've kicked ass and taken names, it'll be just you and me. And whatever this... thing... is between us."

"Wow," Asher said, quietly. Then that brilliant smile broadened out across his face, and it was like the sun was shining on Riley after the clouds parted. "You're right, of course. We straighten up and fly right, we can do it."

"Damn right," Riley cheered. Then, as quickly as the elation had come to him, it was swept away by an anxiety he had never felt before. "But how am I supposed to know how to act?" he asked, genuine concern in his voice.

"What do you mean, act?"

"I don't know how to act straight," Riley said, shrugging.

Asher squinted at him. "Seriously?"

"Yeah," Riley replied, a little defensively. "You've been doing it a long time, but I'm just kind of new at it."

"Oh good Lord, Riley, we kissed. You didn't have a lobotomy."

"What's that supposed to mean?"

"It means that you don't act any differently than you always have. Nothing has changed, and no one will be able to tell anything happened. No one will know."

"I'll know," Riley said quietly. "And, just for the record, everything has changed."

It was Asher's turn to reach out his hand and take Riley's. "I know. And what it feels like now is probably nothing to what it's going to feel like when you wake up in the morning and realize it wasn't a dream: you really spent an hour rolling around in a charity-clothes closet with a boy."

Riley giggled at this—Asher had a way of breaking through his anxiety.

"But you just need to keep calm and carry on, and we'll get through this. And then we can figure out what comes next." Asher sounded much less sure of this last bit, but Riley let it slide.

"I think even a straight guy like me knows what comes next," Riley said, his voice low and a little growly. He put his free hand on top of Asher's, wrapping Asher's hand in his own, much as Asher had done to Sister Angelica. He looked into Asher's wide, kind eyes, and he could see tears beginning to well up. It was more intense than he could take in at the moment, so he turned his head to look out the window instead.

He dropped Asher's hand as if it were a hot iron. Asher pulled back and turned to look out the window as well.

The van had pulled up at the curb outside the cafe.

Riley looked across the table at Asher. "Showtime," he said miserably.

Asher took a deep breath and nodded.

They rose from the table, bussed their cups to the tray at the end of the counter, and strode quickly outside to get in the van. They were apparently the last to be picked up—all of the other bachelors were already in their seats. Once Riley and Asher were settled in their seats (across the aisle from each other) and the van had pulled into the slow conga line of homebound traffic, the producer stood at the front to address the group.

"Excellent work, bachelors. Everyone got at least one hashtag, and most of you got several. We've seen some good traffic on many of them, but the one that's trending now is—" He consulted his tablet and did a double-take. "—the same one that's been trending for several hours: '#BachelorSoup.' Congratulations, Asher and Riley, for making a huge impression by, it appears, scooping soup for homeless people in the worst part of our fair city. Oh, and look—here are some grainy stalker pics taken through what looks to be a broken window." He looked up from his tablet at the men. "Seriously? How cliché can you get?"

"It worked, didn't it?" replied Riley, challenge in his voice. He'd just about had it with the upside-down-ness of this whole venture. They managed to do some good—real good—and now they were being mocked for it, even though by doing so they had helped the stupid show where nothing was real. He shook his head, and caught Asher's eye from across the aisle. He caught sight of Asher's barely suppressed grin and felt the heat sweep up to his scalp. He turned his blushing face out the window, hoping no one had noticed.

No one but Asher, that is. He wouldn't mind if Asher noticed.

They rode in silence back to the house, where there was a live elimination show to be broadcast.

It was a number of hours later when Riley and Asher met, as they often did, in the gym. They hadn't seen each other since the elimination ritual earlier in the evening. They sought to work off the stress of the live television event by lifting and pressing and crunching.

"So that's what it's like to be on the elimination platform," Riley said to Asher as they mounted adjacent treadmills.

"I am so sorry," Asher said, his voice low and contrite.

"Will you stop with that? It's not your fault I was up there."

"But if I hadn't freaked out on the rock descent—"

"Stop it!" Riley interrupted. "If we had shot down that rock and crossed the finish line first, we wouldn't have ended up in the hammock, and you wouldn't have"—he glanced up at the camera—"err, told me that story about Telemachus. Anyway, I knew they wouldn't cut me loose. Not when we did so well for them with the whole 'Bachelors in the Wild' thing today. I think they just wanted to have me up there for the drama."

"Well, it worked. Everyone was kind of shocked to see you up there."

"I was surprised to see both of the other guys cut loose. We're down to eight faster than I thought we would be. Two more rounds and we'll be at the final four." He fell silent for a moment, the sound of their footfalls pounding on the rubber belts the only sound in the gym.

"Doesn't matter how many there are," Asher announced, his voice ringing with a confident swagger. "Number one's the only one I'm interested in." He switched off the treadmill and stepped off the back of it as the belt slowed to a stop. "Sauna?" he asked once he had mopped his brow.

Before he could censor his reaction for the camera, Riley smiled at the thought of being alone with Asher in the superheated cedar closet of the sauna. He wiped the grin off his face and punched the "off" button on his treadmill as well.

They walked to the sauna, Riley feeling a quiver in his chest that he had never known before. He wasn't sure what this meant, especially since they had spent plenty of time in the sauna over the previous weeks. He kicked his shoes off, then pulled his workout shirt off over his head and grabbed a towel from the stack next to the sauna. He wrapped it around his waist and then slipped his shorts and compression briefs off and down his legs, taking his socks with them. He looked studiously at the floor while he did what suddenly seemed like a sensual and scandalous thing, but now he stood up and made himself cast his eyes in Asher's direction. Asher was just wrapping a towel around his waist—his already naked waist, Riley was shocked to see, and he looked away before catching anything more than a shadowy glimpse of Asher's nudity. He quickly opened the door of the sauna and stepped into the waves of dry heat that emanated from it.

They sat in their usual spot, perhaps a little farther apart than normal. Riley looked again at Asher, whose eyes were closed as he lay back against the wall of the sauna. For the first time, he let his eyes wander down Asher's chest, taking in his impressive musculature as if he had never seen it before. There was a mist of exertion and heat glazing Asher's skin, making it glow in the feeble light of the sauna's one bulb.

Riley wondered if this is what being gay meant—looking at another man's body and feeling… what? What did he feel when he saw Asher's broad shoulders, his pronounced clavicles, his hulking but elegantly rounded pectorals? Were those nipples supposed to say something to him? Was he supposed to read some secret in the slabs of abdominal muscle that rippled down into the towel? And what about the things that towel covered, but in covering them only made them more apparent? A flash of panic seared Riley, shot through him like lightning. The things under that towel were things he had never imagined touching—except for his own version, of course—but now… now they were supposed to be the object of his attraction, weren't they? Taking the place of those hidden things that, until a few days ago, comprised his whole universe of sexual desire: those female parts he had always thought to be his sole object. What the hell was he doing?

"Something's different," Asher said suddenly.

"You're feeling that too?" Riley said, relieved.

"What?" Asher looked at Riley, uncomprehending. "No, I meant something's different in here." He looked around the tiny space, scanning for whatever was out of place. "Ah… that's it." He tipped his head toward the other wall, where the hot stones sat waiting to be bathed in water so they could release their steam.

The camera. It was gone. The mounting bracket remained, and lashed to it was a bundle of wire, connected to nothing.

"The steam must really have been screwing with the lens," Asher said. "That means…."

"We're alone," Riley concluded.

Asher turned to look at him, his eyebrows up, as if trying to determine if Riley had the same kind of "alone" in mind he did. "We haven't really… talked… about what happened at St. E. today. Are you…?"

"If you're asking whether I've been freaking out because of what we did, then the answer is yes." Riley shrugged. "But if you asked sixteen-year-old Riley whether he freaked out the first time he got to second base with a girl, then the answer would be yes as well." He grinned.

"Second base? Really? If you think you got to second base with me, you've got another think coming, mister. You'll know it when you get to second."

Riley stopped for a second, frowning. "Come to think of it, what does second base mean when it's… you know…?"

"Two guys?" Asher laughed. "This is so high school, man!"

Riley joined in his laughter. "But seriously, I want to know."

Asher looked him in the eyes and then nodded. "Hang on," he said, then got up and stepped to the rock warmer and picked up the water ladle. He turned to the door and slid the ladle through the handle so that it barred the door from being pulled open from the outside. The door was locked.

Asher sat back down next to Riley and tucked a leg under so he was facing Riley directly.

Riley swallowed hard. Previously when they were alone—at the Beverly Palace, in the hammock, on top of piles of charity clothes—the circumstances were so weird that their kissing was just another strange thing that happened. Here, though, they were choosing to be alone, together, in this hot place, with only towels around them. Riley couldn't help but grin a bit at their luck and ingenuity.

"You okay?" Asher asked, his brow up, eyes wide.

"More than okay," Riley replied. He too tucked a leg under himself, and the two men sat facing each other. Riley reached out a hand, tentatively, to Asher's chest. He stopped suddenly, his hand frozen midway between them, and looked up. "May I?" he asked, as if he was about to open the cookie jar.

"Please. For God's sake, please do," breathed Asher.

Riley reached out farther, crossing the mere foot of hot air between them, and touched his fingertips to Asher's clavicle. He ran his fingers along it, from neck to shoulder, sending goose bumps across Asher's chest. Asher's skin was soft and smooth and glossed with the heat of the sauna. Under it Riley could feel the strong bone of the clavicle and the steely muscle that crested over his shoulder. It was the most intimately Riley had ever touched another man, this simple sweep of his fingertips, and it surged in his own chest, his heart beating twice as fast, spurred on by the scandal of what he was doing. Lights twinkled around the edges of his vision as his heart pounded. He drew two deep, ragged breaths and steadied himself.

He let his hand drift down over the mound of pectoral muscle that undergirded Asher's clavicle, and he swept under it and brushed his thumb across a nipple that was already hard and pointed. Asher sucked in a sharp breath, and more goose bumps shivered their way across his torso.

Riley snickered in delight and brushed his thumb back and forth across the insistently firm flesh as Asher tried to catch his breath.

"Holy shit, guys are easy!" Riley said with a giggle.

Asher reached out and with a deliberate slowness traced the same path on Riley's body—across the clavicle, down across the chest, and to the nipples.

Riley stopped breathing. His lungs seemed ready to explode if he took in even the tiniest breath. With a dry mouth and a shivery shock spreading across his chest, he looked into Asher's eyes, searching frantically for an explanation—how could a single touch do this to him?

"Easy, huh?" Asher said with a sly grin.

"Oh, I can't even... oh my God... it's just so...," Riley blithered as Asher traced intricate paths over his chest and down his arms. Suddenly,

Riley brought his hands up to Asher's face, holding tightly to his strong lower jaw. Asher's hands dropped to his side, surprise on his face.

"Where have you been?" Riley whispered urgently only inches from Asher's face.

"What? Where have I…?"

"I never knew it could feel like this," Riley said, his voice still a hoarse whisper. "It's like your touch goes all the way through me." He shook his head wonderingly. Then he brought Asher's face closer to his, and they met at the lips, and Riley closed his eyes and the world disappeared and the two of them only existed in the heat and the secrecy of this place, where they joined.

It was the first time in Riley's life he had felt himself truly connected to another person. This simple act of sitting close and exchanging these first tentative touches had brought him closer to Asher than he had ever felt to anyone. The kiss they shared, though it was familiar from the times they had kissed in the past, was somehow more overwhelming because they had reached across all that might have kept them apart—out there in the world—and had found this way and this time in this place to become one.

"Does it feel like when you were sixteen?" Asher asked when their kiss had finally run its course.

"No. Not at all."

"Is that a good thing?"

"A very good thing. I was always nervous that I wasn't doing it right, or that I was going to go too far, or that she wasn't as into it as I was. Or maybe, looking back on it, that I wasn't as into it as she was. But with you, it's different."

Asher raised a critical eyebrow.

"Not bad different," Riley blurted, eager to head off any misunderstanding. "Really good different. I never thought about doing this with a guy, but… it's like I know what I like, and I try that on you, and you like it too. It just feels… right. For the first time."

Asher beamed at him. "I know what you mean."

"But you must have done this with other guys, right?"

"I've been with other guys," Asher said. "But guys are not interchangeable. Each time it's different. And this time… well, I'm with you. It just feels right."

Riley smiled as widely as Asher and kissed him again. "This is awesome, but we've been in here too long. We should get to bed before anyone notices."

Asher sighed and nodded reluctantly. "I guess you'll have to wait to see what second base is like."

Riley blinked, scandalized, and then he laughed and playfully punched Asher on the shoulder. "You tease!"

"Gotta keep you coming back for more."

"Oh, I will be coming back. You can count on that. But when we leave here, we need to be straight and narrow, right?"

Asher rolled his eyes.

"Eyes on the prize, my good man," Riley chided. "Eyes on the prize."

"My eyes are on the only prize I want," Asher said, and he laid his hand, just for an instant, on Riley's towel, where the telltale bulge of his eager cock was most prominent.

Riley was shocked—and thrilled, he had to admit. "What kind of floozy do you think I am?" he demanded in an umbrageous falsetto.

"My kind," Asher growled, and he kissed Riley one last time, his tongue flicking out wickedly.

Riley reciprocated but cut it short as they did need to keep up appearances. "Soon," he whispered to Asher and kissed him on the nose.

Asher reached around the back of Riley's head and mussed his hair playfully. "Not soon enough," he whispered back, his smile wide.

They emerged from the sauna separately: Asher first, Riley following a few minutes later.

CHAPTER THIRTEEN

IT STAYS IN VEGAS

"I WORE a tux last time I was in Vegas too. My buddy's wedding. But he got cold feet, and I ended up naked in a tub with two showgirls. Never found out what happened to the tux." The bachelor whose too-perfect hair on the first day had prompted Riley to dub him "The Anchorman" had been sharing reminiscences nonstop since they found out the next challenge would take them to Las Vegas. "You ever play baccarat?" he asked Riley, who had the misfortune to be the only other person in the room.

"No, can't say that I have," Riley replied, trying to convey with his monotone reply that he had little interest in conversation.

"Of all the things they could have us do for a 'James Bond' challenge, seems like a fucking card game is about the lamest."

"Perhaps a car chase with a grenade launcher would be more to your liking?" Riley asked as he finished laying his clothes in his luggage. He hoped this would end their conversation, such as it was.

"Anything but a stupid card game. James Bond always gets the hottest chicks, though. I'm gonna find me some hotties like last time, man."

"I thought this was supposed to be about sweeping Daphne off her feet with your secret agent charm."

"Fuck that. I don't give a crap about Daphne anymore. This whole thing is rigged—the producers are gonna choose who they like, and the rest of us can go whistle."

"You can't really think that," Riley said, though honestly he wasn't sure The Anchorman was that far off.

"Easy for you to say. You're the fair-haired boy. Even when you fuck it up, like in the forest, you still waltz through without a hitch. Must be nice to be the chosen one."

"Well, I guess you'll just have some fun in Vegas and leave the serious work of courtin' to us 'chosen' ones." Riley snapped his suitcase shut and took it with him out of the room.

The van arrived to take them to the airport, and they resumed their usual seats—like schoolkids, they were creatures of habit—and rode in their usual silence. Asher and Riley barely took notice of each other, as they had agreed to do. It cost Riley greatly, however, and he did steal the occasional glance at Asher when he sensed no one was looking.

The flight into Vegas was short and bumpy with the heat rising up out of the desert colliding with the cooler air over the mountains. They lurched into a steep descent and circled the airfield before dropping unceremoniously to the tarmac with a jolt. They were met at the terminal by a bus that was the spitting image of the one they had left behind. With a chuckle Riley considered the possibility that this was the same van and it had been driven at breakneck speed to pick them up at their destination. They climbed aboard, and the van made its way through the melting streets of Vegas in the summer.

Their hotel was one of the monstrous towers on the Strip, and to give this episode the requisite glamour, they would be staying on one of the highest floors, where the rooms were large and lavishly furnished. The bachelors were arrayed in suites along the Strip side of the hotel, with floor-to-ceiling windows stretching the length of the room. Riley and Asher were placed at opposite ends of the hallway, which was a help in their campaign to seem distant from each other.

The bachelors would each have a chance to experience Vegas with Daphne over the next several days. Twice a day for four days she would enjoy the company of a bachelor for activities such as parasailing on a man-made lake or riding the roller coaster at the top of one of the casino towers. The evening bachelors would have the advantage here, since all they needed to do was look handsome in a tuxedo and not spill wine on the bachelorette when they ate dinner at a four-star restaurant.

They drew straws after settling into their respective rooms, and both Riley and Asher ended up having their time with Daphne on the last of the four days: Asher would escort her to the zoo that lay behind one of the casinos on the Strip, and Riley would take her out to dinner at a restaurant where all of the wait staff were also circus performers. That should be annoying, Riley thought when he received his itinerary.

The competitive part of the week would be in the baccarat tournament at the end of their time in the city. None of the bachelors had professed any familiarity with the game—though strategically it would have been an error to admit to it if any did have such knowledge—and so they would receive instruction one morning from an experienced player.

The first three days in Vegas passed without incident or excitement of any kind. The baccarat lesson the first morning was confusing at first, but

Riley felt like he had gotten the hang of the game and its strategy. The key would be to look elegant and detached while frantically recalling the rules during the tournament. On the third day, Riley decided to pass the afternoon at the pool—or rather, the complex of pools—at the base of their hotel. He laid a towel on a shaded lounger next to the artificial beach that was the main attraction. Even though the temperature was well over ninety degrees, the pool beach was well populated, and from his perch Riley surveyed the bobbing mass of humanity that rode the waves created by some unseen machinery at the far end of the pool.

He had never really been a beachgoer, though he had certainly appreciated the many styles of bikini he had encountered during spring break each year in college. Given the harshness of Chicago winters, he had always gladly fled south with his buddies when school let out for a week at the start of spring. They had often chosen Florida, except for one ill-fated year when Mardi Gras came late and spring break came early and they decided New Orleans would be the ideal location. Somehow encouraging women to flash their breasts for beads had seemed less satisfying to Riley than relaxing on the beach and chatting up women in skimpy bathing suits. Plus, they had gotten a bad batch of off-brand Hurricanes and spent two nights and the day between throwing up vigorously.

The crowd here was a little older than those that populated the spring-break beaches of Florida a few years ago, but there were still sights to attract Riley's eye. Many of the younger women wore bikinis obviously designed to maximize tanning potential; some were almost invisible from behind because the thin strap of fabric that constituted the back bottom part of the suit simply disappeared into the cleft between tan buttocks. Not that Riley was complaining. If there had been suits that skimpy on his college vacations, he would have had to spend the entire week lying facedown in the sand hiding a boner.

He had been glancing from bather to bather for several minutes before he realized he was consciously not looking at the men in the water. Shouldn't he be looking at them instead of the women? He wasn't sure what he should be feeling as he gazed out onto that sea of humanity. He closed his eyes and pondered this for a time, and then when he opened them again, he resolved to practice equal-opportunity spectating. He looked around at the people splashing in the water and realized he had no idea what he was looking for. Asher was the only man he had ever felt anything like attraction for, and he had no idea how to generalize from him to the whole mass of men in the world.

His gaze settled on a pair of tallish men in their early twenties, who stood ankle-deep in the surf drinking beer from large plastic cups. They were remarkably pale, as if they had just arrived in town from some sun-deprived northern climate. The one on the left was slightly taller, while his buddy was more sturdily built. They talked as they scanned the crowd— were they looking for prospects, or had they brought girlfriends with them? Riley looked up and down their bodies and found that he viewed them no differently than he would have before ever meeting Asher: they were men, and that did pretty much nothing for him. He looked the other direction up the beach, and all he saw was example after example of the same thing— men in baggy, worn board shorts.

Riley was halfway to convincing himself he could not possibly be gay when he was stopped cold by someone new on the beach. No board shorts on this one: he wore a suit somewhat more modest than a speedo, but just as formfitting. He sipped a cocktail—something with a wedge of lime—and looked out at the scene through stylish sunglasses. What drew Riley's attention was the sleek musculature of his chest. It was powerful without being ponderous, and it flexed and relaxed smoothly as he lifted his drink and looked lazily side to side. His legs were, unlike most of those on display today, as supple and muscled as his upper body; his calves tightened into balls as he rocked gently back and forth. But it was what Riley saw next that really alarmed him: this man had a perfectly round ass. It seemed almost buoyant in its shape, arching gracefully out from the man's lower back before curving symmetrically back in at the top of his legs. It was beautiful, and it was the first time Riley had ever thought that about another man's body. Other than Asher, he said to himself. For he suddenly realized that what he admired in that stranger standing at the edge of the water was what he loved about Asher's body—its curves and ripples, its smoothness and muscled bulges.

It dawned on him then that the only thing that attracted him about men was what Asher had. He wasn't gay, in that sense, at all. What he was, was falling for Asher.

The man down the beach with the stylish glasses and the perfect ass was joined by a woman with perfect breasts and a stylish bikini. They kissed and then stood with their arms around each other, posed as if waiting for the photographer to get the right light on them. Riley turned away, suddenly unable to watch them any longer.

"Hey, I thought that was you!"

Riley turned toward the voice and saw Asher approaching him from the other direction. As he watched the other man approach, he knew from the tingly sensation in his belly that he had been right in his observation—

Asher was somehow the only man he had ever seen who made him feel this way. What was it about him? Riley wasn't sure he cared. It was enough to feel this way, and this way was precisely how he wanted to feel.

"How ya been, stranger?" Riley called back to him as he approached. Their strategic, self-imposed separation had been hard on him, and he thought he could tell from the look of Asher that it had been hard on him as well.

"Well, it's pretty clear I suck at baccarat," Asher said as he plopped down on the lounger next to Riley's. "And this town is pretty damn boring when you can't go anywhere or do anything. How about you?"

"Pretty much the same. Even the people-watching is less fun than you think it's going to be."

Asher looked around, then back to Riley. "Look, they're not even trying to follow us around this trip—I think they're too busy with location shooting with Daphne. What say we head out for an early dinner before they have a chance to track us?"

Riley the strategist was against this plan as it could put the lie to their rivals act. But Riley the suddenly romantic fool was all for it. "Sounds good. Let's go."

They slipped through the lobby of the hotel and onto an upward-bound elevator unnoticed by anyone attached to the show. This was the time of day that the production crews were in transit from the daytime activity to the evening one; the bachelors were left pretty much to their own devices except for periodic check-ins by an assistant to an assistant producer the first couple of days. Once the bachelors got the message that they were going to be watched pretty closely, they gave up on their plans to get shit-faced and hit on showgirls and instead kept to the pool areas and their rooms. The complete absence of any crew on their floor gave Riley the hint that the producers figured their spirits were broken and they no longer required strict surveillance. Still, they moved quickly to their respective rooms to put on the most nondescript clothing they had brought along. In Vegas in the middle of summer, that meant shorts and simple, if stylish, shirts. They would blend in with the more fashionable masses.

They met up in the hallway outside Asher's room, which was the largest of the suites that the bachelors occupied—the hearts inscribed on the doorframe subtly revealed its function as a Honeymoon Suite. Across the hall from his door was the entrance to the stairs; despite the fact that their rooms were on the thirty-fifth floor, they took the stairs down to decrease the odds of running into anyone from the show.

Several minutes later they pushed open the street-level door at the bottom of the stairs and were immediately oppressed by the wall of heat that met them on the other side. But though it was hellish, it was freedom, and they sprinted out of the hotel and through the gardens that decorated the grounds.

"Where should we go?" Riley asked once they had put several blocks of the Strip between themselves and the hotel.

"Someplace where we won't be noticed," Asher replied. He seemed to roll this requirement around in his mind for several strides and then nodded. "Got it," he said, conclusively. He grinned and winked at Riley.

"Whoa there, chief," said Riley, grabbing his elbow to slow him down a bit. "You wouldn't happen to be thinking about a... you know, that kind of bar?"

Asher stopped and looked at him incredulously. "Seriously? You think I would take you to a gay bar, knowing that if anyone saw us in there we would both get bounced off the show? Come on, give me some credit."

"Sorry," Riley replied, ashamed. "That was pretty stupid of me." They resumed walking. "So, where are we going?"

"A place I read about in one of those magazines they put in hotel rooms."

"And how do you know that no one else from the show will be there?"

"You'll see," he answered smugly and kept walking.

In about a quarter of an hour, they arrived at another massive Strip hotel. Asher nudged Riley on the shoulder, and they turned right into the front doors. An icy blast of air conditioning swept over them, giving Riley momentary goose bumps.

The casino was like every other of its kind along the Strip: the muted bling-bling-bling of slot machines, the clicking of the roulette wheel. Asher paused momentarily at a map near the entrance and then nodded, turned, and struck out across the casino floor.

At the back of the vast gaming complex was the entrance to the club Asher had chosen. Unfortunately, while he might have been correct in his intuition that no one associated with the romantic reality show would have normally chosen this somewhat run-down tribute to Old Vegas, tonight was a different story. Outside the entrance to this deliberately tacky nightclub was a corps of bouncers who would have been more at home at the shoulder of a strongman in some obscure dictatorship. They guarded the door with a grim dedication to their task, while before them vibrated a horde of sluttishly dressed lounge lizards in the making, camera phones at the ready. It was quite clear that all were anticipating the impending arrival of at least a B-list celebrity, perhaps even A minus.

Asher stopped as soon as they rounded the corner. "As incognito nightspots go, this one's a bust," he said in a low voice. "The guide said this was a 'no longer bustling destination, ready for refurb.' I kind of assumed that meant, well... not that," he said, nodding toward the mob.

"We should find someplace else before any more excitement develops here. Too many cameras for my taste," Riley said, stepping back.

"Right," answered Asher. Riley followed as Asher walked briskly over to an escalator, which bore them up to the next level of flashing, clanging casino action. Asher scanned the area once they had stepped off. "There," he said, pointing to a doorway off to the right.

They walked over to the entrance to a venue named, according to the luridly bright red neon sign next to the entrance, "V." There was a short queue outside, but it was moving quickly, and they joined it. The line continued to advance briskly, and soon they were inside and standing before the hostess station.

"Welcome to V," the abundantly cleavaged hostess breathed as they stepped up to her podium.

"Two for dinner?" Riley asked.

"Well, of course two," she replied. She winked at him and consulted her seating chart. "It will be just a moment."

"Thank you," Riley said, a bit puzzled at the "of course" part. Was she assuming something about him and Asher?

The phone on the desk beeped subtly, and she picked it up. "V, the first couples-only club on the Vegas Strip, how can I help you?" she answered it, with a smile that was somehow both brilliant and insinuating.

Riley panicked but then considered that at least here they were out of view of the casino at large. If they turned around, they would simply have to find another place to hide.

"Oh, like Valentine," Asher said, suddenly nodding with comprehension.

"We'll see you then," the hostess said into the phone and then replaced it on the desk. She looked up at the men. "Your table is ready now. Please follow Veronica." She nodded to a woman who had approached the podium, dressed—of course—in red.

They walked to their table past many others populated by two and two only. Even the bar was filled with duos, barstools turned toward each other. Riley felt the walls closing in around him as they progressed farther into the restaurant, the weight of couplehood pressing on his chest. Finally they arrived at a small, intimate—of course intimate—high-backed booth against the wall, where at least they would not be visible to the room in general.

Veronica handed them menus after they had settled into the deep red leather. "Valéry will be your waiter this evening," she said in a sultry voice. "Would you like a drink while you peruse the menu?"

"God yes," blurted Asher. This was Riley's first sign that Asher was as flummoxed as he was by the atmosphere of aggressive coupling. "What's good?"

"We have a house specialty cocktail that I think you'll enjoy," she said, raising an eyebrow. "And for you?" She turned to Riley.

"Um.... I'll have the same?" Riley just wanted her to go away so he could have a moment to breathe and assess the mess they had gotten themselves into.

"Fun place, right?" Asher said, rolling his eyes. "Sorry."

"How were you supposed to know we'd end up in Cupid's dungeon? Could have happened to anyone. But if we get recognized here, we are ska-rooed."

"We'll just lay low, and no one will notice."

"Except that everyone's going to notice two bachelors having dinner in a couples-only place."

Asher squinted at him. "Have you taken a good look around?"

Riley scanned the room, wondering what Asher meant. He realized it in short order—they were far from the only two-bachelor table in the place. In fact, there were also two-bachelorette tables scattered about.

"I hadn't noticed. Their take on coupledom is more liberal than I was expecting."

"I did notice, because that's something I have to notice. I have to know whether I'm in a safe place or not. You don't have to notice, because you've never been anything but what people expect you to be. Someday— someday soon, I hope—we'll all have that privilege."

Riley looked out at the room and thought about this for a moment. He had never considered being straight as a privilege, but he could see that Asher had a point.

"Here are a couple of sweethearts!" announced a man in a tuxedo who appeared suddenly at their table.

Riley blushed furiously and was about to say something—he didn't know what, beyond the fact that he wanted to object somehow—when the tuxedoed man swept a silver tray bearing two tall cocktail glasses from behind his back.

"The specialty of the house, the Sweetheart!" he announced grandly and then placed a glass in front of each startled man. The liquid it contained was a pearlescent pink, and it swirled mysteriously in the glass. In the stem of the glass, a tiny red heart was encased, suspended in crystal. "I am Valéry, and it will be my *plaîsir* to serve you gentlemen this evening. Please, sample the Sweethearts before I expire from anticipation!"

Riley looked pleadingly to Asher, who only shrugged in response. He surrendered and picked up his drink, watching it swirl again as he did so. Asher tipped his drink toward Riley, who returned the gesture, and a tiny pinging sound rang out from the contact of their glasses before they lifted them to their lips.

Riley had expected the drink to be cloying and sickly sweet, but it was instead delicate and far more complex than he had imagined possible. By the way Asher's eyebrows shot up, Riley figured he had much the same reaction.

"You are pleased?" Valéry practically panted.

Riley nodded, leaving Asher to answer.

"We are, thank you."

"And now, *messieurs*, how may I delight your tongues?"

Riley couldn't help but giggle at Valéry's recklessness with the English language, much as he tried. Asher fixed him with a stern look, which didn't help.

"We haven't had time to study the menu," Asher said to the waiter. "Would you give us a moment, please?"

"But of course," breathed Valéry. "In the meantime I will bring you an *amuse-bouche* that I think you will love." He nodded formally and shot off across the room.

"Way to keep a low profile," Asher scolded, once they were alone again.

"I'm sorry—he's just funny." Riley took another sip of his drink. "No, that's not it." He smoothed out the white linen tablecloth and then rested his hands in front of him. "I just... this is so... it feels like—"

"Like we're on a date?" Asher finished the thought for him.

Riley nodded.

"And that makes you burst into inappropriate giggling?" Asher gave him the teacherly, stern look again.

"I guess it does. I'm sorry—I've just never done this before."

"Been on a date? Not that we actually are on one, but still, it seems odd that this would be your first one ever."

"No, of course I've been on dates before."

"Okay, but this is the first time you've had dinner with another guy."

"No, I've done that before. Of course I have." Riley's voice was growing defensive, but he didn't know why.

"Then...?"

Riley sighed and wished they weren't having this conversation. "It's just that everyone here is here because they... and we're... and I'm not sure how... oh, never mind. Let's just figure out what we're going to order, okay?"

Asher shook his head, but Riley noticed a hint of a grin play across his face as he picked up the menu.

They reviewed their options for several minutes, then set the menus down when Valéry reappeared, again bearing a silver tray. "A little something to complement the Sweethearts," he said modestly as he set the tray between them. On it rested two tiny bites of unrecognizable yet painstakingly crafted food. "And now, have you *décidé?*"

"Everything on the menu serves two?" asked Riley.

"But of course," replied Valéry, a Gallic growl in his voice.

Riley raised his eyebrows at Asher, hoping he would take the hint. He did, of course.

"Then we'll have the filet, medium, the potatoes two ways, and the soup to start."

"Verrrrry good, sir," enthused Valéry. He nodded to Asher, and his sidelong glance at Riley clearly conveyed admiration for his taste in men.

"You get me every time," Riley said, once they had been left alone.

"You sound surprised every time," Asher replied, smiling.

"I shouldn't be, but I just don't know how you do it."

"Yes you do," Asher said, sipping his drink and looking out over the restaurant.

Riley joined him in his drink, the warmth of which was beginning to spread across his chest. He wondered if his eyes were starting to adjust to the flickering candlelight that filled the room, because he could see their fellow diners much more clearly, and how they truly did have eyes only for each other.

Out of nowhere, Valéry returned with two more drinks. He set them silently on the table, seeming to sense the contemplative mood that had overtaken the men.

"He assumes a lot, doesn't he?" Riley said, though he was glad to have a second drink.

"I ordered a second round," Asher said, as if this should have been clear already.

"When did you do that?"

"After I ordered dinner."

"Huh. I must not have heard." Riley picked up his second drink and started in.

"I didn't say anything. I just looked at the glasses and then nodded to him."

"Wow. Is that some kind of gay code? That's like a superpower." Riley smiled. He quite liked these pink drinks.

"You are hilarious—the innocent abroad, you are." Asher popped one of the tiny morsels Valéry had brought into his mouth. "Oh. My. God."

"Is your bouche amused?" Riley teased.

"Not so much amused as amazed. You've got to try that."

Riley picked up the remaining delicacy and examined its artful layers. Then he shrugged and tossed it into his mouth. It promptly exploded into an overwhelming onslaught of flavors—some savory, some smoky, some sweet—unlike anything he'd ever experienced.

"Wow," he said, once he had chewed and swallowed. "That was incredible."

"It's good to be a couple," Asher said, laughing.

234 | XAVIER MAYNE

"Damn right," answered Riley, and he tipped his glass to Asher before downing the rest of his second drink.

They switched to mineral water to accompany the meal, wanting to stay sharp for the journey back to the hotel. Everything Valéry brought was delightful, and by the end of the meal, when they were sharing the yin-yang dishes of vanilla *pot de crème* and dark chocolate soufflé, Riley wasn't sure there was room in his stomach for all of it. But he forged ahead and then washed down the last of it with the coffee Asher had ordered for them.

The candles were guttering in their crystal wells when Valéry presented the check. Asher reached for it, but Riley was quicker.

"This one's on me," he said with what he hoped Asher would recognize as a tone of voice not to be argued with.

"But—"

"No. You chose the restaurant and the dinner, and it was perfect. I was panicking a little, and you sorted me out. As dates go, this was... well, it was the best I've been on in a long time."

Asher grinned. "So, we're calling it a date now?"

"Call it what you want, I'm just happy to be here." Riley sipped his coffee and sat back against the soft leather upholstery.

They finished their coffee and reluctantly placed their napkins on the table and rose to leave. Asher led the way past the bar toward the exit. Suddenly, Riley felt someone grab his arm.

"Excuse me," said a woman's voice.

Riley froze. They had come so close to getting away with it, only to have their cover blown on the way out. Damn!

The woman appeared to be in her midtwenties, well dressed, but her face was flushed. "Are you two leaving the hotel?"

Perhaps they hadn't been recognized, Riley thought with relief. "Yes, why?"

By this time Asher had realized he was walking alone and come back to see what the holdup was.

"Can I share a cab with you?" she asked. "My fiancé has had a bit too much to drink, and I'd like to get out of here before he comes back from the bathroom."

Riley looked at Asher, unsure what to do. Asher shrugged and nodded.

"Yes, of course," Riley said. "We'd be happy to share a cab with you."

"Oh, thank you so much," she replied, relief evident in her voice. "I'll just grab my purse—"

"Where the fuck you goin'?" slurred a man behind Riley. He whirled around to see the person he assumed to be the fiancé in question, who was apparently more efficient in the bathroom than she had calculated.

"I'm leaving, Paul," she said tersely. "If you find your way back to the hotel tonight, you're welcome to the sofa."

"Fuck you," Paul blurted, and he grabbed the woman's arm as she attempted to move closer to Asher.

"Ouch! Stop it, Paul, you're hurting—"

She was interrupted by Asher gripping Paul's wrist and lifting his hand off her arm. Paul was not a small man, and she was clearly surprised Asher had been able to make him release his grip. He did so with a surprised gasp.

Riley could see the tendons standing out in sharp relief on Asher's forearm—the power that he had built for the rings and parallel bars must still be in there because Paul was beginning to twist and crumple. In apparent desperation, he hauled his other arm back and looked ready to take a swing at Asher, but Riley captured his fist with his right hand and thrust it downward with such force that Paul went with it, crashing to the ground. Asher released his grip as the man fell.

"Shall we?" Riley said, nodding to the woman and Asher. They stepped over the stunned Paul and walked briskly to the door.

Within a few minutes, they were in a taxi, heading for the woman's hotel, which was across from the one where the men were staying. They introduced themselves once they had left the scene at V behind. The backseat of the taxi was a tight fit for the three of them. Asher sat in the middle and was pressed firmly against Riley so as to make as much room as possible for their guest.

"I'm Holly," she said, holding out a hand briskly to each of them. "I am so glad you two happened by at just the right time. Paul gets a few drinks in him and he gets a little crazy. I'd been looking for my chance to get away from him, but I couldn't be sure how he'd react. When I saw a strapping gay couple come through the bar, I knew I would be okay."

"Oh, we're—" Riley began and then realized there was no way to finish that sentence without offending Asher, so he stopped before he could say "not." "We're just happy we could help."

"Not as happy as I am. And I don't know how you were able to get him to let go of my arm so easily. He's a strong guy."

"Must be my Navy SEAL training," Asher said in a booming baritone, but with a self-deprecating smile that restored his modesty.

"Of course he would have laid you out with a roundhouse punch if I hadn't caught his fist," Riley said with a weary sigh, as if bar fights were a nightly occurrence in their lives.

"Almost like being back in the jousting arena, wasn't it?" said Asher. Then he must have realized how much he had revealed because he clapped a hand over his mouth, but Holly seemed not to notice.

"You two are darling. I can't thank you enough. I hope I didn't put too much of a damper on your romantic evening."

Riley laughed in spite of himself. "No, it's just as romantic now as it was before."

"I'll say," Asher rejoined. "You know this clod here wouldn't even kiss me during dinner? It's like he's ashamed of me or something." He smiled playfully as he teased Riley.

"You hang on to this one," Holly scolded Riley. "He's a keeper."

"People keep telling me that," Riley replied. He looked at Asher, and despite the jocular tone all three of them had adopted during the car ride, he surprised himself with the seriousness in his own voice. "I know how lucky I am to have him."

Even in the dimly reflected glow of the casino they'd pulled up in front of, Asher's cheeks burned bright red.

"Ah, here's my hotel. Here…." She handed a bill to the driver. "That's for the whole fare, and keep the change." She closed her purse and turned to Riley and Asher. "Thanks again. And I hope Paul and I can find a way to be as happy together as you two obviously are." She stepped out of the cab, then paused, leaning on the door. "You make me believe in love again." She smiled warmly and shut the door. She waved to them as the cab pulled out to make its way across the street to their hotel.

"I hope she'll be okay," Asher said as they watched her walk into the hotel. "That Paul doesn't seem like a great catch."

"Agreed. Men can be such assholes."

Asher laughed as hard as Riley had ever heard him laugh and was laughing still when they got out of the taxi at their hotel. They had the driver pull up to the side entrance so they could make their way back in undetected.

THE LOBBY was quiet—by Vegas standards—and they slipped into the elevator without being noticed. When they reached their floor, Asher stepped out of the elevator and then gave Riley the all-clear signal they had agreed on. Riley's room was the first they came to, and Asher paused at the door.

"Can we go to your room for a sec? There's something I want to ask you," Riley whispered. Asher nodded, and they walked to his room at the end of the hall.

He opened the door with a swipe of his key card, and he closed it slowly and silently behind them. In the center of the room was a large circular bed, facing a bank of windows that curved all the way across the room. The Strip lay before them, filling the room with the twinkle of a million lights.

Asher set his key and wallet and watch on the table near the door. "So, what did you want to ask me?"

Riley, who had been standing in front of the windows looking out over the city, turned to him and reached out a hand. "Come here," he said, softly.

Asher walked over and joined him in taking in the view. "It's strangely beautiful, isn't it?"

"You were amazing tonight," Riley murmured, almost under his breath.

Asher turned to look at him, a quizzical look on this face.

"After all of the fake crap we've been acting out, you are the real thing," Riley continued. "When that real-life damsel in distress needed help, you didn't hesitate for a second. That guy just crumpled, and you acted like it was no big deal."

"It wasn't a big d—"

"Shh." Riley put his finger on Asher's lips. "It was a big deal. To her. And to me." He paused for a moment, looking at Asher, his face lit from below by the glow of the Strip. "I meant what I said in the taxi." He shook his head in wonder. "Good God—what you do to me," he murmured.

"What do I do to—?"

Asher's question was both cut short and answered fully by Riley's lips. The kiss was sweet and chaste, and Asher must have thought that, as in the hammock, it would be over before it really began. But Riley had other plans. He opened his lips, opened to this man who had some strange power over him, and he reached his hands up and around Asher's strong, tickly, stubbly neck and pulled him into this kiss, this life-changing, leap-off-a-cliff kiss that Riley never wanted to end. Here, standing before the glittering lights of the city below, in this dark and quiet place, everything seemed possible—everything Riley had ever imagined, and a good number of things he hadn't—all could come true because of this man and the possibilities he brought with him everywhere he went.

Before, in the hammock and at Saint E, the kissing had been enough for Riley. It had upended his world, and so he had not had a single thought about what might come next. It was enough that Asher's kiss had ended his life as he had known it. But this time the kiss seemed more about beginnings than endings, and he was suddenly flush with excitement about where they might be heading.

He pulled back from Asher's lips and pressed their foreheads together so he could peer into those glittering eyes, the windows to a soul he wanted to know completely, in all its depths, to its very bottom.

"I do that to you?" Asher whispered raggedly.

"Every time," Riley rumbled, breath coming hot and fast. "No one— and I mean no one, ever—makes me feel like you do. I never imagined I'd be here, with you, doing this, wanting it so much I can feel it in my bones."

"Ohh, fuck" was all Asher could manage to say. He kissed Riley on the neck, the throat, the ear—everywhere he could place his lips, he seemed determined to do so.

Riley took Asher's face in his hands, held him steady, searched his eyes. "I want you to do it," he said, voice hoarse with a desperate hunger.

Asher blinked. "Do... what?"

"You know," Riley growled in reply. "I want you to do it to me. I know it'll hurt at first, but I'm ready. I want you to... to take me."

Asher startled. "Whoa, there. Hang on. Are you saying what I think you're...? No, you can't be."

"How plain can I make this?" Riley whispered urgently. "I want you to… to fuck me."

Asher took a deep breath, then another. "No," he finally said, in a tone that allowed for no argument. "Oh God no."

Riley took a shocked step back. "What?" he was finally able to huff out. "Why not?"

Asher shook his head, a wry smile forming on his lips. "Because that's not the kind of thing you do on the spur of the moment when the bright lights of Vegas have turned your head and made you loopy."

"You don't want to?"

"What I want to do is a completely separate matter," Asher said, his voice even. "What we should not do is clear: that, for one thing."

Riley dropped his arms to his sides, bereft of the animating excitement that had driven him this far. "I don't understand."

"Riley, this is a huge step you're taking just by being here with me, doing this. You shouldn't rush headlong into something even more drastic."

"Why not? I thought that's what… you know… guys did."

Asher nodded. "Some guys do, and most guys have. But not their very first time."

"I'm not scared," Riley protested. "Even if it hurts at first, I'm ready."

"That's not why—look, here's what we should do," Asher said softly, taking Riley's hand in his. "Let's make a deal, okay? I'll take care of what we do tonight and then, if you're still on board, we'll see what comes next." He brushed the back of his other hand along the hollow of Riley's cheek. "Trust me, I know what I'm doing."

Riley closed his eyes and surrendered to Asher's touch. "I trust you," he murmured. "I know you'd never hurt me."

Asher was silent, and finally Riley opened his eyes again and saw tears welling in Asher's eyes.

"Oh, shit, Ash. I've said something stupid, haven't I? I'm sorry. What did I…?"

Asher shook his head, squeezed Riley's hand again. "No, no, you're perfect. It was me just being an emotional wreck as usual. You're just so sweet and so good and so fucking hot I don't know what to do with myself."

Riley grinned and pulled Asher to him. "I didn't come here so you could do anything with yourself." He kissed Asher again, with such intensity that Asher took a step back under the onslaught. But he held strong, and Riley felt the corded muscle under his shirt. It was unlike anything he had ever felt, this strength that rippled just under the surface. Asher was the most gentle person Riley had ever met, and yet such power lay beneath the softness. Riley ran his fingers along Asher's spine and felt the complex web of muscle that spanned out to his ribs.

Asher burst out laughing. "That tickles!"

Riley released his grip.

"Don't you dare stop," growled Asher. "Your hands feel fucking amazing."

Riley wrapped his arms around Asher, this time feeling the tops of his slender hips and that mysterious place where they plunged under the waistband of his shorts. Riley had no idea that a man's body was so different from what he was used to touching. Mischievously, he ran his hands down the back of Asher's shorts, tracing along his perfectly rounded buttocks. Asher responded by surging forward, pressing their pelvises together even more forcefully.

"Riley," he gasped. "I have to ask you something."

"Anything," Riley whispered in response.

"Are you sure this is what you want?"

Riley tightened his grip on Asher's ass, his fingers pressing into the unyielding muscle. "More than anything in the world," he murmured. "More than anything."

Asher beamed at him. "I dreamed of this, but I never thought...." He reached up a hand to wipe his eyes. "I just can't believe that you are here, with me, and that we're.... This isn't how my life works."

"It is now," Riley answered him, certainty in his voice. "And it will be."

Asher clasped Riley to him, folding him in his strong arms, and kissed him again. Then he released him and stepped back, though he held onto Riley's hand. He pulled him toward the bed.

Without a word, Asher began to unbutton Riley's shirt. Riley moved to do the same to Asher's, but his hands were smacked gently out of the way. He dropped his arms to his sides and let Asher take control—just another thing he had never done, never dreamed of doing.

Asher gently opened Riley's shirt and slid his hands under the light fabric. He ran his fingertips along Riley's clavicles and then down and around the fullness of his pectorals. Riley shivered, his mind flooded with the sharp awareness of how Asher's touch was different from that of a woman making the same motions. Where a feminine touch was beckoning, teasing, fluttering, Asher's fingers swept in broad, confident strokes, as if certain of their power to bring pleasure. It occurred to Riley that he had lived his life with just the promise of pleasure, and only now was he beginning to realize that promise. He felt his body coming to life under Asher's sure hand.

Up Asher's fingers rose, sliding the shirt over Riley's shoulders. He felt it slide down his arms and off his body, to puddle on the floor by his feet. Asher ran his fingers down Riley's arms, forcing goose bumps to rise all along their muscled extent. He leaned in and kissed each of Riley's nipples, and Riley gasped in a shock of sudden pleasure as he felt the hot wetness of the other man's mouth close over the sensitive points of flesh. Asher smiled that broad, sunshiny smile Riley had come to love so much. He was clearly enjoying the ability to provoke such delight.

"Here," Asher said as he unbuttoned his own shirt. He slid it off carelessly and then knelt on the bed. He crawled to the headboard, where he stacked up several of the dozen pillows that populated the head of the bed so they formed a gently sloping backrest. Then he settled himself down and leaned back slightly against the pillows. "Come here," he said, opening his arms wide.

Riley mounted the bed on his knees as well, and he shuffled up to where Asher lay.

"Turn around," Asher instructed, and Riley did so. "Now, lie back."

Guided by Asher's strong arms, Riley slowly settled back until he was seated between Asher's legs with his back resting against the other man's chest. Once he had laid himself out, Asher nuzzled up to his ear.

"Look," he murmured.

Riley looked out past the foot of the bed, out the windows, out to the city beyond. Even at this hour, with darkness long settled over the city, waves of heat rising from the pavement made the lights twinkle and flicker, a million candles filling the room with a shimmering glow. But Riley could only take in the sight for a few seconds before closing his eyes, overwhelmed by the sensation of Asher's chest pressed against every inch of his back. He was unprepared for the warmth and softness of the other man's body; he had only ever thought of men's bodies, when he thought of them at all, as rough and hairy and unpleasant in texture and probably smell. But this—this man—was different. When Riley had imagined this moment—he now had no choice but to acknowledge that some part of him had imagined it—he thought he would have to ignore the masculine reality of Asher's body.

But the reality of this moment was not at all what he had imagined. He felt Asher, registered every square millimeter of their bodies in contact. The place on his back where Asher's nipples poked into him, the ridges of his abdominals, it was all there. But the most amazing of all was his breath, the gentle rise and fall of his chest, the slow rhythm of life that contrasted with his own rapidly beating heart. Riley felt his own breathing slow as they lay together, absorbing the calm and serenity and... purity? Yes, Riley thought, purity. This was as pure a moment as he had ever experienced.

He turned his head to the side, reaching instinctively for the man behind him. Asher met him with a kiss on the temple, and on the cheek, and then he nuzzled into Riley's ear, sending shivers down his side. Riley sat up and, still seated between Asher's legs, turned his body around to face him. He leaned forward, his hands planted on the bed on either side of Asher's ribcage, until their noses nearly touched. He looked into those deep brown eyes, wrinkled at the corners with the joy that was practically vibrating out of him, present also in his broad grin and the quick transits his fingertips were making up and down Riley's forearms.

"I can't believe this," he whispered.

Asher's smile grew even more brilliant. "It's Vegas. Things happen."

Riley laughed. "In all of the hotel rooms out there, above all of those twinkling lights, there is no one doing anything close to this."

"Umm, Riley? I know you've been a bit off your game in terms of romance, but I can guarantee you that this is exactly what the vast majority of those people in all of those hotel rooms are doing right now."

"No," Riley said, suddenly serious. "There's never been anyone in the world like us. No one has ever had his life completely broken down, lying in pieces on the floor, and then had someone come along who put it all back together, even the pieces that had no place before. You've done more than help me, Ash. You rebuilt me, made me into something completely new— what I should have been all along and just never realized."

"You are the same amazing person you've always been—you just lost sight of it for a while."

"This," Riley answered, chuckling, nodding his head down to where their bodies met, "is not the person I was. Ever."

"Okay, so that part is new. But I have to say it looks good on you."

"What does?"

"Me," Asher said, and in a flash he had rolled over, flipping Riley neatly onto his back, pouncing on top of him like a jungle cat.

Riley giggled gleefully in his surprise as Asher slid up and down his prone body, friction tickling along the clothed and naked parts alike. Then Asher's mouth was on his own, and Riley wrapped his arms around Asher's lower body, pressing their hips together.

"Oh, fuck," Asher murmured as he began a slow grind against Riley's pelvis. He kissed along Riley's jawline and down to his throat.

Riley had never felt this delicious burn of stubble rubbing along his skin, roughness on roughness. The traction both warmed him and sent shivers down his body. Thrill turned to panic in the moment that Asher's kisses landed on Riley's clavicle, and then under it, and then below that. With the slow and inexorable certainty of gravity Asher kissed his way down the muscled terrain of Riley's chest. Riley knew that this was the moment everything would change. Up to now they had flirted and fooled around, done no more than most adolescents feeling their way through the unmapped terrain of their sexuality. But now they were actually Doing It. He was about to have sex with another man. His breath came quick as an adrenaline rush surged through him.

Asher must have interpreted Riley's jolt and shiver of panic as a surge of excitement because suddenly Asher's mouth, and hands, were everywhere on Riley's upper body. It was an overwhelming onslaught.

"Oh!" Riley called out, clutching the sheets in his fists, writhing crazily. It was too much, far too much, but he knew in that moment it would never be enough, even if they had their entire lives.

Asher slid back up to eye level. "Riley? You okay?"

Riley looked into Asher's eyes and saw in them the answer to his every question, all of his anxieties. He wasn't about to have sex with a man. They were about to create something new between them that grew out of their friendship and their care for each other, and—Riley let himself think the word for the first time—their love. They were about to make love. And that made it perfect.

He nodded. "More than okay."

Asher smiled eagerly. "It's about to get a whole lot more than 'more than okay,'" he growled, and with a kiss and a nibble he was on his way back down.

Riley felt those strong, agile fingers slide along the waistband of his shorts, seeking the opening. They found it, of course, and with a twist and a tug the shorts opened, exposing the Vegas-print boxers Riley had pulled on when he and Asher had decided on the spur of the moment to sneak out of the hotel.

"Kitschy drawers," Asher exclaimed when he caught sight of the palm trees, showgirls, and neon signs that decorated Riley's boxers.

Riley smiled. "I was saving them for date night with Daphne, but for some reason they seemed right for tonight."

"I approve. But I hope you'll understand they have to go."

"That's a sacrifice I'm willing to make," Riley said seriously.

"That's big of you," Asher answered. Then looking down at Riley's boxers, he added, "Very big of you."

Riley laughed. He had no idea that being in bed could be this much fun—why had it never seemed so before? He felt Asher tugging on the legs of his shorts, and he lifted his hips. Asher slid the garment down, over Riley's knees, along his legs, and off his feet. Now only the novelty boxer shorts lay between them.

Asher crouched between Riley's legs and looked hungrily at the place where they met. His eyes flicked up to Riley's and locked there as his hands began their slow, sly progress up the legs of Riley's boxers. It was the most intimate touch Riley had ever felt, and he closed his eyes and tipped his head back, giving himself to it fully. There was no going back. He hardly remembered what he used to be. Asher's fingers traced along Riley's upper thighs, where the hair grew thicker and the skin warmer.

Riley wasn't breathing, couldn't, not until Asher's fingers reached their goal. They roamed and tickled along until finally they reached his manhood, the most essentially male part of him, now doubly so because another man's fingers were closing around its base. Once he was in Asher's hands, literally as well as metaphorically, he could breathe again. The air was suddenly sharp and cold, like the first breath taken in a new world.

Asher delicately traced his fingers along the length of Riley's erection through the boxers, and it pressed even more urgently against the elastic of his waistband. Then Asher took it fully in his grasp, and his hand wrapped all the way around, just as Riley's own did. None of the women Riley had been with could touch their fingers around the girth of his cock. Asher's grip was sure, and his forceful motion as he began to slide his fist along Riley's length made Riley's hips surge upward in a hungry reflex.

"Like that?" Asher teased, his voice deep.

"Oh fuck yeah," Riley replied, his vocabulary having been crippled by the flow of blood to his penis.

"Then lift your hips again."

Riley complied, and again felt a tugging. The boxers slid south several inches, and then his cock broke free, snapping up to slap against his lower belly. Over his balls the fabric slid, and then down and off his legs.

He had been naked in the presence of other men, of course—no one who goes to the gym as often as Riley could avoid it—but this was a kind of exposure he had never experienced. With the women he had been with, nudity had been incidental to the act of sexual intimacy. With Asher, though, it was so central, and so unprecedented, that Riley felt he had never been naked in his life. His essential modesty would normally have made him seek cover, to hide himself from Asher's frank and hungry gaze. But he surprised himself by luxuriating in it instead, basking in Asher's attention as if it were the sun, warming him and loosening his muscles. He spread his arms out wide, feeling the rich softness of the sheets, opening himself completely to the man who had so quickly become the anchor of his new life.

Riley expected—hoped?—that Asher would pounce on his privates like an eagle snatching up a water snake, but instead he felt those strong, warm fingers tracing up the tops of his feet, slithering from the toes up to his ankles, sending shivers all up his legs. He twitched in delight, prompting Asher to repeat this motion with an even lighter, and more tickling, touch. Riley laughed out loud, and his legs shook instinctively. Asher immediately swept up his legs, where the friction was less ticklish and more sensuous. Goose bumps of surprised pleasure spread over Riley's lower body.

"Good God you're beautiful," Asher said with a wondering sigh.

Praise like this would normally strike Riley with a pained embarrassment—he was never very good at taking a compliment. But now, with all modesty and pretense stripped, he could take it in and smile, a little thrill in his heart resonating with joy at having made Asher happy. He was happy that he could make Asher happy, even as he acknowledged that it was his well-formed and hard-won body Asher had admired.

Asher seemed pleased that Riley was touched by his words, and he turned immediately to touching him in a more literal way. He ran his hands up Riley's powerful thighs, over the ridge of the quadriceps muscles standing out in long, low relief. Riley had coaxed these muscles out of hiding over the last several months with endless squats and stair-stepping sessions, and that Asher paid tribute to his labors with several passes of his touch flattered him deeply. But now those hands were working their way higher, returning to the place where the beautifully formed legs met. Asher knelt and bent forward like a supplicant, a worshipper. Riley felt the breath, warm and hot and rapid now, before Asher planted the gentlest of kisses on the smooth skin of his hip, nearby but a world away from that central point that hungered for Asher's caress. With an artist's sense of symmetry, Asher moved to the other hip and kissed it, too, before abandoning the idea of symmetry and kissing a meandering but urgent line directly into the well-trimmed thicket of hair that marked the border of Riley's most private place.

Riley's already achingly hard cock surged and bobbed in anticipation, while Riley himself could hardly draw breath. He wanted—he needed—Asher to complete his journey, in the same moment that he was terrified of what would happen when he got there.

Asher kissed his way along until, finally, he reached Riley's towering erection. Riley waited, still hardly breathing, for him to stuff as much of it as he could fit into his mouth—the women he'd been with had been unable to accommodate him, but he tingled with the thought that a man might be able to do it.

But he didn't.

Instead, Asher buried his nose into the skin at the base of Riley's cock, and breathed in deeply. No one had ever done that before.

"Ohh, fuck," groaned Asher, his eyes rolling back in his head.

"Dude, really?" asked Riley.

Asher laughed. "Oh, you have no idea. Someday, my boy, you will understand." And with that he returned to the task at hand—at mouth—with glee.

Riley could not comprehend how the smell of his crotch could in any way have the intoxicating effect that Asher seemed to be experiencing. In fact, the idea kind of repulsed him. But the feeling that was radiating out across his entire body, his entire being, overwhelmed his hesitation, and he rededicated himself to the abandonment of everything he had known before. If Asher liked it, that was enough for him—as long as Asher finally did what Riley was longing for him to do.

Asher, though, was in no obvious hurry to make with the eagle-and-snake act. He nuzzled around the base of Riley's penis, but when he had worked his way all around he paused over the loose skin of his scrotum. He kissed here, again and again, but then he opened his lips and drew in a fold of the gathered skin. He pressed it gently between his lips and tugged a little bit. Riley was in a hellishly heavenly place. It felt amazing to have this most private part of his body taken inside Asher's mouth, but it was also not what he most urgently wanted. It drove his already frantically bobbing penis to transports of frustrated, steely hardness.

Then he felt Asher's tongue. He was lapping softly at the skin gathered above his balls, and then he went lower. He kissed the smooth, rounded surface of each of Riley's testicles before wiggling his tongue over, and around, and between them, playing the skin taut, letting it gather again. Riley groaned and gripped the sheets.

Transported, Riley was startled to feel flashes of cool air—Asher's panting breath—rushing across his now-wet balls. And then those soft, teasing lips closed over his right ball, pulling it into Asher's mouth.

"Ohmygodohmygodohmygod...," breathed Riley. "Oh God, be careful—"

Asher let the testicle slip out from between his lips, and he looked up at Riley with a sparkle in his eye. "Really?"

"Yes, really. I guess I kind of have sensitive balls, because it almost always hurts."

"What almost always hurts?" Asher asked, his voice still full of mischief.

"When a girl sucks on my balls."

Asher raised an eyebrow. "And is that what is happening to you now? A girl sucking on your balls?"

Riley shook his head, feeling a little stupid.

"You know who else has balls?" Asher asked.

Riley returned his grin. "You do."

"That's right. And do you think that someone who has balls of his own, and knows how good they can feel, is going to mistreat yours?"

"I've never thought of it that way," Riley said.

"Well, now that you have, you can stop thinking." Asher grinned. "Relax, bro—I got this."

Asher's reassurance notwithstanding, Riley still sucked in a breath when Asher sucked in his right ball. But then his worries were obliterated by the insistent, careful, teasing, softly suctioning feel of Asher working his magic. Like most men, Riley had experienced his balls as a source of pain (courtesy of bike bars, errant soccer kicks, and harrowing misadventures with zippers) but never as a source of mind-bending pleasure.

Now, he did.

He felt Asher's sinuous tongue slipping along the surface of his trapped ball, mapping the landscape of its roundnesses and roughnesses. There was pressure and release in delightfully random rushes of sensation; he never knew what he would feel next and quickly had to give up any illusion of control over what was happening to him. He surrendered to it, to Asher. Of all of the things he had ever done in bed, surrender was one he had never even considered. Once he had given himself over to Asher, body as well as spirit, trusting him fully, a shivering warmth radiated out across his entire form. What Asher did to one part of his body was felt in every part. Riley floated.

When Asher released the part of Riley he had held in his mouth, it was only to make room for its companion. This time Riley didn't jump or gasp; this time he moaned and twisted in anticipation of the pleasure that was to come. In this he was not disappointed—Asher knew just how much pressure, how much tension, and how much suction Riley could handle out there on the border between exquisite pleasure and life-affirming, twitchy discomfort. His breath was ragged, and a yearning whine escaped from his throat with each exhalation.

With a wet, slurping noise that was probably more dramatic than it strictly needed to be, Asher released Riley from his mouth. Riley lay panting, glossed with sweat, desperate for more sensation, more contact.

"How'd I do?" Asher asked in a throaty rumble.

"Holy fucking fuck," Riley huffed. "Will you teach me how to do that?"

"Here's a little secret," Asher replied with a grin. "You already know how. All guys do. It's a shame most don't let themselves try."

"Well, I may need a little more tutoring," Riley said with a chuckle. "Do you think you can do that again, like, every night? For, say, ever?"

"I think," Asher mused, "there are other demands on my attention." He lightly traced his fingers up the length of Riley's still iron-hard cock. It twitched.

"I've reconsidered the situation, and I've come to see your point. Please, sir, proceed as you see fit. Right the fuck now, if that's okay with you?"

"Try and stop me," Asher purred, and he seized Riley's member more firmly. He squeezed it gently along its length. A tiny bead of clear liquid emerged from the tip, and his eyes lit up. He leaned close and touched his tongue to the crystal droplet, but not to the slit from which it emerged—

Riley felt no contact. He could, however, see the glittering strand stretch from the head of his penis to Asher's tongue.

Riley growled and made thrusting motions with his hips. He was desperate to get his cock into that man.

This thought, he reflected, should have disturbed him deeply. Fuck that, he thought. Fuck everything that has kept me from being in this moment all my life. Fuck everything outside this room, everywhere but on this bed.

Asher, it seemed, heard this body language loud and clear, for he leaned in again and placed this lightest, flutteriest of kisses on the very tip of Riley's penis.

"Unh, fuck!" cried Riley.

This was, apparently, exactly what Asher was waiting to hear. He smiled broadly and then leaned in and opened his mouth. In one swoop— one life-changing, all-in swoop—he swallowed Riley's cock to its root.

Riley whooped and threw himself backward, writhing and thrashing and moaning. His legs pumped, his arms waved, his head flopped side to side in manic motion. He'd never imagined such a thing was possible—even in porn, no one just swallows down a penis the size of his. But Asher was doing it, and he reared back and did it again. Riley wouldn't be able to take much more of this. A few more transits, and Asher finally pulled off and released Riley's cock to slap wetly against his belly.

"Having fun?" he asked.

"Were you raised in the circus, by sword-swallowers?"

Asher giggled.

"And don't tell me every man knows how to do that," Riley continued. "No one knows how to do that."

"I would be willing to teach you," Asher replied. "But it would require intensive practice. You would need a willing subject on whom to perfect your technique. For this, I humbly offer my services."

"Sounds intriguing. But first I need to see more—you've only just begun, after all."

"Hold on to your gonads, sir, because I'm going to blow your... mind." With that Asher set to work. He repeated his full-throated debut performance but quickly settled into a more focused lick-swirl-suck rhythm that had Riley gritting his teeth.

It wasn't long before Riley felt himself getting close: the heat was rising from his long-deferred erection, breaking in waves over his entire body. Asher's fist pumped up and down the lower half of his cock, while his mouth delivered a devastating suction at the head. With his other hand he lightly massaged Riley's balls. This must have been how he was able to anticipate Riley's impending orgasm, and a split second before the point of no return he stopped. Stopped everything—motion, suction, pressure, everything—and waited for the crisis to pass. It was perfectly played.

Riley screamed. Not a horror-movie scream, high and piercing, but a guttural, rumbling roar from deep in his chest. Everything in his body had been straining for that orgasm, reaching for it, desperate for it, and to have it yanked away in the moment of its realization was torture. His head pounded with frustration, his chest pounded with need, and down lower—down lower Asher was in charge, and he got right back on it. He slammed Riley's red and angry cock back into his mouth, and the man attached to it was instantly blasted back to the pearly gates of impending orgasm. It was whiplash of the most outrageously carnal kind.

Asher seemed to sense he would overplay his hand should he edge Riley again, so this time he went hell for leather, giving all he had to pull all he could out of Riley. Once again, he played Riley's organ like a virtuoso, hitting all the right notes and finally pressing all the keys at once.

Riley expected at each moment to have this orgasm yanked out from under him, so he tried to hold himself back from the precipice as long as he could. Soon, though, he could no more hold it back than he could keep the moon from rising in the sky. Each step, each throbbing, aching, breathtaking step toward that goal echoed through his body—this orgasm seemed to come from everywhere at once. His toes curled, his fingers tore at the sheets, every muscle in his body tightened as he strained to both keep and lose control. Finally, radiating from the epicenter between his legs, the explosion.

Riley would later try to describe this experience, this first orgasm pulled from him, pressed upon him, by another man. He would fail, every time. It was nothing less than the end of the life he had known as his own, and the start of a new one. It was a big bang, a universe-birthing event. Years of hidden need, cravings he didn't know he had, were simultaneously revealed and satisfied. It was everything, complete and entire. He lived.

And he was now very wet.

Asher had, at the very last moment, pulled off of Riley's cock and pumped it with both hands. He had been rewarded with a dozen or more

(Riley was in no state to count) jets of thick, white semen that now covered Riley and the bed.

"Come here," he croaked, reaching out with shaky hands to Asher.

Asher stretched himself along Riley's side and settled on the bed. Riley's eyes fluttered open, and he saw Asher propped up on one arm, looking down at him.

"That was...," he began but trailed off when he was deserted by his words.

"It was for me too," whispered Asher.

Riley considered Asher's words. "But you didn't...."

"Oh yes I did."

Riley blinked and focused a little more clearly. "But how...?"

"You have no idea how hot you are, do you?" Asher shook his head slowly and traced a finger along Riley's chest, drawing little circles around his nipples. "Touching you, tasting you, watching you experience that for the first time? God, Riley, all I had to do was press against the mattress once and I was over the edge." He smiled sweetly. "We got there together."

Riley took in an amazed breath. "That happens?"

Asher shook his head. "No. It doesn't. Only with you."

On a day of so many firsts for Riley, he was touched to his core that he had been able to provide Asher with a first of his own. He felt tears forming in the corners of his eyes. "That's... amazing," he said, a catch in his voice.

"You're amazing," Asher whispered. He leaned down and kissed Riley, softly and sweetly, and Riley knew he was okay. It was all going to be okay.

The air-conditioning was beginning to cool the dampness that still covered Riley's torso, and he shivered involuntarily.

"Here, let me get something," Asher said, sitting up. He threw his legs over the edge of the bed and got to his feet. He padded off toward the bathroom, leaving Riley in a sex-drunk haze of exhaustion and exhilaration. The water ran for a moment, and then Asher returned to the bed bearing a large bath towel that had been soaked in blissfully hot water. Starting at Riley's throat, he gently dabbed and caressed and massaged, working his way down across the chest and belly and the much larger amounts of wetness that had pooled there. Finally, he wiped clean the area around the base of Riley's cock and then swabbed it to the tip with the last corner of the towel. Riley had never felt so cared for.

Asher got up off the bed again and returned from the bathroom in short order. "Here, let's slip under the covers," he said, tugging at the sheets. Riley lifted himself up so that he could slide the sheets down behind him, and Asher slid in next to him.

"Hey, you're naked," Riley said, surprised by the surprise in his voice.

"I needed to clean up too, and I didn't want you to feel underdressed."

"Do you want me to…?" asked Riley, gamely.

"All I want is to lie here with you and try to convince myself that you're real." He kissed Riley, his tongue teasing and insistent. "I still can't believe you're here."

"Mmmm" was all Riley could manage as he drifted into an exhausted slumber.

TIME DOESN'T exist in Vegas, not the way it does in other places. In the hotels and casinos it's always twilight—the promise of the night lived out under the brightness of the day. But when Riley sat bolt upright in bed, he knew it was late. And he knew something was very, very wrong.

He leaned over to the other side of the bed, read the clock. It was 2:24 a.m. Outside, down on the Strip, the lights hadn't dimmed a bit. It was still full speed ahead, things happening there that don't happen anywhere else. Shouldn't happen at all.

Next to him lay the naked form of Asher, the man in Riley's bed. Actually, it was Riley himself who was in the other man's bed. And in this bed they had done things Riley had never done before. Had never wanted to do. Now, with his ardor cooled and the heat of contact abated, what flooded Riley was shame. Shame at what he had done, shame at what he had said, shame at what had been done to him. By this other man.

Shit.

Riley had to get out of here. He slid silently to the edge of this ridiculously wide, round bed, dropped his feet to the floor without a sound. The glow of the strip provided all the light he needed to gather his boxers, his shorts, his shirt. He pulled on the shorts, stuck the boxers in the pocket (hopping around trying to put on stupid underwear was the last thing he needed to embarrass himself doing), and slipped the shirt on without buttoning it. He padded quietly to the door, let himself out. A few steps down the hall and he was at his own room. He got into the shower and scrubbed harder than he ever had in his life. He tried to wash off the entire mortifying evening, the whole sordid horrible affair. Flashes of it came back to him, blared into his head unbidden: the dinner, the touching, kissing, the.... He scrubbed harder, till his skin was red and raw.

What he wasn't able to scrub off with soap, he tried to rub off with the towel. Dry but still unclean, he stumbled over to the dresser and pulled out the first clothes he could lay his hands on—nondescript and mostly black, they would allow him to disappear into the late-night crowd of gamblers and drunks he knew he would find on the Strip.

Opening the door, he looked both ways and found the hallway as quiet as it had been when he fled Asher's room. He walked briskly but quietly along the hallway to the stairway at the end. He shivered involuntarily when he passed Asher's door. It wasn't disgust he felt, he was sure of that, but what was it? Regret? Disgrace? He needed to walk. And think.

He descended the stairs in a controlled fall, hitting every other and sometimes every third step. He crashed through the door at the bottom and this time welcomed the wave of heat that shoved him back—this time it felt like cleansing fire.

A man staggering along the Strip at 3:00 a.m. will attract no attention—or, rather, will attract the attention only of those selling personal services that a lonely man might be persuaded to purchase. Riley avoided these, the heavily made-up women and the slight but jaded men, all hungry in their own way for what he might offer them. He didn't know how far he had walked before ducking into a casino across the street from where they had eaten dinner. Before.

The bar, like everyplace else in this town at this hour, had an air of desperate carnival to it.

"What'll ya have?" asked the bartender. She had a kind face that had seen too many days in the desert and a raspy voice that sounded of tobacco and recklessness.

"Scotch, please. Neat." Riley closed his eyes, covered his face with his hands.

A minute later a heavy crystal glass came to rest softly next to Riley's elbow. He opened his eyes, picked up the glass, and drank it down in one go. He set the glass down, as gently as he could.

"Wow," the bartender said, watching him as she dried some glasses. "That looks bad." She picked up the bottle and poured another for him. She put the bottle back on the bar and stepped back as if to get the big picture on her miserable new customer.

"It is," he said and picked up the refreshed glass. This time he paused to take in the aroma and stopped dead. He looked over at the bottle. "Wait," he blurted. "This is—"

"Yeah, it is. But don't worry—I'll only charge you for rail. You look like you needed something... more."

"You are... a saint, is what you are," Riley said gratefully, and he made himself sip instead of gulping. Because he wanted somewhere to look besides the mirror behind the bar, he studied the label on the bottle. It said nothing different than it did when he drank it for the first time—back at the Beverly Palace, with... him.

"Care to talk about it?" she asked as she stacked glasses under the bar.

"I don't think there are words for it," he said miserably. He took another pull on the smooth, warming amber in his glass.

"Oh honey, I've heard them all," she said with a sage resonance in her gritty voice. "Start with some small ones and work your way up."

Riley gave a mirthless chuckle and tipped up his glass. She picked up the bottle, uncapped it, but didn't tip it toward his glass. "I'll keep pouring, but only if you let out some of what's chewing you up. Deal?"

He looked pleadingly at her but then nodded. She poured, then settled her elbows on the bar to listen.

"You seem pretty good at this—you tell me. I'll give you three guesses."

"I don't need to guess," she replied. "Someone tore you up pretty bad, and just now, judging from the freshness of the wounds. Now the one thing I don't know"—she squinted an eye as if taking aim—"is whether you didn't get what you wanted, or if you got it and it turned out not to be what you wanted after all."

His glass, which had been halfway to his lips, dropped to the bar with a thud. "How'd you do that?"

"Spend a few years behind this bar and you could do it too. Now, tell me—who did this to you?"

Even with two single malts in him, he was able to recognize the artful avoidance of a gendered pronoun in her question. Not "what did she do to you." No, no normal questions for him. Not anymore. Not since Asher fucked everything up by being—well, whatever the hell he was. He took a healthy swig of his third pour.

"One thing you should know," she said briskly, as if changing the subject, "is that working here, I've heard everything. People have told me stuff that would make whatever crap you stepped in seem like a basket of puppies." She looked around the now-empty bar. "It's the end of my shift. All I have to look forward to at home is a sink full of dishes and a cat with digestive issues. You need to talk, I'm a listener."

Riley stared into the faceted glass, studying the reflection of light on the surface of the alcohol.

"You'll feel better, I promise."

He took a deep breath. "It's the second one," he said, still looking at his glass.

"Ah," she said, nodding. "Got what you want, but now you're not sure. Turned to ash in your mouth, huh?"

Riley jolted—he looked in the mirror instinctively, certain that his head had split open. All he saw was a pale version of himself, one that suffered openly, without hope.

"Oh God—honey, what is it?"

"Ash," he said, the one word he was capable of.

"That's just something my daddy used to say," she said. "It means—"

"Regret."

"Yeah, that's it," she said, nodding. "What do you regret?"

He groaned under his breath. "Ash. That's what I regret." He looked up at her, trying desperately to decide if he could trust her with this rawest of wounds, this most monstrous of secrets. "He's what I regret."

She nodded. "Got it." She wiped the bar, though it was already spotless. "That's the hard part done, now you've said it out loud. So tell me, what did he do?"

"Nothing." No, that wasn't right. "Nothing I didn't want him to. At the time, anyway. But then...." He polished off his drink for the third time.

She didn't reach for the bottle—she reached for his hand instead. "Oh, honey, that is the oldest story in the book. People come here and try things they wouldn't ever think of at home, then once the deed is done, they think they're going straight to hell."

"I thought it was what I wanted, but then after—"

She nodded wisely. "You're not the first to have his head turned by a boy in this town. They're good at that—and I should know, because a lot of them are friends of mine."

"No, it wasn't like that. He and I were already friends. We just... got... closer."

She nodded again—this was just another story she'd surely heard before. "Gotcha. Let me break this down for you. He made a move, got what he wanted, and you freaked the hell out. Now he'll move on to the next guy, and you go on with your life. The good news is, if he wants to keep seducing straight hotties—like the one sitting in front of me—he ain't gonna say anything about it. He's got a rep to protect, so yours is safe."

Riley parsed through this line of reasoning, his brain slowed somewhat by the Scottish fog that was quickly lowering over it. "No, that's not it. He didn't seduce me." Riley paused, then blundered ahead. "I was the one.... I told him I wanted...." The tears he'd been fighting back finally overwhelmed him, and his head sank into his hands as he sobbed.

For the next several minutes, he could hear nothing but the blood pounding in his ears and the pathetic sniffling of his clogged nose. At some point, she had poured him another drink, because when he finally got his breathing back under control, and had blotted his eyes and blown his nose, he saw another healthy pool of the amber liquid in the glass.

"Go ahead, drink it. It'll calm you down."

He did as he was told, because he didn't know what else to do.

"Now, this is, as they say, a horse of a different color. What you need to figure out has nothing to do with him—you need to figure out you."

Riley nodded, miserably. He knew that what she said was true. "I was so happy. In that moment I was the happiest I'd ever been."

"And then?"

"And then I woke up. And I realized what we had done."

"Which was what, if you don't mind my asking? Are we talking about a kiss, or...?"

"We.... He and I...." Riley swallowed, hard. "We made love."

"Oh, honey," she said and again placed her hand on his. "First time for you?"

He closed his eyes and nodded.

"Can I just flip to the last chapter and tell you how this ends? I think you deserve that." She apparently took his silence as assent. "Sweetie, whatever you thought about yourself before, now you know the truth. This freak-out is not because you've done something stupid that's going to stay in Vegas. You're freaking out because the truth is scary when it gets sprung on us all of a sudden. But that doesn't it make it any less true. Do you get what I'm saying?"

He shook his head—or, what used to be his head, before he'd filled it with alcohol. He was pretty far gone, which was fine with him.

She put another hand on his, held it tight. "It doesn't mean you're a pervert, and it doesn't mean you've been living a lie, and it doesn't make you a bad person. It just means that you know one true thing about yourself that you didn't before. Now, most people come to this gradually, and they have time to adjust, little bit at a time. You got it all at once, and it kind of feels like a safe's been dropped on you, doesn't it?"

He chuckled and nodded. It felt good to laugh, even at the black humor of a barkeep in a casino in the middle of the night.

"Here's what you're going to do. You're going to get some sleep, and you're going to wake up sometime tomorrow afternoon, and you're going to look yourself in the mirror and see that you're the same person you used to be. You just know something about yourself that you didn't know before. And then you're going to find that friend of yours, that 'Ash,' and tell him you freaked out, and you're sorry, and it was you and not him. Got that?"

He nodded. What she said made perfect sense. And it was the last thing that did.

PAIN. PAIN and the ceiling were the two things he was aware of. One he could see, looming above him; the other he could feel pounding in his temples, twinging in his stomach, throbbing behind his eyes. He slowly became aware of his situation. He was in his room, on top of his covers. He was fully clothed, though seriously rumpled. Midmorning light was streaming through the windows.

How had he gotten here?

He sat up but immediately realized his mistake as the throbbing in his head intensified suddenly. He flopped backward as gently as he could and tried to piece together what had happened last night. The part with Asher he remembered, of course—though he found he could now look back on it without the flash of shame that had plagued him at first. He recalled leaving Asher's room, and showering, and then he was at a casino bar, and then... what? How did he end up here, alone and hungover to an extent he hadn't imagined possible?

He flopped his head to one side and happened to glance at the clock. It was just after noon. But what day was it?

Think, Riley.

Fuck. It was Friday. His day with Daphne. And Asher's.

Asher.

Fuck.

Riley again struggled to sit up, fighting the pain in his head. He closed his eyes when the dancing lights of headache flashed too brightly, and finally they receded. He swung his legs off the bed, steadied himself on the side table, slowly rose to his feet. Once he was confident in his ability to remain upright, he walked haltingly toward the bathroom. On his way, he noticed something in his hand—it must have stuck to it when he was leaning on the side table. He shook it off, and as it fell, he saw it was a cocktail napkin. He picked it up—slowly, oh, the throbbing—and smoothed it on the bathroom counter. It was from the bar whose name had been lost in the fog of last night, but he knew when he saw it exactly whose writing was on it. He leaned close and squinted hard.

"Talk to him," it read. "He needs to know."

Riley found the toilet just in time. He threw up everything he had in his stomach, and more besides, until he felt sure that the turkey he ate last Thanksgiving was about to come up. Finally, exhausted, he slumped to the side of the commode and tried to remember how to breathe.

He was there for a while.

He crawled to the shower, opened the heavy glass door, and hauled himself to his feet once again. The water, when it finally came, was too hot, and then too cold, and then just too much. He stood unsteadily under the torrent, spitting it out when it filled his mouth or nose, rocking back and forth because—well, he didn't know why. He leaned against the cold marble tile, and finally the tears came. They came in great hacking sobs, in pitiable sniffles, in shaking shuddering cries of anguish that echoed around the palatial lavatory. He was a snotty, bleary mess—he sniffed, trying to clear his clogged nose, and then spat a great glob onto the floor of the shower. Spat out all of that misery and regret, spat it out like....

Ash.

The name hit him like a shaft of light: he had been wandering in the darkness, and that name came to him, to save him. There was no shame now, only clarity and truth and… purity. He had burned off the conflicted feelings and twisted shame, and all that remained now was the pure power of the love he shared with Ash. The man in his life.

Suddenly, he could breathe again. He felt a physical weight lift off his chest. His head no longer throbbed, as if admitting Asher to his life had displaced the pain, leaving his head clear and his heart light. But there was still something missing. He knew where to find it—down the hall.

He washed the remnants of last night off his body and out of his hair, and he stepped lightly out of the shower. He toweled off, shaved, and dressed in a flurry. He couldn't wait to see Asher; his heart fluttered at the thought. He stuck his head out into the hallway to make sure the coast was clear and then slunk quickly down the hall, past all of the other bachelors' doors, and arrived at Asher's. He knocked quietly and listened intently. No response. He knocked again, a little more loudly. Nothing.

He walked back to his room and only then recalled that Asher's date with Daphne was going on right now. They were at the zoo, talking to the animals, while Riley had been agonizing (and barfing, and crying). They had clearly gotten the better end of that deal.

Riley opened his door and heard the phone ringing. He ran to it and picked it up eagerly.

"Hello?"

"Riley? We need you to meet the limo downstairs at three, in your tux."

"Isn't that kind of early for dinner?"

"We have some shooting we need to do first, while you're fresh. Three o'clock, okay?"

"Got it," he answered and placed the receiver back in the cradle.

At 2:55 he stepped once again into the hallway, dressed in the brand-new tux that the show had provided for the occasion. He pushed the down button for the elevator and stepped toward the doors marked by the flashing light. They slid open, and Riley's heart stopped.

It was Asher, back from his zoo date.

He had been leaning against the corner of the elevator, and his eyes only opened when the doors slid out of the way completely. He shook his head and pushed off from the wall toward the door. He nearly tripped when he saw Riley standing there.

The sight of him took Riley's breath away. His reservations, his doubts, they were all swept away by the presence of this man in his life. He smiled and opened his arms to him.

Asher set his jaw and brushed past him into the hallway, clipping his shoulder on the way. He didn't slow down.

"Ash?" Riley called.

Asher turned the corner and was gone.

"THE GAME is Baccarat *Chemin de Fer,*" the croupier intoned silkily. The competition was about to begin.

Over the last twenty-four hours Riley had tried every way he could think of to get Asher to talk to him, or at least listen, without success. Asher wouldn't answer the door or the phone, and he resolutely walked away from him when they happened into the same space. Now they were required to be in the same place, though Asher had managed to place himself at the far end of the table from Riley. He wouldn't meet Riley's eye.

The game progressed without much excitement—whoever came up with this idea had clearly been more enamored of the James Bond feel of baccarat than the reality of the game, which was largely one of chance. There was some strategy but really only in the betting. It was a lot like watching people play blackjack, which in terms of excitement was just above televised golf. They would probably create tension out of whole cloth with quick cuts and dramatic music, but the World Series of Poker this was not.

To Riley, the game was heart pounding. The only strategy he cared about was Asher's, and that strategy seemed to consist entirely in betting against Riley. When Riley had the Bank, Asher bet big, clearly hoping to drive him out of the game. Riley losing a hand seemed to be the only thing that lightened his mood.

Riley did not enjoy himself.

Of the eight bachelors competing, three were broke before the first round of the game had been completed. Riley went out next, distracted as he was by Asher's apparent bloodlust. Play continued long enough that most of the deposed bachelors drifted off, knowing they would not be needed for a close-up, but Riley stuck around to see Asher win the final hand and be declared the victor of this competition. After the obligatory interviews with Asher and Daphne, it was past midnight. Riley waited in the lobby by the elevators for Asher to come by, but when he caught sight of Riley he turned and walked out of the hotel altogether.

Riley could have chased him down, but before he could even take a step, he rejected the idea. Clearly Asher didn't want to talk to him, and Riley could hardly blame him. But, he thought as he rode the elevator back up to the top of the hotel, wouldn't Asher have expected him to need some time to adjust to this not inconsequential change in his life? He seemed to understand what a huge thing this was to Riley, and he was so reluctant to even entertain the idea of their being together that in the end Riley (he blushed to recall it) had had to practically force himself on Asher.

But this utter silence? The complete rejection? As he took off his tux and got ready for bed, he had no choice but to admit he had hurt Asher far more than he had realized. Only emotional devastation would have this profound an effect—and Riley was well acquainted with emotional devastation. He had broken Asher's heart, without meaning to, and pointlessly. He needed to find a way to make it right.

"WELL, SHIT," Kaitlyn spat, watching the last of the footage from the baccarat table. She turned to Omar. "You never heard me say this"—she heaved a great breath—"but I was wrong."

Omar jolted, then looked heavenward.

"What are you doing?" she asked.

"I assumed since you admitted you were wrong I would shortly witness the return of Vishnu."

"Very funny. But seriously, I can admit when I've been beaten. I really thought those boys belonged together—after the soup kitchen, I figured they were working on being the next Bill and Melinda Gates. But it's clear that whatever spark they had has been extinguished."

"So, now what?"

"Now nothing, I guess."

"But we have established that Asher really is gay, right?" Omar said, in the manner of a prompter reading a line to a forgetful actor.

"Maybe."

"Maybe? Perhaps you're working with a different definition of 'gay' than I am."

"He told Riley he was gay, but since then he's done nothing but push him away. It may be some strange attempt at strategy, for all we know."

"And that means we're going to…?"

"Do nothing," Kaitlyn said definitively. "We keep the competition going, and they all stay in. Whatever drama there was between Riley and Asher is over now, and they're still competing. Score one for cutthroat competition, and zero for the last flicker of romance." She sighed, but with resignation. "It all makes the last few events easier. Run them out to the South Pacific, do the hometown visit, and done."

Omar tipped his head, looked thoughtful. "Seems like the fun has gone out of it for you."

She nodded. "Yep. Story of my life. But we just need to keep moving." She shook her head, sighed again. "Why don't you pull up the itinerary for Tahiti, and let's make sure everything's ready."

Omar set to work, but it seemed the fun had gone out of it for him as well.

CHAPTER FOURTEEN

DESERT ISLAND

THE SIX remaining bachelors settled into their seats for the long flight to Tahiti. There they would transfer to a much smaller plane of the wheezing, propeller-driven sort and finally arrive the next morning at the tropical resort on Bora Bora that would be their home for the week. This was a rest and relaxation week that the bachelors and Daphne would enjoy; at the end, they would accompany her to her hometown to meet her family. She would make her final selection, as would America, upon their return to LA.

The rattling shuttle bus that retrieved them from the airport shook and shimmied its way to the dock, where it drove slowly and carefully onto a small ferryboat. They chugged across the lagoon, finally coming to a lurching halt at the chipped-concrete pier on the far side. This tiny island existed solely to support the resort the bachelors would occupy—there was quite literally nothing on the island otherwise but a few low buildings that housed the staff. Walkways extended in thin arcs from the core of the resort, and arrayed along each like leaves on a fern was a series of bungalows. They stood on stilts in the shallow water of the lagoon. The bachelors were each assigned one of the bungalows that lined one of the arms, three on each side, and Daphne occupied a larger structure at the very end.

Riley's bungalow was the first on the right, so he was the first to be dropped off by the bell captain, with his suitcase. He opened the door and walked in to find a beautifully wood-finished space, clearly designed with romance in mind. There was a large bathtub situated in front of floor-to-ceiling windows with a view of the ocean; a bed on a platform under a huge skylight; and a trapdoor set into the floor. Riley lifted it to find a ladder that dropped directly into the bright-blue water below. Atop the structure was a terrace with a fire pit and loungers. It was gorgeous, out here on the edge of the world. There was only one thing needful.

Asher.

Just at that moment, Asher emerged into the sunshine at the top of his bungalow on the other side of the walkway. Riley watched him, hoping he would turn and look over, but if he saw Riley, he gave no sign. After his quick survey of the area, he ducked back down and was gone. Riley stepped slowly down the spiral staircase and stood in the silence of his lovely, lonely bungalow.

The beach was located at the base of the walkway, surrounding the main resort buildings, and that was where the primary shooting would take place. The producers had assured the bachelors this week was to be relaxing, and they should focus on just "being themselves." As if that meant anything anymore. The lack of formal competition should have made the bachelors happy, but a week of simply lounging around the beach made most of them crazy. Riley could tell just how crazy by the level of posturing and machismo on display during time on the beach. The only men who seemed to know how to make conversation with Daphne were Riley, Shane, and, of course, Asher. They took turns talking with her in the shade of the verandahs and palm trees, while the other three bachelors strutted and posed.

Riley felt that his and Asher's position in the game was as strong as ever, but their situation with each other was as bad as it had ever been. Asher had won Vegas week, while one of the other bachelors (who did, Riley could admit to himself, look amazing in a tux) had won the viewer's vote. Riley couldn't begrudge him his victory, but he wished keenly to congratulate him, to celebrate with him. To be acknowledged by him. That would be a start.

After two days in paradise, Riley was on the verge of going completely insane.

HE KNOCKED on the trapdoor in the middle of the night. Above him slow footsteps sounded across the floor, paused, and then finally reached the hatch. It swung open.

"Riley? What the fuck!"

Riley climbed up the ladder before Asher could have second thoughts about opening it. He hefted himself as quickly as he could through the opening and plopped rather less elegantly than he wanted to onto the floor of exotic tropical woods. He scrambled to his feet, sending water droplets onto every surface. He stood, panting and looking pleadingly at Asher.

"Please," he said, breathlessly. "Please listen."

Asher seemed to recover at least a small part of his composure. He tied the robe he had apparently just thrown on with a vigorous knot. "Go," he said bluntly, as he held the trapdoor, ready to slam it shut. "Just go."

"No, please. Please listen to me. I want to explain what happened."

Asher sighed. "You don't need to. I understand it all—even the parts that you are, apparently, only starting to work out for yourself."

"I made a mistake," Riley said, his voice thick. Now that he was finally here, and Asher was finally listening to him, it was all he could do to keep from bursting into tears. But he was determined to get through this. "A huge mistake. I know that now."

Asher's eyes flashed. "I've been called a mistake by better men than you," he hissed. If he was aiming to wound, he had done it. "Now get the fuck out."

Riley blinked back tears. "No," he said in a choked voice. It was low and strained, but it carried the seriousness of his resolve. "Not until you listen."

"Listen to you tell me how it seemed like a good idea at the time, but it turns out you're not really into guys after all? Listen to how it's not me, it's you? Listen to you reconstruct your wounded masculinity after the damage I've done to it with my evil seductive ways? Why the fucking fuck would I want to listen to that? Because I've never heard it before?" Asher's voice was rising, starting to break. "Let me tell you one thing: I have been here and I have done this, and I won't do it again." A sob caught in his throat. "Don't do this to me."

Riley was shocked by the sudden turn of Asher's anger to misery. "That isn't what I was going to say. I wouldn't say those things."

"It doesn't matter what you were going to say!" Asher was crying out now, in pain and in frustration. He took a deep breath and wiped his eyes with the palms of his hands. "I could handle any of that if you were some kind of Vegas fling, a one-night stand, don't-ask don't-tell casino hook-up," he said, his voice lower but just as strained. "But I fell in love with you, Riley. I knew the risk, and I did it anyway. I let myself believe that you knew what you were about, against my better judgment. I let you in. Into my—" His voice cracked, and he struggled to complete the thought. "—into my heart."

"Asher, I—"

"And then... and then you bolt from my bed, without a word. I could have handled that, maybe I even expected it. But then you show up at my door with some tramp you picked up in a bar, drunk out of your fucking mind, just to show me how fucking hetero you are. No one's ever treated me that way, not the most closeted, angry, repressed guy out of his mind with homo panic—no one has ever treated me that way."

"What? What are you talking about? I didn't—"

"Oh the hell you didn't. Don't try to tell me that you were too drunk to know what you were doing. You knew exactly what you were doing. You brought her to my room to show me, to rub my nose in it. That's when you went from confused to just cruel. That was just… cruel." He was crying freely now. "I swear to God you are the last straight man I will ever—"

"Damn right!"

Asher shook his head. "What?"

"I'm the last straight man you will ever," Riley said emphatically. "You were with me on my last night as a straight man, and my first night as a gay one."

Asher's mouth opened, but no sound emerged.

"I know who I am, Ash. I finally know who I am. And what you mean to me."

Asher shook his head. "I don't understand."

"I'll explain everything. But can I dry off first? This is kind of uncomfortable."

Asher looked the soaked and rumpled Riley up and down. "Most people would have put on a swimsuit before going swimming."

"I didn't really think it through. I saw your light on, and everyone else had gone to sleep, and so I just dove in. I didn't want to lose my chance." For the first time Riley saw something like warmth on Asher's face, but it was gone almost before it appeared. Still, he felt hope stirring in his chest where there had only been desolation before. He stripped off his T-shirt. "Can I have your other robe? Assuming that you don't have someone else here using it, that is."

Asher rolled his eyes. "I don't think I'll be having anyone in my bed for some time. You kind of ruined that for me for a while." He walked to the bathroom and returned with the robe. He handed it over to Riley.

"Thanks," Riley said. It felt like the first normal word he had spoken since his emergence from the water. He threw the robe around his shoulders, then slipped off his soaked shorts and underwear. He tied the robe and then kicked the wet clothes over to the waterproof apron surrounding the trapdoor.

Asher stood, waiting.

"Hey, have you been up top at night?" Riley asked.

"No."

"Come on. You need to see this sky." Riley bounded to the spiral staircase. Like everything in Asher's bungalow, it was a mirror image of his—the stairs even spiraled the opposite direction. He reached for Asher's hand, but the other man pulled it back. Riley was undeterred. He stepped to the side and swept his hand before him. "After you," he said with a bow.

Asher walked up the stairs, and Riley followed close behind. He was shocked at the reaction he had to Asher's smell—woody, clean, and spicy. He was certain he would not have been able to describe it when not in the man's presence, but his body responded to it like a drug. Riley was a little light-headed by the time he got to the top of the stairs.

The layout of the rooftop was ingenious: there was a central area where the two-person lounger sat, surrounded by low planters that obscured them from the prying eyes of the neighboring bungalows but opened them to the sky and to the ocean in the distance. Knowing that turning on the lights would reveal them to any passersby, they felt their way through the pitch-black night from the top of the staircase to the seating area. They settled into the wide lounger, side by side in the warm tropical breeze, under the wide sky full of stars.

They lay without speaking for several long minutes. Then, Riley screwed his courage to the sticking place and started.

"I am so sorry," he said. It was as good a place as any to begin. "I acted like an idiot—like a panicked, adolescent idiot. You didn't do anything wrong. You were amazing. Are amazing. You are more than I could ever deserve."

He could hear Asher breathing in the darkness next to him, but he remained silent.

"When I woke up a couple of hours after... afterward, I just freaked out. It was like I had broken through some deep-seated monstrous repression, and it came roaring back in the still of the night. I needed to get out—I couldn't breathe."

He heard Asher take a short breath, perhaps a sob?

"It wasn't anything you did—it was all me," Riley continued. "I went to my room, and showered, and threw on some clothes, and got out of the hotel. Ended up in an empty casino dive drinking expensive whiskey with a sympathetic bartender. She just let me talk and helped me see what an epic asshole I'd been. I don't remember what happened after that—I woke up the next day."

Asher finally made a sound. It was a low chuckle. "I can fill in the rest for you," he said. "Your new friend brought you back to the hotel, and you apparently told her you belonged in my room, so at four in the morning, she pounded like Hannibal's army until I opened the door."

"Oh, shit."

"Yes, I think that's what I said at the time. You were a complete mess, and she was—well, you have a pretty good idea of what it looked like. I thanked you both for gracing me with a visit, and I shut the door—pretty hard. I may have slammed it, in fact. The maintenance guys had to see to the hinges the next morning."

"You must have thought I was a complete bastard."

"Again, I may have used those exact words."

Riley reached out his hand in the darkness, toward the sound of Asher's voice. He touched the other man's shoulder and then stroked the stubbly cheek. He thought—he hoped—that he felt it move slightly toward him, but he couldn't be sure. "I am so sorry," he said.

"You broke my heart," Asher whispered after a silence that seemed to Riley to stretch out for minutes. "I fell so hard for you. I didn't want to, because I knew it wasn't going to end well, but you wore me down. And then you left."

"I was out of my mind—that's all I can say about it. You have to understand what a huge thing it was for me—I just couldn't deal with it all at once like that."

He heard Asher move on the lounger next to him, and when he spoke again his voice was louder, more sure. "You didn't have to deal with it alone! I figured the first time might be rough, but I held you and watched you sleep for an hour, amazed that you were finally there with me."

Riley didn't know what to say. He had never imagined the experience from Asher's side, how it must have felt to wonder whether he was going to be abandoned by another man who thought he might try being gay for a while.

"I was going to leave the show," Asher finally continued. "I called the producers and I was about to tell them I was done, I was going home. I couldn't bear the thought of having to see you again. But then I thought of my sister, and how much she needs me, and I decided to stick it out. When those elevator doors opened and I saw you standing there, I just about lost it. I can't tell you how much I wanted to run into your arms, to pretend you hadn't skipped out on me, hadn't slept with some tramp to remind me—remind yourself—that you were straight. I went back to my room and cried until I was dehydrated. I worked my way through the minibar, and the next morning all I wanted to do was beat you at baccarat so you would know how much you hurt me."

Riley let this hang in the air for a moment or two.

"I will never hurt you again," he said, his voice small but steady. "I am yours for as long as you will have me."

More silence.

"I wish I could believe that," Asher finally replied. "I want to, but—"

"You have no reason to trust me. But I took a leap of faith with you in Vegas—I trusted you even though it meant changing everything I thought about myself. But I took that chance. And it was the best thing I've ever done. I didn't see that right away, but I know it now. I want to be the best thing in your life, like you are in mine."

Asher's breath caught, as if he were suppressing a sob or a laugh. Riley couldn't tell which.

"Look at that sky," Riley said. "This is what it must have looked like when Telemachus and Pisistratus lay down together and looked up at the stars. They didn't know what lay ahead, but they were sure of each other." He turned in the darkness toward Asher. "I am sure of you, and I am sure that next to you is where I want to be."

He again heard the catch in the other man's breathing, and this time he knew exactly what it meant. Asher had heard him, understood him. A wave of relief swept through Riley. He had come home.

Riley rolled onto his side so he was pressed up against Asher. He leaned in and instinctively found the other man's ear. "I love you," he whispered into it. "More than anything in this world."

"Oh, Riley," Asher murmured, his voice thick with emotion. He reached up to Riley's face, and—again, with what must surely be a lover's instinct—found it in the dark. He ran his hand along Riley's jaw, to the back of his head. "I love you," he said, the words low and unhurried.

Riley then felt the one thing that he needed in all the world—Asher's lips. What had been an impossibility a short time ago—another man's mouth on his own—was now a necessity, was life itself. He kissed him back with all of the force that longing and desperation and the fear of having lost him forever brought to bear. There, under the stars, they kissed like they were born to complete each other. Riley rose without breaking contact with Asher's lips—he never wanted this kiss to end. He pushed Asher back gently until he fully reclined against the back of the lounger, then rolled onto him. Riley lay astride Asher, their bodies pressed together in the silence and the darkness. The only light came from the stars, the only sound from the waves of the lagoon lapping against the stilts of the bungalow far below.

It was when Riley released the other man's mouth and gently kissed his chin, his cheeks, his eyes that he felt the tears that rolled down in the dark. "What's the matter?" he whispered, panic edging into his consciousness.

Asher was silent for a moment. "Nothing," he finally whispered in return. "Nothing will ever be wrong again if you're here with me. Fuck, I thought I had lost you forever—I didn't know how I was going to face another day."

Riley kissed the damp tracks of Asher's tears, erasing the salty evidence of his sadness. "I will always be here," he murmured resolutely. "Nothing will ever keep me from you again."

Asher's sharp intake of breath was followed instantly by his pressing his lips to Riley's with a desperate passion. They kissed until Riley felt something he hadn't before—a lengthening, a hardening where their hips met. Knowing that he had this effect on Asher filled him with pride—and a little bit of panic. He hadn't done this, any of this, before.

"Will you do something for me?" Riley whispered into Asher's ear.

"Anything."

"Tell me if I'm doing it wrong."

"You kiss like it was an Olympic sport. You're not capable of doing it wrong."

Riley laughed. "I've actually kissed people a few times in my checkered past. But I've never done any of the things I'm about to do to you."

Asher brought his hands up to rest on either side of Riley's face. "You don't have to do anything," he said with a slow intensity. "It's enough just to have you here, in my arms. I don't need anything else."

Riley leaned in and rested his cheek on Asher's. "I need it. I need you, Ash. And tonight I'm going to show you how much."

"Oh, fuck," murmured Asher, tipping his head back. Riley could feel a shiver twitch along his entire body.

"That's more like it," Riley whispered and kissed his way down Asher's throat to the top of his chest.

He slid his fingers into the open neck of the bathrobe, pushing back the fabric slowly. He glided his fingertips along the smooth, firm surface of Asher's skin and was rewarded with an explosion of goose bumps. He felt along each rounded, solid pectoral muscle until he reached the nipples, full and stiff and beckoning. He slowly circled a thumb over each one, teasing them to even greater prominence. Then he lowered his head and took the left one into his mouth, kissing it and allowing it to penetrate him, to occupy his mouth. Asher let out a low moan, his back arching, thrusting his chest up toward Riley's mouth.

"How am I doing?" Riley asked, sly mischief in his voice.

"Fucking amazing" came the immediate reply—a redundant reply, as Asher's body language had already conveyed the same message.

Pleased, Riley kissed his way over to the other nipple and then, without warning, swooped down on it with a vigor that surprised both men. As he slowly, gently tugged at the skin with his teeth, Asher moaned and writhed. Riley felt the muscles pulling and stretching under his skin, spasms surging their way across his chest. This, Riley realized in a flash, is how men and women are different—he loved women's breasts because they were part of, but delightfully independent from, the structure of their bodies; they remained soft and yielding and responsive even as their mistress arched and moaned and climaxed. But with Asher, the structure of his chest—the geography Riley was blindly traversing in the dark—was entirely determined by his movements, by the tension and tug of his gymnastic musculature. It was a whole new world every time he shifted, every time he was caught unawares by a new pleasure. The pure unity of the body's deep structure and its surface dazzled Riley. He could read Asher, know what he was feeling deep inside, by tracing his fingers—and his mouth—across the smooth and ridged surfaces of his body.

As entranced as Riley was by Asher's exotically robust chest, he drew his fingers downward, to trace the underside of the pectorals and then to sweep out over Asher's ribcage. Riley had noticed, and admired, the sharply ridged obliques on several occasions; now he became more intimately acquainted with them by running his fingertips over them in lazy swooping spirals. They stood out more strongly as he did so, and he heard Asher take in a breath.

"Ticklish?" Riley lifted his head and asked into the darkness.

"Desperately," replied Asher, clearly short of breath. "But it's wonderful—please don't stop."

"Your wish," Riley whispered and slowed the motion of his hands to a luxurious pace that allowed him to feel every goose bump raised on Asher's torso. This landscape of excitation was something completely new to Riley, who had never taken this much time to study the body of anyone with whom he had shared a bed. With women the excitement was always partly, and sometimes mostly, visual. Here, deprived of his sight by the inky blackness of this moonless night, his other senses took over. And he was overwhelmed.

As he pushed open the bathrobe to gain access to Asher's belly, he recalled the gasps of wonder that often accompanied its exposure during the challenges. Every time Asher took off his shirt, onlookers reacted with startled envy (most men) or frank desire (most women). Riley himself, he smiled to think, had experienced both reactions, often at the same time. But now this legendary package of tight muscle, this ridged promised land of gymnastic power, was his and his alone. With slow, ecstatic purpose he ran a finger down the deep valley marking the middle passage from chest to the wonders that lay to the south. Riley leaned in and kissed each square ingot of abdominal muscle, feeling the fine hairs brush against his lips, tickling them, making his glee complete.

"You are so beautiful," he sighed.

Asher chuckled. "You can't even see me."

"I don't have to. I could spend the rest of my life tracing your body with my hands, feeling how it all fits together so perfectly."

Asher sat up and pulled Riley's face to his. "I fucking love you," he growled and then pressed his mouth to Riley's with a kiss that took his breath away.

"Now you lie back," Riley said once he had recovered the use of his lips. He pushed on Asher's powerful chest. "I still have a lot of territory to cover."

He again kissed Asher's stomach, but this time he continued, feeling the muscles lengthen and smooth out as they reached over his lower belly. He planted a dainty kiss on Asher's navel, then wriggled his tongue around inside, delighting in hearing the giggles that resulted. Still he moved down across the smooth, taut expanse of skin that sloped down toward Riley's goal. He wasn't expecting to run into Asher's penis so suddenly, but his chin made contact well before his mouth reached Asher's groin. Not wanting to jump to the end of the game immediately, Riley steered to the side of the stiff slab of flesh and continued his progress down. The fine hairs of Asher's lower belly gave way to thicker and slightly longer hair that marked the border of the undiscovered country. Remembering what Asher had done, Riley nuzzled his nose into the base of Asher's cock and took in his essence. Instantly he felt his own manhood surge in response—the smell that had struck him on the stairs was concentrated a hundredfold, and it made his head swim. He understood Asher now on a level he hadn't imagined previously. He wanted to pretty much live here, breathing in this amazing essence.

But this night wasn't about him—it was about making Asher see how much he loved him. Riley knelt between Asher's legs and swept both of his hands in over the ridge that marked Asher's hipbone toward the center of his body. His hands circled the root of Asher's cock and began to close around it. He ran his fingers upward from the broad base along its considerable length to where its head flared. There he encountered a small rivulet of slightly sticky wetness. He slowly pulled his finger away, feeling the thread stretch and lace his other fingers, and he rubbed his fingertips together, slipping them against each other, glorying in what Asher had produced for him. He brought his fingers to his open mouth and ran them along his lips, tasting another man for the first time in his life. The sweet, sticky intimacy sent a shiver down his spine despite the warm, still tropical air.

"You taste," he moaned, breathless, "so fucking good."

Asher's only reply was a groan and a thrashing noise, as if he were tearing at his bathrobe in desperation.

Delighted at this reaction, Riley returned his hands to their rightful place on Asher's hard penis and slid them lightly up and down. "Like that, do you?"

"I'm… going to…," Asher huffed, his voice reduced to a hungry whine, "fucking… explode!"

"But I'm just getting started," Riley replied, his voice innocent.

Asher laughed, a crazy, somewhat unhinged laugh. "You forget…. I started months ago."

Startled, Riley stopped stroking Asher's erection. This brought another groan and an insistent thrusting, but he refused to grant any friction. "Tell me."

"Tell you… what?" moaned Asher.

"Tell me about when you 'started.' When was it?"

Riley expected Asher to be frustrated by this demand, but he instead seemed happy to have a distraction.

"It was at the jousting competition." Asher's voice was calmer now, just a bit.

"When we fought together?"

"No, before that. When we were getting made up."

"I didn't even see you then," Riley replied, baffled.

"I was two stations away from you. You hardly looked around, though. You seemed absolutely panicked by the whole thing. And then, right before it was time to compete, I saw what happened."

Riley took what felt like his last breath. "You saw…?"

"Everything. It was the hottest thing I've ever seen in my life. When he put the towel around you, and then leaned in close to you while you wanked? That just about did me in. Un-fucking-believable."

Riley was silent for a moment. "You must have thought I was a complete pervert."

"No—not at all. I saw that you were there to win. But I also saw that you were at war with what your body wanted. And that's when I let myself hope, in just one small corner of my mind, that we might be able to be… close."

"So when you teamed up with me, you were really hoping that…?"

"Oh, I was out to win. Or at least come in second. But I knew if I was going to make it work with anyone in the competition, it was going to be you. And here we are!"

"Yeah, because you planned all of that crazy shit that happened to us." Riley chuckled. "Right."

"All I had to do was stay close to you, and I knew it would all work out."

"You're brilliant. Now let me see if there's something I can do to show my appreciation for your hard work." He again gripped Asher's steel-hard cock and began to slide his fingers up and down its length.

"Oh, fuck," Asher moaned, and again Riley could sense flailing motion from the upper part of his body. "I'm not going to last long," he added.

"I'll take that as a compliment," Riley growled, and he hunched down over Asher's crotch. He licked his lips, reminded himself to keep his teeth out of the way, and then—for the first time—he opened wide and let another man enter him. He swirled his tongue around the substantial cock head in his mouth, wetting it to reduce friction, preparing it and himself for what was to come. He panicked a bit, realizing what he was doing, what he was about to do, but then the taste of Asher filled his mouth—that sweetness, that pure essence of the man—and he relaxed. He edged a little farther down, eased a little more of Asher into him.

"Oh! Oh! Oh!" Asher's staccato moan, quiet and desperate and plaintive, reached Riley's ears like music.

Then came the surge.

The head of Asher's cock seemed to double in size, and Riley heard him take in ten or more jagged, strangled breaths, as if he were trying to hold back a tsunami.

In this he failed.

Riley slid his hands to the base, where Asher's penis was rooted to his tensing and now thrusting body, and he pressed down firmly—Asher's thrusts were growing more urgent, and he knew he couldn't handle an entire erection the way Asher had back in Vegas. This pressure seemed to drive Asher to new heights, though, and he gasped aloud several times before a final urgent thrust that he held, frozen in his seizure of ecstasy.

Riley knew he should pull off as Asher had done to him, letting him shower the rooftop garden. But he didn't—couldn't—because he had let go of Asher once, and he would never do that again. He wanted Asher to know that he was all-in, that he had embraced who he was and who Asher was to him. What they were together, now. And so he held on; he kept the head of Asher's now ridiculously large manhood firmly in his mouth and sucked twice as hard for good measure.

"No, I'm gonna…." This was as far as Asher got.

Riley responded by pressing down even farther with his mouth, by wriggling his tongue even more energetically around the head of Asher's penis.

"Oh God…." Asher's voice was weak and resigned, and he didn't move or speak or even seem to breathe again.

The first pump of semen flowed into Riley's mouth like a beam of sunshine on a summer's day, and it filled him with warmth and, to his surprise and delight, with joy. Then the second one came, with twice the volume and four times the force. Riley welcomed it as well and swallowed hard. Then the orgasm got fully underway. Swallow, breathe, hang on; swallow, breathe, hang on—this was Riley's mantra as the orgasm crashed its way through Asher's body, the full force of it flooding into Riley's mouth. It was overwhelming, yes, but hanging on for the wild ride was his way of showing Asher how much he cared, how much he… loved him. Riley was in love, he knew that now with a clarity that lightened his heart; it was proven by the sticky surfeit in his mouth.

With a great heaving groan Asher began to breathe again as the tip of his cock slipped from Riley's mouth. Riley held firm to it with his hand, though, and bathed it with gentle nuzzling licks and kisses while it began to soften—though only slightly. He would have been content to remain like this the rest of the night, nestled between Asher's legs, making slow and deliberate love to this wonder of a penis he still held in his grasp. But Asher reached down in the darkness and pulled him up by the shoulders. Riley could not resist the imploring tug he felt, the urgency in Asher's grip. He slid slowly, luxuriantly, up along the body now slick with sweat, until they were once again facing each other.

"That was the best thing anyone has ever done to me. Ever," breathed Asher, his voice low and quiet and dazzled.

"Thanks, but since it was my first time, I'm sure you've had better."

"No." Asher's voice was firm. "No. It was you. It was beyond anything I've ever known because it was you. This is everything I've ever wanted—you are the one I've been waiting for all my life."

Riley kissed him, trying to convey by the motion of his lips the workings of his heart. "I never even knew what I wanted," he said, finally. "I'm the luckiest man in the world. Before I was aware of what my life was missing, you showed up and gave it to me. You've given me the joy without the hungering for it, the completion without ever having felt the lack. You're a miracle, and I will never let you go."

Without another word—they needed no more—they lay together under the stars, friends and lovers, two halves of one heart.

THE ROSY fingers of dawn were beginning to play at the edges of the wide sky when Riley's eyes opened. In the pink predawn light, he looked down with joy at where their limbs overlapped and entwined, an entanglement of contented rest. Asher stirred as well and opened his sleepy but clear eyes.

"You're still here," Asher said, and Riley was ashamed at the almost imperceptible note of surprise in his voice.

"I will always be here," Riley answered, and he kissed Asher's nose. This led to more kissing, until both men felt the urgency of their bodies' contact.

"But right now I have to go," he said, with a wry grin. "Got to keep up appearances, right?"

Asher made a face that on a puppy at the pound would result in instant adoption. "Do you really have to?"

"What choice do we have? If I stay here, we're basically out of the game."

"Would that be so bad?" Asher asked. "Everything I need to be happy in life is right here with me." He kissed Riley again as if to drive the point home. His argument was buttressed by his erection poking Riley's leg.

"Do you really want to cause that kind of scandal? We're almost there. Just another week, and we can win this thing."

"Won't it cause a scandal then anyway? Why put it off?"

"Because if we hang in, your sister will get the treatment she needs, and when the dust settles, we'll be able to start our lives together."

Asher looked him right in the eyes and spoke slowly and seriously. "I would give up anything to be with you."

"I think I've given up a lot too—a lifetime of heterosexuality, for one," Riley said with a grin. "But we don't have to give up anything if we stick with the plan. The hometown visit will be a cakewalk, and then we have a few weeks of publicity to do, and then we're done. Things go back to normal, and we spend the rest of our lives doing this."

Asher seemed to mull this over for a moment. "Promise?"

"You have my promise." Riley kissed his cheeks. "You have my heart." He kissed his eyelids. "You have my love, for my entire life." Riley pulled Asher to him and kissed his lips, teasing him with his tongue.

Asher sighed and nodded. "You're right. Of course. We spend one more week pretending to be fierce competitors, a few weeks on tour, and then the rest of our lives finding new ways to fit together." He shook his head. "How did we end up here?" he said with a smile.

"We've been very, very good boys, clearly. The universe owed us a miracle, and here we are."

"I don't think I know how to be this good," Asher replied with a laugh.

"It's going to be light soon. I need to go."

Asher nodded, and they rose from the loungers and wrapped their robes around themselves. Riley led the way down the staircase and over to the trapdoor. He untied his robe and slid it down off his shoulders. He handed it to Asher and stood unabashedly naked in front of him.

"I love you," he said, his voice unsteady with the sadness of having to leave.

"I will always love you," Asher replied, a tear appearing in his eye.

Riley picked up his clothes, which were still damp and tangled where he had left them the night before. "No sense trying to put these on. I'll just skinny dip back to my place."

"Watch out for sharks," Asher said, laughing. "There are dangly parts that I very much want to have back."

"The only mouth they're going into is yours," Riley said with a growl and a grin.

They kissed one more time, and then one time more. Finally, Riley opened the trapdoor and made his way down the ladder. The water was warm and welcoming, and Riley reveled in the feeling of it surrounding his entire body. He swam quietly back to his bungalow and climbed his own ladder. Just as he closed the trapdoor, he heard a knock; he wrapped a robe around himself and went to the door to be greeted with the early breakfast he had forgotten he'd ordered yesterday. He thanked the waiter and silently thanked the universe for keeping his—and Asher's—secret.

They were going to win this.

CHAPTER FIFTEEN

HOMETOWN GIRL

FRESH FROM their week in the tropics, the final six bachelors were bound this week for the hometown of Daphne, the bachelorette. She hailed from a small, dreary town in the dead center of the less lovely of the Dakotas. It was so small that the arrival of the cast and crew completely overwhelmed it. There was only the one tiny motel (in 1950s fashion it called itself a "motor court" without irony), and it offered only a dozen or so rooms. Six would be occupied by the bachelors, forcing the crew to double up—and, in the case of the more junior members, triple.

The bus clattered into the dusty town early in the evening after a full day of travel. Riley glanced out the window, looking up from his book for the first time since they had departed the airport several hours before—there was simply nothing outside the bus to draw his attention away.

"And I thought last week was a remote location," he muttered. His body ached from its serial confinement aboard a large jet, a small turboprop, and now this stifling bus. "Where the hell are we?"

"I suspect we fell off the edge of the world about an hour ago," replied Asher from several rows back. "That would make this... hell, I reckon." He smiled broadly, somehow full of good cheer even in this extreme.

The bus rattled to a stop in front of the motor court. "Gentlemen, you'll be staying at the Dew Drop Inn, the town's finest accommodations." The assistant producer failed to mention that the Inn was also the town's only accommodations. "Here are your room keys." He handed out actual metal keys with large plastic key chains shaped like some local rock formation. "Tomorrow you will accompany Daphne to her family's annual summer picnic, where you will meet her relatives. Remember that their impression of you will weigh heavily in the decision she must make at the end of the week, as two of you go home and the final four enter the last round."

Riley settled into room 11, almost at the end of the row of doors. The only rooms beyond his were Asher's, number 12, and then one of the other bachelors in lucky 13. The room was dingy, of course, paneled with dark, clearly fake wood, and decorated with fixtures and furnishings that seemed to have been gathered from the "free" pile at thirty years' worth of garage sales. The bedspread, a lurid affair in an aggressive 1970s floral design, was tattered on the edges and somehow slick to the touch. Riley decided not to touch.

He saw Asher walk by: the windows of the rooms all looked out onto the parking lot, and the comings and goings of each were visible to all. Riley heard the door open at number 12 and close again. The walls seemed to be made of construction paper for all the soundproofing they offered. He gave Asher a few minutes to settle in, and then he knocked lightly on the wall to signal him. Asher understood the message and stepped back out into the parking lot, where he stood looking around as if to take in the spectacle of the sunset or enjoy some local vista. No such beauty presented itself.

Riley stepped out of his room and sidled up next to Asher. "Nothing quite like the majesty of the Great Plains, is there?"

"Nothing," Asher replied. "I can't believe I waited this long to see it."

They laughed ruefully.

"You know the only thing that could make this better?" Asher asked.

"I can't think of a single thing," Riley replied. "I mean, there's a positively belching smokestack over there, and I think I saw a quaint little slaughterhouse on the way into town."

Asher leaned casually closer to Riley as if trying to get a better view of the smokestack. "Ripping your clothes off and licking you from head to toe," he whispered. "I think that would make it better." Then he cleared his throat and straightened up.

"Fuck," was all Riley could say in return. If this is how guys flirted, he regretted coming to it so late in life.

"But first, we picnic." Asher said, all business again.

"Right you are," Riley rejoined, with a jauntiness he hoped sounded sincere, should there be a microphone nearby to pick it up.

"Until tomorrow, then," Asher said with a curt nod of his head.

"Fuckyoulater," Riley said in a rush only Asher could have understood. His shocked expression clearly indicated that he had done so. He nodded in agreement.

The men parted and returned to their rooms. Riley did what he could to release the tension built up during their conversation; he imagined Asher doing the same on the other side of the cardboard wall, and that brought him to orgasm almost immediately. He was able to sleep quite well that night.

THE NEXT morning they rose early to climb on the bus and be driven to the largest park in town, where Daphne's family would convene their picnic. Of course, the picnic would be held in the afternoon, but the bachelors needed to be there hours in advance to make preparatory remarks for the cameras about how nervous they were to be meeting the family of the supposed love of their lives. Riley and Asher had this stuff down cold—they could emote to the camera about how much they enjoyed Daphne's company, and how much they liked her as a person, and how excited they were to finally meet the people she had told them about so often. All of this had the virtue of being true. They really did like her and were in fact looking forward to meeting her family. With the exception of Shane, the other bachelors—the straight ones—didn't seem to even know the names of any of the people they would be meeting today, because for them this competition was even less about Daphne than it was for Riley and Asher.

When the family arrived, led by Daphne, the cameras were there to record the first meetings between the bachelors and her parents, her older twin brothers (who made television-ready protests about how very ready they were to defend her honor should any of them treat her ill), and her younger siblings, two sisters and a much-younger brother, eight years old, who had Down syndrome. The crew took several hours carefully repositioning the cameras and sound equipment to capture all of the spontaneous family interaction.

Riley and Asher maintained a careful distance from each other during all of the filming with Daphne's family. Whenever they found it necessary to cross paths, they looked the other way and pretended not to notice each other. Once or twice they couldn't avoid bumping shoulders or elbows, and Asher, in keeping with his well-known sunny disposition would beg Riley's pardon rather loudly, and then under his breath he would add something just for Riley's ears. "Excuse me," Asher said when they reached for the same bottle of water from the large iron washtub full of ice, "I need something cool after looking at your ass all day." Riley blushed furiously when Asher whispered this last bit and dropped the bottle of water back into the tub. Asher grinned and picked it up, then walked away with a backward wink.

While incalculable amounts of meat roasted on the grills, filling the park with a carnal smoke, Daphne's family arranged some games for the kids and, of course, for the bachelors. All six were drafted for the three-legged race, in which pairs of bachelors would compete against Daphne's twin brothers. The bachelors were paired up by proximity, and as Riley and Asher had just been silently flirting with each other near the potato salad, they were drafted into the competition as a team. Before they knew what was happening they were standing with their legs pressed against each other, one of Daphne's sisters wrapping twine around their ankles. They were also bound just above the knee, preventing any independent movement of their conjoined leg at all.

"Well, this is awkward," Riley murmured to Asher, through the grin that he kept immobile for the cameras.

"Weren't expecting bondage?" Asher whispered. "Welcome to third base."

Riley laughed, then covered his laughter by pointing at another pair of bachelors who were having great difficulty being tied together due to the difference in their height.

"Being pressed up against you like this is causing me... difficulties," Riley continued.

Asher's eyes flicked down to Riley's crotch. They widened, and then he looked up to Riley's face. "Whoa, that is a... difficulty. A hard problem, one might say. A bone of contention."

"Shut up! You're making it worse!"

Asher turned his head as if to look over toward the starting line of the race. This brought his lips into direct contact with Riley's ear. "I will make it all better tonight. Promise." He made a kissing noise that startled Riley. "You won't have any problem with swelling when I'm done with you."

"Fuck," Riley huffed out. "Stop that!"

"Never," whispered Asher.

"Let's get this race going!" shouted Daphne's father, who seemed delighted to offer the bachelors a chance to embarrass themselves in front of his daughter and the television audience. The contestants assembled at the starting line, and Riley and Asher found themselves next to Daphne's brothers. They were well over six feet tall and wore plaid work shirts with the sleeves cut off, showing the farm-raised muscle of their tanned arms. Their jeans looked practically painted on, worn almost colorless at pressure points such as the knees, crotch, and around the snuff can in their back pockets. Their sharp, clear blue eyes glinted at Riley and Asher from under the tattered brims of their baseball caps.

Asher seemed to have noticed Riley taking in the sights. "Nothing better than a country boy, eh?" he whispered to Riley. "Except maybe a matched set, tied together for easy carrying back home."

Riley, shocked, turned to Asher with wide eyes.

"What? I saw you gawking first. Don't give me that look, mister."

Riley knew Asher was right—he had been looking. Had he always noticed other men and just never had a place in his mind for awareness of it? Had Asher freed something in him that had always been there, or was he changing him?

"Ready... set... go!" called Daphne, the official starter of the race.

Her brothers immediately shot out in front of the pack, leaving the bachelors in their dust. Riley and Asher were close behind, however, with Riley calling out "In! Out! In! Out!" to keep their cadence even and to eliminate the stumbling that had paralyzed the other bachelor pairs. They closed in on the twins and would have overtaken them had Riley not stumbled when he realized how the tightly packed Wranglers in front of him undulated side to side with the powerful strides of the twins. It was mesmerizing. And disturbing.

Riley and Asher finished second behind the twins; one of the other bachelor pairs fell within three strides of the finish line; and the last pair had turned on each other early in the race and made more progress shoving each other than running toward the finish line.

"Nice job," the twins said, in unison, as they shook Riley's and Asher's hands. Riley was struck with the calloused strength of their hands, warm yet work-hardened.

"Thanks, but you guys are Olympic at the three-legged race," Riley replied, smiling.

"We do everything together, so it's kind of an unfair advantage," the one on the right said, smiling brilliantly. "But we'll take the glory when we can get it," said the other with an identical grin.

One of Daphne's aunts arrived with a knife of alarming dimensions and cleanly slit the bonds between the men.

"Looks like lunch is ready," said the first of the twins. "You guys eat meat?" He cast a narrowed gaze on Riley and Asher, as if expecting they might be big-city vegans and therefore morally suspect.

"Hell yeah," replied Riley with what he hoped was a good ol' boy grin. He wasn't sure how to make one of those, but he tried.

"You guys go on ahead," Asher said. "I'll catch up in a minute."

Riley looked at him with a quizzical expression, but Asher just nodded quickly and turned to kneel next to a child who had been watching the race and cheering. Riley walked a short distance with the twins to where the grills were disgorging their fleshy payload, but he kept an eye and ear on Asher as he did so.

"Hi, I'm Asher," he said and extended a hand to the boy.

"My name is Charlie," the boy replied, and he studied Asher's face for a long moment before nodding to himself and taking the man's hand. "Daphne is my sister. I love her."

Asher smiled. "I'm sure you do. I have a sister I love too."

Charlie seemed to take this as a bond of no small importance between them—he nodded slowly and then extended his hand to Asher again. "I'm going to get me some lunch," he said. "Come with me."

Asher stood, beaming, and walked hand-in-hand with Charlie over to the table where Riley stood awaiting a plate piled with the seared remains of a great many animals. Asher flashed him a quick grin but returned his attention to Charlie immediately.

"So, what's your favorite?" he asked, leaning down close to the boy and whispering conspiratorially.

"I like ribs. Momma says I like brisket the best, but she just says that because ribs are messy. That's why she says that."

"But you like ribs because they're messy, right?" Asher prompted.

Charlie nodded gravely, then burst out with a delighted laughter. "I get really messy!"

"Well, then, Charlie, let's get some ribs." Asher turned to the caterer the show had brought in to help Daphne's family with the food. "My good friend Charlie and I will have some of your finest ribs—and please make them extra messy." Charlie bounced and cackled, clapping his hands. Asher took the two heavily laden plates and turned toward the gingham-bedecked tables set out for the lunch crowd, and Charlie scampered right behind him, still laughing joyously.

Riley watched them all the way to the table, and he chuckled to himself when Charlie insisted that Asher stuff a huge napkin into his collar. They tucked into the ribs, and soon, as Charlie had predicted, their faces were covered with the sauce.

"Sir? Would you like anything else?" The caterer held out a plate Riley had been ignoring while he watched Asher and Charlie.

"No, thank you. This looks great." Riley took his plate and walked over to where Daphne sat with her sisters in the shade of a great gnarled tree.

"This seat taken?" he asked Daphne.

She shook her head and gestured for him to sit down. Her sisters gawked and giggled at having someone they'd seen on TV suddenly sit down at their table.

Riley nodded to them. "Ladies," he said in his best Prince Charming voice.

They giggled again and exchanged a look with each other.

"Why don't you two go see if you can help out anywhere," Daphne said to her sisters. "Now that you've finished eating, can you leave me in peace for a moment?" Her words were polite but her intonation was all big sister. They rose and ran off.

"Your family does this every year?" Riley asked, as he began to navigate around the pile of food on his plate.

"For decades now. But it's much more of a circus this year, like everything else." She sighed. He had never seen her looking so tired; she seemed as exhausted as Riley felt.

"You know, they put us through a lot, but it's got to be even harder on you, since you're basically locked in a house—"

"And carted around to be impressed by how manly and amazing and honestly conceited all of you are." She turned suddenly once this was out of her mouth. "Not that I think that about you! Sorry, I'm a little tired right now. I think you're great."

Riley smiled. "I'll bet you say that to all the bachelors."

She rolled her eyes. "Yeah, not so much. Most of them don't even seem interested in getting to know me. At least you talk to me—about things other than yourself. I would have gone insane on that island last week if you hadn't been there to talk with. How lucky that we had just been reading the same book!"

It hadn't been luck at all, actually—Riley had observed her choice of novel and had asked one of the production crew to get him a copy so they would have things to talk about. But he nodded and smiled. "Great minds, you know."

She laughed and took a sip of the devastatingly sweet punch that had been ladled out by the gallon to picnic attendees. Apparently it was a no-alcohol event, which was probably for the best, given the presence of so many cameras.

Riley took advantage of the pause in conversation to take a few bites of lunch and take a look in Asher's direction. He and Charlie were jabbering and laughing and demolishing the worms-in-dirt dessert that had been laid out for the kids—and Asher, apparently. He smiled at the childlike wonder on Asher's face. He really was in his element when relating to a child. He must find such joy in the classroom, Riley thought.

"I think he's amazing, too," Daphne said, leaning close to Riley.

Riley shook his head. "What? Sorry—what?"

"Asher. I think he's a great guy. No one else even noticed Charlie, and Asher's his best friend now."

Riley was stumped. "Uh, yeah, I guess. But I just see him as a competitor. You know, another guy who wants to be with you."

Daphne smiled. "I don't think that with me is where he wants to be. And I see the way you look at him. Don't shake your head at me—I may have grown up in the sticks, but I have eyes." She gave him another of her big-sister expressions, the one that says "you better come clean."

Riley had no choice but to stick to his guns. "Well, we did team up at the beginning. It just made sense to have an alliance against such a big field. But now we're in it to win it."

She nodded, a hint of a grin playing around her mouth. "Um-hmm." She took another sip. "I like you, Riley. And I like Asher too. Whatever is going on between you two is for you to figure out. I just know that the only fun I've had while doing this show is with the two of you. You're great together, and sometimes it doesn't make sense to break up a team." She stood and picked up her empty plate. "I need to mingle. See if I can get the other bachelors to tear themselves away from trying to impress my family—did you see Trey lift up his shirt and ask my Nana to feel his abs? Ugh. But still, it's kind of my job…."

"Well, it's nice to talk with you," stumbled Riley. He was still not sure what Daphne knew, or thought she knew, about him and Asher.

She put her hand on his. "You too," she said warmly. "However this turns out, I'm glad I met you."

THE PICNIC wound down after another round of games, and, inexplicably, a piñata in the shape of a steer's head. Charlie, assisted by Asher, was the one who broke it open. As the bachelors made their way to the bus that would take them back to the motor court, Charlie ran after Asher and wrapped his arms around him in a hug that nearly knocked the man over.

"I hope Daphne chooses you," he said.

"I do too. But even if she doesn't, I'm very glad to have met you, and we can still be friends, right?"

"Right!" Charlie said, giving Asher an emphatic thumbs-up.

Once the bus pulled away from the park for the short ride back to the motel, Riley moved to the back to sit across the aisle from Asher.

"You sure did make a friend back there," he said.

Asher chuckled. "Charlie's great. Kids like that are always so positive, and they will tell you the God's honest truth, every time. I learned some good stuff about Daphne, by the way."

Riley regarded him with raised eyebrows.

"Oh, nothing scandalous. She's always been his favorite, and he misses her a lot."

Riley nodded. Asher turned to look out the window at dusk falling over the dusty town.

"You know what I miss?" Asher said out of the blue.

"What?"

"Sucking your dick," Asher replied in a low voice.

"Dude, you have got to stop doing that!" Riley replied in a scandalized murmur.

"If you ever stop reacting like that then I might."

"So this is just a game to you? Teasing me?"

"It's only a tease if I don't follow through." Asher tipped his head down, like a librarian looking quite seriously at Riley over his reading glasses. "I will—definitely—follow through."

"Tonight?" Riley breathed.

"Come to my room at midnight, and I will do things to you that you've never dreamed of."

Riley struggled to take the next breath. All he could do was nod. And adjust his pants to allow for his rapidly growing penis.

DARKNESS FELL on the town, rendering it even more deathly quiet than it was during daylight hours. As 11:00 p.m. came and passed, Riley noticed that headlights passing by on the highway came farther and farther apart. As the ancient clock on the nightstand ticked on toward midnight, more than ten minutes elapsed between flashes of light from the road.

Riley's heart pounded in his chest as he watched the hands of the clock jerk uncertainly toward the twelve at the top of the dial. He wasn't sure whether it was nervousness or excitement about what might happen when he ventured next door. Perhaps it was a mix of both, which was pretty much always the case when Riley thought about sex—regardless of where, or how, or with whom. He was coming to the conclusion that sex kind of made him crazy. But at least in this he didn't feel alone; he suspected it made lots of people crazy. Probably.

Tick, tick.

Riley brushed his teeth for the third time. He wasn't sure what Asher had in mind, but Riley figured a minty fresh mouth wouldn't go amiss. He had showered after the picnic and then again just before eleven. Again, he wasn't sure what the evening would involve, so he soaped everything twice—even the parts to which he would normally give rather cursory attention. The idea of scrubbing his ass before a date would have made him queasy a month ago, but now it excited him in a way he didn't really have words for. The notion that these formerly neglected parts of his body might be put to innovative uses by Asher gave him a butterfly in the belly.

At 11:59, he slowly and silently opened the door of his room and checked up and down the walkway that ran between the row of rooms and the parking lot. The coast was clear. He took a deep breath, swallowed hard, and stepped out into the still summer evening. Crickets chirped in the background, and some inconsequential bugs swarmed around the streetlight that stood lonely guard over the few cars in the lot. Riley walked the ten feet between door number 11 and door number 12 on light feet and stood before the door at precisely midnight. He lifted his hand to the door to knock when it swung open silently. Suddenly, there was a hand on his neck, and he was yanked into the room. The door swooshed shut behind him, and before he could even get a word out, Asher was on him—everywhere at once.

If Riley thought he knew all of Asher's moves when it came to kissing, he now learned he was mistaken. Asher the teasing, gentle smoocher was gone, replaced by this ravenous, mauling beast who laid siege to Riley's mouth and conquered it instantly, thrillingly. Riley could only stagger back in surprise at the onslaught, but Asher slid a hand along the small of his back and held him firmly in place. It was only when Asher broke the kiss so he could start tearing at Riley's clothes that he could catch his breath.

"Whoa, dude, you're—" Riley managed to get out.

"You bet your ass I am," Asher replied, unbuttoning Riley's shirt and throwing it open. "Watching you at the picnic with your tight jeans and your sexy smile, charming all the bumpkins—holy fuck I wanted to shove all that potato salad off the table and climb the fuck on you, right there in front of everybody." He yanked Riley's shirt down his arms, grabbed him by the shoulders, and crashed into his lips again.

Riley had never seen Asher act this way, consumed with this urgency, and to know he was the cause of it made his chest pound. He ran his hands along Asher's heaving chest, up to the neck of his T-shirt, and he laid hold of it with both fists. He forced his tongue into Asher's mouth, and when Asher reared back in surprise, Riley pulled as hard as he could. Asher's shirt gave way, rent from top to bottom in one smooth motion. Riley pushed Asher back, hard and fast, and he stumbled back onto the bed, the remnants of the garment fluttering as he fell. Riley pounced on him and locked his mouth on one of Asher's nipples—they suddenly seemed to him the most beautiful thing in the world.

Riley had kissed Asher's chest before, but this time he used his teeth. He wanted Asher to feel the dangerous energy that was throbbing in him, to know that the safety was off.

Asher knew—his gasps and then his moans told Riley they were on the same page.

Still attached by the teeth to Asher's nipple, Riley slid his hands down to his waist and began to unfasten his shorts. He got the button undone and eased the zipper down—it was only then that he realized Asher was going commando. When Riley's hand slithered into the opening, he felt the hot, hard flesh spring to his grip. The surprise of this ready access made him open his jaw, releasing Asher's nipple, now red from his impassioned attention. He slid his way up to look into Asher's flushed face.

"Well, aren't you frisky tonight?" Riley asked him, grinning.

"I didn't want anything to get in the way. All I've been able to think about since the island is doing this with you. I must have jerked it three times a day thinking about this very moment, and it still wouldn't go down."

"Let me see if I can help you out with that," Riley replied. He was about to slide down to take the situation in hand when he felt Asher's hands on his shoulders again.

"First, I have to tell you," Asher said.

"Tell me what?"

Asher smiled, but there was sadness in his eyes as well. "I love you. I've fantasized about doing this with you from about five minutes after I met you, but I'm not here just because you are sexy and gorgeous. You are, of course, but I wouldn't be here unless we were, you know, in love. I'm not a slut, is what I'm trying to say."

"Ash, everything we've ever done together has been because I've asked you to do it. You've been patient and wonderful, and I love you the way I've never loved anyone in my life. But tonight I need you to be a slut. Bust out the advanced playbook and give me your best shot or I'm going to fucking explode." He fixed Asher with a raised eyebrow and a sexy snarl. "Come at me, bro."

Asher's face ran the gamut of expressions while Riley spoke, until finally he set his jaw and nodded with a wicked grin. "Oh, it is on," he growled. He threw both his arms and his legs around Riley and kissed him with a frenetic energy that made Riley see stars; they pressed their bodies together, reveling in the friction that forbidden contact creates.

Suddenly Asher released his full-body hold and rolled out from under him, leaving Riley on all fours. He darted to the end of the bed, kicked his shorts off, and from behind quickly unbuttoned Riley's pants and slid them down to his knees. "Lift," he said brusquely, tapping on Riley's knees, and Riley immediately straightened his legs, allowing Asher to slide his pants down to his ankles. "Back down," Asher ordered, pressing on Riley's buttocks, and he lowered himself to his knees once again. Asher yanked the pants the rest of the way off, taking the socks with them.

Riley was left naked save for his boxer shorts, on all fours on the bed. He felt vulnerable, but also safe in Asher's hands. Well, mostly safe—Asher's demeanor had taken on a bit of an edge. Riley shivered in anticipation.

Asher laid his hands on Riley's buttocks, pressing against the muscles that lay just beneath the surface. Riley was pleased that his months of squats and running had given his ass a shape that an athlete ten years younger would have been proud of. Asher's gentle, admiring touch made him feel doubly pleased. Then Asher's fingers strayed into the cleft between Riley's strong, round ass cheeks, and Riley jolted forward instinctively. No one had ever touched him there. But as soon as he moved, he felt Asher's arm loop around the front of his hips, holding him in place, while the other hand continued more forceful explorations. Then suddenly, the arm was withdrawn, and Riley felt both hands roaming his ass again. He sighed in relief at the restraint being removed, but his respite was short-lived: Asher's fingers met in the slender space between Riley's cheeks, and they gripped the thin fabric of the boxers. With a great tearing noise, they were rent apart, and without any warning Riley's most private place was fully on display.

Riley was shocked. No one had ever done anything like this to him. Here, on hands and knees in a cheap motel room, wearing only the shreds of a pair of boxers, he was in the control of a man who knelt behind him and was even now planning an assault. On Riley's ass. Be careful what you wish for, a voice in his head tut-tutted. Yes, he had asked for this, recklessly, back in Vegas, but Asher had said no. What he meant, obviously, was not yet. Now, though, anything was possible.

But instead of any kind of invasive attack, what Riley felt was a kiss. Asher planted a kiss, tender and slow, on his left buttock. Then one on the right. Then another on the left, this time slightly closer to the cleft. He repeated the action, slowly and deliberately, alternating sides as he worked his way in. Riley was breathless with anticipation.

"You have no idea how beautiful you are," Asher murmured between kisses. "Of course, you've probably never seen yourself from this particular angle. But let me assure you—I've seen a few asses, and yours is by far the finest I've ever had the pleasure to encounter."

"Why don't you kiss it, then?" Riley challenged. He had come suddenly to realize that slow and deliberate lovemaking was not what he wanted from Asher. Not tonight.

"You may want to find something to hang on to," Asher said, warning in his voice. "I'm about to come at you, bro."

"Bring it," Riley said. This was the last thing he was able to say for a while, as his mouth was occupied chewing on the pillow into which he pressed his face for support.

Asher dug his fingers into the cleft between Riley's muscular cheeks and pried them apart—not drastically, but enough to expose Riley in a way he had never experienced before. Whatever he felt about that violation was instantly forced from his mind by what came next—Asher's lips pressing against his anus. Riley tried to cry out and take in a sharp breath at the same time and found he could do neither. But Asher's kiss was only the beginning.

Without warning, Asher surged forward, pressing his face into Riley, destroying his last scrap of privacy. Then Riley felt the warm, wet, wriggling invasion of Asher's tongue. Asher's tongue was going up his ass, and there was nothing he could do about it.

Actually, there was nothing he wanted to do about it. No one had ever touched him there, no one had ever kissed him there, and certainly no one had ever done this. Suddenly Asher's tongue seemed enormous, as if it were capable of ripping Riley in two. It shot into him, spasmed about, and then retreated, only to come barreling back into him with renewed vigor.

"Oh—oh!" was all Riley could say; Asher probably didn't even hear it, as his face was well buried in the pillow. The feeling of being completely possessed by this man overwhelmed him. They had no secrets now; there was nothing between them and never again could be. He had given himself entirely to Asher.

It was only when this realization dawned on him that he began to feel—or let himself feel—how astoundingly pleasurable this was. Riley had suddenly gained a new sex organ. He surprised himself by pushing back against Asher's face, urging him deeper inside. His abandon was complete when he reached back and pulled his buttocks wider apart, granting Asher an obscene vantage point and unprecedented access. He took full advantage, thrusting Riley forward again with all the force his gym-honed body could muster.

Finally, when Riley was close to hyperventilating, Asher pulled off of him with a sloppy smack of his lips. "Flip over," he growled.

"What are you going to do?" Riley asked, knowing even as he said it that he would do whatever Asher asked of him.

"I want to look in your eyes when I eat you," Asher said, his sly grin revealing how much he enjoyed talking dirty to Riley.

Riley lay on his back, and Asher grabbed his legs and pushed. Riley doubled up, hips in the air, feet against the headboard. He was thankful that several months of yoga classes allowed him to be Asher's sexual origami.

Asher knelt against Riley's back and again his fingers found their way to his ass. But this time Asher could lock eyes with Riley as he snaked his tongue out and brought it down onto, and into, Riley's quivering ass. Riley's eyes rolled back in his head, an instinctive response to the sensations exploding through his body, but quickly returned to himself and met Asher's eyes. Asher grinned as he again and again lowered his mouth to Riley's anus, assaulting it with his tongue, kissing it, sucking at it. Riley was panting wildly, and still Asher attacked. Soon his legs were rubbery and twitching as the sensations threatened to overwhelm him. Finally, Asher released the pressure and let Riley's legs flop back down on the bed. He kissed his way up Riley's torso, slipping past his cock and balls and up his chest until they were again eye-to-eye.

"I had no idea," Riley whispered, unable to put any more words together than that.

"That your ass could feel that way? Yeah, I remember my first time too. But your ass is a work of art—that was amazing."

"I guarantee you it was better for me."

"This is not a contest. Of course, if it were, I would totally win." Asher laughed and kissed Riley on the nose.

"So, was that third base?" Riley asked, mischievously.

"Oh, honey, we are out of the ballpark altogether."

Riley blinked hard and looked urgently into Asher's eyes.

"What?" Asher asked. "Did I say something wrong?"

"You called me honey," Riley said, his voice a little unsteady.

"I'm sorry—was that the wrong thing to say?"

Riley shook his head fervently. "No—no, it's perfect. I just never thought I'd hear that from a guy. But I love hearing it from you."

Asher smiled, and they kissed.

"Now, there's something I've got to do," Asher said. He kissed Riley on the nose one more time and then rolled off. "Back on your hands and knees, mister," he instructed.

Riley didn't think—he simply complied.

Asher returned to the foot of the bed and then turned and faced away before lying back on the bed and sliding his head between Riley's knees. In this position he was looking directly up into Riley's crotch, the dripping head of Riley's thick cock brushing against his lips. He kissed it and then ran his tongue around the head, wetting it, tickling Riley while also inflaming him. Asher lifted his head and kissed Riley's balls before opening wide and taking both of them into his mouth at once. Riley gasped but then relaxed immediately and let Asher take his balls however he wanted them. His surrender was freeing—for the first time in his life he could just let go and enjoy physical contact with another person rather than trying to manage his partner's pleasure before his own. He simply gave himself to Asher.

Asher, meanwhile, slipped his middle finger into his mouth and wetted it abundantly with saliva. He then raised his hand to Riley's ass, up there above his head, and poked at Riley's back door. Riley jolted a little at the intrusion, but he trusted Asher and would let him do what he wanted. What Asher wanted, apparently, was to fuck Riley with his finger. By way of welcome, Riley pushed back against Asher's invading digit, and it slid in up to the first knuckle. Riley was shocked at the intrusion and at how enormous that finger felt—Riley knew it was strong and slender, but in his ass it felt positively gigantic. He quickly accommodated to it, however, and was soon pushing back on it as if he were in heat.

When Asher's finger slid the rest of the way in, he began to move it about, running it across the surfaces inside Riley's ass. Soon he found what he was evidently looking for—Riley's prostate. He ran his strong finger along it, and Riley's head just about exploded.

"Oh, oh, fuck!" he called, louder than he had been before. "What the fuck are you doing in there?"

Asher's mouth was full of dick at the moment, so his answer was delayed while he cleared his throat. "That's your prostate," he said helpfully. "You aren't going to believe what this thing can do."

"It can make me pee on you, apparently," Riley moaned, desperate to understand what could be causing that urgent sensation.

"Don't worry—you may leak a bit, but it's not pee. It's precum, and it's normal to let some slip when someone's working your prostate. Now hang on. You're going to love this." Asher slipped Riley's achingly hard penis back into his mouth and moved his head rapidly up and down, all the while pressing and rubbing and coaxing his prostate into madness.

The orgasm hit Riley like a freight train. No warning, no buildup—whatever Asher was doing was magical, able to conjure up orgasms fully formed and already underway. The entire apparatus between his legs jolted into a spasm of joy so electric that all he could do was grip the sheets and try to hang on: to the bed, to his sanity. Then, the pressure in his ass spiked, and he broke through to a realm of orgasm he hadn't known existed. Every muscle drew tight and seized as Riley tried desperately to hold his body together against the savage force that had laid siege to it. He yelped, he grunted, he tried to breathe. And then, with every scrap of strength he had left, he thrust himself forward, deeper into Asher. The fluttering in his groin felt almost delicate, but it quickly filled Asher's mouth—Riley could feel the hot wet stickiness spread along the length of his cock as it surged in and out of Asher, overflowing his clenching lips.

At some point—he wasn't sure when—he had collapsed over to the side and then lay panting on the bed. Asher didn't release his grip, though, and continued to kiss and lick at the tip of Riley's cock until the sensation grew to be too much and Riley had to squirm away. He laid his hand on Asher's head and ruffled his hair playfully. Asher slid up the bed to lie alongside his lover and was about to wipe his mouth with his hand when Riley stopped him.

"No, don't," he said, and then he leaned in and kissed Asher's chin right where it was glazed with his own semen.

Asher's eyes widened.

"What?" Riley asked, amused. "I can't expect you to taste it if I'm not willing to, right?" He kissed the side of Asher's mouth where another pearly drop nestled.

"You're amazing," Asher whispered.

"No, I think you're the amazing one. That thing you did with your finger? Holy fuck how did I not know about that? It's like you pushed the orgasm button—hard."

"Then I was doing it right," Asher murmured.

"I gotta try that," Riley said, bouncing back from his post-orgasmic bliss almost immediately.

"Riley, wait," Asher said. "Go slow. I want to last a little longer this time, but you're just so... well, I'm kinda on a hair trigger here."

"Then we'll just have to shoot it off a few times." Riley grinned and kissed Asher on the nose. "Because there is no way I'm going slow. I've got years to make up for!" Riley rose up from the bed and pushed Asher over until he rolled onto his belly, lying flat on the bed. He threw a leg over the prone man, and lay flat atop him. He kissed Asher's ear, and then his neck, and then down his spine, a kiss on every vertebra. Then he reached the place where the base of Asher's backbone dipped down and his round buttocks arched up—two dimples in the muscle marked the boundary between his back and Riley's destination, which lay below. Riley planted a kiss on the top of each cheek and then licked his lips; a slightly salty tang was the evidence of Asher's excitement. He then kissed his way down the middle, continuing his straight path, and was soon pressing his own cheeks against Asher's.

"I get it now," he said, his voice playfully lilting.

"What do you get?" Asher asked. Though he was lying still, he sounded a bit out of breath.

"How beautiful this is—you are." He ran his fingertips across the flawlessly smooth skin of Asher's ass and delighted in the goose bumps that emerged. Riley, like most men, had always been fascinated with women's breasts, but Asher's ass had all the round fullness of the most beautiful breasts Riley had ever contemplated. But it was pure muscle, which made it even sexier. Riley resisted the urge to motorboat—he wasn't sure, but he figured that might be viewed as inappropriate. He'd have to ask. Later.

When he looked back on the transformation his life underwent during this time, it was this moment that would stand out to him as one of the most significant. Until he met Asher, "beautiful" was a word he would never have used to describe another man. And he would certainly have never expected to find himself here, with his face less than an inch from another man's buttocks. But in this moment, all he felt was excitement and perhaps a thrill of the forbidden. It wouldn't be forbidden for long.

Riley remembered what Asher had done, and he let his fingers drift into the tight space between the smooth globes of muscle before him. He teased and tickled and was pleased to hear Asher moan and see him writhe. Riley wriggled between Asher's legs, pushing them apart so he could better reach his target. Asher complied, spreading his legs with a sigh, and his buttocks clenched rhythmically as Riley settled himself before them. Suddenly, he slapped Asher's right buttock with a stinging swat of his hand.

"Stop that!" he ordered, his voice as gruff as he could make it.

"What?" Asher's voice was tentative and meek.

"I saw what you were doing."

"I wasn't doing anything!"

Another swat, this time on Asher's left buttock. He jumped, and a handprint flushed into color instantly, a companion to the first.

"You were fucking the mattress," Riley growled. "You were sliding your hard cock up and down. Mister 'let's go slow' suddenly can't wait for me, huh?"

"I'm sorry... sir," said Asher, but this time his voice was thick with excitement. He clearly enjoyed the route they were now taking.

"That's better," groused Riley. His voice bore no trace of the wide grin that had spread across his face as he played this little game, and Asher couldn't see him. He was thrilled that he could get a little rough and Asher took it in stride.

Riley placed the palms of his hands flat against Asher's buttocks, his index fingers and his thumbs forming a diamond directly over the darkest recess of the cleft between. He pressed down and spread his hands apart, and Asher opened to him. The furrow was hairless and smooth and clean; the tightly gathered knot where Asher's body opened to him twitched as it met the light. Riley leaned in close, so close that his breath fanned the delicate flesh, and Asher gave a shiver that worked its way up his spine all the way to the top of his head. But Riley froze bare millimeters away and ventured no closer.

Asher's hips began to twitch again, as if impatient for contact.

"Something you want?" Riley asked, his voice low and taunting.

"You know what I want."

"I need you to say it."

Asher was quiet for a moment. Riley blew softly, the way he might into a lover's ear. The target was different, but the effect was the same. Asher shivered again and swore under his breath.

"I want you to...," he began but trailed off.

"What? You want me to what?" Riley prompted.

"To lick me." Asher's voice was a mere whisper.

"To what, now? I didn't quite catch that."

"To lick me. I need you to stick your tongue in my ass." Then, in an almost unhinged, desperate growl: "Fuck me with your tongue, dammit!"

Provoked by Asher's urgent plea, Riley did away with any further preliminaries. He pushed his hands even farther apart and lunged, spearing Asher with his tongue, breaking through the tight ring of muscle in one voracious thrust.

Asher gripped the headboard with both hands and cried out at the violation he had craved, had asked for, demanded. Riley was thrilled to have taken the more experienced man so forcefully.

Having staked his claim, he withdrew his tongue and kissed the place it had emerged from after it snapped closed. But he didn't want Asher to get too relaxed, so without warning he plunged his tongue back in, even more deeply this time, and he thickened up his tongue as much as he could—he wanted Asher to feel him take his ass.

Without moving his lips from Asher's ass, Riley put his hands on Asher's hips and pulled him back. Asher lifted his hips, giving Riley what he wanted—access to the hard and dripping cock that had previously been hidden underneath. He reached around Asher's hips and gripped his cock with both hands and began a firm milking motion while he continued to thrust his tongue in, out, and around.

"Oh...," groaned Asher. His chest was still on the mattress, his head on the pillow, and he continued to slap his hand against the headboard as if the stimulation would soon unhinge him completely.

Riley could feel the spasms start. The wrinkly but strong muscle surrounding his tongue twitched once, twice, and then clamped down hard. Deeper pulsations rippled through Asher's pelvis—Riley could feel them on his tongue, in his hands. He continued his milking motion without pause, and the tension built. Finally, Asher gave a small gasp, an almost plaintive sound, and bucked back against Riley face as his cock surged to steely hardness.

"I love you," Asher whispered and for the next two minutes said nothing coherent. His ejaculation was vigorous, a dozen emphatic splashes onto the sheet, a scattering of hot pearly pools.

Riley continued to milk, continued to thrust his tongue into Asher, until, as Riley had, he flopped over in exhaustion. He lay, glazed with sweat, breathing like a sprinter, his eyes unfocused. Riley was proud of the devastation he had caused. This didn't seem like the work of a beginner. He laid himself alongside Asher, spooning against his heaving back, and ran his hands up and down the other man's body. He was happy—happier than he ever remembered being.

"I love you too," he whispered into Asher's ear.

Asher arched back and wrapped his hand around Riley's neck, pulling him close. "That was fucking amazing," he whispered.

"You should have seen it from my angle," Riley replied, laughing.

"I'm considering whether to forgive you for the spanking," Asher said with a critical eyebrow raised at Riley. Then he giggled. "That was awesome, by the way. And then I think I kind of made a mess on the sheets at one point."

"Totally my fault. I would have gladly swallowed it, but I really didn't want to pull my tongue out of that muscly gymnast ass." Riley paused, then giggled. "That really didn't sound like something a straight guy would say, did it?"

Asher burst out laughing. "I don't think you have to worry about your straight-guy credentials anymore." He kissed Riley, nibbling a little at his lips. "They've been revoked."

"Fuck yeah," Riley growled.

The men embraced and rolled around the motel bed for a while, kissing and clinching and luxuriating in having so much time to spend together. Finally, when they lay on their backs contemplating the cracked ceiling above them, Riley spoke something that had been in the back of his mind for a while.

"Hey," he said, turning to his side so that he could look at Asher stretched out next to him. "This is really fun, but I was kind of wondering…."

"Ready to go again? Finally!" Asher replied with a laugh.

"Well, of course I am. But this time, do you think we could do something more… mutual? I love doing you, and I think I might love you doing me even more." He paused here to kiss Asher once, then twice, then once more. "But isn't there something we can do… together?"

"We haven't even scratched the surface of what we can do together," Asher replied. "Here—let me show you." He sprang up from the bed and padded over to his suitcase.

"You even walk sexy," Riley called to him from the bed.

"All part of the service we provide," Asher replied with a laugh as he hurried back to bed with a small bottle in his hand. "Now, wait until you try this," he said excitedly. "Lie back," he instructed.

Riley complied, not sure what to expect. Asher flipped the lid on the bottle, squeezed some of the contents into his hands, and spread an even coating of slick liquid all over Riley's body, from his chest to his groin. A sweet smell filled the room.

"What is it?" Riley asked.

"Almond oil," Asher replied, squirting a little more oil on Riley's torso.

"Dude, don't you think you're overdoing it? I thought lube just went on the parts that get inserted."

Asher smiled as he snapped the lid shut and put the bottle down on the nightstand. "Oh, just you wait." He began to massage Riley's chest, stomach, and pelvis.

Riley loved a good rubdown, and Asher was certainly expert at it, but it wasn't really what he was in the mood for, unless there was another amazing happy ending in the offing. But quickly Asher stopped stroking him and lay down atop his oil-slicked body.

"Well, this is going to get sloppy," Riley observed.

"Oh, you have no idea," Asher growled, and he began to slide up and down Riley's body, their muscled chests slipping against each other, their oiled abs slurping together and apart as Asher moved. He looked deep into Riley's eyes, fixed him with a gaze of such intensity that Riley could only look from one eye to the other, seeking the meaning in the stare.

Then, as Asher kissed him, he knew. He felt it. Their penises, well-oiled by the motion of their bodies, rubbed against each other, their shafts slickly slipping along, their heads poking and retreating in random yet purposeful motion. They thrust into each other, never breaking eye contact, consumed with each other's proximity.

They were making love.

"Oh, God, this is perfect," Riley breathed.

"Because it's you," Asher responded. "I've never done this with anyone else."

This was enough to bring Riley to the brink of orgasm before he'd even had a chance to enjoy the sloppy friction of their union. The idea that Asher was doing something with him for the first time... well, that leveled the playing field in a way he'd never expected, and it made what they were doing even hotter.

"I want to get there together," Riley murmured, kissing Asher's neck while they slid and jostled.

"It's gonna be a quick trip," Asher replied, his voice groaning and urgent.

"You... feel... so... fucking... good," Riley huffed as they writhed.

"Your cock is amazing," Asher growled. "It's huge and hard and I will never want anyone else's ever again."

Riley stopped moving and looked at Asher with wide eyes. Then, he screwed them shut and began to jerk like a fish out of water. "Come come come come," he chanted. "Come with me, right fucking now!"

The urgency, the thrusting, the chanting—they were swept up in it and drove each other toward their goal without rest, without mercy. Strings of precum emerged from both engorged members and added their hot stickiness to the slick essence between them.

"I love you," Riley's voice creaked out.

"I love you," Asher answered, his quiet voice both a prayer and an answer to one.

They repeated this to each other over and over again, until finally they did what Riley had wanted—they came together, arching, thrusting, shaking with spasms of love and joy and wicked pleasure. They gripped each other tight and filled the space between them, the thin, slippery gap, with the thick white evidence of their passion. And still they grappled, stretching it out, never wanting it to end.

Finally, exhausted, they collapsed together and kissed and exchanged soft words of love and devotion and joy.

They were complete, together.

CHAPTER SIXTEEN

END GAME

"KAITLYN, HE'S here." Omar ducked back out of her office and headed off down the hall.

"Shit." Every year she thought she had seen the worst this damn show could dish out, and every year she was proven wrong. This one, though. Fuck, this one. She couldn't imagine any season being worse than this one—if one ever turned out to be, she would simply have to burn down the house and slip away under cover of darkness.

She had worked so hard to nurture the faltering steps that Riley and Asher had taken toward each other, only to see them flame out in Vegas. Now, though, when there were only four contestants left and she was out of options for managing their departure from the show, this happens.

She rose from her desk, tried to shake off the complex mix of anger, dread, and exhaustion that surrounded her like a dark cloud. Might as well get this over with. The conference room was just a few steps from her office, and as she strode she willed herself back into professional form, pulling her hair back into a fresh ponytail and straightening her blouse. Despite her efforts, she still looked like she had slept at her desk. Which she had. Again.

"Thanks for coming. Please, sit." She motioned the bachelor into the chair from which he had risen. He was chivalrous, she had to give him that. She sat opposite him and looked him up and down once, taking his measure.

"Can you tell me what's going on?" he asked, politely but with an undertone of feeling taken for a bit of a ride. Which he had been, having been rousted from his bed at 6:00 a.m. and brought across the city to the production offices. "I'm happy to help however I can."

"I need to talk with you about a matter of great concern for the show," Kaitlyn began, carefully keeping her tone neutral. "It's not our usual practice to meet with contestants like this."

He leaned forward, his brow furrowed. He didn't speak, but his arched eyebrows prompted her to continue.

"It's about Asher."

Riley dropped back into his seat, apparently stunned. Then, the stricken look was magically replaced with a good-sportsmanship-award-winning smile. "I hope this is about eliminating the competition—I think he's a real contender."

"Riley, can we be perfectly honest?" Kaitlyn asked, her voice kind but with a sharpness to it that Riley sensed immediately.

He nodded. "Of course."

"I've been watching you and Asher for some time. As you know, we are under a lot of scrutiny this season, particularly with the Gavin and Liam spectacle. This is not a matchmaking show between the bachelors."

Riley scoffed and shook his head. Kaitlyn held up a hand, and he stopped.

"I watched the footage from the cliff top dinner," she continued. "The massages, the after-dinner heart-to-heart."

She had his attention.

"I've been watching you ever since—at the Beverly Palace, during the challenges, all of it. And I was rooting for you to find true love. Someone should, given that it's the theme of the show. But then things went sideways in Vegas—" She held up a hand to silence his interjection at the mention of the Vegas episode. "I didn't have cameras in your rooms, if that's what you're concerned about, but I saw what happened at the baccarat game. Suddenly, the most telegenic partnership in the history of the show isn't speaking to each other. No words exchanged as far as I can tell during an entire week in the tropics. Distant glances at the family hoedown. It was enough to make me give up on love."

Riley, she could see, was completely lost. He didn't seem to know if he should object, and if so, to what. Time to drop the bomb.

"And then, perhaps I was too hasty." She looked across the table at him. "I know what happened at the motel."

The color drained from his cheeks, and the life seemed to leave him. His shoulders slumped. He tried twice to say something but didn't appear to know where to even start.

"I thought so," she said, not without empathy. "Trey was in the room next to Asher's. He heard some strange noises, and he claimed he saw you leave that room before dawn the next morning."

"Nothing happened in the motel."

Kaitlyn shook her head slowly. "Are you saying that wasn't you leaving Asher's room after making the headboard knock all night?"

"Look, you know Asher and I have been fighting it out pretty hard the last few weeks. I mean, I respect the guy, but sometimes his goody-goody act gets to be a bit much. Like that thing in the soup kitchen—right?" Riley rolled his eyes. "I went to his room to call him out about how he had made a play for Daphne at the picnic by sucking up to her brother Charlie. Seemed like a dick move to me, and I told him so. I may have shoved him against the wall at one point, and he pushed back. We were hardly making the headboard dance."

Kaitlyn studied Riley, bored into him with her eyes. If he was bullshitting, he was really good at it. She decided to take a different tack. She fixed him with a skeptical look.

"Here's how I see this going down," she said, like the cop in a low-budget procedural recounting the criminal's thought process. "You are the favorite to win this thing. Daphne loves you, and so does the audience. It's really between you and Shane at this point. You're the one and two going into the final round. Trey is still in it because he's gorgeous, and he has a fan base of fifteen-year-olds with speed dial. Daphne can't stand him, but she can't shake him because he brings in the numbers every single week. Then there's Asher. Daphne loves him, but like a brother. That thing with Charlie at the picnic cemented his place—she thinks he's great, and so does the audience. But he's not the marrying kind, that's clear. So he's our number four."

Riley blinked as if trying to take in all of this information.

Kaitlyn continued. "So, depending on how the voting goes, and what Daphne feels like when she wakes up on Sunday morning, you or Shane will walk away with the prize. But so help me, if it turns out that you and Asher are the real couple...." She shook her head. "Let's just say that the network will pursue all of its options, legal and financial. It would get very awkward for you, very quickly."

Riley stared at her, face devoid of emotion.

"So that's where we stand. Let me assure you, Riley, that I am the biggest cheerleader for equal rights you're ever going to meet. If you and Asher are meant to be together, and this show has brought you that opportunity, I'm thrilled. But I need you to tell me that, right now, and we'll get you out of the show. We'll figure out how to manage it, and you'll be released—except for the part where you disappear for six weeks and don't breathe a word about the show to anyone—as per your legally binding agreement—and once the dust settles you can be blissfully happy together. I'll be happy for you. But you will not take my show down—that's the line I'm drawing."

She set her jaw and stared him down across the table. He sat in silence for a while, clearly aware of how serious she was.

"I auditioned for this show on the rebound from a bad breakup," he said in a quiet voice. "She left me at the altar, which sounds like a cliché or an exaggeration, but it actually happened to me. I'm here because I wanted to get my mojo back, so the next woman I meet won't be looking at a pile of rubble where my heart used to be. If you've seen me as emotionally vulnerable, you're right. If you watched me and Asher become friends, and you've seen me lean on his support as I got my shit together, you're right again. He's helped me a lot. But this is a competition, and we're opponents. I've never forgotten that, and neither has he. I'm going to win this thing, and from what you've said, I just need to beat Shane for the top spot. That I can do."

"And you and Asher...?"

"There is no me and Asher," he said with a dismissive chuckle. He shook his head as if the very idea were beyond the pale.

Kaitlyn sat for a long moment, replaying the conversation in her head, poking at it from several angles. Finally, she nodded. "All right, then." She stood. "Thanks for your time, Riley. This has been helpful."

He rose as well. "You have a very tough job," he offered as he walked around the table toward the exit. "I don't envy you the stress of it."

"You have no idea," she muttered, but then brightened up by sheer force of will. "Thanks again. The car is waiting outside to take you back to the house. I look forward to seeing how things play out in the next forty-eight hours."

"As do I," he said with a gracious nod, and he strode purposefully to the door. In a moment, he was gone.

"I hope to God he was telling me the truth," she said under her breath. She turned to seek out Omar—they had contingencies to plan for, as well as two hours of primetime to fill.

THE FOUR remaining bachelors spent the final day of the show recording reflections on their experience in the competition. The house was crawling with production assistants from the moment Riley returned from his meeting with Kaitlyn until late in the evening, leaving him no opportunity to bring Asher up to speed.

Riley sat at the foot of his bed in the half darkness, listening to the quiet of the house. When he had arrived here, weeks and weeks ago, the dorm had bustled with bachelors posturing and intimidating one another. Now he could only hear his breathing and the sound of Trey, who shared the room with Riley, brushing his teeth energetically. Riley had never really understood Trey's appeal to the show's audience: he was about as shallow as a person could get and still cast a shadow. His popularity came exclusively from his appearance, which, Riley was now free to admit to himself, was stunning. Trey had the lithe yet impeccably muscled physique of an Olympic diver—smooth and limber and compact—and a dimpled face that was destined to decorate the cover of teen magazines for years to come. And yet what came out of his mouth was so unbelievably muddled that five minutes of conversation would lead any thinking person to wonder if Trey hadn't wandered away from a care facility of some kind. His stupidity was rivaled only by his unwavering focus on himself and the value of his physical attributes.

Riley recalled their first encounter. "Dude, you want to know how I make these calves pop?" Trey had asked him, flexing his lower leg at Riley. Riley tried several times thereafter to engage him in conversation on topics both general and specific, but he had discovered no deeper reserves of insight in Trey. Daphne was, based on her remarks at the picnic, of the same mind. But Trey had flexed and posed his way into the final round of the game simply by always knowing where the cameras were and presenting his best, most tanned and toned, side toward them. He flexed, and the teen girls (and, Riley suspected, a fair number of men) dialed.

Trey returned from the bathroom, his nightly ablutions complete. There were still six beds in the room, but the men slept in the same bunks they had claimed upon arrival that first week: Riley next to the door, Trey in the last bed in the same row. This left one bed empty between them.

"Dude, get the lights?" Trey asked as he lay down.

Riley reached up, switched off the lamp, and lay back. He stared at the ceiling for a few minutes, until he heard Trey's breathing settle into a slow rhythm, and then spoke softly into the darkness. "Guess this is our last night, huh?"

No answer.

Riley waited another few minutes until he was certain that Trey was deeply asleep. Then he pulled back the sheet covering him and swung his feet to the floor.

"Psst! Trey!" he whispered, more loudly this time. Still no response. He stood and walked carefully over to Trey's bed. His eyes had adjusted to the darkness of the room, but he was wary of stubbing his toe and waking his roommate. He reached Trey's bed and touched the other man's shoulder, gave it a little shake. No reaction—Trey was certainly a deep sleeper.

Riley took a deep breath and steeled himself for what he was about to do. He reached out a hand and took hold of Trey's covers. He pulled them back, slowly, until Trey was laid out before him, unclothed from head to upper thighs. The man lay on his back, facing away from Riley. His breathing was deep and regular, the ridges of his well-defined ab muscles sharpening and then softening with each breath. In the dim light, Riley could make out all of the curves and hard angles he had come so quickly to know on Asher, but he could also see—for the first time in his life—that a man's body had as many mysteries, as many uniquenesses, as a woman's. He would never have dreamed that the change in his sexuality would bring with it changes in the way he saw everything.

Riley held his breath for a moment, listening hard to be sure that there was no one lurking about the house. Satisfied with the silence, he untied his pajama bottoms and let them slide to the floor. He took a deep breath and grabbed hold of his penis.

KAITLYN AND Omar focused on editing the snippets of reflective musing the bachelors had done upon their experiences during the season. As usual, they were the last ones here, having carried the entire show between them. Kaitlyn was just finishing her (mostly pointless) attempt to make Trey look sentient in his recollections and would next edit the footage taken of the leading contenders, Shane and Riley. Omar had already taken care of Asher—as usual, his native sweetness and wit had made that job a snap—and he was now compiling the montage of memorable moments from the entire season.

"It'll be nice to have this season wrapped," Kaitlyn said, not looking up from her editing. "I'm going to sleep for about three weeks."

"I think I forgot how." Omar laughed. "But I'm going to miss this."

"Seriously? You will miss—this?" Kaitlyn gestured around her with a haggard twirl of her hands.

Omar's hands retreated from his keyboard and came to rest in his lap. "These have been the most exciting months of my life," he said simply. "I'll be sorry when they are over."

"Wow." Kaitlyn had no other words. "I guess if you needed a sign that this is the right career for you, that's the clearest one you're ever likely to get. Most people would run screaming from this place. In fact," she said with a look around her, "it looks like they have. Again."

"That's the part I don't understand. They have a chance to learn from you, to work with someone who's been in this business forever—"

"Hey! I'm in my early thirties, mister."

Omar's eyes widened. "That's not what I—"

"Oh I'm just kidding," she teased. "Please continue."

In a more dignified tone, he did. "We've had so many hours locked in this room, making a show out of whatever awkwardly shot, badly voiced, out-of-focus footage the crew manages to capture, that I think I could make forty-four minutes of primetime out of any miscellaneous crap I lay my hands on. Now, this may be the Stockholm syndrome talking, but I'm honored to have been trapped for weeks on end in this windowless prison with someone as talented as you are."

"That's about the sweetest thing anyone's ever said to me!" Kaitlyn held one hand to her chest and fanned herself with the other. "Now let's get back to it—we've got a two-hour live primetime special to fill."

RILEY'S COCK was being stubborn. It refused to respond to his strokes, and while the naked, supine Trey would have been the answer to a million fevered prayers, Riley felt nothing when he looked upon him. It was only when he closed his eyes and thought of Asher that he responded—in an instant he was fully hard. He wanked away vigorously, because he wanted to be right on the edge when he took the next step. When he felt a drop of precum slip down onto his hand, he knew he was getting close.

In a smooth, fluid motion he lay himself down on the bed, right next to Trey. He was careful not to make contact with the other man's body, but he was close enough to feel the hair on his leg brush against the hair of Trey's. He kept up his rhythmic stroking, and within a minute he was again on the verge of an orgasm. This time, though, he didn't stop. He felt the tingle building in his groin, spreading throughout his body, as more slick gel emerged from the tip of his penis, lubing his tightly gripping hand as it sped along his hard shaft. Twitching broke out across his entire body signaling the point of no return, and he reached out his other arm in a glorious stretch that opened him to the impending waves of pleasure.

His outstretched hand felt along the edge of the nightstand next to Trey's bed until he found the button. Just as the orgasm seized his body, he pushed it, and then turned his concentration to aiming his streams of semen so as to achieve greatest effect. Several of them he directed to Trey's flaccid penis, and then once it was glazed he shot several streams on his hip. The last few Riley kept for himself, dripping them haphazardly around his groin. They were a proper mess by the time the spasms ran themselves out.

Now, he just had to wait.

KAITLYN AND Omar jumped when the alarm sounded. Even with all of the shocks and surprises of this season, they had still never heard the alarm—until now. They both stood instinctively and scanned the monitors to see what was going on.

The silent alarms that had been installed on every nightstand and in the bathrooms of the house were intended to protect the cast members. If anyone witnessed behavior that was unruly or dangerous, they could press an alarm button and security personnel would respond quickly and silently. No one had used it thus far because the bachelors had gotten on quite well with one another during the competition—unlike in previous seasons, the crew had not had to break up a single fight.

"Security, what's going on?" Kaitlyn barked into her phone.

"We've got a silent triggered in number two dorm. We're on our way!"

RILEY HEARD a door open in a remote part of the house—they were on their way. Only one more thing he needed to do, and it was what he was least happy about. Still, it needed to be done. He reached out and took hold of Trey's penis. It was soft, but a couple of strokes with a firm grip changed that right away.

Riley shuddered at the thought of what he was doing. Asher's penis was one thing—he had only touched that after he realized he was in love with Asher. This time he was just touching another man—one he barely knew—and it felt ugly and strange. But it was what he needed to do, and so he did.

Trey, still asleep, was nonetheless responsive. His already large cock grew quickly, firming up under Riley's insistent grip, until it reached full hardness about fifteen seconds after Riley had begun stroking it. Perfect, Riley thought.

It was at that moment security burst through the door.

KAITLYN SWITCHED the main monitors to the number two dorm cameras just as the security officers turned on the lights. She couldn't believe what she was seeing. Both occupants of the room, Riley and Trey, were in the same bed, and they were fully naked. And, now that she squinted and leaned forward, she could see they both were fully erect.

"Oh, for fuck's sake!" Kaitlyn shouted and slammed her fist on the control panel. "What in the fucking fuck is this?"

"Oh God, are they…?" Omar asked between the fingers he had laced over his face. "Tell me they aren't!"

"Well, they may not be right now, but that's only because they just finished." Kaitlyn flipped off the audio feed from the house and sat silently, letting what she had seen sink in. Slowly, she lowered her head to the control panel. "We're dead," she moaned softly. "We're just dead. We will be the only show in history to be cancelled on the day of our finale."

Omar put his hand on Kaitlyn's shoulder. "There is a silver lining," he said quietly.

"What's that?" she muttered disconsolately.

"You were right about Riley. That's something, right?"

She lifted her head with a jerk. She looked at him, trying to figure out how he always knew the right thing to say. "It's a curse, always being right," she said, a grin only barely starting to flicker at the corner of her mouth.

"It is your cross to bear. But the question is, what do we do now?"

"Give me a sec," she said, closing her eyes. His confidence in her, that she would be able to answer his question even in this moment of devastation, heartened her. "Got it," she said, definitively.

"I never doubted you," Omar replied with a reverent nod.

"WHAT THE fuck are you doing?" Trey demanded when the lights came on and he realized he was not alone in bed.

Riley looked from Trey to the two security guards and back again, as if trying to come up with a story that would excuse their situation. Slumping his shoulders as if giving up, he sighed. "We can't get out of it this time. We might as well be honest."

"I have no idea what you—" Trey sputtered. He turned to the guards. "I have no idea what this faggot is saying. I wasn't doing anything."

"Honey, they can see what we've been doing," Riley said in a calm, soothing voice. He nodded down to their glistening, just-now-softening penises.

"Oh, fuck!" Trey yelled, leaping from the bed as if their cocks were cobras. His penis bobbed out in front of him, a jutting testimony to the fact that he had, in fact, been doing something.

"All right, lovebirds, let's get some clothes on. You have some explaining to do at HQ."

"There's really nothing to explain," Riley said, a convincing note of misery in his voice. "We were just excited about tomorrow, and he started to feel frisky, and before I knew it we were going at it. I must have hit the button when… well, let's just say my boy has got quite a talented mouth." Riley giggled and reached for his pajama bottoms, which were still lying where he had dropped them earlier.

"Oh. My. God. Why are you doing this?" Trey asked Riley, apparently disregarding for the moment that he was still naked. He turned back to the guards. "He's making this up to disqualify me. He's trying to get me eliminated."

"Buddy, from where we stand it looks like both of you are outta here. Plus," the guard paused, a look of disgust on his face. "If he made the whole thing up, why is there spooge dripping from your dingus?"

Trey looked down, horrified. He looked back up to Riley, and his mouth opened and closed several times in mute outrage. Then he ran to the bathroom and began a noisy and expletive-filled disinfection process.

Riley turned to the guards. "Sorry. He gets like this when he's embarrassed. I told him it wasn't a good idea to do this on the last night, but he was so horned up. Then once he comes he gets all crazy like this. You know men, right?" He smiled broadly at the guards, both of whom stared back at him, speechless.

"WELL, HERE we are again," Kaitlyn said wearily, staring across the table at Riley. "It was less than twenty-four hours ago that you sat in that chair and told me you weren't gay, that you were in this to win it. If you will pardon my bluntness, which at this hour is all I have to offer you, you lied to me. You sat right there and lied to me, and I took you at your word. Which, I now find out, was worth absolutely nothing. I'm screwed, my show is screwed, and you are perhaps the most screwed of all, which to me is the silver lining in all of this screwed-ness." She finally paused to take a breath. "Now, tell me, Riley, what the fuck is going on."

Riley's expression was contrite. "I'm sorry, Kaitlyn," he said in a low, quiet voice. "I couldn't help it. I should have told you the truth. The truth is that Asher awakened something in me, something I had no inkling of before I met him. And once I had realized it about myself, he wanted nothing to do with me. I know you think Asher is gay, but he's not—at least not where I'm concerned. That's what we were really fighting about in the horrible motel in the middle of nowhere. I wanted to, he certainly didn't, and that's where we left it. Then, tonight, Trey's nerves must have gotten to him because he was all over me, and... and I just let it happen. I didn't intend for this to happen— it's not the way I wanted it to go. But when Asher pushed me away I.... I thought I was some horrible monster that no one would ever want. That Trey was even interested in me meant a lot." Tears were falling down Riley's cheeks now—he invoked them by thinking of what Asher would feel when he heard the news. This was the part of the plan he hated the most—but he couldn't think of any better way to accomplish the goal.

Kaitlyn softened. "Look, I feel bad for you as a person, I do. And I would like to go on the record as saying you are certainly not a monster, and that out there somewhere is the perfect guy for you. But right now my concern has to be getting my show back on track."

Riley nodded and wiped the tears from his cheeks.

"I'll do anything I can to help," he said, meaning every word. He would like to minimize the damage for all involved if he could.

"You've done enough," she said, not without compassion. "Trey, of course, denied the entire thing, said he woke up and you were in his bed. He claims to have no idea how he came to be covered in... well, you know."

Riley shook his head sadly. "I know what it's like to be in his situation, denying who you are. It's sad, really. But given some time he'll work through it." This was the part of the plan Riley was most ambivalent about; clearly Trey was innocent of what he was now suspected of, but he wasn't going to win anyway. No one involved would want the reason for his disqualification made public, so there wouldn't be any lasting damage to his reputation. Ethically, Riley was on thin ice, and he knew it. Love makes us do what we never imagined we would, he thought.

"Here's what's going to happen. You are contractually bound not to speak about your experience on the show until after the promotional period has ended. That's the six weeks after the final show airs, during which time the chosen bachelor—Shane—and Daphne will tour everything from talk shows to county fairs and show the world how much they love each other. Asher will do the consolation tour, talking to anyone who will listen about how nice guys don't always finish first, and generally showing the human side of the competition. Then, once the six weeks are up, we move along to casting the next season and everyone fades away while buzz ramps up about who the new bachelors are going to be. At that point you can do whatever you want to whomever you want."

"If you don't mind my saying so, isn't it kind of cruel to parade Asher around like that? What's the point?"

Kaitlyn smiled wryly. "Because we need people to believe that the contest is real, and the runner-up is proof of that. He's cute and sweet and nice, and everyone will see that the competition must have been fierce if he didn't walk away with it. Women will be throwing themselves at him, mark my words."

Riley nodded, as if he were happy for Asher and all of those women who were preparing to launch at him.

Kaitlyn continued. "That's why we have to keep him focused on the tour, and not let any news emerge about how the end of the show went down." She regarded him, trying to determine how much she could trust him. She decided she had no choice but to trust him, if she were honest about it. "Riley, I'm just going to say this once, and I need you to listen to me. You cannot, under any circumstances, no matter what the reason, you cannot have any contact with Asher during the six weeks after we wrap. He's simply worth too much to the future of the show. The network and its pack of slavering legal rottweilers will be watching everything he does, and everyone he talks to—one text message from you, and it's all over for him. He disappears, and so does the quarter-million consolation prize. Are we clear?"

Again Riley nodded, his expression desolate. "Yes, we're clear. You don't have to worry about me. I'll be back in Chicago by the time the show airs tomorrow."

"Actually, you'll be in Chicago before breakfast. There's a car outside waiting to take you to the airport, where you'll board the red-eye. The show sprang for business class so you can get some sleep. You're welcome."

Riley chuckled mirthlessly and rose to leave. At the door, he glanced back. "I just—I only wanted.... I'm sorry." He turned back and walked down the hallway with as much dignity as he could muster. It wasn't much.

"I hope you find what you're looking for," she muttered, shaking her head. But there was still much to do tonight, so she could spare no more thoughts for Riley. As she picked up her clipboard, a small, folded piece of paper slid off the top, and she picked it up from the floor. "Asher" was written on the outside. She opened it, read the message, shrugged, and folded it back up. She would decide what to do about that later.

"So what you're saying is that we're the final two," Shane said with a skeptical squint.

"That's right. The other two contestants were disqualified late last night."

At this revelation, Shane nodded, while Asher jolted in his seat.

"I heard something about that from the crew," Shane said in a slow Aussie drawl. "Seems our bachelors were discovered *in flagrante*."

Asher paled, his mouth dropping open. He closed it with a visible effort. "What did he say?" He looked from Shane to Kaitlyn, clearly in shock.

"Riley and Trey were discovered last night in bed together. They have both been sent home for violating the terms of their contract with the show." She watched Asher's face and saw shock turn to horror.

"But—"

"They are no longer your concern," Kaitlyn interrupted him. "Tonight we have two hours of primetime to fill, and our only job is to make it the best finale we can. We had planned to eliminate two of the contestants at the end of the first hour, and we will stick to that plan—we have everything we need from Trey and Riley recorded, and we are all going to pretend that they were in the game until tonight. All of us, understand?" She looked significantly at the men—her expression brooked no argument, and the men made none. "Now, let's run through the rough outline of the show, and then we'll fill in the details."

She spent the next hour fleshing out the sequence of interviews, reflections, live satellite Q&A from viewing parties across the country—all of the elements that would make this evening's show a logistical nightmare. But Shane and Asher proved to be ready pupils, and she began to see a flicker of hope that they might pull this off.

"The car will bring you to the theatre this afternoon at two so we can run through again and get the blocking down. Don't worry about what to wear—we'll have wardrobe for you there. Any questions?"

The men shook their heads with a somewhat overwhelmed look in their eyes.

"Thank you, gentlemen. I'll see you this afternoon."

They rose to leave. "I'll meet you in the car, mate," Shane said. "Got to make a quick stop." He headed down the hall to the restroom.

"Asher, wait," Kaitlyn said as Asher was about to leave the room. "I have something for you."

He stopped and turned back to her. His eyes were red, and he looked as if he were about to cry. "What—" His voice was thick. He cleared his throat and tried again. "What is it?" he managed to ask.

"It's from"—she leaned toward him as she handed him the folded slip of paper she had found on her clipboard—"Riley," she whispered.

He gasped quietly and put a hand to his mouth as he took the paper from her. He looked at his name written on the paper and shook his head as if he didn't recognize the word. He unfolded the paper and read what was written inside.

"HE STARED at it, and you could see every emotion in his face. He was surprised, and happy, and angry—all at once. Then he just grew calm, and he took three deep breaths with his eyes closed. Then he turned to me and said 'Thank you,' and left. It was the strangest thing."

Omar tipped his head thoughtfully. "What did the note say?"

"Do you think I read people's private notes?" Kaitlyn asked, her voice indignant.

Omar crossed his arms and lifted a critical eyebrow.

"All right, so what. For the good of the show! But I have no idea what it meant. He sure seemed to know, though."

"At the risk of repeating myself, what did the note say?"

"It said 'We were joined at Pylos.' That's it. That mean anything to you?"

Omar shook his head. "No idea. Did you Wikipedia it?"

"Of course. I'm not so old that I don't know how to look things up on the Internet," she replied indignantly. "But it was no help. It's a perfectly lovely town in Greece, but as far as I know neither of them has ever been there."

"How do you know?"

"We do background checks after the Great Fraud of Season Four. I'm sure you've heard of that one?"

"Where all of the final candidates had lied about their past?"

"Yeah, about their education, career, felony record, history of mental imbalance resulting in institutionalization, that kind of thing." Kaitlyn shook her head at the memory. "Anyway, since then we've done background checks on people before casting them. And then we ran another, more intensive round of checks after we discovered Liam and Gavin had managed to slip through. We got a rundown of any international travel they've done in the last ten years, and neither of these guys has been to Greece."

"A code of some kind, then?" Omar asked.

"I don't know. At this point I didn't see how it could hurt anything to let him have it—by the end of the day this will all be over. I trust Riley when he says he will lay low for six weeks, and plus he's in Chicago by now. He seemed like he was going to go home and lick his wounds."

Omar reached out and touched Kaitlyn on the arm. "I'm sorry it turned out this way—I was really pulling for true love."

"Thank you." She sighed, and sadness washed across her face. Then she shook it off and resumed being the professional she prided herself on being. "Now, let's get to the theatre. The show must go on." She smiled grimly and led the way.

"YOU LOOK like hell, man."

"Don't pull any punches, buddy. Tell me how you really feel." Riley chuckled bleakly and took the beer Kevin was holding out to him. "Thanks. It's been kind of a long day already."

They sat on the porch of Kevin's house, the noontime haze of a late summer Chicago Sunday glaring around them. Biscuit was curled up on Riley's feet, a spot he hadn't stirred from since Riley had arrived from the airport just before breakfast. Kevin took a deep pull on his cheap beer, and regarded his friend with empathetic eyes.

"Want to talk about it?"

Riley knew how he was supposed to answer this question: as was their custom, Kevin expected him to say, "Hell no, I'm a guy." But he couldn't bring himself to do it. "It was rough. God, it was the toughest thing I've ever been through."

"It looked intense all right. That stuff you did in the mountains? I don't think I could have done half of that, with the rock climbing and the kayaks and everything."

Riley shook his head, took another drink. "That was the easy stuff. It was what you didn't see that was the hardest."

Kevin squinted at him. "What the hell they do to you? This was supposed to be about you getting your mojo back, not getting your ass handed to you."

"It's not what they did, exactly." He paused, looking for the right words. "When you're thrown into that kind of situation, with a group of strangers, you learn a lot about yourself. Stress brings out some serious shit, man."

Kevin sat down his beer. "When you texted me and said you were coming home, I didn't expect smiles and sunshine, but shit, man. This has got you pretty fucked up."

Riley looked out into the middle distance, silent.

Kevin leaned toward Riley. "You can tell me anything, you know that. Don't be like those vets who come back from war and don't talk about it and then go apeshit all of a sudden." He searched Riley's face. "God, Riley, what the hell?"

Riley snapped back to himself and turned a smiling face to his best friend. "It's nothing. Jet lag, mostly. Plus, I didn't even make it to the final round, so that sucks, right?" He polished off his can of beer. "I'm good, really. Now, what are you going to grill tonight? I need to drown my sorrows in meat."

Kevin regarded his best friend skeptically but shrugged and laughed it off. "Let's go pick some stuff out of the freezer. My cousin in Wisconsin hooked us up with a half-side of beef, so you can drown yourself and still have leftovers!"

Riley tossed back the last swallow in the can of beer and rose to follow Kevin back into the house.

By the time the show came on, they had worked their way through a sizable pile of beef. Riley and Kevin and his family gathered around the television with bowls of ice cream and strawberries to watch.

"Uncle Riley, why you not on TV now?" asked Kevin's older daughter, who had just turned three. "We watch you."

"I didn't make it to the end," he answered, smiling at the beautiful little girl. She had Kevin's eyes and her mother's blonde hair. "But good sports cheer on the winners, right?"

"Who's gonna win?" she asked.

"I hope Shane wins, myself," he said. "Asher's a great guy, but I kind of think he's going to end up in second place."

Suddenly she flapped her arms at him. "Shhh… it's starting!" She was serious about watching TV, apparently.

The first hour of the show was torturous for Riley, with montage after montage of his exploits and those of the other bachelors. He had seen none of the finished show and was surprised to find he was the early favorite to make it to the end. His heart pounded every time Asher was on the screen. Had Kaitlyn given him the note? Or was he thinking that he had been abandoned—again?

It was at the end of the first hour that Kaitlyn's creativity kicked into high gear. The hosts described the results of the telephone voting and how many millions of votes had been recorded.

"And the two bachelors who have been eliminated, based on your votes, are"—the longest television pause ever broadcast followed, and then, finally: "Trey and… Riley." A huge groan went up in the theatre, clearly audible on the broadcast, and was echoed in the Chicago living room where Riley sat.

Kevin clapped Riley on the shoulder. "Tough break, man. I voted for you. Several times, in fact."

"Thanks. I appreciate it." Riley knew the viewer vote had nothing to do with it—he had eliminated himself. But what choice did he have? This was the only way for Asher to get what he wanted.

The first hour of the show concluded with excerpts from the reflections the dismissed bachelors had recorded the previous day. These had been selected to make them seem like reactions to being voted off—Kaitlyn had been sure that the men were asked leading questions like "You've just found out that you didn't win. How do you feel about that?" This, Riley realized now, got them talking in the right verb tense and everything—it was very crafty; he had to give her that. He watched himself reflect on his own dismissal with words he had recorded before he had arranged for his own disqualification. It was a little surreal.

The second hour was given over to Daphne and the two remaining bachelors chatting and viewing excerpts from their dates over the course of the show. For the first time, Riley could see Shane's appeal—he was confident and suave, and the accent certainly didn't hurt. But it was the date footage with Asher that struck him most deeply. He was so thoughtful and so sweet—everything Shane was not—that Riley found himself falling in love all over again.

In the final quarter-hour of the show—between blizzards of commercials—the choice had to be made. Each man was given a chance to say some closing words to Daphne. Shane's were polished, delivered in the gravelly outback voice he used when he wanted to be extra sexy. When it was Asher's turn, he talked about the things he had come to love about Daphne, which seemed to please her, and then the camera came in for a close-up on his final words.

Asher looked away from Daphne for the first time. "I promise you this," he said, directly into the camera, "No man will keep me from you."

Those words. Those words.

"Riley, you okay?"

"What?" Riley turned to Kevin, his face pale.

"You gasped like you saw a ghost," Kevin said, his voice full of concern. "Are you crying?"

"All right, girls, let's go finish watching up in mommy and daddy's room." Kevin's wife picked up the baby and took the older child's hand. "Let's let Daddy and Uncle Riley have some space."

Riley wiped his face, delighted to be crying tears of joy rather than worry and despair and all of the other emotions that had swept over him in the last twenty-four hours. "Yeah, I'm okay. Really."

The show was back from commercial. Daphne took center stage, and she had a few words to say to each man. Shane was complimented for the way he made her feel like a lady, and Asher for his warm heart and kindness. She chose… Shane.

"Whooooooo!" Riley shouted and jumped to his feet, pumping his hands in the air. "Fuck yeah!"

"Well, I'm glad the girls weren't here to see that, though I imagine they heard it," Kevin said with a concerned glance at the ceiling. He switched off the television.

"Sorry. I've spent too much time in LA—I'm not used to being around people anymore." Riley's face glowed with happiness.

"Let's head downstairs. I'm going to pour us a drink, and you're going to tell me what the hell is going on with you, because you're kind of scaring me right now with the crying one minute and whoo-hooing the next." Once they had descended, he ducked behind the bar and began rummaging through the cabinet. "I've been saving this for something special, and since it looks like I'm going to have to have you committed to an asylum soon, we might as well enjoy this now." He placed the bottle reverently on the bar.

Riley looked at the label and burst out with manic laughter.

"Okay, dude, I'm seriously freaked out right now. What the fuck?" Kevin looked at the bottle, then to his friend, then back again.

"I'm sorry. It's just that there have been some bizarre twists and turns in my life lately, and at each of them a bottle of that Scotch shows up. This is the third time. I'm starting to think I owe the nice folks at Bruichladdich a thank-you note."

"You can thank me while you're at it," Kevin said as he poured. "This bottle set me back a couple hundred."

"Well, I have a story to tell you that will make it all worth it," Riley said cheerfully as he raised his glass of the exotic yet now-familiar amber liquid.

"You gonna finally tell me what's been going on with you?"

"Think you can handle it?" Riley said, still smiling but with a serious undertone. He had forged ahead bravely thus far, but what he was about to do scared him shitless if he stopped to think about it too much.

Kevin, with a lifelong friend's intuition, set down his glass. "There is nothing you can tell me that will change how I feel about you. If you stole something, I'll help you hide it. If you killed somebody, I'll grab a shovel. If you fell in love, I will smack you for being a drama queen about it and then help you plan the wedding." He held up his fingers in a Vulcan salute. "I am, and always shall be, your friend."

"It's the third one," Riley blurted, and then tossed back his Scotch.

"Well, that wasn't so hard, was it? Good for you, man, good for you!" Kevin tipped up his glass and then poured more. He lifted his glass and nodded for Riley to do the same. "Here's to you, and to the lucky woman of your dreams, whose name is…?"

"Asher." Riley slugged back his drink before Kevin could react.

"Sorry, didn't catch that," Kevin said, tapping his ear. "Ashley?"

"No." Riley took a deep breath. "I said Asher. Asher from the show. Asher the runner-up. Asher the first guy I ever... yeah, Asher."

Kevin set his glass down slowly. He looked at Riley through half-closed eyes, his expression inscrutable. He walked around the bar to stand next to Riley.

Riley turned to him, suddenly terrified. He'd never seen Kevin like this, his face a mask of mute confusion. Then, suddenly, Kevin yanked Riley to him in a hug, squeezing him so hard that Riley saw stars.

"I am... *so* happy for you," Kevin murmured, his face pressed against Riley's head. "That's awesome." He released his grip on Riley but kept his hands on his shoulders. "Now, you know he was just on television professing his love for a woman, right? I don't mean to rain on your parade and all, but isn't that kind of a complication?"

Riley laughed. "Yeah, you'd think so. But that thing he said at the end—that he would let no man come between them?"

"You mean right before you freaked out?"

"Yeah. There was this thing that he said to me once, about these two characters from the *Odyssey*. When I left the show yesterday, I left him a note with the first part, and he answered back with the second part. It means we're good." Riley giggled, another wave of relief that his plan had actually worked washing over him. "Well, in six weeks we're good. We're kind of in limbo until then."

"I think you should start from the beginning and tell me the whole thing," Kevin said, and he sat on the leather couch to listen.

CHAPTER SEVENTEEN

HAPPILY EVER

IT WAS exactly six weeks and one day later that Riley stood in the corridor of the elementary school, looking through the small window set in the door of Asher's classroom.

Asher taught at an arts magnet school, which explained the brightly decorated corridors and the ambient music—jazz and classical and something that sounded modern and experimental. Riley had flown in a week earlier to make arrangements for this moment, and while he was beside himself with excitement to see Asher, he was still excruciatingly nervous.

The class finished its morning ritual of announcements and a song and then broke into studio groups: some put on painting smocks, while others picked up lumps of clay from the bin in the back of the room, and still others booted up computers and fiddled with styluses while they waited for the drawing software to load. Asher moved from group to group, ensuring that everyone had what they needed to create. He positively glowed in the classroom, and Riley simply beamed to watch him work.

"We gonna head in, chief, or stand in the hallway all day?"

Riley turned to the impatient Kaitlyn with a look of mock scolding. "Can't you let me enjoy this moment of anticipation?"

"I've been anticipating this moment even longer than you have. I'm gonna bust with anticipation unless you open that door and get to making him the happiest man in the world!"

Riley smiled at the love underneath the rough words. He had come to appreciate the producer more and more in the past month. Once Daphne and Shane had announced their engagement, two weeks into their post-show tour, there was really no need for Asher to continue to play the chipper also-ran. They let him come back home for the start of the school year. She had called Riley to let him know, despite the embargo, and she was thrilled when he finally told her the truth; they had immediately begun to plan this day. And now that it was here, she had a matchmaker's impatience to get to the good stuff.

Riley nodded to the principal of the school, and she turned the door handle. She slipped into the classroom without revealing the crowd in the hallway and walked into the room with a purposeful stride.

"Mr. Morgan, may I have the attention of your class please?" She smiled sweetly at the assembled children.

"Of course, Principal Chang. Class, please turn your attention to Principal Chang. Thank you."

The class was remarkably well behaved, Riley thought. Or perhaps the sudden appearance of the principal was an unusual event that piqued their curiosity.

"Thank you, Mr. Morgan. Now, class, we have something very special to do in this classroom today, and I am so glad that we are all here to share it with Mr. Morgan."

Asher's head turned quickly to the principal. He clearly hadn't been expecting this.

"Now, who can tell me what happens when two grown-ups fall in love and want to spend their lives together. What do they do?"

"They get married!" shouted the class in unison.

"That's right! Very good. Now, do you know what it's called when one grown-up asks another if they would like to get married?"

"A reposal!" shouted a girl in the front of the class, as she jumped up and down and waved her arms.

"Excellent! We call it a *pro*posal, and it's a very exciting moment indeed. Now, boys and girls, I want you to be very quiet and put on your very best party manners, because something very special is about to happen. Ready?" She looked around the classroom at twenty faces full of barely contained excitement, and she nodded toward the door.

It opened, slowly, and Riley stepped into the classroom. He was dressed in a tuxedo and was carrying a spray of red roses.

Asher turned and gasped, his hand over his mouth. Tears sprang to his eyes in an instant.

Riley walked to the front of the class where Asher stood. He handed Asher the roses, and then he got down on one knee. "Asher Morgan, I love you more than life itself. Will you do me the very great honor of becoming my husband?" He opened a small box containing two gold bands and held it up to Asher.

"Oh my God, oh my God," Asher said, shaking his head. "Yes, yes, yes yesyesyesyes!" His tears were flowing freely now.

Riley took one of the two rings and placed it on Asher's finger. Then he stood and handed the other one to Asher, who put it on Riley's finger.

"I love you so much," Asher whispered to Riley, and they kissed.

"Yay!" shrieked a girl in the front row, and she was joined by the rest of the class in hooting and clapping their joy at seeing their teacher so happy. Such was the commotion that at first no one noticed the singing. But soon a hush fell over the room and all could hear the delicate notes of the sixth-grade choir, who had filed in after Riley had begun his proposal. They had been rehearsing "Simple Gifts" for a fall recital when Riley had called the school to make arrangements for the proposal, and the slow, lovely notes created an ethereal calm over the room. When they finished, applause broke out from a group of adults who had slipped into the room to watch the proposal. Kaitlyn and Omar stood next to Kevin and Asher's sister Meg. There was not a dry eye in the bunch.

"THIS IS the problem with gay marriage," Kaitlyn whispered to Omar. "Once these guys start planning proposals, no straight guy will be able to compete."

Omar laughed and nudged her in the ribs. "This must feel good, being right in the end."

"Yeah, I get that a lot. Pretty used to it by now." She smiled and wiped her eyes, and then turned to watch the happy couple embrace and accept the congratulations of all in the room.

RILEY AND Asher watched the sun set over the Mediterranean. Their wedding had been in May, at the end of the school year, and while there had been many decisions to be made about the wedding, their choice of honeymoon spot was never in question. They would come to Pylos.

"I can't believe this place," Asher said, gesturing at the brilliant white walls, the deep blue of the pool that extended to the very edge of the cliff overlooking the sea.

"Kaitlyn comes through once again," Riley added.

"This is what the Beverly Palace was trying to be."

Riley put his arm around Asher, kissed him on the cheek. "It's better than that—this is the place you dreamed of. The place I've been dreaming of since you told me the story of Telemachus and Pisistratus."

"It was just a story until I met you. I never thought I'd actually have a Pisistratus of my own. And then you came along, and just when I needed you most, you slayed the last suitor."

The sky deepened from pink to purple, and the first stars began to glimmer above them.

"Meg sure looked good at the wedding," Riley said.

"Her hair grew back with the most amazing texture, and she was back to being the girl I grew up with." He looked at Riley. "She's got her whole life ahead of her because of you."

"That was all you," he replied. "I just gave the plan a little nudge at the right moment."

"We make a pretty great team."

"I have an idea," Riley murmured as he began to unbutton Asher's shirt. "How about a little swim?"

"Sounds amazing." Asher began to undo the buttons on Riley's shirt as well.

Soon they were reveling in the feeling of the warm water gliding over their naked bodies, their aimless paddling interrupted by their inability to keep their hands off each other. Their embraces were at first fleeting and playful but then grew more urgent and intense as the sky darkened and the majestic romance of the setting sank in.

"So, Telemachus, how about some anointing with olive oil and then a little Greek-style wrestling?"

"I thought you'd never ask, Pisistratus." Asher took Riley by the hand and led him up the steps out of the pool and over to the bed that lay open to the stars.

Next to the bed a table held two large white towels and a small carafe of oil. Asher dried Riley off, caressing him gently with the luxuriantly soft towel, and then poured a little of the fragrant oil in his hand and rubbed it all over his body. Riley returned the favor, drying Asher and then smoothing him with the oil. They lay together on the bed and looked up at the stars.

"This is where they were when they found each other," Asher whispered, awe in his voice. "We're lying under the same stars."

"What do you think happened next?" Riley murmured. "When you imagined them, what did you think of them doing?"

Asher turned to kiss Riley softly on the lips. "I imagined them just like this. Limbs intertwined, exchanging stolen kisses when they thought they were alone. I don't know that I thought about them doing much more than that, at least at first. But in my fantasy version, once Pisistratus killed that suitor, then—watch out. I figure Telemachus would have let him pound him pretty good as a thank-you for that."

"Is that an invitation?" Riley growled.

Asher kissed him again. "You know I've been saving myself for my wedding night." He paused. "So, yes—consider yourself invited," he said, laughing.

"We've waited so long for this—those lucky Greeks didn't have to hold off for two clear test results six months apart."

"But this way it's more authentic—after what Odysseus went through, there's no way Telemachus would ever fuck with a Trojan!" Asher laughed delightedly at his own literary joke, at least until he realized that Riley's expression was more one of lust than humor.

Riley rose and laid himself atop Asher, pressing their lips together while slipping their hard, oiled bodies along each other. He was instantly erect, as was Asher, and just as in the motel, the friction was intoxicating. But Riley wanted more tonight, and he looked expectantly into Asher's eyes. He was not disappointed.

"I want you to do it," Asher said, repeating the words Riley had said in Vegas.

"Do what?"

"I want you to fuck me," he breathed, his voice pleading. "You disposed of the last suitor, and I am your prize."

Riley's reply was a deep, guttural rumble in his chest. He reared back and placed the head of his oiled cock at the spot his tongue and his fingers knew so well. He felt that knot of muscle for the first time with the tip of his steely hard penis and thought he might come just from the feel of rubbing it up and down along the opening he'd dreamed of breaching for so long. "Are you ready?" he asked, his voice an urgent groan.

"I give myself to you, tonight and forever," Asher replied, his voice solemn.

"Fuck, you always know what to say," huffed Riley as he began to press against Asher's tight ass. The head nudged in, and he was overwhelmed with the thrilling heat. He felt Asher shiver beneath him, but as he stared into those eyes, the eyes of the man he loved, he knew it was all right.

"God, you're huge!" groaned Asher, throwing his legs around Riley's waist and pulling him closer. "More, please, more."

Riley pushed, and his cock slid in smoothly past the spasming muscle. Asher sighed as Riley's hips met his buttocks. They were joined now.

Riley had never felt a love so entire. He kissed Asher, nuzzled his neck, nibbled at his ear, all the while keeping a slow but building rhythm. Soon, though, his gentleness gave way to faster, harder thrusts.

"Yes, yes," Asher chanted. He voice was rising to a higher pitch with each thrust, and soon he was incoherent with passion. "Oh, oh God—I'm going to…!"

Riley pulled back so he could give Asher a couple of strokes to get him all the way there, but before he could even reach for his cock he felt Asher's ass grip his own cock tighter than ever. He kept thrusting, knowing that in this position he was pounding directly at Asher's prostate—he could feel it start to swell, and he pressed his erection against it as hard as he could.

Asher gripped the sheets and writhed as his cock surged and then blasted a nearly continuous rope of white fluid all over his chest and neck. Riley laid hold of it and gave it several vigorous strokes, which sent Asher into an even higher orbit—he screamed and a new volley of semen erupted from his cock. It was this second ejaculation that sent Riley over the edge. Every muscle in his body seized up, and he froze midthrust; then those special muscles deep in his pelvis snapped into action and he flooded Asher with jet after jet of hot cum. Riley surged forward and then resumed his wild thrusting until he was completely emptied. Then he collapsed onto Asher, their torsos slick with a double load of spunk. They panted, spent, elated.

A few minutes later Riley rolled off and the two men lay together, again looking at the stars.

"I imagine it went something like that," Riley said finally.

"I think Telemachus would have been walking funny the next day," Asher moaned. "That's quite a weapon you've got there."

Riley laced his fingers with Asher's. "It's a good thing we have two weeks here, because I think I'm going to need to do that a few more times. And I expect you to return the favor."

"Oh, don't worry about that—your ass is mine."

"Forever," Riley said, as he snuggled tighter into Asher.

THE NEXT morning, the two men sat at the table by the pool eating a light breakfast in the warming air.

"So, what do you think about Kaitlyn's offer?" Asher asked.

"It's intriguing," Riley replied. "And it's not like my work is thrilling me these days." His insurance company had allowed him to move several hundred miles away to live with Asher, but the truth was that the work, now done primarily by phone and computer, just didn't excite him anymore.

"I just wonder whether anyone would watch it," Asher said, sipping his orange juice. "It's a kind of radical concept."

"Yeah, it is," Riley agreed. "But it's also kind of inspired. I mean, the whole bachelor/bachelorette concept is pretty long in the tooth, right? But the idea of getting a bunch of guys together whose friends and family think they might be gay, and then seeing if they develop feelings for a bachelor or a bachelorette, well—I think I would watch that."

"You're just saying that because you lived it," Asher replied with a laugh. "And I'm really glad you did. Do you think they can find enough people to sign up for it?"

"How many people out there know someone who seems gay but insists he's straight? People go on TV for all kinds of reasons, you know," he said with a grin.

"Well, if Kaitlyn's involved, I think it's got a shot. She's pretty smart about this kind of thing."

"She knew about us long before I did, I'll give her that. And she did give us this amazing wedding present," he said, looking around the villa. "So, I think I'll give it a try. Might as well change up everything in my life at once, right? A year ago I was straight and miserable, and now I'm married to the most amazing man in the world and going to host my own reality show. How lucky am I?"

Asher leaned across the table and kissed him. "I'm the lucky one. My dreams all came true when I met you."

"I never even dreamed I could be this happy in love, and yet here you are. I think that makes me the luckiest one. But we have the rest of our lives to settle this—let's take it slow."

"Speaking of taking it slow," Asher said with a cocked eyebrow, "I believe there was something we were going to do today."

Riley grinned broadly. "I've given you my heart and soul." He rose and reached for Asher's hand. "You might as well have that too." He led his husband back to bed, heart fluttering with the promise of the new devotion he was about to experience.

They were joined at Pylos.

XAVIER MAYNE is the pen name of a professor of English who works at a university in the midwest United States. Versed in academic theories of sexual identity, he is passionate about writing stories in which men experience a love that pushes them beyond the boundaries they thought defined their sexuality. He believes that romance can be hot, funny, and sweet in equal measure.

The name Xavier Mayne is a tribute to the pioneering gay author Edward Prime-Stevenson, who also used it as a pen name. He wrote the first openly gay novel by an American, 1906's Imre: A Memorandum, which depicts two masculine men falling in love despite social pressures that attempt to keep them apart.

Please visit Xavier Mayne's website at http://www.xaviermayne.com.

Romance by Xavier Mayne

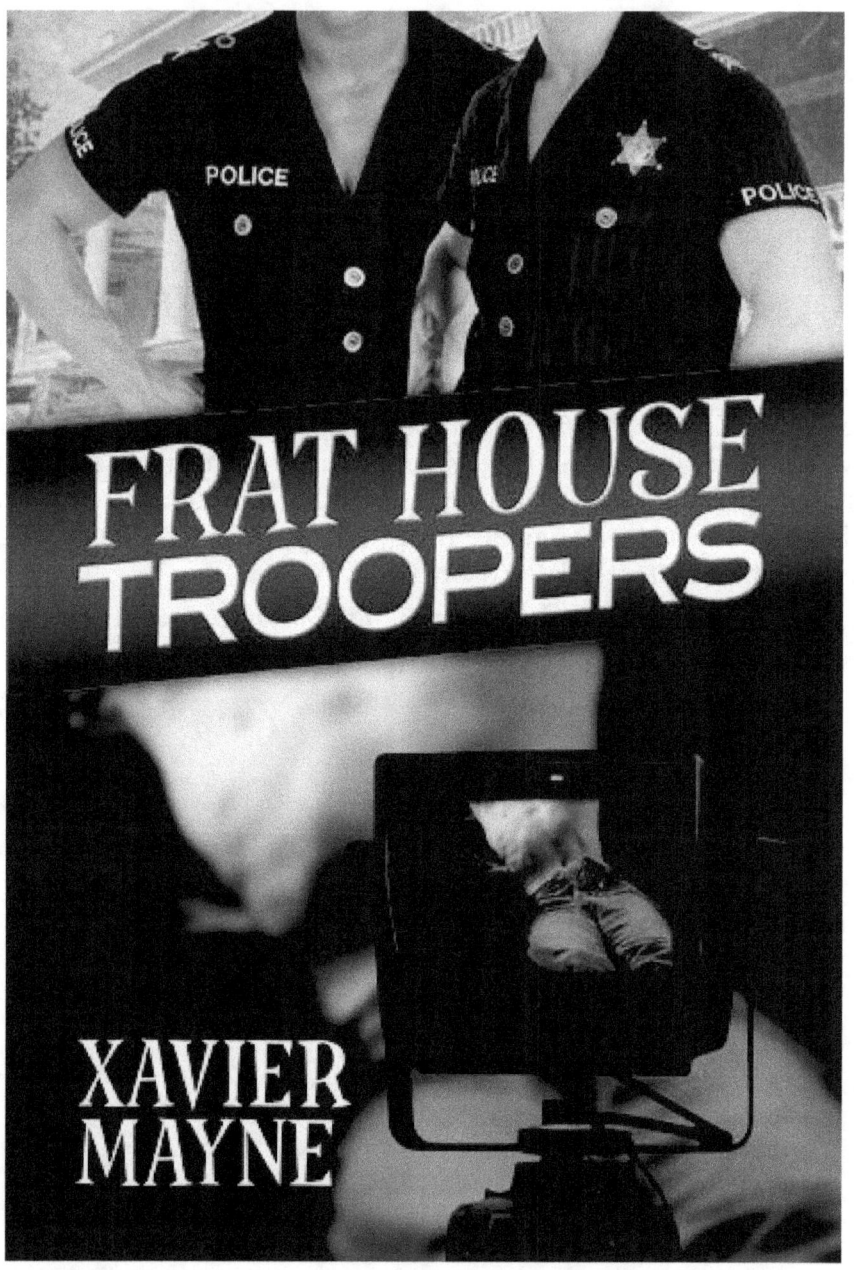

http://www.dreamspinnerpress.com

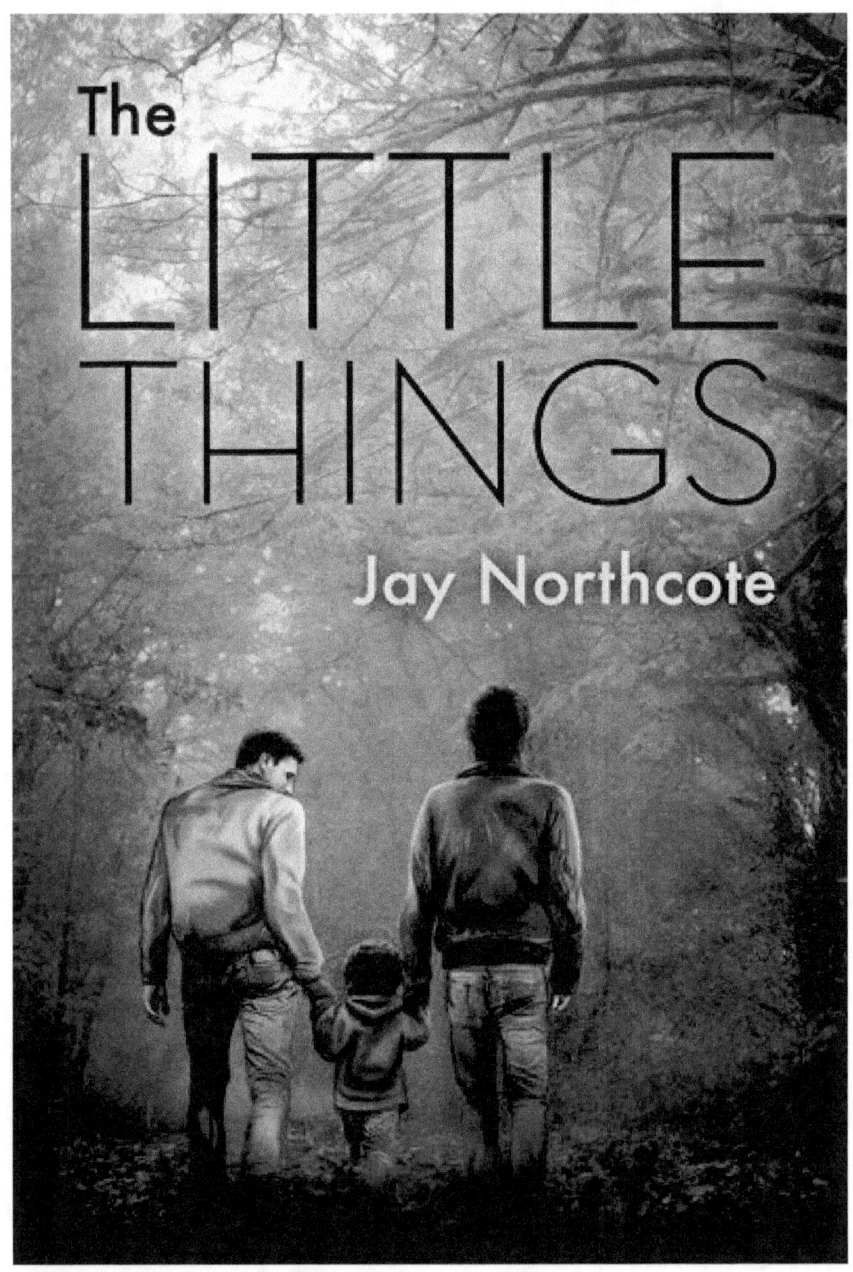

Also from DREAMSPINNER PRESS

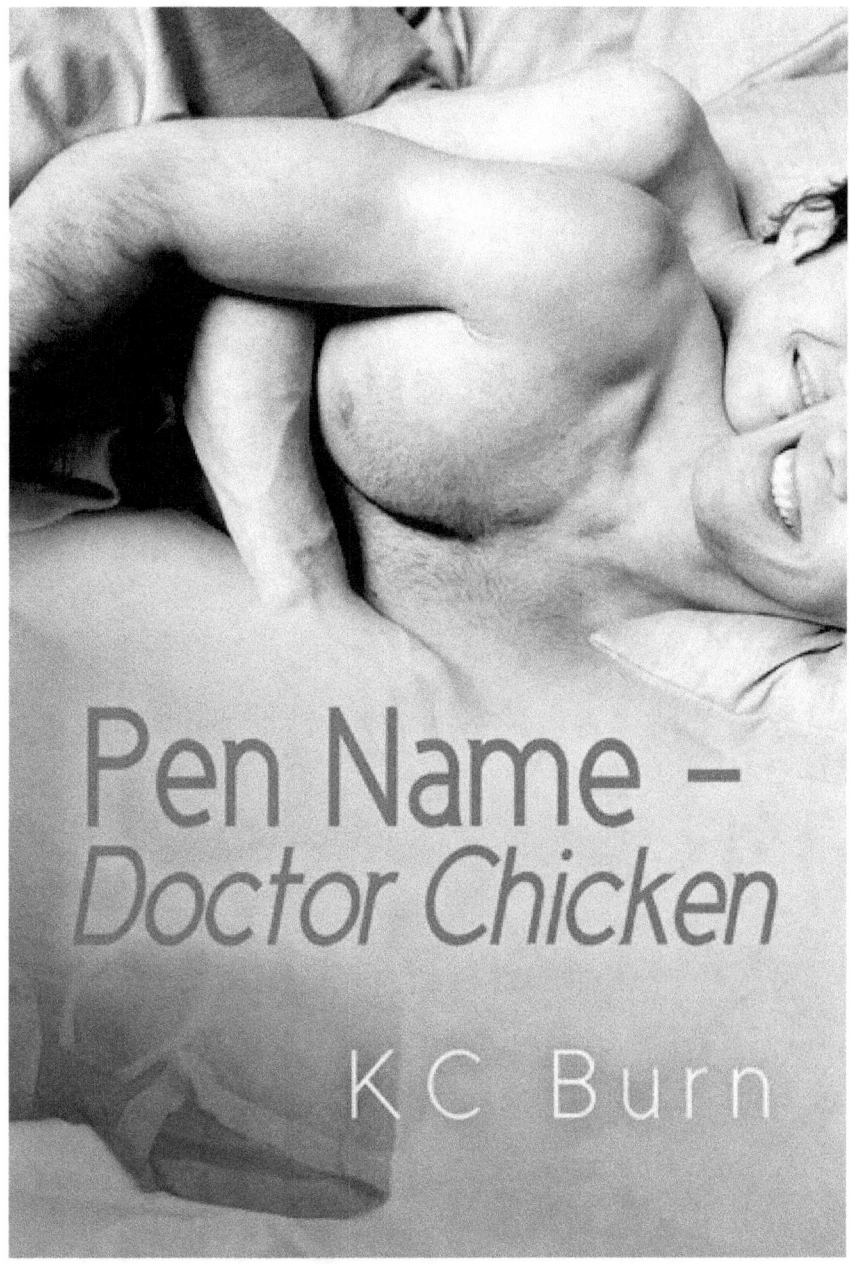

Pen Name –
Doctor Chicken

KC Burn

http://www.dreamspinnerpress.com

Also from DREAMSPINNER PRESS

SEX &
SOURDOUGH

A.J. THOMAS

http://www.dreamspinnerpress.com

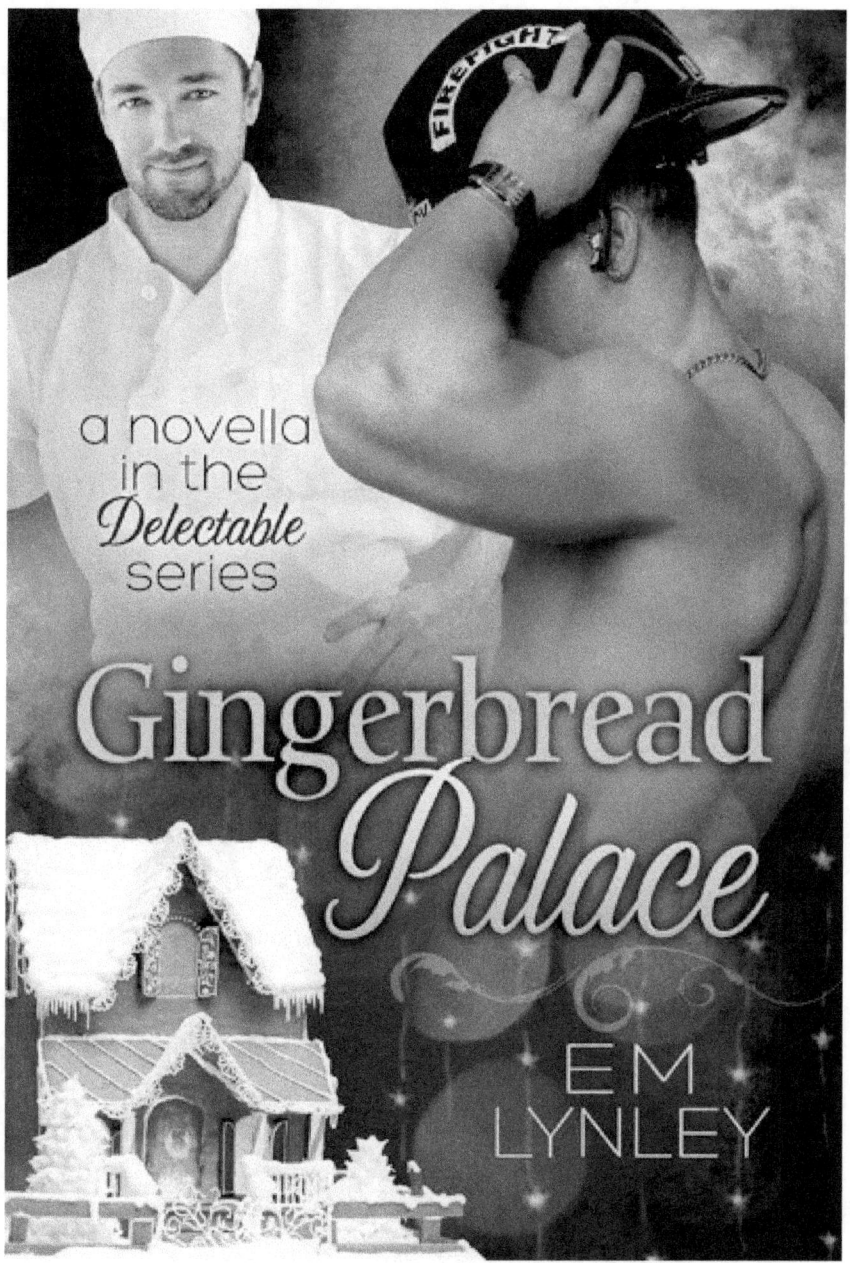